THE HEART SNATCHER

T. H. CARRINGTON

The Heart Snatcher

First published in Great Britain 2024 by T. H. C. PUBLISHING

A CIP catalogue copy of this book is available from the British Library.

Cover design and photography: Tiffany Carrington

eBook ISBN: 978-1-0686637-0-3
Paperback ISBN: 978-1-0686637-1-0

For my Mum and dad, whose love and support is unlike any other. Thank you for never stifling my imagination as a child.

A special thanks to my loving husband Chris, for always believing in me even when I didn't believe in myself.

This book has strong themes of mental health and mental illness as well as topics that some people might find upsetting.

Prologue

He wondered what the red liquid was that crawled across the floorboards out from under her body. He didn't recognise the face staring back at him at first. She was a stranger; a silhouette of someone he loved. Her eyes were wide and empty, staring at him with her jaw pried open. A red hollow space in her chest. He took a step closer; the wooden floor felt cold beneath his bare feet and the hem of his PJs dragged across the floor at his heel. He could hear the sound of rushing water as the bathtub behind her began to overflow, trailing down the sides and seeping across the floor towards where she lay. The faint sound of sirens echoed throughout the night as blue lights penetrated through the window behind him, illuminating the woman's pale face with a blue glow every few seconds before throwing her back into darkness. He knew then who it was.

"Mum?" he whimpered as he stepped forward again wondering why she wasn't answering him. The soles of his feet felt wet. He looked down and saw that they were being submerged in the thick, sticky red liquid.

"Ethan!" a voice screeched as footsteps pounded across the floor.

A shadow loomed over him as he was snatched from behind and lifted up into the warmth of their arms. His legs and arms wrapped around the person like a baby ape to its mother. He didn't see who it was as they pressed his face into their neck, keeping one hand pushed to the back of his head. The sweet smell of jasmine and vanilla filled his nostrils. He felt the cold air piercing the thin layer of his PJs, hitting his clammy skin as his body was carried towards the open front door. He couldn't tear his eyes away, straining to look up over the person's shoulder to see her lying on the floor. The blue lights still lit up her face as she continued to watch him leave. That was all Ethan remembered of that day.

Chapter One

Sixteen years later.

"Ethan!" Detective Inspector Anna Jones shouts, but it's too late, he's already jumped out of the passenger side of the car before it's stopped moving.

Police cars surround the area along the road, with journalists and news reporters standing behind the blue and white police tape blocking off the forest. He doesn't look at them as he rushes across the tarmac. An officer tries to step in front of him.

"Sir, you can't –," the officer begins but Ethan shoves his Detective Sergeant identification in his face without stopping.

He ducks under the tape and sprints into the forest. His eyes don't blink as he goes up over the mound of dirt and grass, looking down at the river below him. Forensic photographers flash pictures and place down markers around the body. Her body. His partner. Carla.

He clutches the fabric of his t-shirt around his stomach as his mind and body grow numb. Blue lights radiating from the police cars light up her face with a blue glow that's all too familiar to him. His knees shake and give in as he stumbles forward. Collapsing to the ground, he can't tear his eyes away from Carla's body lying by the water's edge, the river overspilling onto the land behind her. The sound of rushing water fills his ears.

Her skin is tinted a sickly green colour, and her blonde hair is in tangled knots. Her brown eyes and mouth are wide open as if forever frozen in a state of fear, a deep hole in the centre of her chest with veins and arteries spilling out. Her ribs protrude from her ripped flesh, but he can't see her heart anywhere amongst the mess. He can smell the stench of death over the forestry scent even from this distance.

Ethan's seen many scenes like this before, but he's always blocked out his emotions. Not this time. Burning vomit in the pit of his stomach sets his insides on fire as it fights its way up to his throat. He puts his hand over his mouth to stop it going further before feeling a pair of hands grab his shoulders and pull him back.

"Ethan, you can't be in the cordon!" Anna shouts, dragging him back.

He staggers to his feet, but his knees tremble as he is still trying to fight back the vomit lodged in his throat. She guides him back to the edge of the outer cordon but it's too late, they've already been caught.

"What the hell are you doing?" Crime Scene Manager Milly Young shrieks.

She's wearing an all-in-one white forensic suit that covers her from head to toe with her flaming red hair tucked inside her hood.

"It's fine," Anna blurts.

"No, it's not! You can't be in my cordon. You're not even wearing PPE; you'll contaminate my crime scene!"

As if on cue, the vomit wedged in his throat gurgles up. He turns away as the burning liquid spills out of his mouth.

"See! Contaminating my scene!" she screeches.

"Show some compassion," Anna barks as he feels her hand gently rub up and down his back like an attentive parent to a sick child.

Milly sighs. "Look I get it, but I need to make sure that all the evidence doesn't get contaminated. Once my CSIs are done, then the scene is yours."

Ethan hears the sound of leaves shuffling as she storms away. He remains hunched, panting with the bitter taste of vomit on his tongue. He feels Anna's hand go up onto his shoulder. Her touch now makes him feel cold. He brushes off her hand and stands upright, but he's still lightheaded.

Anna stares at him with a sympathetic look. He knows this look. It's the same one people gave him when his mum died. It's a 'poor Ethan' look. One he never wanted to see again.

"I'm fine," he chokes out. And there's the next look. The 'are you sure?' look. "I'm okay, really," he says but it's not convincing. She guides him further towards the police tape, staying close to his side.

"Take the rest of the day off."

"I can't."

"I think you should."

"No," his voice raises, but he didn't mean to, especially not towards his DI.

"Fine, but no one's going to think less of you if you did. Hell, take the rest of the week off if you want."

He should do what she says but he can't go home now. He needs to know what happened.

"Who called in about the body?"

He'd heard about them finding a body that matched Carla's description, although he hoped it wouldn't be her.

"The guy didn't leave a name and he didn't stick around either," she says, and he frowns. "I know, weird, right?"

Anna falls silent, her eyes scan the area as they walk towards the forest edge. The image of Carla's dead body won't shift from his mind and his head still feels full of air. He tries to ground himself by using the 5-4-3-2-1 method. He uses Anna for the five things he can see: Her neatly tied-back brown hair, large brown eyes lined with black makeup, immaculate dark brown skin, her formal suit; and her high heels. Touch is next. He runs his hand down his leather jacket, picking at peeling fabric on the seams. He then puts his hands in his pocket but screws his face up as he struggles to name what strange texture is in there. Feels like used chewing gum.

Anna stops, turning to face him and he's taken out of his thoughts before he can finish his 4th acknowledgement.

"You know how some killers return to the crime scene?" She pauses, and he nods. "Don't look, but there's a guy who's acting kind of weird."

He automatically turns to look, but then he feels a whack on his arm. His head whips back to her.

"Ow!"

"I said don't look!"

"In what way 'weird'?" he asks rubbing his arm.

"Well, he's got a camera, but I can't see a journalist ID badge around his neck," she says glancing over and then back to Ethan. "He's also apart from the others. You see them?" She nods towards the crowd of journalists and photographers gathered on one side of the police tape trying to get a snap of the body with their flashing cameras. *Sick bastards*, Ethan thinks to himself as he watches the cordon officers struggle to keep them at bay. He turns back to her and nods. "Well, they're over there trying to get a shot of the body, whilst he's on the other side with his camera pointed at me and you."

Ethan frowns and looks around. Finding the guy isn't difficult. His face is hidden behind a camera. The figure lowers his camera slightly. He sees Ethan looking and he does exactly what Ethan expects him to do. He runs.

She turns to give Ethan a look that resembles a 'I told you so'. Ethan doesn't hesitate as he bolts after the man, ducking under the tape.

"Stop! Police!" he shouts, but the man doesn't stop.

He's fast, but Ethan's faster. His feet pound on the tarmac, the muscles in his legs strain and his stomach churns uneasily. The distance between them decreases as he closes the gap. Ethan grabs him by the waist pulling him down in the form of a rugby tackle. They crash to the ground, tumbling over one another and scraping across the tarmac. He falls on top of the man who lands face down. Ethan turns him over, balancing his weight on one arm. His jaw drops as he sees the guy's jet-black hair, piercing blue eyes, and pale skin; his lips are parted in shock as he stares up at Ethan.

"Riley?" Ethan says, but he doesn't recognise his own voice.

Riley doesn't say anything, as he stares at him.

"Nice catch, Skipper," he hears Anna say as she approaches them. "You," she says, pointing at Riley. "Why the fuck did you run?"

Ethan looks up at her as she stands over them. It only takes a moment of distraction for Riley to squirm out from under him and try to scurry away.

"Don't move!" Ethan demands as he grabs him to pull him back.

Riley turns and a force strikes Ethan's face, twisting his head to the side with a crack. All his adrenaline has just been knocked out of him, as his vision blurs and noises around him muffle. A sharp burning pain upsurges around his eye and cheekbone. His hand goes to it, feeling his skin instantly swell beneath his fingertips. He thinks about his 5-4-3-2-1 method and how that's another one for his 4th acknowledgement.

***

Ethan paces the floor in the clinically white hallway in front of Anna who's leaning up against the wall. He can feel her eyes watching him with every step. Catching his reflection in the glass on a door, he realises how dishevelled he looks: Swept over, scruffy brown hair; tired brown eyes with dark rings around them; and coarse stubble framing his face. He can't remember the last time he shaved. He can't even remember the last time he took a shower. The skin around his eye is inflamed red and still throbs from when Riley whacked him in the face. He runs his fingertips along it, feeling the raised bruised skin before continuing to pace. He takes out a packet of cigarettes from the back pocket of his jeans and lights one up.

"You really shouldn't smoke in here," Anna warns.

"I don't give a shit."

She would usually argue with him, but she remains quiet, allowing him to take a satisfying drag of his cigarette.

"You know, it might not even be her. It could be someone who looks like her," Anna says a little too flippantly for his liking, although she's most likely just trying to reassure him.

"It's her."

Silence falls between them and he doesn't look at her.

"Are you sure you want to do this? Any one of the other officers she's worked with can identify her."

"I need to do this," he mutters.

It's not about identifying her; he needs confirmation. To see her for himself. It's the same reason that when one of your pets dies, you show the body to the other one so they can move on. Although he's not sure how he ever will.

"Don't you want to at least do it by photograph or through a window?"

"No. I need to see her in person."

"Ethan Brown?" a voice says, and Ethan spins on his heels to see a tall skinny man approaching them. He quickly hides the cigarette behind his back and waves away the smoke. "We're ready when you are."

Ethan thought he was ready but now he's second-guessing everything. He nods and goes to follow the coroner before feeling Anna's hand on his arm. He turns to look at her, but she doesn't say anything. She flashes a soft sympathetic smile and there's no need for any words.

They follow the coroner in silence to a lift and Ethan ditches his cigarette butt on the receptionist's desk, knowing he'll probably feel bad for that later. The doors close and the metal box jolts, taking them down into the mortuary. Ethan can feel the temperature growing colder as goosebumps spread across the surface of his skin. The lift beeps and grinds to a halt making him startle. The coroner then leads them through into a clinical room, similar to an operating theatre. It's cold and lifeless. There's a table in the middle of the room, with a white sheet draped over it, and a lump in the shape of a body under it. He stands on one side of the table near her head whilst the coroner stands on the opposite side and pulls on latex gloves. Ethan watches as he takes hold of the cloth between his index finger and thumb. He stops and looks up.

"Are you sure you're ready?" he asks.

Ethan gives a short nod, whilst trying to swallow the lump in his throat. He feels Anna close behind him.

The coroner peels back the fabric as if not to hurt her, stopping at her chest. Ethan stops breathing. His stomach turns in the same way it did when he saw her lying next to the river. If he had anything left in it, he's sure it would have come back up.

It's her, there's no doubt that it's Carla. Her blonde hair is pulled off her face and disappears beneath her head. Her eyes are now closed, and her lips are together. The coroner carefully lifts the cloth on one side to reveal her arm. A tattoo of two interlocked hearts, one small and one large, on her upper wrist is the final confirmation. He chokes out a noise but nothing that resembles words. He nods and the coroner quickly goes to cover her body.

"Don't," Ethan croaks. The coroner stops and looks at him with wide eyes. "I just… I just need to say goodbye."

He gives Ethan a sympathetic look. "I'll give you some time alone."

The coroner walks around the table and disappears behind him. The sound of the door opens and closes behind him but he can still feel Anna's presence lingering.

Carla doesn't even look human anymore. The backside of her body is a reddish-purple colour from where all of her blood is no longer circulating, it's just sitting inside her as gravity pulls it down like water in a glass. She was lying on her back when she died. The top side of her body facing upwards is a cold pale colour. He can see the split flesh at the top of her chest disappearing under the fabric as it grows bigger. It's like looking at his mother's body again. The images of his mum, Natalie's body lying on the ground with her chest ripped open, emerge in his mind. He's not sure why but he goes to reach out.

"Don't touch the body," Anna says before his hand finds Carla's body.

Her voice makes him jump and then freeze as it echoes around the room. He hears her footsteps, and he turns to look at her as she appears beside him.

"Sorry," she adds looking at his face.

That's when he realises that his cheeks feel wet. He wipes them and shakes off the feeling, looking back at her body.

The pigmentation around one of her eyes is consistent with pre-mortem bruising. His eyes follow the discolouration and lacerations along her shoulders, running down her one exposed arm. Defence wounds. There's a ring of bruising and cuts circling her wrist, clearly from restraints.

"She was restrained," he says, as a way of getting his voice working and his mind focused on his job rather than his emotions.

"It appears that way. They put her time of death between 1 am and 3 am last night."

She died in the early hours of this morning on this day of all days, the anniversary of his mother's murder. That's not a coincidence. He looks down at the marks on her body.

"What else do you know?"

"Her heart is unaccounted for."

He clutches the fabric around his abdomen, feeling like he might throw up again.

"Could an animal have done that?" he asks.

She shakes her head. "The cut is consistent with a power saw. Most likely surgical," Anna explains. "On initial examination, the pathologist suggests that the cause of death is blood loss, but a full post-mortem will take place soon."

"Blood loss," he mutters, looking at the glimpse of the hole in her chest. "That would mean she was probably alive when the killer…"

He trails off as he imagines her being strapped to a table fully awake as the killer cut open her chest.

"The blood splatter on her body suggests that too," she says with sadness in her voice. "But we can't be sure of anything until the full post-mortem is conducted." She pauses analysing his face. "Plus, she would have passed out long before the killer... you know."

He swallows down a little vomit.

"What did the CSI's find?"

"The lack of blood at the crime scene suggests that the body was placed there post-mortem."

Ethan scans Carla's empty shell of a body.

"And the lack of water tension in her skin tells me that she wasn't dumped *in* the river."

"So, the killer either fucked up which means they're an amateur."

"Or they purposely placed her in front of the river for someone to find her," he finishes her sentence.

The image of her body lying in front of the river re-emerges in his mind, the sound of rushing water pouring onto the land. Like an overflowing bathtub. For some reason, it feels like a twisted way to remind him of what happened sixteen years ago. He shakes the image from his mind, reminding himself to stay professional.

"Where's Riley?" he asks, but this time she doesn't respond straight away.

"Being questioned."

"What's he said?" She doesn't answer, so he looks at her. "Anna?"

"Look," she says with a sigh, moving away from the body and forcing him to follow her. "I've already told you too much. I can't tell you anymore."

"Why not?"

She swallows hard and adverts her eyes.

"Because you're not allowed on the case."

"What!"

"The DCI has demanded that you stay away from this case."

"Who's the DCI?"

"Ash Morris." He rolls his eyes. "He's just trying to protect you, Ethan."

"How the fuck is taking me off the case protecting me?"

"You're too emotionally involved."

"You mean I'm a liability."

"Look, I know you and Carla were partners but –"

"It's more than that!" he outbursts. She gives him a suggested look, and he knows what's going through her head. He knows how it sounds. "Not like that! She was – she –"

"It's fine."

"She was like a mum to me," he says and his voice breaks. There's that look of pity in Anna's eyes again. He sighs and pinches the bridge of his nose, squinting his eyes shut. "I need to know what's going on. I could help, I –"

"I know," she says, and his head whips up to look at her as the room falls into silence for a moment before she continues. "It wasn't my call."

"Then I want to speak to Ash."

"I'm not sure how much that'll help."

"Please, Anna. You can talk to him; request for me to help with the case."

"You don't think I've already done that?" she defends herself. They exchange a look for what feels like forever before her shoulders slump. "Fine, I'll talk to him *again*, but I can't promise anything."

He knows that trying to talk Ash into letting Ethan be a part of Carla's case will be difficult, but he has to try. One thing is for sure; whether he's on the case or not, he will find out who did this to her.

Chapter Two

Anna knocks on Ash's office door that looks as though it's made from pristine wood and has a smart silver plaque across it that reads DCI Ash Morris. Ethan lingers close behind her.

"Come in," Ash's voice calls from the other side. Anna leads as she pushes open the door.

Ash is standing behind his desk, dressed in a smart grey suit. He looks up when they enter, his expression hardening as soon as he sees Ethan.

"No, get out," Ash demands, pointing his bony finger towards the door.

Anna takes a deep breath.

"Sir, I think Ethan could be valuable in giving us insight into Carla's case."

"How'd you figure that?"

"The victim is Ethan's partner, and the suspect is his friend; he's already at the centre of this investigation."

Usually, Ethan would speak up, but he's stunned by the word 'suspect'. Riley? A suspect? Not possible.

"Which is exactly why he shouldn't be here!"

"Wouldn't we usually question friends and family of the victim *and* the suspect?" she asks innocently, but her tone is sarcastic.

"So, go and question him then."

"Technically, I don't have to agree to be questioned unless you're arresting me," Ethan challenges.

"Are you blackmailing me?"

"Well, if you want my help…"

Ash glares between them, landing his final gaze on Ethan. "Fine, but I'm only giving you one chance. If you fuck up even a little, you're out!" Ash warns.

Anna closes the door and for some reason, the sound of it

shutting makes Ethan's body jump.

"How long have you known Riley Darlington?" Ash asks, looking at him, cold pale blue eyes seeking him out from under his light grey eyebrows. His combed silver hair appears darker in this dimmed lighting.

"I've known him since we were eight, so about seventeen years."

"And you two were friends?"

He stares at Ash with a deadpan expression. "Yes," Ethan lies, careful not to let it show with his facial expressions.

Ash nods slowly. "And what can you tell us about his schizophrenia?"

"What?"

"You didn't know?"

Ethan shakes his head.

"When was the last time you saw him?" Anna asks.

He struggles to collect his thoughts.

"After he went to university, so, I guess it's been about... eight years." Fuck. Eight years. Has it really been that long?

"On Mr Darlington's medical records, it says that he was diagnosed with schizophrenia and hospitalised eight years ago for about a year and a half," Ash explains.

"Why do you have his medical files? I thought we could only access those in extreme cases," Ethan asks, folding his arms.

Ash stares at him unblinking. "We're talking about murder; you don't get more extreme than that."

"Come on, you can't actually think Riley killed Carla?" Ethan says in disbelief. Not Riley. Anyone but him.

"He confessed to finding the body but didn't identify himself. He hung around at the crime scene for no other reason but to watch and take photos. Then he tried to flee from the police. I think it's pretty obvious who killed your partner."

"No, there's no way!"

"And why not?"

"Do you really think if he did it, he would have called the fucking police? Of course not."

"Skipper's got a point," Anna chips in.

"I think this," Ash says holding up Riley's medical file. "Explains why. He's delusional and probably not in control of his actions."

"What about motive?" she says, sending the room into silence.

Ethan dabbles with the idea that Riley could have killed someone. That somehow, he did kill Carla. What is the motive? Why would he possibly do it? The others are also silent.

"There is none," Ethan says finally.

"Again, I don't think this is going in his favour," Ash says holding up the medical file again.

"Oh, will you put that fucking thing down! Riley isn't capable of murder."

"Not the Riley you once knew, no. But what about this Riley?"

He points to the file again. Ethan's knuckles turn pale.

"I'm telling you; he didn't do it!"

"Ethan," Anna pacifies, "you know that the first person we have to eliminate as a suspect is the person who found the body. Riley also has no alibi for the time of Carla's death and it's a bit of a coincidence that *your* friend found *your* partner's body and was taking photos at the crime scene."

"He also hit you earlier, too," Ash adds.

"Then I'll talk to him," Ethan says. They both look at him.

"Absolutely not," Ash says. "I know you and Carla were close and I'm sorry for your loss, but you can't be on this case, especially now. You should go home."

"Let me talk to him. Let me help."

"I said no."

"But I can get through to him more than you can."

"He's right and you know it," Anna says, jumping to his defence. "Ethan could help with figuring this guy out, considering he already knows him."

Ash narrows his eyes at Anna and then back to Ethan before saying, "Fine, but I don't think it's a good idea."

Ethan agrees, it's not a good idea. But he has to see him.

***

Ash storms ahead out of the office as Ethan struggles to keep up. He leads Ethan through a series of hallways towards the holding cell. DC Oliver Harrison is standing upright next to one of the doors. He's got short curly black hair with a baby face and black skin, large round dark eyes look up at them both.

"Ethan's going in to speak to Mr Riley Darlington now," Ash explains to him as they approach.

"But aren't we supposed to inform Riley's next of kin that we've taken him in first?" he says with eyes flicking between them. Ash gives him a look and Oliver adds with a mousy tone, "Sir."

"We've tried calling his parents and no one's answered."

"Isn't there someone else?" he asks, voice cracking. Ash narrows his eyes. "Sorry, Sir, it's just protocol to have an appropriate adult with a suspect with mental health conditions when we question them."

"We're not questioning him, yet. Now, run along."

"But –"

"Do what I tell you, *DC* Harrison."

Ethan glares at him. They don't usually call each other by their titles or last names, only when doing introductions, meaning Ash is only saying it to make a point of his ranking.

"Yes, Sir," Oliver mumbles, and Ethan watches him leave.

"He's got a point," Ethan says.

"Don't worry, we'll get him a specialist-appropriate adult to sit in on the official interrogation," Ash says, unlocking the door.

"But –"

"Do you want to speak to him or not?"

Ethan realises how close Ash is to not letting him see Riley anyway, so decides to stay quiet.

"You've got ten minutes and then I'm moving him to an interrogation room for questioning," he explains. "We've padded him down and taken his shoelaces and belt."

"Why?"

"Just precaution," he says with a shrug.

Ethan's hand goes towards the handle, but Ash grabs his wrist, making him jump.

"Be careful, Ethan. He might be dangerous or unpredictable. Don't forget, we've also got cameras in there and I'll be watching. If you feel threatened, say the safe word: Oranges."

"Why oranges?"

Ash shrugs.

"Well, you're hardly going to talk about what kind of fruit you like. Remember when you're in there, keep your distance from him. I know he used to be your friend, but he might not be the same person you used to know."

"I'll be fine, it's not like I'm going into a lion's den."

"As I said, it's just precaution," he says, stepping back from the door.

Ethan grabs the handle but hesitates. Why is everyone on such high alert? Is Riley really that dangerous? No, not innocent little Riley. He couldn't hurt a fly. That had always been the problem, Riley could never defend himself and it was Ethan who had to fight his bullies at school. He was what people called a 'nerd' and was too weak to hit back. But is the man in this room still the same boy he used to know all those years ago?

He pulls the handle down and swings the door open before he changes his mind. The room looks bigger than it is thanks to the minimalistic interior design consisting of plain white walls and a single metal bed on the far side of the room with padded restraints hanging from the rails of the bed frame.

Ethan stands there frozen to the spot as Riley's head whips around, looking at him with wide eyes. He's standing in the middle of the room as if he had been pacing. He's wearing a long sleeve shirt with dark blue jeans and his hair is scuffed up. Ash's warnings about Riley keep going over in his head. The look of surprise on Riley's face is replaced with a warm smile, as he lets out a sigh of relief.

"Ethan," he breathes.

There it is. There's the real Riley. The kind and gentle person Ethan knows. His body loosens as he closes the door, trying to swallow the lump in his throat. He doesn't know what to say. Anything he had planned to say is lost in his brain.

"I'm so glad you're here," he says, coming towards Ethan.

He remembers what Ash said and the sudden movement makes Ethan throw his back against the door. Riley freezes, stopping a short distance away from him. His smile drops and his eyes are wide in surprise.

"Oh, I get it," Riley says stepping back.

Ethan breathes out heavily. He doesn't know why he's on edge. It's *Riley*. He's a five-foot-four timid bag of pale skin and bones. Ethan towers over him and can easily defend himself.

"So, what safe word did they give you?" Riley asks with an unsteady tone to his voice and lines creasing along his forehead. Ethan doesn't answer. "Probably something like asking if I want a glass of water or some kind of food like pizza topping. Or a fruit."

Ethan feels his eye twitch and he knows he saw it. Riley turns away as if thinking deeply.

"Maybe something like apples, pears or bananas," he says as if thinking out loud. He spins on his heel to look at Ethan. "Or is it oranges?"

As quick as that, the harmless man standing there a moment ago is gone. That wild look returns in his eyes. Ethan tilts his head back, staying where he is. He remembers one thing he needed to ask.

"What were you doing at the crime scene earlier?" Ethan asks, not being able to raise his voice above a whisper.

Riley lowers his head, cocking it to the side. Shadows appear around his narrow eyes.

"Am I being interrogated, Detective?"

There's a tormenting tone to his voice. Ethan's eyes dart up to the camera in the corner of the room. A little light on the side of it shows it's working. He looks back to Riley, realising he's taken his eyes off him. He stands there, waiting for an answer. It's all a game. Answering a question with another question.

"Did you kill Carla?" he manages to raise his voice louder.

Riley scoffs a laugh.

"Judging by your reaction you've already made your own assumptions about that," Riley says as he begins to pace in front of him.

Ethan doesn't move, his back still pressed against the door. He follows Riley with his eyes.

"That's not an answer."

"Is it a crime to go for a walk in a forest?" he asks spinning back round to look at Ethan.

"That's strange because you always used to bitch about living in the countryside when we were teenagers" Ethan says watching as Riley's jaw clenches.

"My psychiatrist recommended I take nature walks."

"Your psychiatrist?" he asks. Riley nods. "And you just so happened to find a body?"

"Yes."

The answer comes out so simple that Ethan doesn't know what to say now. There's an uncomfortable silence as they stare at each other, neither of them backing down.

"Why did you run then?" Ethan asks and he scoffs another laugh.

"Because I'm not stupid. Someone like me finding a body, of course, I was going to be suspect number one. Come on, Detective, it doesn't take a genius to work that one out."

He sits on the bed with his knees spread and his elbows resting on them. Ethan can't work out what he's thinking. One of Ethan's skills is that he can read people, being an expert in criminal behaviour, but with Riley he's never been able to work out what goes on inside his head.

Ethan takes the chance to fill the space. He steps off the wall and walks into the middle of the room gaining control of the situation, but he struggles to recall his thoughts.

"If that's true, then why did you hang around after making the call about the body?"

"I wanted to make sure the police found her." He hesitates before looking up at Ethan with wide eyes. "Then I saw you."

There's a pause as their eyes lock and Riley's face softens.

"But you ran from me."

"Because I knew what it looked like. I knew I'd be a suspect if I was caught there, but I wanted to see to you."

"Why?"

"You looked upset, and I wanted to talk to you. I wanted –"

"Where were you last night between 1 am and 3 am?" he asks, cutting Riley off. He has to keep his emotions detached.

Riley's face hardens again. "Home."

"Can anyone vouch for that?"

He shakes his head.

"Doesn't mean I did it," Riley bites.

"But no one can confirm it?"

Riley pulls himself off the bed and before Ethan knows it, Riley's standing directly in front of him. He looks up at Ethan, those dark shadows around his eyes illuminating his bright blue irises. Their bodies inches away from touching. Riley's sweet but masculine aftershave fills his nostrils and it's a scent that sends him back to when they were eighteen.

"Doesn't mean I did it, Detective," Riley says with a tormenting innocence to his voice.

Ethan can feel his breath on his neck as he speaks. Riley glides around him, brushing his body against his as he moves. Ethan doesn't know if it's accidental or purposeful. He lets out a breath of air and spins around, not wanting to turn his back to Riley. He's facing away from Ethan. His shoulders look stiff and tense.

"Bit of a coincidence, don't you think?" Ethan manages to choke out.

"What is?" he asks but doesn't look at Ethan as he answers.

"I haven't seen you for eight years and now you just show up, finding my partner's dead body."

"A coincidence is all it is," he says spinning on his heels to look at him with his hands behind his back.

"You haven't denied it," Ethan says but Riley frowns. "Not once have you said that you didn't kill her."

"Do I have to for you to believe me?"

Ethan's taken back. Should he just trust him? Is that what Riley is expecting?

"I need to hear you say it."

"Please don't treat me like I'm a stranger, Ethan." That's the first time he's used Ethan's name. "You know me."

And you left me, Ethan thinks, biting his tongue to resist saying it.

"Say it," Ethan demands stepping towards him, closing the gap. He realises that he's standing too close to him, and he should probably step back. But he doesn't.

"Ethan," Riley soothes and moves his hand from behind his back to brush Ethan's. But he's not in the mood to play any more of these games. He grabs Riley's wrist, holding him in place.

"Say it!" he demands.

Riley looks at him surprised. His mouth opens but no words follow. Then Ethan feels it. His hand shifts and his fingers brush a small bump on the surface of Riley's wrist. He frowns, looking down at Riley's hand. Ethan turns it over, and then slides Riley's sleeve up with his other hand. The fabric rises, revealing a raised white scar running from his wrist up his forearm. Ethan glides his thumb across it. He doesn't know why, maybe as a way of trying to soothe it or because he doesn't believe what he's seeing.

"I didn't kill her," Riley's voice cracks. Ethan looks at him as his eyes fill with hurt and betrayal along with tears. "I shouldn't have to say it for you to know that.".

Riley moves his sleeve back down to cover his scar. Ethan can't find any words to say.

"Ethan," he says as he moves forward. Ethan doesn't know if it's for comfort or not, but his instinct is to move back.

He can't do this. Ash is right, he's too emotionally involved. It's Riley. It's Carla. He never should have come into this room.

"I have to go," he blurts, turning towards the door.

Riley's hand grabs his arm, spinning him around.

"Don't go," Riley pleads, clutching either side of his arms.

Ethan's eyes dart to the camera in the corner of the room. He tries to push back but Riley doesn't loosen his grip. His tight fists holding onto the leather of Ethan's jacket.

"Please don't leave me here!" he begs.

Ethan hears the door swing open and footsteps march in behind him. He's shoved out the way as two male uniformed officers, much larger than Riley, approach him.

"No!" Riley shouts, trying to hold onto Ethan as the two officers grab him and force him down onto the bed. Ethan backs away, still staring as they use the restraints hooked on the bed frame to clasp around Riley's wrists. His legs kick rapidly as he tries to fight a losing battle.

"Ethan!" he calls as he tries to throw his head back to see him. But Ethan can't stay here. He retreats into the hallway and throws his back against the wall breathing heavily.

"I told you," Ethan hears Ash say.

Ethan turns his head, glaring at Ash as he leans against the wall, looking at him with a smug smirk. He imagines punching it off his face.

Chapter Three

Ethan's not sure what happened next. His mind is experiencing blanks. It's like time is passing, but he can't recall it. All he knows is that one minute he was in the holding cell with Riley and now he's outside an interrogation room with Anna. He leans back against the wall, pinching the bridge of his nose. His head begins to pound, and he can feel the vein in his right temple throb.

"Are you sure you don't want to go home?" she asks.

"I'm fine," he says but even he's getting tired of hearing himself say it. He takes out a packet of his cigarettes, but Anna's hand comes down on top of his.

"Not in here," she barks.

He rolls his eyes and puts them back into his jeans pocket.

"We're taking him in for questioning," Ash's voice bellows down the hallway. Ethan turns to look at him as he approaches along with another officer whom Ethan's not seen before. "It took so bloody long because we had to get a specialist appropriate adult."

"You ready?" she asks Ethan but before he can answer, Ash cuts in.

"He's not allowed on this case, so he can't go in with you."

"I need a DS on this case, Sir. More than one."

"I know, that's why I've brought in DS Lucas Turner," he says gesturing to the officer beside him.

The bags under Lucas's eyes and the withdrawn look on his face tell Ethan that he either has young kids keeping him up at night or he's up all night partying. A shining gold wedding ring on his finger makes him think it's the first option.

"You're Ethan Brown?" Lucas asks coming forward with his hand outstretched and tilting to the side in an attempt to balance the two bags on either shoulder. "I've heard a lot about you."

He looks down at Lucas's hand and then glares up at his face.

"You're fucking joking!" he snaps and Lucas jolts. He looks like he might cry or throw up. "Why the fuck is some amateur working on my partner's case?"

He looks to Ash. Lucas glances between them, like a child caught between two arguing parents.

"How do you know he's new?" Anna asks.

"Doesn't take a genius to work it out," Ethan says, looking him up and down and noting how overdressed Lucas is in his pale green shirt and immaculate tie. Lucas looks offended.

"He may be new, but I can assure you that Lucas is perfectly capable of handling this case," Ash explains but Ethan scoffs a laugh.

"And what about me?"

Ash glares at him. "We've been through this. You can't work on a case that you're too emotionally invested in. You've already proved that when I let you speak to him earlier."

"I'm the best one for the case and you know it. I've got a good track record of closing cases, and my emotional involvement can help with the case. I know things he doesn't."

"I've already caught Lucas up to date on this case and I've made my feelings about you being involved clear. So, drop it!" Ash snarls.

Ethan's mouth opens but as he's about to argue, he sees him. He watches as two uniformed officers guide Riley down the hallway along with his appropriate adult. He looks at Riley's face. Piercing blue eyes begging him to do something. Anything. Then Ethan looks down. Handcuffs fastened tight around Riley's wrists in front of him. His eyes stay with Ethan even as he disappears into the interrogation room.

"Why the fuck is he in cuffs?" Ethan shouts stepping towards Ash.

"Isn't it obvious? He's dangerous."

"He's not dangerous."

"He attacked you. Twice!"

"He didn't fucking attack me!"

He feels Anna's hand on his back as she leans around him to talk to Ash. "I think what Ethan's trying to say is that we only use cuffs if someone is erratic. He didn't look erratic to me."

"We shouldn't take any chances with a suspect like this," Lucas chips in taking out a file from one of his bags and examining it. "Says in his medical file that he attacked another patient in the psychiatric hospital."

"And this is why I'm recruiting Lucas on this case. Any objections, Anna?" Ash says, lifting his left eyebrow.

"No, Sir," she resigns.

"Good. Now, I've got more important things to be doing right now," he says as he strides down the corridor and disappears around the corner.

Lucas follows Anna into the interrogation room and there's no way that Ethan's going to walk away now. He needs to know what's happening in there.

He charges into the room next to theirs where there's a computer screen showing the live feed from the security camera inside the interrogation room. It's a small stale room that smells like one too many takeaways. He stares down at the monitor as Anna and Lucas give the usual housekeeping to Riley. Ethan never thought that he would see *him* in one of these rooms.

"You haven't accepted our offer of a lawyer," Anna says, half a statement and half a question.

"Do I need one?" he asks with a naïve tone.

He seems so vulnerable and small in the interrogation chair as he fidgets with his hands, twisting them against the cuffs. It makes the guilt in Ethan's gut swell. He leans forward closer to the screen.

"Well, I would if I was arrested for murder."

"But I didn't do it."

"What were you doing when you found the body?" Lucas

asks. Riley stutters slightly and Lucas raises his voice. "Oh, come on, it's not a difficult question."

"Give him time to speak," the appropriate adult says.

"I was just walking," Riley blurts.

"Why didn't you identify yourself when you called about the body?"

"I'm guessing it's because you thought you'd be a suspect," Anna defends Riley before he can say something, "because of your condition. Isn't that right, Riley?"

He nods and his shoulders relax. Lucas slams his hands onto the table making Riley jump back in his seat. "But you stuck around at the crime scene for what? A day out? Do you have a thing for dead bodies?"

"You shouldn't be talking to him like that," Riley's appropriate adult warns.

"Settle down, Lucas," Anna says and then leans over the table towards Riley, switching back to a sympathetic tone. "I want to help you, but I can't do that if you don't help me."

Ethan gets it now. Lucas is bad cop and Anna is good cop. It's not something they're ever trained to do because it rarely works but sometimes during interviews, each officer will naturally gravitate towards either one. There is something sickening about doing that to someone with a mental health condition, though. It's against protocol and if Riley's appropriate adult isn't going to intervene then Ethan will. He goes towards the door to stop this from continuing, but then he hears the door to the interrogation room burst open and he watches as all their heads whip round.

"What the hell is going on?" a tall man shouts from the doorway. Oliver is standing behind him. Ethan gawps at the screen with a dropped jaw.

Anna and Lucas vacate the room, pushing the man back into the hallway whilst Riley's appropriate adult stays behind.

Ethan opens the door and steps into the hallway, watching the argument unfold in real life. The door to the interrogation room slams shut. Ethan watches from a distance as they all bunch together in the narrow hallway. A mass of raised voices and protests merge into a mess of non-formulated sentences and unheard words. Ethan decides not to approach them; he prefers being a fly on the wall.

The tall man gestures furiously. He's wearing a dark suit, complimenting his black slicked-back hair and his dark eyes. He looks late forties with a strong jawline and chiselled face. Ethan recognises his face from when he was younger. The Darlington's family friend who always lingered around Riley's parents when Ethan and Riley were kids.

"What the hell are you doing?" the man shouts.

"Who the fuck are you?" Anna exclaims.

"He works with Riley's dad," Oliver explains, gesturing to the man.

"I'm a family friend," the man corrects Oliver.

"Why is he here?" Lucas asks, directing his question at Oliver.

"Regulations. We had to inform a family member that Riley's here but considering we can't get hold of his parents, we got in touch with their *family friend*," he explains. Ethan's eyes dart between them. "He has a right to be here with Riley, Ma'am, it's –"

Anna raises his hand to cut him off. "Fine, just go."

He gives a hesitant look and then walks away.

"Right," Anna says, dropping her harsh tone as she turns to the man, stepping forward with an outstretched hand. "I'm DI Anna Jones and this is DS Lucas Turner. You are?"

He glares down at Anna's hand but doesn't accept it.

"Dr Vincent Hale," he says with emphasis on the word 'Dr'. "And what you're doing is abuse of police powers."

Anna and Lucas exchange a look. Ethan doesn't want to be detected but he wants to see how this plays out.

"Why don't we go and talk about this somewhere more comfortable," Anna suggests, gesturing for them to leave.

"I'm not going anywhere until he's released."

"Look, we have probable cause for questioning him."

Vincent chokes out a laugh. "What probable cause?"

"Mr Darlington found the body of a dead detective. He tried to flee the scene and then assaulted one of my officers. He was acting erratic, so we contained him for his own safety."

"For his safety," Vincent scoffs.

"He remains a person of interest in this investigation," Lucas chips in.

Vincent looks between them. He doesn't speak, but it's not from stupidity. He's choosing his next words carefully. Ethan can see the clockwork in his mind turning.

"Have you assigned him an appropriate adult to help him with communication?"

"Yes."

"Does he have access to his medication?"

"Yes."

That's a lie. He's not seen them do this once. Vincent's eyes narrow.

"Does he have a lawyer?"

"We offered him one, but he hasn't accepted it," Lucas answers this time.

"And you've got his statement?"

"Yes."

"Then why is he still here? Unless you have concrete evidence that he was involved in the murder, you have to let him go. I know his rights, even if he doesn't."

"He's still a person of interest and we still have some more questions," Anna says.

Vincent pauses, contemplating his next words.

"And I'm sure you've already looked at his medical records?"

"We deemed it necessary."

"Then you must know that he's medicated, receives regular therapy, and hasn't experienced psychosis for two years? He's not a risk to himself or anyone else."

"We also saw the report about the attack in the psychiatric hospital," Lucas says crossing his arms in front of his chest.

"What that report doesn't tell you is that he was only defending himself. The other patient attacked him first."

"Is that what he told you?"

They glare at each other.

"It was a minor incident and he was in a low-security hospital. If Riley was dangerous, he would have been kept in a high-security hospital."

"Yes, but –"

"I'm a doctor, detectives, and I can assure you that Mr Darlington is in a stable condition. His actions aren't any different from anyone else being arrested for something they didn't do. Your judgement is based only on his condition."

"Oh really? Well, he attacked my officer, twice!" Anna exclaims.

"He didn't attack me," Ethan mutters but it comes out louder than anticipated and now all their eyes are on him. So much for being a fly on the wall.

It feels as though Vincent's eyes are burning through him. He lowers his head. There aren't many people who can make him feel small, but Vincent appears to be one of them.

"And this is the officer who was supposedly assaulted?" Vincent asks looking straight at him, clearly not recognising him.

"Yes," Anna answers for him.

Ethan runs his fingertips along the raised skin on the side of his face.

"How did it happen, Mr…" Vincent pauses waiting for him to finish the sentence.

"DS Ethan Brown," he says.

"Ethan?" Vincent repeats with a frown and then there's the look of realisation. "Oh, I recognise you. You're Riley's old *friend*. From when you were kids."

Ethan gives a short nod. Vincent steps towards him extending his hand. Ethan frowns. Strange how he refused to shake Anna's hand but wants to shake Ethan's. He accepts it and Vincent tightens his grip too hard to be pleasant. It's more like intimidation. Ethan doesn't answer his question.

"Tell me, are you pressing charges?" Vincent asks, still gripping Ethan's hand.

"No, at least I don't think so."

With some effort, Ethan wiggles his hand free. He glances at Anna and Lucas who scowl at him.

"About the so-called attack, do you mind telling me what happened?" he asks, and Ethan feels obliged to answer.

"Riley – I mean, Mr Darlington – fled the scene, so I chased him and tackled him. He tried to flee again so I restrained him. During the struggle, he elbowed my face."

Their scowls harden. Has he said something wrong?

Vincent nods, processing the information.

"Seems more like an accident to me." There's a pause. Ethan frowns. He supposes it could have been an accident. "And the second assault?"

Ethan takes a deep breath, now feeling under pressure. As though he's being interrogated.

"He just grabbed my arm when I went to leave."

Strange how he finds himself defending Riley now, but what Vincent is saying seems to make sense and Ethan doesn't like the way they were treating Riley. Vincent turns back to Anna and Lucas, and he lets out a sigh of relief.

"So, your officer chased and tackled Riley, you arrested him and locked him in a room, all because he found a body? You also have no further evidence that he had anything to do with the murder other than the fact he's got schizophrenia. And *he's* the dangerous one?" Vincent's tone is stern, almost disciplinary. He's not quite shouting but not just talking either. This looks bad and they all know it.

"He was acting suspicious and taking photos at the crime scene. Then he tried to flee from detectives..." Anna begins.

"And with good reason, it seems," he interrupts. "You'll be lucky if he doesn't sue you all for this."

"Sometimes brute force is necessary when a person of interest is not compliant."

"But there's no reason for him to still be here. All I see is the police stigmatising a vulnerable person because of his mental health condition."

"Look, until we can verify where Mr Darlington was last night..."

"Last night?" he repeats.

"Yes, between 1 am to 3 am."

"Well, I can tell you exactly where Riley was," Vincent says, causing a silence to fall straight afterwards. Ethan's head perks up. Vincent draws out the silence as if to tease them. "He was at a family function with me and all his family and friends."

Anna and Lucas exchange a look.

"That's not what he said earlier," she says crossing her arms. "He said he was home alone."

Vincent chokes on a short laugh. "Right, probably because you scared him, and he couldn't think straight. He is vulnerable after all. But it's the absolute truth, you can ask anyone of them. So, if you're done questioning him and your officer isn't pressing charges for the so-called assault – which I'd advise he doesn't – then I'd suggest you release him. Now."

Ethan looks between all three of them. Anna unfolds her arms and deflates with submission. She opens the door to the interrogation room and Vincent follows her, slamming the door behind them. Lucas turns to Ethan with that scowl still on his face.

"You've just compromised this case!"

"I can't compromise something that's been bullshit from the start. He's right..."

"Our only suspect is being released because you opened your mouth. And why? Because he's your friend. Ash is right, you should stay away from this case."

"Who the fuck do you think you're talking to, Newbie?"

Lucas's eyes sharpen. "Ash will definitely be hearing about this."

He charges down the hallway and disappears around the corner. Ethan is now alone.

"Snitch," he mutters to no one.

He begins to pace, a million questions racing through his mind. Within a few hours, he found out that Carla is dead, and then Riley was arrested as a suspect. But now what? It's only noon, yet the morning feels like a whole day has passed. The door to the interrogation room opens and the appropriate adult leaves first and doesn't hang around. Then Anna, Vincent, and Riley. He approaches them, but Vincent glares at him.

"What are you still doing here?" he spits.

Ethan ignores him, looking at Riley. "Can I talk to you for a minute?"

Riley looks surprised and maybe even concerned. His mouth drops open but before he can speak, Vincent interrupts.

"Haven't you put him through enough?"

Ethan doesn't respond, he doesn't even look at him. He looks at Riley, waiting for *him* to answer.

"Yeah," Riley manages to say and then clears his throat. "I'm okay with that."

Vincent glares at Riley before letting out a sigh.

"Fine," he says and goes to move with Riley, but Ethan raises his hand, hitting Vincent's shoulder.

"Just Riley," Ethan says, sharpening his eyes.

"No way!"

"Riley, please," he begs looking at him.

Riley looks between them as if trying to decide who he trusts more.

"I think you've caused him enough stress. He's not answering anymore of your questions," Vincent says, grabbing and pulling Riley's forearm to guide him around Ethan. But his body doesn't shift from where he's standing. His eyes are glued to Ethan's. Vincent looks back at him with a frown. "Riley, let's go."

He draws in a deep breath. "I'll only be a minute. I want to hear what he has to say."

"Riley…"

"I'll be fine."

Vincent doesn't release him and there's a silent battle between them as their eyes lock. Anna's eyes shift between all three of them. Ethan almost forgot that she is still here. He grabs Vincent's wrist to pry his hand off Riley.

"He said, he'll be fine," he says, glaring at Vincent who returns the look and reluctantly releases his grip.

"You got a pen?" Riley asks him.

Vincent frowns. "Why?"

He doesn't answer, just holds out his hand. Vincent reaches into his shirt pocket and hands over a ballpen. Ethan places his hand on Riley's arm to lead him away, out of hearing range from them both.

"He's a touchy fuck," Ethan says glaring past him at Vincent, as they stop to the side.

"Can you blame him?"

Their eyes lock and its strange how different Riley is now. He seems normal. Even attractive. Ethan questions where the man went who was in the holding room earlier, but he realises that he was most likely projecting the stigma of Riley's condition onto him. Now he sees clearly.

"Um, I'm sorry about the, uh," Riley says gesturing to the bruise of Ethan's face.

Ethan doesn't know why. After all Riley's been put through, he's showing *him* sympathy?

"It's fine," he says, shrugging it off and moving back before

Riley's hand can touch his face. "It doesn't hurt."

"It was an accident. I didn't mean –"

"It's really okay."

Riley gives a weak, sympathetic smile. Ethan's the one who called him over. He's the one who wants to ask him, well, everything. Does Riley still care about him? Is it a coincidence that he found Carla's body? Why did he leave Ethan all those years ago? But for some reason, no words pass his lips. Ethan's still not sure if he can even trust him. He doesn't know if Riley did have something to do with Carla's homicide or not. He forces himself to believe not, but he can't shake the feeling that they're linked somehow.

"Can I?" Riley asks holding up the pen.

He gestures for Ethan to give him his hand and he hesitantly offers it. Riley takes it and the skin-to-skin contact shocks him. It's a touch that for some reason feels more intimate than sex; caring and delicate. His eyes are fixated on Riley as he writes numbers on the back of his hand.

"If you ever need me for anything, just ring," he says, finishing and freeing Ethan's hand.

Riley looks up at him with another sympathetic smile. Why does he want anything to do with Ethan after this? He exchanges a short smile in return, but Riley doesn't move. He clears his throat.

"It sucks what happened to your partner," he says.

Before Ethan can react, Riley turns and gestures to Vincent. He walks past Ethan, followed by Vincent who scowls at him. He turns to watch Riley leave, wanting to go after him but his body doesn't move. As Vincent catches up to Riley, he places his hand on his back as Riley turns to give Ethan a last look.

Seems weird that Riley said that. People usually say shit like, 'I'm sorry for your loss' which feels pitiful. But what he said feels different. More empathetic rather than sympathetic.

"I didn't realise you take numbers from guys, Skipper?" he

hears Anna say and his head whips around to look at her. She smirks, gesturing to the digits on his hand.

"No! It's just – I don't," Ethan stutters trying to reconcile his fragmented thoughts.

"Relax, I'm only joking."

"Not funny."

The smile drops from her face. He wipes the pen mark from his hand, and it smudges. He pulls the sleeve of his leather jacket over it. Anna takes a deep breath, staring down the hallway and Ethan follows her gaze as Riley and Vincent disappear around the corner. He's gone. Again. *The one that got away*, Ethan thinks as he looks after him even though he's no longer there.

"Well, I guess we're back to square one." She looks at him. "I have to go and fill in the forms for Riley's release, but do you mind sticking around?"

"Why?"

"I just need to ask you some questions." His frown deepens, so she continues. "I need to conduct a formal interview with people who knew the victim and you're the only one who was close to Carla. Plus, you could have been the last person to see her alive. Besides the killer that is."

He nods but doubts he will be much help.

Chapter Four

Anna ushers Ethan through the door and out of the hallway. He stops in the doorway.

"Why are we in here?" he asks.

"It's just procedure," she replies with a shrug before gesturing with the file in her hand for him to take a seat.

He looks into the interrogation room. There's only a table with two chairs on opposite sides of it. It's not designed for comfort.

He steps through and Anna closes the door behind him. Ethan goes to take the seat closest to the door, but Anna gestures for him to take the chair on the other side. He looks at the chair where they'd usually ask criminals to sit in before walking around the table and sliding into it. She plops herself in the chair opposite him, both arms on the surface in front of her with relaxed shoulders and posture. Ethan straightens up but keeps both arms on the table. The room smells like rust. A metallic scent that sticks to the back of his throat.

She lays her file on the table before pulling out a recorder. Ethan frowns at her but she doesn't notice. She barely looks at him.

"This interview will be recorded for both yours and my safety. Is that okay?" she asks and this time she looks at him. He nods. "Good," she says, pressing the record button and opening up the file. "My name is DI Anna Jones. Please state your name for the record?"

"Ethan Brown."

"You're a Detective Sergeant, correct?"

"Yes."

"You've been a DS for a little over a year. Correct?"

Ethan knows where this is going, and he knows the reason she's asking these types of questions in this particular way, getting him to answer in an affirmative manner over and over. It's a method they use to get a person of interest talking and saying the word 'yes'. They use it when interrogating suspects, but he plays along.

"Yes," he says with a low sigh, glancing at the file and then at Anna.

"And your date of birth is the 8th of April 1997. Correct?"

"Yes."

She takes a deep breath looking down at her file.

"How did you know Carla Milhouse?" Anna says looking up at him with wide dark eyes.

He was expecting the question, but he still feels off guard.

"She's my work colleague and my friend. I mean, was." The last word in the sentence trails off as he slumps into the chair. His mind is still stuck in the past. He predicts the next question and he's prepared, regaining his upright posture.

"Have you ever been romantically or sexually involved with Carla?"

"No."

Anna's eyes search his, as she gives an unconvincing nod.

"And you lived together?"

He clears his throat. "Um, yeah, we did." Anna's eyes burn into his. He feels the need to elaborate. "It was for financial reasons. Cheaper for us to share a *two*-bedroom flat than to live in separate flats."

She takes a moment to think, calculating her next move. "So, you worked and lived together, but were just friends?"

"Yes."

"Huh. Wow, I can't imagine living and working with someone. You two must have never gotten a break from each other," she remarks with an unnatural laugh.

"We were good friends," Ethan explains not really knowing where this is going.

"Well, even good friends argue, especially spending that much time together. Did you ever argue?"

"Sure, sometimes."

"Did you argue a lot?"

There's a look in her eyes that tells him this isn't a harmless interview anymore and her tone has switched from light to serious. Is he a suspect now?

He flashes a quick smile. "Like you said, it's impossible to spend that much time with someone and not have the odd bicker."

She still stares at him as if she's trying to figure out if he's guilty or innocent. When did this interview change into an interrogation?

"We're going to need access to the flat," she says.

"Why?"

Ethan knows why, but his defensive side comes out. The thought of SOCOs rummaging through her belongings makes him shudder.

"There might be something she left behind that could determine what happened to her."

He hesitates before pulling out his keys and holding them out to her, but she doesn't take them.

"Saves you breaking down my door," he says with a smirk, placing it on the table with a metallic clang. It screeches as he slides the keys across the surface of the table. He has nothing to hide anyway.

"Thank you." She grabs it and slides it into her pocket. "And when was the last time you saw Carla?"

"Last night."

"Do you remember what time?"

"Not really."

"And what do you remember about last night?"

"Surely you can pull up the report I gave early this morning when I declared her missing," Ethan grunts, annoyed that he has to relive this again.

"It helps us and you to go over the details again, so if you don't mind…" she says gesturing for him to answer the question.

He draws in breath, recalling the events of the night. It's too painful. He remembers vividly how she looked. The way her hair was kinked and crippled from being tied up all day and then let down during the course of the night. How the strobe lights flashed across her face, her dark eye makeup making her eyes look like slits. As the night continued, her leaking mascara turned the slits into panda eyes.

His nostrils flare as they become smothered with that sweet smell of vanilla and jasmine. He half closes his eyes, and his shoulders loosen, feeling a sense of warmth overcome him. A breeze brushes along his shoulder blades trailing from one side to the other. She emerges from behind him, gliding her way around the table towards Anna and standing behind her with her back to him. Her shoulder-length dark blonde hair falling like a waterfall onto the leather of her brown jacket. Her body turns and he catches a glimpse of her face.

"Do you need me to repeat the question?" he hears Anna's voice say but it sounds muffled, and he can't tear his eyes away from her.

Carla turns to face him with her wide chestnut eyes.

"Why are you looking at me? Go ahead, answer her," Carla says, theatrically gesturing to Anna.

His focus snaps back to Anna, who frowns at him. He stutters trying to get his voice working. "It – it was a good day at work." He pauses to swallow the lump in his throat. "We'd just closed a case, and she wanted to go out to celebrate." His eyes are darting between Anna and the table, trying his best not to look at her.

"What case was it?"

"It was a homicide linking to a drug ring."

"Did the suspect make threats at you both, particularly Carla?"

"Nothing that we don't usually get."

"I'm going to need access to that case file and any other cases you both worked on in the run-up to her disappearance."

Ethan closes his eyes for a few seconds before reopening them and looking across to see if she's still there. Carla eyes him with a smirk and folds her arms across her chest.

"So, where did you both go to celebrate?" Anna continues.

Ethan's mouth opens but no words follow. He freezes, remembering raised voices, glass smashing and how makeup-stained tears ran down from Carla's eyes.

"Just the pub."

"That's a lie!" the hallucination of Carla exclaims. He looks at her as she grins at him, before darting his eyes back to Anna.

"What pub?" Anna asks.

"The Harp."

"Anywhere else?"

"No."

"Liar," Carla interjects.

His eyes glance towards her but he tries to fixate his gaze on Anna who frowns at him. Can she tell he's lying? Tiny beads of sweat form on the surface of his skin and the room feels hot with stale air.

"How did the night end?" she asks.

He takes a deep breath but it's shaky. Like his story. He clears his throat. "She disappeared."

"Disappeared into thin air?" she questions.

"She said she was going back to the flat and she'd see me later."

"So, you stayed out?" Ethan nods, realising how stupid that decision was now. How he should have gone back to the flat with her. He feels tears swell in his eyes, but he shakes it off before Anna notices. She moves on. "What time did Carla leave?"

"I got her into a taxi at 10.30 pm, I think."

"Liar!" Carla calls.

His head whips towards her and then to Anna. Lines crease on her forehead. She looks behind confused and then back to him.

"So, what time did you get back to the flat?"

"About 1 am." His voice cracks.

Anna's eyes narrow. "The Harp closes at eleven. So where were you from then to 1 am?"

Shit.

"Yeah, well I went to a club afterwards as well."

"So, you lied before about just going to the pub."

"Slipped my mind."

"What club?"

"Oh, come on Ethan, tell her the truth," Carla exclaims stepping forward.

Ethan tries his best to ignore her but his eyes dart between them both.

"Why do you keep looking over there?" Anna asks, pointing in Carla's direction.

"Why don't you tell her about our little argument?" Carla asks perching herself on the table. "Can you even remember what it was about? Do you really remember how that night ended?"

In a blind panic, he lashes out. "I'm sorry, am I being fucking interrogated?"

Anna doesn't show any emotion. "Just procedure, Skipper."

"Well maybe you should spend less fucking time interrogating me and more time finding out who killed her."

The chair skids out from underneath him as he jumps up. Both Carla and Anna's eyes follow him as he leaves.

"You can't hide it forever, Ethan. They're going to find out one way or another," Carla calls. He slams the door leaving them both in the room. His body is rigid and tensing.

He sees flashes of Carla's body which are replaced by his mother's. They don't know about his mother's murder and given how generic the last name Brown is and how long ago Natalie was murdered, they wouldn't ever look into it. Besides, she was murdered in his hometown Shere in Guildford, and Carla was murdered in London. But Ethan knows better. He knows it's the same killer and he knows what to do next. The only thing he doesn't know is what he and Carla were arguing about last night before she was murdered.

***

Ethan stops just short of Carla's desk as a figure looms over it.

"Hey!" Ethan shouts. "What the fuck are you doing?"

The man turns around with wide green eyes.

"Lucas!" he says through gritted teeth.

"Ethan."

"What the fuck are you doing at my partner's desk?"

"My job."

Ethan narrows his eyes.

"Get out my way," he says, pushing Lucas aside and approaching the desk.

Lucas steps back in front of him. "I've got a feeling I've caught you on a bad day, so let's -"

"Oh, only like the worst!" Ethan exclaims making him withdraw into himself. "My partner's body has just been found, my best friend was arrested, and I'm being told I can't work on the case, but some fucking amateur is!"

Lucas doesn't respond straight away. He places his hand on his hip and perches his lips. "Look, I apologise for earlier. I should know that you're grieving right now, and I should have been more considerate. Is there anything I can do?"

Ethan glares at him.

"Yes. Get. Out. Of. My. Way," he demands as he goes to step forward. Lucas puts his hands up in defence.

"Why? What are you doing?"

"Looking for something."

"I can't let you do that. This isn't your case. It's mine."

"And how can I trust a newbie with my partner's case?"

"You've clearly got trust issues."

That stings because it's true. Anyone he's ever trusted let him down in some way or another.

Lucas takes a deep breath, and a sympathetic look crosses

his face again. "Look, I know this must be hard for you, but I promise I'll find out who did this to Carla."

Classic rookie mistake. Never promise the victim's loved ones that you'll solve the case. In reality, there are so many cases that never get solved and get pushed to the cold case department where they collect dust. But he knows that Lucas isn't going to let this go easily.

"Fine," Ethan says with an exhausted sigh, flopping down in the closest chair to him with his head hung low and his shoulders slumped forward. "You're right."

Lucas's face softens more. "You're doing the right thing," he says as he awkwardly pats Ethan's arm in some form of attempted comfort. "And I'm so sorry for your loss."

Ethan's stomach turns and he feels sick at Lucas's pity. He doesn't want pity. He wants what Riley gave him earlier. Empathy and understanding. Ethan will never understand that saying. 'Sorry for your loss'. What has Lucas got to be sorry about, anyway?

"Can you do me a favour?" he asks, glancing up at Lucas who nods. "Can you get me some water? I can't remember the last time I drank anything."

That's true. He can't remember the last time he drank or ate. Lucas nods before turning away. Ethan watches him leave and as soon as the doors close behind him, he jumps up and begins rummaging through Carla's desk.

He scans over its surface which has paperwork spread out across it. Carla never kept personal possessions on her desk. Work was work. But when he thinks about it, it's probably because she didn't have family or friends. Just like Ethan. As far as he knows, Carla only had one sister who lives in America and the two weren't close.

He tears through the drawers, right down to the bottom, flicking through numerous folders and files before coming across it. He opens a cardboard box from the bottom drawer and freezes.

He frowns down at a photocopy of Natalie Brown's case file. He remembers how he wanted to take the file out, but Carla protested. She told him that he wouldn't want to know what happened to her and that it would do him no good. So why did Carla have it?

His confusion deepens as he rummages through the rest of the paperwork that's in the box. Notes, scribbles, and a series of unformulated numbers. He looks to the door, knowing he doesn't have long. He collects the case file and paperwork in the box and stuffs it into the inside of his jacket. He places the rest of the paperwork back in the drawer before rushing towards the door.

Chapter Five

Ethan drops into the chair next to Oliver's desk. He looks at Ethan with wide eyes.

"What?" he asks.

"Nothing. I just think it was pretty ballsy of you to let Vincent into the interrogation room earlier."

Oliver shrugs. "I didn't do anything wrong."

"How did you get hold of Vincent?"

"Riley was allowed one phone call and he used it to call him." Ethan's not sure why but he feels guilty that Riley trusted someone else to step in and defend him when Ethan failed. "I only led him through when he arrived."

"Why?"

"I just – I just didn't like what Ash had planned. It's against protocol when it comes to dealing with people with mental health disorders."

"Ash did get him an appropriate adult."

"Yeah, not a good one. Riley was entitled to have a friend or family member there. I didn't do anything wrong in taking Vincent through."

"Ash still won't be happy about it."

"I'm just waiting for him to call me into his office.

"He can't do much more than slap you on the wrist for this though."

A small smile tugs at the side of Oliver's mouth. "True."

"Ethan Brown!" he hears Lucas shout. Ethan turns to see him charging across the office towards him. "I told you to leave it alone!"

Ethan rolls his eyes, rising from his seat. "I don't know what you're talking about."

"You didn't think I would notice? You had no right to go through Carla's desk!" he exclaims, but Ethan ignores him, walking past him. He feels Lucas's hand grab his arm to stop him. "I'm still talking to you!"

Ethan shoots him a glare and then shrugs off his hand. "Get the fuck off me!"

Lucas's shoulders tense. "This is my case. Not yours. Don't fuck this up for me!"

Ethan gets it. Newbie trying to show off. He sees this case as his moment to shine and advance his career. To be known as the DS who solved another detective's homicide.

"Go fuck yourself!"

Lucas takes hold of his arm again and Ethan loses it. He grabs Lucas by his collar and pins him against the nearest wall. The back of Lucas's head smacks against it. He raises his fist but freezes after hearing his name being called.

"Ethan!" he hears Anna's voice shout before she comes into view, trying to wedge herself between them both. "Let go!"

She pushes him back and Ethan releases his grip on Lucas. Their eyes locked together in a mutual hate.

"Come with me, we need to have a chat," she says to him before turning to Lucas. "You, go cool off outside."

Ethan and Lucas still haven't looked at her. They continue to glare at each other as Oliver goes to Lucas's side whilst Anna holds Ethan's arm in a way that's gentle yet firm as she leads him towards Ash's office. Ash is standing at the window looking out at them. Ethan averts his eyes. He knows that the little chat she wants to have with him is a scorning, but she won't make a scene in front of everyone. He feels the room heavy on him, but he doesn't look at any of the other officers as he's led into the office.

Ash moves towards his desk with his arms folded. He hears Anna close the door behind him. He feels like prey being trapped and circled by predators.

"Sit," Ash demands, and Ethan can't refuse. He rolls his eyes, throwing himself down into the chair in front of Ash.

"Right, I know what this is about, okay, so spare me the

lecture and tell me my punishment."

"Not this time, Skipper," Anna says from behind him. He cranes his neck around to get a glimpse of her. There's no smirk or humorous tone. Only a stern, professional voice. One she has never shared with him before.

"I told you to leave this case alone, Ethan, but you refused to listen to my orders," Ash says.

"Look, I had a quick look over Carla's desk."

"It's not just that!" Ash shouts, forcing Ethan to sink a little into his chair. "It's everything. You convinced me to let you talk to a suspect and then you cocked up the interrogation because of your emotional attachment. And now, you're picking fights with your colleagues!"

Ethan clenches his fists.

"We think that your personal relationship with Carla and Riley has corrupted your view," Anna explains in a calm yet serious tone.

"But you still couldn't leave it alone. You had to keep fucking interfering."

"Fine. I won't interfere anymore, cross my heart," Ethan mocks, drawing an invisible cross over his chest with his finger and raising one hand.

"You think you're funny? You think any of this is funny!" Ash asks. Ethan opens his mouth. "Don't answer that!" he shouts, and Ethan closes his mouth. "You need to realise that your actions have consequences."

"Fine. Stick me on desk duty for a while then, I don't care."

"No, you need to be seriously punished, the same as anyone else in this place. The problem with you is that you think you're indispensable, but you're not."

"What are you going to do?" Ethan asks, narrowing his eyes.

"You're suspended."

"What!"

"We just think that maybe you need some time off. To heal

from everything. You've just found out that Carla is dead, you need some time to grieve," Anna pacifies. "We're able to look past what you did to Lucas because of what you've been through today. Any other time, you'd be under investigation."

Ethan doesn't turn to look at her, but her voice does something to calm him. "How long?"

"Two weeks, unpaid," Ash says without any movement in his face.

"That's bullshit!" Ethan bursts out.

"Ethan," Anna says from behind him.

"No, you can't do that. What I did doesn't warrant that."

"Do you want to make it four weeks?" Ash says through gritted teeth.

His mouth drops open, but no words exit. It's a fight he can't win. "Fine," he bites, pulling himself out of the seat and turning towards the door. He doesn't look at Ash as he walks towards it. "I'll go collect my things."

"You can't," Anna says stepping in front of him "I'll call you when you can collect your stuff."

He frowns at her. "Why not?"

"We need it for evidence."

"Evidence? What, am I some kind of a suspect now?"

"It's the procedure, Ethan. We have to rule out anyone close to Carla. You must understand that."

"Not to mention your account of last night doesn't make any sense," Ash says from behind him.

Ethan turns to look at him. "I was drunk, so I'm sorry if I'm not the most reliable eyewitness. You can't expect me to know exactly what happened and what time it happened."

"You also didn't report her missing last night."

"I did report her missing this morning before I was told about the body."

"A bit late don't you think?"

"I thought she was at the flat! I even tried calling her over and over all last night. You can check for yourself." Ethan takes out his mobile and throws it on Ash's desk.

"Oh, we will."

"It's procedure, Ethan," Anna says again, drawing his attention back to her. There's a look in her eye that tells him this isn't personal. "Trust me," she whispers so much so that even he can barely hear the words.

He pinches the bridge of his nose. "Fine."

"You also can't go back to your flat," Ash says.

"Let me guess, you need CSIs to go through it first?"

"We need to secure all evidence first, so if there are any skeletons in your closet that we should be aware of, then you better tell us now."

"I've got nothing to hide," he says through gritted teeth. It's a lie, but not for the reasons they think.

"You'll need somewhere to stay while your flat is being investigated. Do you have any friends or family you can stay with?" Anna asks concerned.

Of course not. After his mother died, no other family member loved him enough to stick around and no friend would ever put up with him.

"I'll figure something out," he says.

She nods, stepping to one side to let him through. She grabs the door handle, opening the door for him.

"We may need to question you again, so don't even think about taking any holidays," Ash's voice calls as he heads out the door.

"Ah, that's a shame, I heard Italy is nice this time of year." Ethan turns to flash him a smug smirk before leaving his office.

As he walks across the open office, he can feel everyone's eyes on him, but he doesn't give anyone eye contact. He's not giving them the privilege of seeing him at his worst. He needs to get out of here. As he passes Lucas by the door, he can't resist showing him the middle finger as he leaves.

It hits him as he steps out of the building and the cold evening air sticks to his skin, the night he found his mother's body flashes like strobe lighting in his memory. He presses his back against the brick wall. He's lost everything. His friend, his job, and his flat. He also remembers that he's left the keys to his motorbike along with the flat keys with Anna and there's no way he's showing his face back in there. He pinches the bridge of his nose, contemplating where he could sleep tonight. He doesn't have anyone he can stay with and it's not like he has the money to stay in a hotel or B&B for, well, who knows how long.

He takes out his cigarettes and lights one up. The smudged blue digits on the back of his hand catch his eye. He stares at it. Realising that he's left his mobile with Ash and Anna, he walks down to the nearest phone box as the sun begins to set casting an orange glow across the sky. It's not in use. There are only a few phone boxes left in London that still work thanks to the invention of mobiles.

"Fuck," he mutters to himself as he slams the little phone box door and walks down the road to the next one. He gets lucky with this one.

He shuts himself inside and counts the spare change he has in his wallet before feeding it into the machine. Squinting to read the smeared digits on the back of his hand, he dials the number and presses the black receiver to his ear, looking around as it rings. What if Riley doesn't want to see him? He can't blame him if he doesn't. But Ethan has no other option. He doesn't know what he's going to say and before he can formulate a plan, he's out of time. The ringing stops.

"Hello?" Riley's voice says down the phone. His mouth opens but no words follow. "Hello?" Riley says again. Ethan's sure he'll hang up now if he doesn't respond so he forces out the words.

"Riley, it's Ethan."

There's silence for a long and painful ten seconds.

"Ethan," he says with a hint of surprise.

"Yeah, I – is it okay if, um," Ethan stutters, trying to formulate a sentence. "Can I see you?"

There's a pause. "Riley?"

"When?"

"Now."

A longer pause.

"Where?"

Ethan thinks for a moment. "Your place?"

The line falls silent again.

"Why?"

Ethan sighs. "I just need to see you right now, okay?"

"You're not going to interrogate me or anything, right?"

His heart sinks a little. Is that what he's worried about?

"No, of course not," Ethan says and then sucks in air as he tries to think of how to explain. "I need someone to talk to."

There's a moment of silence and Ethan wonders how long he has on the call before the machine cuts out on him.

"Okay."

He exhales. It's only one word that makes the world fall off his shoulders.

Chapter Six

Ethan takes the tube to get close to Riley's flat and walks the rest of the way as the sky now turns to night. He navigates by remembering the set of instructions Riley gave him over the phone. He lives in the more touristy part of London that has all the museums and art galleries around making the flat easier to find. Ethan has to stop to ask a stranger for directions before he finds it. It's split-level and Riley is on the first floor. He climbs the concrete steps leading up to the front door. This is a bad idea. He shouldn't have called Riley at all. He brings his fist up to the door, his hand hanging in the air as he contemplates whether it's too late to turn around and run. He knocks lightly in the hopes that Riley won't hear and then he can say at least he tried.

He waits for a moment. His body tenses as he hears the sound of footsteps on the other side of the door. He can hear multiple locks being unfastened before the door is pulled open and two piercing blue eyes look up at him.

"Are you okay?" Riley asks and he has no idea how to answer that question, so he shakes his head. "Come in."

Riley widens the door and steps to the side to let him through. He lingers for a while, body edging forward and then backwards in hesitation before he forces himself to move inside. Riley closes the door behind Ethan before scurrying up the stairs. The hallway is small with a shoe rack, coat hangers and a staircase leading up to the rest of the flat.

Ethan looks at the shoe rack and wonders for a moment if he should take his shoes off, before ditching the idea and following Riley up the stairs. He walks through a hallway and into the living room on the left. It's open plan living with the kitchen on the right as he walks through the door where Riley is filling up a kettle. Ethan keeps his distance.

The living room looks like it's out of a home magazine. He

runs his finger along the console table and inspects his fingertip. Nothing. The smell of bleach and fragranced cleaning products smothers his nose. Every piece of furniture is parallel and in line with each other. The back of the dark blue sofa is lined up with the edge of the blue patterned rug under it. A matching armchair to the left of the sofa inclosing the living room area. The glass coffee table is centred perfectly between the sofa and the television. Paintings hang in clean silver frames against the deep blue walls. The colours that surround him take him back to the riverside, to the moment he found his mother's body next to the bathtub. His chest feels tight as his heartbeat quickens and his breathing becomes shallow. He grabs the collar of his shirt, yanking it down.

"Coffee?" Riley asks, taking him out of his thoughts.

Why is he being so nice to him? Ethan wants to ask but can only mutter a simple, "Uh, sure." He pauses. "I have my coffee –"

"With the smallest amount of milk possible?" Riley interjects. Ethan must look surprised because Riley smiles and adds, "I remember."

Ethan finds it weird that Riley recalls how he takes his coffee. He looks around at the pristine flat again. Ethan rang about thirty minutes ago and that's not enough time for Riley to clean the flat to this level.

"Were you expecting company? Like, before I called you?"

Riley looks around surprised by the question. "No, why?"

"No reason," Ethan shrugs looking around. He watches Riley as he grabs cups from the cupboard along with a coffee jar, which is strange considering Riley never used to drink coffee. He frowns. "So, you drink coffee now?"

"I don't," Riley says pulling the lid off the coffee jar. "I just keep coffee in the cupboard for guests."

"Mm." The sound escapes Ethan as he watches Riley peel the foil off the new coffee jar.

"I actually can't have caffeine at all. You know, because of," he says pointing to his head. Ethan watches as he takes out a carton of plant-based milk and looks at it before looking at Ethan with round eyes. "Is plant-based, okay?"

"I guess." He doesn't really know; he's never had it before. "So, you're vegan?"

Riley nods. "Yeah, have been for the last couple of years."

"Huh…" he utters. That's new. An uncomfortable silence fills the air. "What do you do now?" Ethan asks.

Riley pours the kettle water into the mugs. "I'm a photographer."

"Ah, should have guessed," Ethan says, but it comes out more sarcastic than he intended. He remembers that Riley studied photography at university. He doesn't think Riley noticed the sarcasm as he continues to talk.

"Yeah, I work for a studio but also do some freelancing," Riley explains.

Ethan only notices how far away he is when Riley holds out Ethan's coffee, but then decides to place it on the table instead. He scoots it along the wooden surface towards him. Riley steps back and props himself up on the counter, sitting with his legs dangling over the edge. Ethan steps forward and takes the mug. He looks down at the plant-based coffee as if it's poisonous. If it was anyone else, he would leave it on the side, but he doesn't want to be rude to Riley, so he takes a strenuous sip. It's not as bad as he had anticipated, just different.

"So, that's what you were doing in the forest when you found Carla's body? That's why you had a camera?"

"Oh, so we're back to that again?" he asks surprised. "Detective," he adds.

Ethan realises that it sounded like an interrogation more than a harmless question, but he didn't mean it that way. There are traits in his job that have become embedded in his personality.

"It wasn't like I took pictures of her body or anything," Riley defends himself. "So, I'd like my camera back at some point."

"They haven't given it back to you yet?" Ethan asks. He shakes his head. "They're just holding onto it for evidence."

"I need it back for a wedding in a couple of weeks."

"You should probably let the detectives know that."

"I just did," Riley says with confusion.

"Yeah, well…" He pauses, scratching the back of his neck, feeling the heat trapped under his shirt escape through a small gap at the hem of his top. He places down his mug. "That's actually why I'm here. I can't work on Carla's case because of my emotional involvement."

"Right," Riley hesitates, and Ethan can see that he's thinking. "But, you weren't – like – I didn't think you…"

"We weren't a couple," Ethan spits and it comes out harsher than intended.

"Huh, didn't think so."

"Yeah, well, now I've been suspended."

"Suspended?"

"For trying to interfere in the case."

"Oh." A silence hangs in the air. "So, you aren't here to interrogate me?" Ethan shakes his head. "Then, why are you here?"

Ethan sighs, coming forward and placing his hands on the back of the dining table chair. He could tell the truth, but he doesn't know which truth to tell him. He could tell him that he has no one else to turn to; that he needs somewhere to stay; or that some part of him for some reason is convinced that Riley is involved in Carla's murder somehow and he wants to know how. "I need somewhere to stay for a while," Ethan clarifies.

"Why?"

"My flat is full of CSIs, and I won't be able to go back there until they're done collecting evidence."

"But Carla was found in the woods, not in your flat?"

"Yeah, but they still need to go through her belongings in case there are any clues as to what happened to her."

"Oh, so you two lived together?"

That awkward silence creeps back in.

"Yeah, we were *roommates*."

"Right. And now you want to stay here?"

It sounds bad. Like he's just using Riley and expecting that he'll let Ethan stay with him. After what Riley was put through today, he knows he's asking too much.

"I don't mind sleeping on the sofa for a few days. If that's okay?"

"I've got a spare room you can use."

"Thanks," he says flashing a relieved smile.

"I can't believe it's been eight years," Riley says tilting his head to the side. His eyes scan over Ethan from head to toe. "You look good."

The compliment catches Ethan off-guard as he knows he most likely looks like shit, and he stutters trying to formulate a simple 'thank you'. He stops and frowns at him when he remembers how Riley left him eight years ago without an explanation. The fucking coward didn't have the guts to break up with him in person, not even a phone call or a text. He got his father to tell him instead.

"I'll show you your room," Riley says jumping off the counter as if sensing the awkwardness.

He darts past Ethan and heads out into the hallway. Ethan follows him to a bedroom on the left but he lingers in the doorway, watching as Riley darts around the room collecting stuff in his arms and straightening the bedcovers and bedside lamp.

"It's a little messy," Riley says but trails off.

He looks around the room. It's not. In fact, it's cleaner than most hotels Ethan's stayed in. There's a double bed pushed to the back wall, a chest of drawers to the side and a wardrobe. There's also an easel in the corner along with canvases leant up against the wall near the window. Riley follows his eyes towards it.

"Oh yeah, sorry, I use this room for my painting as well as a guest bedroom. You know, for when people stay," he explains, his words trailing off at the end. Ethan doubts that he gets many guests.

He rushes over, collecting his paints and canvases and then attempting to grab the easel. Ethan would offer to help, but he's distracted by one of the paintings on the canvases. It's coloured with red and black paint as a small figure stands in front of a large monster. The creature has a row of bloody fangs and red eyes. He wonders if the painting has stemmed from one of Riley's hallucinations.

"All yours," he chimes, flashing Ethan another smile as he shuffles past him in the doorway. Riley had smiled at him earlier today, but this time, it was a genuine one.

He watches as Riley walks to the end of the hallway and uses his elbow to open the door on the right. He presumes that it's his bedroom and knows that following him in there might be too personal. Riley reappears with empty hands and then gestures to the door opposite him which is next to the spare room.

"Um, the bathroom is in there. Feel free to use any of my stuff. Maybe not the toothbrush though," he says with an awkward laugh. "I've got a spare one in the cabinet you can use."

The uncomfortable silence returns as they look at each other. Ethan opens his mouth to say thank you, but for some reason, no words come out.

"Um, we can watch TV if you want?" Riley offers as he walks back down the hallway towards the living room. "I don't know what's on though. Or maybe we can stream something."

"I'd like to get an early night. It's been a long day."

"Right of course," he says sounding a little disappointed. "I'll let you get some sleep." Neither of them moves. Riley clears his throat. "Goodnight."

"Night," he says, his voice cracked. He watches as Riley disappears into the living room after flashing a quick smile. Ethan retreats into the spare room.

"So, that's Riley, huh?" he hears Carla say from behind as he closes the door.

He spins on the spot to see her standing in the middle of the room with her arms crossed and a smirk on her face.

"Fucking hell!" he shouts jumping back against the door.

"He's cute," she continues nodding in the direction of the living room. "A little strange, but cute."

"No, you're not here! You're dead!"

"Well, you got the second part right."

He squeezes his eyes shut for a few seconds as he mutters, "She's not here, she's not here," to himself and then opens them. She stares at him bewildered.

"What the hell are you doing?" she asks. He shuts them again and waits longer before reopening them. When he does, she's now standing directly in front of him. "Boo!"

"Jesus Christ!" he exclaims, sliding to one side to escape her. "I've gone fucking mad!"

"Probably," she says with a shrug.

"How the fuck are you here?"

"Does that really matter?"

"You're not a ghost or anything right?" he speculates as he pokes her shoulder with his shaky finger to see if it would go straight through.

She scoffs a laugh. "Of course not, what do you think this is, X-Files? No, I only exist within here," she says tapping his forehead. "Grief does funny things to people."

"Right…"

Her eyes look past him in the distance. "Now, what about him?"

"Riley?"

"Yeah, what's his deal?"

"What do you mean?"

"Can you trust him?"

"No."

"Then why are you here?"

Ethan thinks for a moment. He can't work out why Riley's being so nice to him. Why does he care? Why does he even want Ethan here? It doesn't make sense. There's a lot that doesn't make sense about today. The way Carla was murdered, her having his mother's case file, and Riley's involvement. And now he's having a conversation with a dead woman.

"Because it's one of two things; he found your body, so he either knows something that he's not telling me – maybe he's seen or heard something - or he's the killer."

"I'd suggest sleeping with one eye open from now on then."

He remembers Natalie's case stuffed in his jacket. "Why were you looking into my mother's homicide?"

"Ah, do I really need to explain why I can't answer that question?"

"Right, you're not actually here."

"I only know what you know."

"I really have lost my mind," he utters to himself.

"You can deal with that later, but for now we've got work to do."

"We?"

"Well, you obviously need me otherwise you wouldn't be seeing me."

He glares at her. "How do I need you?"

"Isn't it obvious? We've got a killer to catch. *My* killer," she says and something in her eyes lights up as a smirk tugs at her lips, the same way it always did whenever they got given a case.

"This is crazy," he says, "but you just might be able to help."

He could use this figment of his imagination to his advantage to help solve the case, even if in reality he's talking to himself.

"We need to look at the facts in my homicide. My heart is missing. Now, why would the killer take it?"

"As a trophy maybe."

"But why the heart?"

"Maybe the killer had his heart broken emotionally so they - "

"Yawn! Think bigger. The likelihood is the killer's reasons are much more complex than that." She pauses and analyses his face. "You think this is linked to your mother's case, don't you?"

"Her heart was also ripped from her chest."

"But that was sixteen years ago."

"They never caught who did it though."

"So?"

"You were also killed on the anniversary of Natalie's murder. That's not a coincidence."

Her mouth opens and then closes as if contemplating it. "Good point. So, we've either got a copycat, or it's the same killer."

"It's the same killer."

"How do you know?"

"I just know. It's the same crime scene. The killer placed your body next to a river in the same position that I found my mother's body in."

"Seems like that was meant for you."

Ethan goes to the chest of drawers and rummages through each one.

"What are you looking for?" Carla asks from behind him.

"Paper."

Riley had his art supplies in this room, the likelihood is that he's left something behind and it's not long before Ethan comes across a sketch pad and some pencils. He sits on the floor and starts writing down notes of everything he remembers about Carla's murder. Where her body was found, the time of death, and how her heart was extracted. Every detail.

"Shall I make us some ghost coffee?" she asks with a smirk behind her words. He turns to glare at her as she lays across the bed with her head perked up like a seal.

He then pulls out Natalie's case file from his jacket and opens it to the first page where there's a profile image of Natalie.

A young blonde woman with green eyes smiling naively at a camera, unaware that this photo would be used in her murder profile.

"Do you mind if I find out what happened to you?" he mutters to the images.

"Such a gentleman," Carla says amused.

He rolls his eyes. He knows it sounds stupid, but he does it with every case he's worked on. Asking the photo of the victim that question seems respectful, like he's permitting himself to investigate them. After all, he was about to dive into every personal detail of this person's life, including the most personal moment of all; their last.

Ethan finds the post-mortem report and reads through it, comparing it to what little he remembers about Carla's initial evaluation. Natalie was stabbed first and then her heart was removed post-mortem with the kitchen knife. Whereas Carla's was taken whilst she was alive, although she would have passed out along the way.

"So, it can't be the same killer then."

"Just because the killer changed tactics, doesn't mean it's not the same killer. It means they've evolved."

"Which means there's probably more victims."

Coldness washes over him like someone is freezing his blood from top to bottom when he sees it. Her body lying there in her own blood as the bath behind her overflows with water. It's a sight he's not been able to go one day without seeing in his head but seeing it in this crime scene photo takes him back to that moment. The sound of the water, the stickiness of the blood submerging his feet and the voice calling his name. He compares it to the new image that's now been burned into his memory: Carla's body by the river in the exact same position. They were both found near water. A way in which the killer torments Ethan.

"But the killer would have to know you have a fear of water and that you can't swim," Carla says.

"Riley's the only one who knows that."

"Exactly."

"No, Riley couldn't have killed you," he says with a yawn.

"Why not?"

"Because whoever killed you, also murdered Natalie which would have made Riley ten at the time, and a ten-year-old couldn't have committed murder." She gives him a look. "Right?"

But it is strange how Riley supposedly found Carla's body, lying by the water's edge. Chest ripped open like prey, the same as his mother's. He looks back at Natalie's post-mortem report and begins laying down each piece of paper across the floor in front of him.

No DNA was found on the body. His dad was suspected as he had no alibi that night but there was no evidence. Ethan was in his bedroom when she was killed. He was too young to understand anything back then. Still, old enough to commit murder. But he couldn't have killed a grown woman and take her heart. Right? He shakes away the thought, rubbing his tired eyes, but it still lingers in the back of his head. After all, he's seen younger offenders.

He remembers how his dad used to beat him. Was there a reason for that, other than his grief? Was he punishing Ethan for killing his mother but didn't want to convict his own son? Did he kill his own mother? Did he kill Carla when she came too close to the truth? Seems strange that two people in his life are dead. He tries to push those thoughts aside. He can't be the killer. It can't be him. He scratches at his face, trying to keep himself awake and focused.

Then there's his and Carla's argument the night Carla was murdered. They were both drunk and swaying from side to side outside some club. He can't remember what they argued about, but he remembers her eyes were bloodshot from the tears that streamed down her face, and he remembers her shouting at him, or was he shouting at her? Why was he shouting at her?

His body sways to the side and his eyelids drop.

Chapter Seven

Ethan wakes up to the smell of fried food and murmured voices coming from the other side of the door. He rolls over realising that he's laid on the floor still fully clothed. He climbs to his feet and stumbles out of his room, leaving the papers scattered across the floor. Riley is standing at the back of the sofa with a remote control in his hand. The voices on the television become clear.

"Police are still looking into what might have happened to DI Carla Milhouse. Reporter Alice Simmons has more -," the news reporter says, as an image of Carla's smiling face appears on the screen.

The sight of her takes Ethan back. It then changes to a new female reporter standing with a microphone next to the forest where Carla's body was found. Ethan joins Riley's side, both staring at the TV.

"It's a tragedy that's shocked the nation as the body of a detective was found in this forest behind me. All we know is that police are treating her death as suspicious. A man was also arrested and later discharged but police say he is still assisting with their investigation. At this point, police are still reluctant to give out any more details," the reporter goes on to explain. Ethan glances at Riley whose eyes are fixed to the screen. "They are also investigating whether brute force was necessary when making an arrest, which the police have been scrutinised for countless times."

Ethan frowns, feeling as though he's late to the party and must have missed something.

"My arrest," he hears Riley say. They look at each other briefly before Ethan's attention is drawn back to the TV.

At first, he doesn't recognise himself as he watches the low-res footage of a past version of himself tackle Riley to the ground. It looks way more aggressive than he remembered it being.

"Great," he breathes through gritted teeth.

"It's all-over social media," Riley says, getting his mobile out his pocket and pulling up the first social media app on his phone. He holds it up for Ethan to see. A video plays with the same footage that was on the TV.

"Someone's even remixed us to dubstep," he says pulling up a video where someone's looped them crashing to the ground with a repetitive dubstep song playing in the background.

Comments at the bottom of the screen spring up and he catches what some of them say. 'POLICE BRUTALTY!', 'Fuck the police', 'OMG this is the funniest version yet!' and it goes on.

"Fuck social media!" Ethan says batting the mobile away.

"I guess you don't want to see the mountain of videos about Carla's investigation then?"

"What do you mean?"

"People on social media have already started speculating about what happened to her. There're tones of videos about it."

"Fucking social media detectives," Ethan growls.

"You don't have social media, do you?"

"No, just a bloody waste of time."

"Good. I've had to shut mine down," Riley says and when Ethan frowns, he continues, "Some people I used to know have recognised me from that video and I've been inundated with messages all night."

"Wankers!"

"I want you to know that I didn't say anything to the other officers about pressing charges for what happened, you know, you tackling me."

"No, but I bet Vincent did."

"I'm not pressing any charges."

"Why not?"

They stare at each other for a moment.

"I just want this all dropped. Forgotten about," Riley says, switching off the television and throwing the remote onto the sofa, before turning towards the kitchen, “I’ve made you breakfast.” He places a plate on the kitchen table. The smell of fried food now makes sense as the plate has toast, bacon, eggs, and sausages on it.

“Why?”

“Well, you got to eat.”

“I thought you were vegan?”

“I am, but I’m presuming you’re not. So, I went out this morning and bought you some stuff for breakfast.”

“You didn’t have to,” Ethan murmurs, shifting his weight from one leg to the other. He’s not even sure he’ll be able to eat.

“It’s fine, I just forgot how bad dead animal smells.” He lets out a nervous laugh.

Ethan looks at the clock on the back wall of the kitchen. It’s nine in the morning. It was twenty-four hours ago that they discovered Carla’s body and he saw Riley for the first time in years. Strange how now he finds himself standing in Riley’s flat as he cooks him breakfast. Ethan’s never had a guy cook him breakfast before. He always left before the morning to avoid that uncomfortable scenario.

“You’re not eating?” Ethan asks.

“I already did.”

“Right,” he says now feeling even worse. He watches as Riley begins to clean up and he remembers what he wanted to ask him. “What made you turn vegan?”

Riley stops, his shoulders tense and Ethan wonders if he’s asked a personal question. He turns to look at Ethan.

“I don’t know. One day I just woke up and didn’t like the look of meat, or the smell,” he explains, and Ethan notices him clasping his hand over his wrist and twisting his hand around it repeatedly. It could be mistaken for nerves, but Ethan knows that he’s touching the scars on his wrist.

“Right, because the look of meat and blood reminds you of,” Ethan says but doesn’t finish his sentence as he gestures to

Riley's wrist with a rasher of bacon.

"I guess so."

Ethan really can't eat now. He drops the piece of bacon back on the plate with the image of Carla's body in his head. Even though he hasn't eaten properly in the last twenty-four hours, he feels sick.

"Do you always talk like that?" Riley says hopping up onto the counter.

"Like what?"

"A detective."

It's a habit Ethan forgets he keeps doing. "I guess." That uncomfortable silence returns. "Can I go and shower?"

Riley nods as he gets up and walks down the hallway towards the bathroom, leaving a full plate behind. It's a small square space with an over bath shower, toilet, and sink with a glass cabinet fixed to the wall above it. One thing Ethan does note is how clean it is, but he's not surprised. He catches his reflection in the cabinet mirror, realising that he looks like shit. His eyes glance down at the handles.

"Do it," Carla's voice says. He can't see her, but he can feel her breath on his neck. He shakes his head. "Do it!" she demands, and it's the only push he needs to go through with it. He opens the cabinet and inspects the inside. Toothbrush, toothpaste, deodorant, and small rectangle boxes of medication accompanied by a pill organiser with the days of the week written on each compartment. He hesitates before snatching one of the boxes that has a label on it with Riley's full name. Antipsychotics. Ethan opens the box to find two blister packs inside. He places it back where it was before closing the cabinet and looking around. Nothing else.

"Maybe you'll find more personal belongings in his bedroom," Carla says with a tang of excitement. He shakes off the idea.

"I can't," he mutters.

"Why not?"

"I just can't."

"Do you want to know if he's hiding anything? If you can trust him?"

Ethan opens the door and creeps out, looking down the hallway towards the living room and kitchen. He can hear the sound of plates and cutlery cluttering around. He looks at Riley's bedroom door. There's a moment of hesitation before he rushes across and swings it open. He shuts it behind him, careful to place the handle down with minimal noise.

He turns to face the room. A double bed pushed up against the wall on his left. There's a chest of drawers, a wardrobe, and an easel with a canvas on it but it's covered up with a sheet. Canvases are propped up around it. Beige walls surround the rest of the room with blue bedding and rug. He can't waste time. He begins to open drawers and cupboards, but all he finds are neatly folded clothes, sketchpads, pencils, and paints. He goes to check the drawers next to the bed but hesitates. Like ripping off a plaster, he opens the first drawer, then the second, then the third. All he finds are books, art supplies, and headphones. It almost seems too clean. Too innocent.

He then drops to the floor, searching under the bed. A single shoe box, thick with dust on top is underneath. Ethan reaches to grab it, stopping as a pair of shoes walk into his eyeline from the other side of the bed. He throws his head up, making him feel lightheaded as he looks up at Riley.

"What are you doing?" Riley asks, crossing his arms across his chest.

Ethan tries to kick his brain into working, but everything is dizzy.

"Oh, this is your room. Sorry, I thought it was mine."

He watches as Riley's jaw twists, and he tilts his head sideways. A thing he always did when they were younger when he wasn't amused by something Ethan said or did.

"What are all these?" Riley says holding up some papers.

"What the fuck are you doing with those?" Ethan shouts climbing to his feet as he recognises his mother's homicide file in Riley's hand.

"I could ask you the same thing."

"You went through my stuff?"

"Seriously?" Riley laughs gesturing to Ethan and the rest of the bedroom.

"This is different."

"How?"

"Because you're the suspect here, not me!"

"Let's not forget, you're the one who called me. You're the one who came to me."

"Yeah, because I had no fucking choice."

A flash of hurt flickers across Riley's face. "You don't think I already know that I'm your last bloody choice!"

"Can you fucking blame me?" he shouts, and this time Riley remains silent, staring at him with wide eyes. "You haven't made it easy for me to trust you."

"How haven't I?" he asks, his voice weak.

"For starters, finding my partner's body."

"That's not exactly my fault."

"Then trying to flee from the scene."

"You mean when you tackled me?"

Ethan shoots him a look. "After everything that's happened, how can you expect me to trust you?"

"And how can I trust you?" Riley says with no emotion in his voice this time. "How do I know that you didn't kill Carla?"

"Riley, you know I didn't kill her."

"How do you figure that?"

"Because you don't invite a killer to come and stay with you and you certainly don't confront them all alone in your bedroom."

He watches as Riley tries to hide his reaction and maintain a poker face, but Ethan sees through him. He's been caught out on a bluff.

"Yeah, well you also don't go and stay with someone you think is a killer either."

True for most people, but Ethan isn't most people. He still doesn't know if he can trust Riley, but he's determined to find out what happened to Carla, whether or not it kills him. "I still don't trust you."

"Oh, I'm sorry, but aren't you the one who's been suspended from their job? Why? Because they don't trust you? Because maybe they think that you were the one who killed Carla?"

"As far as suspects go, I think they're pointing the finger at the schizophrenic, not the fucking detective!" Ethan says it because he knows it'll hurt him, and guessing by the look on Riley's face, it works. In the moment it seemed like a good idea, now, he wishes he hadn't said it. "Don't touch my fucking stuff!" he shouts as he grabs the paper from Riley and marches out of the room.

"Hello, is this DI Anna Jones?" he hears Riley's voice say.

Ethan's body turns rigid before skidding back into Riley's room where he's standing with a mobile phone pressed to his ear.

"How the fuck did you…"

"Yes, you gave me your card in case I remembered anything."

Riley doesn't break eye contact as he talks into the mobile.

"You wouldn't," Ethan warns as he shakes his head.

"There's something I think you should know."

He lunges forward to grab the mobile and end the call. "What the fuck are you doing?"

"Showing you that you're not the only one with leverage here," Riley says through gritted teeth, snatching back his mobile. "I could tell her and the rest of your little detective buddies that you're still investigating a case that you've been suspended from. I wonder what they'd think of that?"

"You think that's leverage? I could easily get rid of these before you've even ended the call," he says holding up the file.

"True," he says cocking his head to the side. "That's why I took photos of it all so I can show them that you stole a confidential file and I'm pretty sure you'll be more than just suspended for doing that."

He looks at his mobile in Riley's palm, wondering how fast he could knock it out of his hand.

"And I've uploaded them to the cloud," Riley adds.

"You bastard."

"I knew you'd react like this, so I did what I had to do."

Ethan pinches the bridge of his nose. "Fine, what the fuck do you want?"

There's a moment of silence as Ethan watches the clockwork turn in Riley's mind. He tilts his head back and chin up. "I want to help."

"You want to what?"

"You heard. I want to help you figure out who the killer is."

"I think you've watched one too many crime shows."

"Do you want me to call Anna again?"

"Why the fuck do you want to help?"

"Well, you said it. With the police pointing their finger at me, they're not looking for the real killer."

"You have an alibi."

"Yeah, friends and family. Not really a solid alibi and I can tell they don't believe it."

Ethan gets it, Riley wants to prove his innocence, to get concrete evidence that he didn't kill Carla, like Ethan is trying to get evidence to prove that he didn't do it either. Not just to prove it to his colleagues, but to himself. "Don't you have a job to go to?"

"I have holiday to use up and sick days."

Ethan thinks about his options. He can refuse and risk losing his job for good after they find out he took a confidential file, or he can let a suspect help with the case. "Alright, fine."

Riley beams before it turning serious again. "For this to work, we have to trust each other, so you have to promise me that you'll trust me, that we'll work together as a team and tell each other everything," Riley says. "Deal?"

Ethan hesitates. "Whatever," he says which prompts Riley to give him a look. "Fine. We have a deal."

"Great! Where do we start?"

Chapter Eight

"Right, let's start from the beginning," Riley announces from behind a large cork board as he walks into the kitchen with it.

"Whoa, what the fuck is that?"

"A corkboard."

"Why is it here?"

"Isn't this what you detectives use?"

"We have whiteboards."

"Oh, well this will have to do."

Ethan watches as Riley places the board on the kitchen counter, leaning it back against the cupboards.

"We start with Natalie's homicide," Ethan says turning to the case file that's on the kitchen table along with the notes on Carla's homicide.

"Why? What does your mother's homicide have to do with Carla's murder?"

Ethan realises then that he hasn't explained it to him yet. "There's some links between the cases that we need to look into."

"Okay," Riley says leaning over and picking up her file.

Ethan's instincts kick in and he grabs it at the same time to protect it from Riley's prying eyes. He doesn't like the thought of just anyone reading the details of his mother's murder or even worse, seeing the photos of her mutilated body. Both of them stare at each other as neither one let's go. Ethan's hand is partly on top of Riley's which feels too intimate to be comfortable.

"What happened to trusting each other?" Riley raises an eyebrow.

"It's hard to trust someone who's blackmailing you."

"Then why don't I call Anna and get this over with?"

"I'm still letting you help; I just don't want you looking at this file. Not even I've read through it all yet."

Riley's jaw twists but he let's go. Ethan throws himself down into the nearest chair at the table and opens the file. That's when he notices that Riley is still hovering around him.

"What links both Carla's and your mother's cases anyway?"

"Uh," Ethan utters trying to work out the best way of telling him, but his voice doesn't cooperate. "Both their hearts were cut out."

Riley stares at him. "What?"

"Sorry," he coughs, clearing his throat and speaking louder. "Both their hearts were cut out."

"I heard you!" Riley snaps and they fall silent. Ethan can see the information churning over in his mind.

"Didn't you notice Carla's heart was missing when you found her body?"

"I thought an animal had done it."

"No, something much worse than an animal."

"Why take their," he begins and pauses to swallow hard. "Their hearts?"

"I don't know."

"Well, what the hell are they doing with it?" Riley asks, his face rising as he becomes more panicked.

"I don't know, maybe he keeps it as a trophy -"

"A trophy?"

"Or maybe he eats it –"

"Eats it!"

"I don't know!"

Riley stares at him wide-eyed.

"Ethan, what the hell are we dealing with here?"

He doesn't know how to answer. Even for him, this is way over his head, but at least he's familiar with it all, having investigated murders. Riley has no experience in this area at all. "A very sick person. Not a monster. Not some unstoppable villain. Just a very sick, twisted individual," he says. "But hey, I completely understand if you want to walk away from all this."

"Nice try. I'm still helping."

Ethan deflates. “Fine.”

Silence fills the room as Ethan focuses his attention back on the case file.

“You never told me that your mother’s heart was removed.” Riley’s voice is low, and it sounds more like a question.

“I never talk about that night.”

“I know, but you could, to me,” he says looking up at Ethan.

“Well, now I don’t have to,” Ethan says gesturing to all the notes scattered on the table. “You’re pretty much going to find out everything from all this anyway.”

“What about what’s not in that file?”

“I don’t know what you mean.”

“It must have been awful to witness that, especially considering you were just a kid.”

“I don’t really remember it,” he lies. Ethan remembers it vividly. He can even hear the sound of running water and smell that iron stench.

“You can talk to me about it.”

“I said I don’t remember!”

Riley turns away and starts pinning Ethan’s scribbled notes to the board and he wonders if he was too blunt. Ethan picks up from where he left off last night, reading and taking notes about her post-mortem. He turns the crime scene photos upside down so that Riley doesn’t become exposed to them but also because Ethan doesn’t want his mother’s dead body staring him in the face.

“Have you got any beer?” Ethan blurts.

Riley looks up with a frown. “No, why?”

“I could use a drink right now,” he mutters.

“Sorry, I don’t drink,” Riley says, returning to his notes.

“Why not?”

“I just don’t.”

That’s new and he wants to know why. He wonders what else has changed and if he really is the same Riley he’s always known and even at one point, loved. Ethan realises that one thing has changed. He has schizophrenia now. Ethan takes a stab in the dark.

"Let me guess, because of your condition?"

Riley's head shoots up. "Oh, well done, *Detective*. Now can we just focus on the murder?"

"Fine."

Ethan notices how he's pinning Natalie's case notes next to the notes Ethan made from Carla's initial crime scene observations, dividing the board in half, and drawing comparisons between them. A small line creases in the middle of Riley's forehead as he reads. That hasn't changed. Whenever Riley had to study for exams or when he painted, he'd always get that crease of concentration. Ethan hates how much he adores it.

"I can see what you mean about there being links between the murders," Riley says.

"Yeah, the obvious thing being that their hearts were removed."

"So, what do you think? A copycat?"

"It's the same killer."

"How do you know?"

"Carla was murdered on the anniversary of Natalie's murder."

"Coincidence?"

"I don't believe in coincidences. Plus, the killer placed Carla's body in front of a river and positioned her exactly how I found my mother's body. Call it a hunch or whatever, but I just know it's the same killer."

"I thought you couldn't remember anything about the night your mother was murdered?" he says crossing his arms.

Shit. "Well, maybe I remember some things from that night."

"Huh."

"Which brings me to my next point; the killer must be someone we know," Ethan says, and he watches as Riley's body tenses.

"What do you mean?"

"Well, the killer targeted Natalie and Carla and because he knew both of them, the likelihood is that we know the killer too."

"You mean *you* know the killer, Ethan. They're only linked to you." Ethan nods. "So, the killer has to be someone older to have been old enough to murder your, you know."

"You don't think a child could commit murder?"

"Unlikely."

"So, we're looking for someone at least in their late thirties," Ethan says and then trails off into his own thoughts.

"What about your dad?"

"What about him?"

"It's just – I know they always accuse the spouse first," Riley stutters trying to explain. Ethan knows why he's nervous and he knows why Riley is asking.

"He didn't kill Natalie."

"How do you know?"

"Because I *know*. Colin is many things, but I can't imagine he's capable of murder." *Maybe hitting a child, but not murder.* "There's no way he killed Natalie."

"Why do you keep calling her Natalie and not *mum*?"

Ethan's shocked by the question and takes a while to formulate a response that makes sense.

"Less personal, I guess."

"Do you remember much about your mum?"

"Not a lot. Just snippets."

"Like what?"

"I don't think we've got time for this," he barks, pushing the chair back as he gets up and approaches the corkboard.

Riley sighs. "Fine. Have you got anything else for me?" Riley asks as he starts rummaging through the scraps of paper on the table.

Ethan glances around as his hand grabs the crime scene photos. "Don't!" Ethan begins as he lunges towards Riley but it's too late.

Ethan watches his expression and how much paler Riley looks which is worrying considering how pale he is already. Riley's eyes don't blink as they fill with all sorts of conflicting emotions, but he still can't tear himself away from the image. Ethan knows that feeling and it doesn't get any easier with time or experience. But his reaction has also proven something else; that Riley really is innocent.

"Riley," he rasps as he slides the photos from his hand. Riley still looks into the space where the photos once were. "Riley," he repeats but louder.

His watery eyes snap up to look at Ethan as if being pulled back into reality. "I just –"

"I know."

There's a drawn-out silence as Ethan watches him collect his thoughts. "When I found Carla's body, I thought it was a hallucination, that it wasn't real, so it never really…"

"Felt real," Ethan finishes for him.

There's another long silence. Riley's excitement has now disappeared. "You're right, it is exactly like Carla's," he says.

"Yeah, but what I can't work out is why now? What's triggered him to go sixteen years to flag back up on the radar now?"

"Him?" Riley questions. "How do we know the killer's a he?"

"Most violent serial killers are men. Only 15% of serial killers are female and most of those wouldn't kill in such a gruesome manner. Also, most female killers murder men."

"It's rare, yes, but not impossible. We shouldn't rule out that our killer is a female."

He's got a point and Ethan accepts the possibility that the perp is female. "Fine, what's triggered *them* to flag back up now?"

"I've heard that some killers can leave years between their kills."

"That's not what I meant," he says and Riley frowns at him. "I don't think the killer ever stopped."

"What do you mean?"

"I think there are more victims. The only difference between Carla and Natalie is that Natalie's heart was cut out post-mortem and Carla's was cut out whilst she was still alive…"

"Whilst she was alive!" Riley interjects. Ethan looks at the board realising that Riley hadn't got around to pinning that note up yet.

"Sorry, I thought you'd read that bit. Anyway, the killer has evolved over the last sixteen years; you don't make that jump from two kills."

"You do realise what you're saying, right?"

"Yeah, that this has been an active serial killer for sixteen years, which means they're probably not going to stop."

Riley doesn't respond as he stares into space with a blank expression and Ethan's not sure if he should say anything. Riley turns and rushes around the flat, locking the windows and closing all the curtains.

"I don't think some glass and a piece of fabric is going to keep a serial killer from getting in here," Ethan says getting up from the chair. Riley shoots him a glare before continuing to make sure all the windows are secure. "Look, if you want to back out."

Riley spins around to face him. "If you think that there are more victims then where are they? Why haven't we heard about other murdered women with their hearts ripped out?"

"Police probably haven't found the bodies yet. Either that or our killer is smart, and they've killed across different counties to avoid being detected."

"So, what did you mean earlier about the killer being triggered now after sixteen years?"

Ethan takes a deep breath. "Natalie was killed sixteen years ago, and it must have been one of their first kills because they left her there for the police to find. But then the killer goes undetected for sixteen years to now murder Carla and leave her body for us to find. Why do you think that is?"

Riley stares at him. "Because of you?"

"I think the killer wanted me to know that they murdered both Natalie and Carla."

"Are you telling me that you've got a serial killer's target on your back and you're staying in my flat?"

He shrugs. "I guess."

After a brief pause, Riley spins on his heels and rushes out the room. He hears Riley's footsteps down the stairs and Ethan thinks he might be leaving but then he hears the sound of locks on the front door fasten. Ethan decides not to tell him that a few locks on a wooden door probably won't stop a serial killer either.

Chapter Nine

"Breathe," Ethan tells him as calmly as he can, given how frustrated he feels. "Just breathe."

After ordering takeaway and going through the rest of the initial crime scene observations, they'd barely gotten through the gory details of Natalie's post-mortem when Riley had to go and puke in the bathroom. Then he started hyperventilating whilst sitting on the floor next to the toilet, so Ethan grabbed the takeaway bag for Riley to use to breathe into. Ethan squats down in front of him, watching the bag inflate and deflate.

"I told you if you want to leave this all, you can," Ethan says in his last attempt to get Riley to let this go.

"And I told you, I'm still helping! I need to do this," he pants, tearing the bag away from his mouth to answer.

"Well, you can't keep holding me up!"

They'd spent the morning sorting and pinning notes to the board, and most of this afternoon Ethan spent trying to pacify as he can't seem to stomach the gory details of Natalie's dead body. Riley hands him the bag and staggers to his feet, but he loses his footing and stumbles to the side. Ethan grabs his arm to steady him. "I'm fine," Riley snaps and moves himself out of Ethan's grasp.

Ethan rolls his eyes and vacates back to the kitchen. He rummages through the paperwork trying to find something less gross for Riley to deal with and uncovers the sequence of numbers that Carla scribbled.

As Riley returns, Ethan turns and shoves them towards him. "Here, sort this out!"

"What's this?"

"Some notes I found with Natalie's file."

"Whose are they?" Riley asks, struggling to collect them.

"Carla's. That's definitely her handwriting."

"But it's just a load of numbers?"

"And?"

"Do they mean anything to you?"

"No, but they have to mean something, so figure it out."

"I can help with other stuff."

"No, you can't, you've already puked twice!"

"There has to be something else I can do. What else is in this file?"

"Physical and digital evidence, interview statements, that sort of thing," he says flicking through it and pulls pieces out.

"What will all that tell you?"

"A lot. There could be something in there that didn't make sense back then but will now." He grabs the digital and electronic evidence documents and shoves it towards Riley. "Here take this."

Riley takes it and Ethan pulls out his cigarettes and places one between his lips.

"Jesus, you smoke now?" Riley asks.

"No shit!" he says lighting it up.

"You can't smoke that in here!"

"Where else am I supposed to go?"

"At least go over by the window."

Ethan rolls his eyes and sits on the window sill with his knees up as he opens the window and directs the smoke from his cigarette outside.

"You really shouldn't smoke," Riley utters.

"Spare me the lecture."

Riley mutters something that Ethan doesn't quite catch but he lets it go. Ethan spends the rest of the afternoon going through the rest of the post-mortem without Riley and then gathers all the pieces of evidence found at the crime scene looking for anything that could link to Carla's. It's a long shot but it needs doing. The photos show that Natalie was packing her bags and was halfway through packing Ethan's bags. Why was she leaving? Why weren't his father's bags packed too? And where was she taking him? That doesn't make any sense.

He sorts through every photo and all the logged items whilst retreating to the window every now and again for a cigarette in between whilst Riley sorts through all the digital evidence like emails, messages, transactions, etc., but nothing and no one stands out. They order takeaway and eat while working. Riley lies across the sofa on his stomach, keeping his head upright on his elbows as he examines the scribbled pages of numbers. Ethan makes a start on the interview statements. Riley yawns and the bags under his eyes seem to grow heavier as the hands on the clock gather on the left side of the face.

"Maybe we should call it a day?" Riley suggests.

"I can't. Not yet. I just need to go through these statements."

"Did they," he says, taking a long pause. "Interview you when you were a kid?"

Ethan stops with the file in his hand. "Yes."

"Would you rather I looked through it?" he asks.

Ethan raises an eyebrow. "Nice try."

"What?"

"So, you can find something and hide it from me? No way."

"You have trust issues," Riley mutters.

He doesn't respond as he starts reading his father's statement. He knows Colin didn't kill his mother, but he wants to know his account of the night and where he was. The raw typed-up summary of the video recording depicts a grieving husband who's in a state of shock. He wasn't the one who found Ethan by his mother's body. He flicks the page to his statement, looks away and then looks back to it. He remembers being sat in that chair in the family room. He remembers the female detective asking him what he saw or heard before finding her. He remembers saying nothing for hours before they coxed out of him that his mother had put him to bed, and he was awoken by a banging noise. He walked out to find her lying there. It wasn't entirely true. The truth is, he heard shouting, he heard banging, and then he heard silence. Ethan was too scared to leave his bedroom. Even though he tells himself that as a child, there was nothing he could have done, he still carries that guilt.

"Have you figured it out yet?" he calls to Riley, shaking off that feeling. No reply. "Riley?"

He looks towards the sofa but can't see him. He gets up and walks over to find Riley lying on his side fast asleep. He sighs and returns to the kitchen table to pick up the file again.

At the end of his statement, he says that he was found by his mum's friend. Ethan remembers the woman's blonde hair falling off her shoulders as he peered over at his mother's body. He flicks through the pages to the police report from the first responder and begins reading. The neighbours called the police about a domestic disturbance and found him along with Natalie's friend outside the house. She was interviewed and released without further suspicion. He finds the report of her interview and frowns at the piece of paper. Carla Milhouse's name along with the date, time, and place of the interview. It has to be a mistake. He reads every detail over and over again trying to find any mistake that proves this doesn't belong in Natalie's homicide file. He reads her summary report. How she knew the victim, why she was there, and how she found Ethan and carried him out.

The scent of jasmine and vanilla fills the air around him. His eyes look up through his hair at her as she leans against the wall. The first thing he noticed about her when they first met on a case was the way she smelt. Her fragrance that he always found comforting and familiar although could never work out why, until now.

"It was you?" he says with a cracked voice. Carla's eyes narrow. "It was you!"

He remembers his mother's lifeless body sprawled out across the bathroom tiles. The blood seeping out from her across the floor. The sound of running water.

“Ethan!” a familiar voice calls his name. It’s the voice from his memory. The same voice that scooped him into their arms. A much younger Carla lifting him up and taking him away from his mother’s corpse.

“You were there the night she died,” he exclaims, pushing his chair back as he projects himself out of it towards her.

“Damn, I thought I took that secret to the grave,” she says with a slight smirk.

“You think this is fucking funny!”

“Shh, you’ll wake Riley.”

“I don’t fucking care!”

“Will you just fucking calm down!”

“You lied to me!”

“I didn’t lie to you. I just didn’t tell you.”

“It’s the same thing!”

“Well, I don’t know how you don’t remember me!” she shouts, sending him into silence. Her posture shifts into a rigid yet calm composure. “You could never pronounce my name, so you called me, La-La.”

Ethan looks into her chestnut eyes and realisation washes over him. He remembers that name and he has more memories of Carla alongside the ones of his mother but he’s not sure if it’s only his mind filling in the gaps with imaginary images. He moves away from her trying to put distance between them as he runs his hand through his hair, grabbing and tugging the strands in a tight fist.

“This whole fucking time and you never told me!”

“How could I?” she cries and her cracked voice is like icy water on a red burn. He looks at her as her eyes line with tears.

“That’s why you were looking into her case.”

“She was my friend and I wanted to do it for you. Everything I did was for you.”

“You still should have fucking told me!” he shouts as he kicks over the kitchen table. It crashes to the ground with a large thump.

"Ethan?" he hears Riley's voice say. Ethan turns to look at him as he peers over the back of the sofa. His eyes puffy and tired.

"Sorry."

"What's wrong?" Riley says. A thump on the floor distracts him from answering Riley's question. Riley lets out a sigh. "That's my downstairs neighbour."

Ethan still has more rage to release, and he needs someone to aim it at. So, he begins stomping on the floor over and over again. Both his feet rising and thumping the ground in sync with each other.

"Go back to sleep, you fucking assholes!" he shouts.

When exhausted, he stops and looks at Riley whose eyes are now wide and staring at him.

"You done?"

Ethan thumps his foot one last time. "Yes."

***

Ethan fills Riley in on his latest discovery and he doesn't realise how long he'd been going through Natalie's file until he notices the sunrise through the gap in the curtain. A slither of light peeks into the living room where Riley stares at Carla's interview summary. He's been gawking at it most of the night whilst asking what, how and why Carla never told him.

"Are you done staring at that?" Ethan asks taking a drag on his cigarette next to the open window.

"Sorry, I still can't believe Carla was Natalie's friend and you never knew," Riley says as he goes over to the board and pins it with the rest of the interview statements.

"I guess I just don't remember her all that well," Ethan says. It does make sense given how familiar Carla felt to him when he first met her, but he could never work out why. He flicks the stub of his cigarette out the window.

"Well, this has to be a lead, right?"

Ethan looks at him. He's beginning to sound like a detective now and Ethan's not sure if that's good or bad.

"It can't be a coincidence," Ethan says taking out another cigarette and lighting it up. Riley gives him a disapproving look. "What? I'm stressed!"

Riley's landline starts to ring and he's quick to answer it.

"Hello?" he says on the phone. He doesn't speak for a few seconds before holding it out towards Ethan. "It's for you?"

"Who is it?" he asks through his cigarette. No one knows he's here.

"Anna."

Ethan rolls his eyes, ditching his cig and getting up to grab it. He looks at the phone in hand and then at Riley. "Why the hell do you have a landline anyway?"

"My mobile doesn't always have a signal and if I need someone in case of an emergency, I've got a landline."

"Right, because of your condition, I get it," Ethan mutters before bringing the phone to his ear. "What do you want?" he says into the phone.

"Hello, Skipper!" Anna's voice bellows down the phone.

"Why are you calling here?"

"You left your mobile here and I thought to myself, where would young Ethan be without a phone, a flat or any family to turn to?"

"So, you figured I'd be here. Great detective skills."

"Didn't take a genius to work it out."

"What do you want?"

"For you to come and collect all your crap for starters. We've searched through your desk but didn't find anything useful. Also, your motorbike is still here."

The blood rushes to his face. He had stormed out in such anger, he forgot all about his bike and he had too much pride to go back for it.

"When can I collect it?"

"Today preferably."

"Fine, I'll be there this afternoon."

"Oh and bring Krispy Kremes! You fucked up so you owe us, don't forget," she shouts down the phone.

"Right, because being suspended isn't enough of a punishment, I still have to buy you all doughnuts."

"That's right," she says, and he can hear a smirk behind her words.

"Fine," he says and hangs up before she can answer back. "I've got to go out."

"Where are you going?"

"To the station."

"Why?"

"I've got to pick up my stuff and bring in some doughnuts," he explains but it confuses Riley more as a deep frown appears on his face. "It's just some stupid thing we do. When someone messes up, that person has to buy everyone doughnuts."

"Doughnuts… that's a bit cliché, isn't it?"

"That's the point. It's supposed to be funny."

"Hilarious," Riley mumbles.

"You coming with me?"

Riley chokes out a laugh. "Why on earth would I want to come with you?"

Ethan shrugs. "Fine, you can stay here if you want. I'm sure you'll be fine, after all, your locks will keep a serial killer out. Maybe."

He can see that Riley's thinking it over. "I'll drive," he says finally as he collects his keys off the counter.

"We'll walk and take the tube," Ethan interjects. Riley looks at him waiting for an explanation. "I could do with the fresh air. Plus, isn't walking good for your condition?"

He doesn't want to tell him about the motorbike, otherwise, he really won't come along and for some reason, Ethan wants him there. Riley nods, placing the keys back down.

Chapter Ten

Riley side-eyes Ethan carrying the box of doughnuts as they walk down the hallway of a building he never wanted to come back to again. Riley's throat feels tight, and his chest feels like it's being crushed. He takes a deep breath before speaking.

"So, it's true then?" he asks.

"What is?"

"That all you guys do is sit around all day eating doughnuts."

Ethan gives him a disapproving glare. "It's not all we do, but some sugar sure does help."

Riley nods, lowering his head. As they walk through into the open office, Riley brings his hand to his mouth to bite away at his fingernails. It's a chaotic mess of detectives, copiers and desks scattered around the room. It's like any other office, except there are some whiteboards with notes scribbled on it along with photographs, but that's the only sign of any stereotypical detective work.

As the door closes behind them, Anna cranes her neck around from her desk, and a smile lights up her face. She leaps from her office chair and shouts to the rest of the room, announcing their entrance.

"Oi, Skipper's here!" she shouts.

Riley frowns, leaning in closer to Ethan. "Skipper?"

"It's a nickname they give Sergeants," he explains as Anna approaches them. Her eyes land on Riley.

"Oh, and he's brought his pet."

He frowns, feeling insulted to be referred to as Ethan's pet.

"Ma'am," Ethan says, offering the box of doughnuts which she snatches and places on the desk.

A girl with red curly hair bounces up to them.

"Did you get custard ones?" she asks. Ethan nods, but the red-haired woman is distracted when her eyes find Riley. "Who's this?"

"This is Riley. Riley, this is Milly," Anna says as she takes a doughnut and waves it in the air gesturing to them both.

Milly's eyes grow wide, staring at him. Riley watches as she pulls Anna to the side, lowering her voice so he can't hear. At least she thinks he can't hear her.

"Riley, as in the suspect in Carla's case?" she whispers to Anna.

"Yeah, but he's not a suspect anymore."

"Isn't he, you know," Milly uses her finger to spin circles in the air next to the side of her head and makes a short whistling noise.

"I can see you," Riley says. She looks at him with round eyes.

"He has an alibi," Ethan says, and Riley lowers his head.

"An alibi that checks out," Anna adds. Milly's mouth forms an O in realisation. "Custard," Anna says, holding out a doughnut to her. Milly swipes it, shoving it into her mouth.

"Ethan," Lucas calls, approaching them with a box in his hands. "I've got your stuff here."

He holds it out towards Ethan, and Riley already knows that look in his eyes. Like he's about to punch someone.

"Keen to get rid of me then, Lucas?"

"Just trying to help. Plus, it was in my way."

"What do you mean?"

"Well, it was on my desk."

Ethan looks at Anna and Riley follows his gaze. She finishes off her mouthful before speaking.

"Well, we're tight on space, so we've temporarily given Lucas your desk."

Riley's body tenses, already feeling Ethan's anger radiating off him.

"How nice of you," he says, grabbing the box off Lucas, but then discarding it onto the closest desk. "You better not fuck up my chair, Newbie. I got the seat perfect on that thing."

"Don't worry, I'll have it exactly as you left it when you return. Well, *if* you return," Lucas says as he turns to Anna.

Riley knows what Ethan's going to do next. As Ethan's fist locks back behind his head and shoots forward towards Lucas, Riley's hand catches it, forcing it back down. Riley catches Anna shooting Ethan a look to which he responds with an overly sweet smile whilst placing his hands behind his back. Lucas goes to pick up a doughnut, but Anna bats his hand away.

"I don't think so, Sarge. I want that report on my desk first," she taunts and winks at him.

"I'll come back later then," he says with a smirk. Then he turns to Ethan. "I'll be sure to keep your seat warm for you."

Riley's body tenses.

"Fuck you, Newbie," Ethan spits.

"You're not really my type." He winks at Ethan before walking away. Ethan's eyes still burn into his back as he walks out the doors.

"Doughnut?" Anna asks holding out the box towards them.

"No, thanks," Ethan says. She then holds it in Riley's direction and before he can decline the offer, Ethan jumps in. "He can't, he's vegan."

"Oh, you're one of those." Riley frowns, wondering what that's supposed to mean. "Do you want me to get you some carrot sticks then?" Anna says with a smirk and a laugh erupts out of Milly through a mouthful of food.

"I don't just eat carrot sticks," he says, realising that it's the most he's talked to them since being here.

"Right, celery sometimes too, then?" Anna mocks.

He shifts his weight from side to side, not finding her jokes as funny as Milly does.

"He's not used to our type of humour," Ethan says, and a look is exchanged between him and Anna that makes them stop.

"Your motorbike is also out the back. Here you go," Anna says, picking up a key off her desk and holding it out to him.

"Motorbike?" Riley says, shooting Ethan a glare. "You didn't say anything about a motorbike."

"Slipped my mind." Ethan grabs the key from Anna. "Right, I have to go and get my coffee from the kitchen," he says, changing the subject.

"Can't you just leave it here?" she asks.

"You can get fucked if you think you can suspend me and then drink my coffee!"

"Fine, but you'll have to leave your pet here," Anna says, pointing to Riley and he hopes that nickname doesn't stick.

Ethan goes to leave but Riley rushes forward and grabs hold of the fabric on his jacket.

"You can't leave me here alone with them," he says with hushed frustration.

"Don't worry, I won't be long. I'll be back by the time they eat you alive."

Ethan grins before disappearing. Riley looks around concerned that he's just left him with Anna and Milly.

"Your kind of cute for a schizophrenic," Milly says, cocking her head to the side and running her eyes up and down him. Riley's body tenses.

"Milly," Anna says like a parent.

"Sorry, it's just – you don't look like you have schizophrenia. You seem so, normal," Milly tries to explain but it only cuts him deeper.

"I am normal," he croaks.

"I didn't mean it like that! It's just – I – I meant," she stutters.

"It's fine," Riley interjects. "I'll have to try and show it more next time." He gives a weak smile, and she returns it.

"So, do you like hallucinate shit a lot? Like right now?" Milly asks with wide eyes and an enthusiastic tone.

"Don't be stupid!" Anna exclaims.

"No, it's mostly controlled through medication," he answers.

"Fascinating," she says leaning forward and resting her elbow on the desk and her chin on her knuckles. Riley's not sure if 'fascinating' is a word he would use for it. "So, what kind of stuff do you hallucinate?"

Riley glances at Anna who rolls her eyes. "That's kind of personal."

She squints as if trying to inspect him. "You must be really wild in the bedroom."

"Milly!" Anna shouts.

"What? I heard that people with schizophrenia are, you know, a little kinky."

Milly stares at him as if waiting for an answer. She doesn't expect him to answer that, right? He squirms on the spot, wanting to be anywhere but here right now. "Don't believe everything you hear."

"Shame." She grins with a wink.

"Haven't you got work to do?" Anna says. They exchange a look before Milly bolts, heading out the office. His shoulders slump, and he bites his nails to try and relieve his nerves.

"She doesn't mean any harm," Anna says. He looks at her. "She just doesn't have a filter over her mouth."

"It's fine. I get stuff like that a lot."

"But you shouldn't," she says, and it catches him off guard. Their eyes lock and she gives a short smile before turning to look at the paperwork on the desk, but he keeps his eyes on her.

"Weren't you the one who arrested and interrogated me yesterday?" he asks, confused as to why now she seems to be on his side.

She looks at him and their eyes meet again. "You've got me wrong, Riley. I only treated you as a person of interest because you found the body and then tried to run. Not to mention smacking my DS in the face. It wasn't about your condition. Well, not for me anyway."

He guesses that makes sense, so he nods. Their eyes are still locked together and there's something sincere in the way she looks at him. It's different from before and it's different from the way the others look at him.

She's the first to break eye contact as she looks back down at her paperwork. How did he not notice before how attractive she is? Probably because the last time they saw each other, she arrested him and interrogated him. Although some men get a kick out of that. She's flawless in every way and out of his league. But Riley thinks that about a lot of people.

She glances up at him, catching him still looking at her. Great, now he looks like a creep. He darts his eyes away but realises that's worse. He looks back at her and she's still eying him. He gives her a crooked smile, trying to wipe the sweat from the palm of his hands onto his jeans. She chokes out a laugh and he's worried what she finds amusing. Does she think he's creepy or cute? He adverts his eyes towards the ground, not sure what to do now.

"You got a girlfriend?" Anna asks and his head whips back up to her. "Or boyfriend?" she adds with a shrug.

He hesitates and stutters, debating how to answer the question. "Neither unfortunately."

"Huh," she utters, as she looks him up and down with a smile tugging at the ends of her lips. "I find that hard to believe."

She raises an eyebrow and Riley feels the heat rush to his face. Is she flirting with him? Is he blushing? Anna's smile widens as if enjoying the effect, she has on him. She looks down. "Are you an artist, Riley?"

He frowns, wondering how she would know that. She gestures to his hands which have dried paint in the creases of his skin.

"Oh, yeah," he mutters, inspecting his own hands. He's not sure why that impresses him given that she's a detective. He decides to make it into a joke. "You should have been a detective," he says but his voice is too shaky. Her face breaks into a wide smile.

"I'll bear that in mind," she laughs and then pauses. "You must be a good friend to let someone you haven't seen since school stay with you."

"Who?" Riley says frowning. She raises an eyebrow. "Oh, yeah, Ethan. Well, we did use to be, close."

"Oh, what happened?"

He shrugs and begins to shift on the spot again. "I don't know."

"Just old friends that drifted apart?"

"You could say that."

"And now?"

He thinks for a moment not knowing what him and Ethan are anymore. "I don't know, I guess I feel sorry for him."

"Right, because of Carla. I know they were close."

"Yeah well, it's not just about Carla."

"What else is it about?"

"His mother."

"What about her?"

"You don't know?" he asks. She shakes her head. "She died when he was ten."

"Oh shit," she says with wide eyes. "Why wouldn't he tell me that?" she then mutters. It sounds rhetorical, but he still answers the question.

"You know what he's like. Too much pride."

"And arrogance."

He chokes out a laugh. "That too."

"How did she die?" Anna asks.

"Murdered."

Riley looks at her, realising that he's said too much. Her eyes are large and her jaw drops.

"Did they ever catch who did it?"

He doesn't answer. Something shifts in her eyes as she blinks away what Riley could only describe as fear. Then she does something which surprises him. She leans across the table, taking one of his hands into both of hers. He feels the heat rush to his face again as she rubs her thumb across the surface of his skin.

"Look, I'm only trying to help him, same as you. But he won't let me, and I can't help if I don't know what's going on."

He looks down at her hand as she caresses his skin. Her fingertips sliding under the hem of his sleeves and finding his scars. He winces but then feels something different. Comfort. He looks at her as she offers a sympathetic smile.

"No, they didn't catch who did it," he chokes.

"How was she murdered?"

"I don't know, Ethan doesn't talk about it much. I can't blame him though; he was the one who found her body."

"Jesus, that's rough!"

He replies with a short grunt.

"You really must be a good friend to stick by him," she says.

Her fingers trace invisible circles on his skin as her gaze lifts and then a catty smile spreads across her face. Their eyes locked together. Anna's smile drops and she pulls away, straightening herself. He frowns.

"Right, I'm ready to get the fuck out of here," Ethan's voice sounds from behind him, making Riley jump. He turns to see Ethan throw the jar of coffee into the box.

"You know you should really keep your desk tidier, Skipper. Took us hours to clean it. I mean what am I? Your mother?" she says in a tone that slices the atmosphere.

"You should have just left it a mess then, Ma'am. I'm sure Luc wouldn't mind," he replies with a grin.

They glare at each other, and Riley starts to feel caught in the crossfire, glancing between them both.

"Let's go, Riley," he says, collecting the box off the desk.

Anna turns towards him as if Ethan's not there anymore. Her expression softens again.

"Don't be a stranger," she says and places her hand on his upper arm for a few seconds too long to only be a friendly touch. Her lips grow into that catty smile again as she retreats and walks away.

He can't help but watch her as she leaves and then he feels a force jab him in his arm. He whips around to see Ethan scowling down at him.

"I said, let's go," Ethan growls as he storms away.

"What's this about a motorbike? You didn't say anything about a motorbike," Riley shouts jogging to keep up with him as they leave.

Chapter Eleven

Ethan empties the contents of the box into the compartment under the seat. He slams it shut and tosses the box on the ground while an uncomfortable Riley stands to the side of the motorbike.

"Here," Ethan says grabbing and holding out a helmet.

"Why do you have two?"

"One was Carla's."

"Right," he says inspecting the helmet with a hesitant look. "This one was hers?"

Ethan shrugs. "I'm sure it'll fit your tiny head."

"Look, there's no way I'm getting on that thing!"

"Why not?"

"Do you have any idea how many accidents involve motorbikes?"

"You do realise that pretty much all accidents involve cars, right?"

Riley shoots him a glare. "I'm not doing it!"

"Don't be such a fucking baby and put the damn helmet on."

Ethan shoves the helmet into his abdomen but Riley glares at it and then him. His jaw twists with stubbornness before grabbing it. "Fine," he mumbles under his breath, turning it around in his hands.

He tries to slide it on his head, but it gets stuck. Ethan rolls his eyes and thumps on the top of the helmet so it shifts down over Riley's head. He straightens it and then adjusts the clips for Riley, tightening them around his chin before securing it. His fingertips tracing Riley's soft skin along his jawline.

His eyes meet Riley's. Blue eyes shining out from under the black helmet that frames the sides of his face. Ethan places both hands on either side of the helmet and something in Riley's face lights up. Ethan shakes the helmet from side to side and that loving gaze vanishes in Riley's eyes.

"What the hell!" Riley exclaims.

"I have to make sure the helmet is secure. Unless you want your pretty brains splattered on the tarmac." Ethan swings his leg over the motorbike and puts on his helmet. Riley hesitates by the side of the bike. "Are you fucking coming or not?"

"I'd prefer 'or not'."

Ethan shoots him a glare. Riley's shoulders slump and he approaches the bike. He tries to lift his leg over it but accidently knocks the bike and almost falls over himself. Ethan rolls his eyes. Riley finally manages to hop up on the back. Riley's weight shifts behind him from side to side.

"Are you quite done?" he snaps, and he can feel Riley's scowl burn into the back of his head.

"It doesn't seem very safe," Riley says with hesitance in his voice.

"Relax, there's a bar under the seat that you can hold…"

Ethan stops, feeling his arms slide around his waist. Riley's hands clasp together over his stomach as their bodies fasten tight together. His head tucked behind Ethan's shoulder blade. That knot in the pit of his stomach reties itself. The same knot that he used to get when they were teenagers. Before Riley left him. Ethan shakes off the feeling and unties Riley's hands from his waist.

"There's a bar under your seat you can hold onto," Ethan repeats and he feels Riley lean back to grab it.

Ethan releases the brake and speeds off. Riley's arms wrap back around him and his hands form tight fists gripping Ethan's shirt.

"Slow down!" he hears Riley call from behind.

Ethan eases off the accelerator, allowing the bike to slow. He also decides that weaving through traffic isn't a good idea, not with how nervous Riley is. He follows behind the slow-moving car in front of them for what seems like forever. Checking his mirrors, he notices a black car behind them that seems familiar.

It's a number plate he recognises from when they first set off. He could be paranoid, or they could be being followed. His mind always goes to the worst-case scenario, so he has to test his theory.

He makes a detour, turning last minute at the next junction and taking unconventional roads. The car follows his movements as he predicted. Turning onto the main road they recently came off, the car follows them, keeping a distance far enough to try not to be recognised, but close enough that Ethan knows that they're being followed. They stop in traffic, and he eyes the car waiting a few vehicles behind. Ethan has the advantage, because it's harder to follow a motorbike. He leans back to speak to Riley.

"Hold on tight," he says, but he has no time to explain.

With the rev of the engine, he swings the motorbike around and does a U-turn in the road. Riley's arms tighten around his abdomen, and he feels his helmet press into his back. Ethan speeds off in the opposite direction, passing the car that was following them. The car has dark tinted windows so he can't see inside, but Ethan flips off the car anyway. He looks in the side mirror as the car also tries to make a U-turn in the road to follow them.

Weaving through the traffic he takes his chances squeezing into every minor gap possible. Some blast their horns and others shout curses, but Ethan ignores them. He's focused on getting away. He peers over his shoulder as the car attempts to follow but it falls behind. Ethan turns off the main road and onto a side road, leading them out further away from buildings and into open space with more rural landscapes until he can't see the car following them anymore. He keeps speeding onward, paranoid that the car might reappear.

Ethan skids the bike around a sharp bend. He doesn't see the car coming the other way. He barely has time to react. He misses it by inches as the sound of a car horn blasts. Riley's hands grab at Ethan's arms. He can hear Riley's voice shouting, but he's not sure what he's saying. It sounds like he's shouting for Ethan to stop the bike. To slow down. But the more Riley pulls at his arms, the more Ethan's hands pull the throttle back, causing the engine to rev louder and louder, overpowering Ethan's thoughts in his head. The needle jumps into the red.

Riley pulls at his arms again and this time, the bike rears up. There's a blur of motion as the road in front of him disappears from view and all he sees is the sky and handlebars in front of him. The bike flips backwards, skidding out from under him. He scrapes across the tarmac before his body is mercilessly tossed around over and over again. As fast as things escalated, they slow down to nothingness as he stares directly at a bush. He's lying on his side with half his face in the grass and dirt. His body feels numb and detached from his mind.

Disorientated, he tries to look around. They're in a field just off the side of the road. The bike is on its side and Riley is lying a short distance from it on his back. Riley. He looks so motionless and fear pumps straight into Ethan's veins, motivating his body to move. As he tries to lift his body, he realises his right arm is twisted unnaturally and hangs limp. He struggles to his feet, but his knees buckle, and he falls to the ground again, so he crawls across the grass towards Riley using his one working limb. He can't feel the pain of his dislocated arm. Yet.

"Please don't be dead. Please don't be dead. Please don't be dead," he mutters to himself repeatedly as he approaches Riley's side.

He's staring up at the sky. His eyes round from shock. Ethan can't see any blood or visible injuries as he scans his body.

"Are you okay?" Ethan asks.

He doesn't speak at first as he stares up at him with his mouth open. "I – I think so."

Riley goes to move but Ethan stops him. "Don't move!" He could have a head injury and if he moves, it could cause more damage. "How many fingers am I holding up?" he asks, using his non-injured arm to hold up two fingers.

Riley squints. "Tw – two." Riley's eyes widen. "You're hurt," he says, half a question and half a statement.

Ethan looks down at his dislocated arm. "I'm fine."

"No, you're not," Riley says as he starts to get up.

He tries to stop him again. "No, stay still. You could have a head injury."

"I'm okay," Riley says getting up and balancing on his knees. He leans in towards the injury, inspecting his arm. "It looks like it's dislocated."

"I know, it's fine."

"We should get you to a hospital."

"No," Ethan blurts out.

"It's got to be put back."

"It can't be that hard to do." Ethan looks up at him. "Your parents are doctors, surely you know how to put it back?"

Riley narrows his eyes. "Fine."

He staggers to his feet, almost falling over as he stands. He moves behind Ethan, placing one hand on his shoulder and grabs hold of Ethan's arm with the other.

"Right, I'm going to count down from three and then I'm going to pull."

"Okay," Ethan says as he mentally and physically prepares himself. Then, he second guesses letting Riley do this. "Wait, is this going to hurt?"

"No. What the hell is that?" Riley says pointing in the distance in front of Ethan.

"What?" he asks confused.

The next thing Ethan feels is the cracking of his bones locating back into place as Riley yanks his arm back. Pain surges through it, gathering in his shoulder.

"Motherfucker!"

"You okay?" Riley asks coming around to look at him.

"You said it wouldn't hurt!"

"Well, I wasn't going to tell you that it would!"

Ethan rotates his arm around in large circles to create some stimulation. "Fucking hell."

"What the hell were you thinking?"

"What?"

"I told you, didn't I? Bikes aren't safe."

"Well, if you hadn't pulled my arms, I wouldn't have lost control."

"Maybe you shouldn't have been driving like a bloody lunatic! Are you trying to kill us?"

"Oh, I'm sorry for trying to protect you from the creepy car that was following us!"

"Someone was following us?"

"Yes."

"Who?"

"I don't fucking know, do I?"

"Oh," he utters before collapsing in a heap on the grass.

Ethan looks behind him at the bike lying on its side. "We'll have to roll the bike back."

"Okay, I just need to sit down for a bit first."

He looks exhausted as he lies back on the grass, staring up at the sky again. He's still got his helmet on. He's not visibly injured but an accident takes its toll mentally. Ethan nods and then collapses by his side, both of them on their backs staring into a blue void. Neither of them says a word but that's what he likes most about Riley. He doesn't need to say anything. As the sky fades to a dusky pink, he knows they better head back. They both get up and work together to get the motorbike standing again. Ethan tries to take most of the weight, but he struggles. He doesn't tell Riley that his body aches and throbs because he knows that if he tells Riley, he'll insist on taking him to the hospital. Ethan knows he should see a doctor, but he decides against the idea. Them having a motorbike accident doesn't look good with everything else that's going on right now.

"It's a long way back," Riley says with exhaustion. "Maybe we should just stay somewhere else so we can rest for a bit."

"Like a hotel?"

Riley looks around at his surroundings and then pulls out his mobile. "You know, I don't think my family's cabin is far from here."

"Your family's cabin?"

"Yeah, their holiday home in East Sussex. If we are where I think we are, it's closer than my flat."

Riley holds up his mobile to show him the route. Ethan nods and accepts the closer option given how much pain he's in but wonders if it's a good idea to go to a secluded cabin whilst there's a serial killer targeting him.

Chapter Twelve

Night has now fallen as Riley and Ethan each hold onto one handlebar of the motorbike, using it to support their weight as they roll it along the side of the road and dragging their feet behind them. Riley directs them using Maps on his mobile. His phone also being the only light source guiding them as there are no street lights along this road. It takes them a few hours before they reach a forest with a dirt track running through it. They follow the path up as a cabin next to a lake emerges into sight.

He watches as Ethan kicks the stand on the bike before tripping on a large stone. His arms reach out to catch Ethan. He looks at Riley surprised.

"I'm fine," he says, but Riley knows it's not true. He says that way too much.

He notices Ethan holding his side.

"How badly are you hurt?"

"Not bad."

He watches as Ethan continues to hold his side and stumbles up the steps of the cabin. Riley collects the rusty key from under the plant pot, unlocks the door, and holds it open for him. Ethan sways from side to side making his way indoors. Riley walks behind him, making sure he doesn't fall. He's obviously more hurt than he's letting on.

His parent's cabin is charming and traditional, with dark wooden beams, walls, and flooring. A large red rug in the centre of the living room and large floor to ceiling windows running along one side of the cabin where the view of the lake is. Riley remembers coming up here as a child and teenager all the time. That same childhood smell clings to this place even after all these years. He can't quite distinguish what the scent is though, except for wood, forestry, and water. The coldness in the cabin seems worse than the outside air. Riley switches on a side table lamp that emits a warm glow around the cabin.

"It's a bit cold in here," Ethan says.

"Yeah, my parents didn't install heating."

"Why not?"

"They only use it during the summer, so there's no point."

"Oh."

He watches as Ethan limps his way into the living room looking around the place. Riley realises that when they were younger, Ethan was never invited to come here. He turns to look at Riley.

"What?" Ethan asks.

"Your hurt."

"It's not that bad."

"You need to let me have a look."

"I said, I'm fine."

"Let me help."

Riley slides off his helmet and goes over to the sofa to pad out the dust and make it seem more appealing.

"Come on, take it off," he says gesturing to his shirt. He senses Ethan's hesitation.

"It's just a few bruises, I'm sure I won't die."

"I should still take a look, so take it off." There's a pause. "Come on, Ethan, it's nothing I haven't seen before."

Ethan's eyes sharpen and the air now feels stuffy and humid despite the cold. "That's different."

"Look, it's either I help you, or I'm taking you to the hospital."

Ethan glares at him before pulling the hem of his shirt up. Riley watches as he winces in pain, struggling to free himself. Riley goes over to help him, grabbing the fabric and tugging it up. Ethan grunts from the force as it goes over his head and then slips off his arms. Underneath the purple bruising blotted all over his body, is a landscape of sculptured muscles that are highlighted more in the dimming light.

"Sit," Riley says trying to clear his throat.

He goes to the kitchen to get ice from the freezer and wraps it in a tea towel. When he turns around, Ethan is sat on the sofa, still holding his side. Riley approaches, dragging the coffee table closer to him and sitting on it. He gently moves Ethan's hand away from the dark purple bruising which has stained most of his right side. He lowers the ice-wrapped towel onto his skin, watching Ethan's face as he winces. Riley knows that he won't say anything. He's always acting tougher than he is as if he has a point to prove. But Ethan doesn't need to be like that with him.

"Is this what you do for a living?" Riley asks, trying to take his mind off the pain.

"What? Get into accidents?" he asks and Riley nods. Ethan laughs. "No, that's not an everyday occurrence. I mostly do other stuff."

"What kind of stuff?"

"Just paperwork, interviewing suspects, talking to relatives, stuff like that."

"Do you have a gun?"

"No."

"Have you ever killed anyone?"

Ethan shakes his head with a slight laugh. "I get the feeling you think my job is more exciting than it actually is."

"Have you ever saved anyone before?" Riley asks and lifts his gaze to look at Ethan's chestnut-coloured irises.

"I like to think that every criminal I put behind bars is saving someone's life down the line."

"Huh." He thinks about his next question. "Have you ever used your job to pull anyone before?"

"No," Ethan laughs with shock.

"Well, nowadays, detectives are considered sexy."

Riley focuses on the bruising and does not allow himself to get too distracted.

"Do you?" Ethan asks.

"Do I what?"

"Think detectives are sexy?"

Riley looks at him with a slight grin. "Depends on the detective."

He could have sworn that Ethan's cheeks flashed red, but the lighting is too dark to tell for sure.

"Yeah, well what about you?"

"What about me?" Riley asks.

"You know, being a university student, you must have done all sorts of stuff. Parties, drinking, drugs…"

Riley chokes a laugh. "I'm hardly going to tell a detective if I've ever taken drugs or not."

"Technically I'm suspended."

"It was never really my thing." He pauses. "Turn around."

Ethan turns his back to Riley, and he attends to the bruising there. There's something other than bruising on his skin. Small pale indentations are scattered across his back. Like shallow cut marks. Similar to the ones on Riley's wrist, but smaller. Not made by a knife, but by the buckle of a belt. He thinks about their positioning too. As if Ethan was in a foetal position when those marks were made. Riley traces his fingertips across one of the scars. He's seen them before, but it hits differently this time. He feels Ethan's back tense in defence.

"You can talk to me, you know? About what your father, you know, did to you."

Ethan doesn't respond at first and Riley regrets saying anything. "Yeah, well, you should have seen the black eye I gave him one time."

"You don't have to do that."

"Do what?"

"Act like it doesn't hurt. Like you're emotionless," Riley says, watching Ethan's body tense again.

"I guess I have to. Part of my job."

"Don't try to make it sound heroic. It doesn't make you a hero. It only makes you arrogant and frustrating to be around."

Ethan chokes out a faint laugh. "Do you think that's why I don't have any friends?"

"I'm your friend."

"You know what I mean."

"In the end, all you do is hurt the people around you."

"Yeah, well, hurt people hurt people, right?"

"That's not completely true. Hurt people only hurt themselves." Riley pauses and swallows the lump in his throat. "And in the process of their self-destructive mission, they unintentionally hurt the ones around them. They don't mean to, it just happens. What you're doing is different. You're deliberately pushing people away and hurting them."

Ethan doesn't say anything which is strange for him to not come back with a quirky or sarcastic remark. Instead, they sit in silence as Riley soothes the bruising over Ethan's skin until the ice melts and all he has is a damp cloth.

"You should get some rest," Riley says after a while, getting up and rearranging the pillows on the sofa for him to place his head down.

Ethan collapses the rest of his body across the sofa.

"Set an alarm for the morning," Ethan says. "I want to be out of here at sunrise."

Riley sets an alarm on his mobile and places it on the table. "Okay, just be sure to wake me up if I miss it."

Riley shifts from side to side in the armchair until he gets settled.

"Don't you have your own room here?" Ethan asks.

"Yeah, but I don't want to leave you."

Riley switches off the lamp. Darkness and silence linger between them.

"Do you think we need a code word?" Riley asks.

"What do you mean?"

"Like a word that we can use if we're in trouble? A word that only we know that means we need help without us saying it."

"Sure."

"What word should we use?"

The silence goes on for so long that he wonders if Ethan will ever answer him.

"What about 'oranges'?"

Riley thinks for a moment. "That could work." He pauses. "Ethan?" he says but he doesn't respond. "Are we going to die?"

"Why are you asking?" Ethan questions out from the darkness.

"Because of the car that was following us. You don't think that was the, you know?"

"The killer?" That silence creeps back in again. "I don't know."

"Are you saying you don't know if that was the killer, or you don't know if we're going to die?"

"Both."

Riley stares into the darkness for what feels like hours before his eyes give in, and sleep consumes him.

***

Ethan's bare feet move along the cold wooden floor towards the ajar door. He can hear his mother's raised voice along with another. The other voice is familiar, but he can't quite figure it out. His mum turns to look at him in shock and that's when the sound of an alarm rings through Ethan's ear and he jolts awake.

He's lying on his side, facing the sofa cushions. He stares at the colour of the red fabric, trying to recall the nightmare he's forgotten but has still left his heart in his mouth. It takes him a while to realise where he is and then he remembers how they had stumbled back to Riley's parent's cabin. He stirs, grunting in pain with every movement as he reaches across the coffee table to turn off the alarm on Riley's mobile.

He looks over at Riley who is fast asleep in the armchair, half curled into a foetus position. There's a peaceful, content look on his face as gentle sunlight saturates through the window and lights up his skin with a warm glow. He doesn't move much in his sleep, only soft breathing. He decides not to wake him.

He notices Riley's arms are crossed over his chest and his body shakes. Is he cold? Ethan can feel the crisp bite in the air as he peels back his leather jacket off his body allowing the cold to crawl over his now exposed skin. He places the jacket over Riley's torso. He stirs but then relaxes.

Remember, he left you, Ethan reminds himself. Riley was the one who didn't want him anymore. It's strange how fast hate replaces love.

The need for a cigarette to relax his mind becomes overwhelming. Ethan pulls his shirt back on, trying not to muffle his grunts of pain. He goes to the large window with the sliding door and steps out, gliding the door shut. He looks through it at Riley who's still sleeping.

Ethan walks down the dirt sloop towards the lake pier, pulling his cigarettes out his jeans pocket and lighting one up. Listening to the wooden slates beneath his feet creak, he looks out at the vast landscape as the sky turns into a mix of pale pink and purple, reflecting off the clear motionless water. The cigarette burns away too fast, and he tosses the stub across the pier. The sight of the vast deep water makes Ethan queasy, so he sits on the edge of the wooden structure. He imagines what it would be like to be submerged in it. Nothing around him but water. Lost into nothingness. Ethan wouldn't stand a chance. He can't swim.

The sound of footsteps on the wooden pier makes Ethan crane his neck back to see Riley walking down towards him.

"You didn't wake me," Riley says, falling somewhere between a statement and a question. He joins Ethan at the edge of the pier, holding his jacket close to his body. Ethan shrugs.

"You looked like you needed to sleep."

"Thanks," he croaks, holding up Ethan's jacket. "Do you want it back?"

Ethan looks at it and wonders if the goosebumps on his arms

are obvious or not. Riley's body shakes in the bitter breeze.

"No, you keep it."

"Are you sure?"

"I'm not cold."

Riley then does something that surprises him. He slides his arms into the jacket and zips it up. The fabric swallows his body, and the sleeves overhang his hands. It's strange to see him wearing Ethan's tatty, old jacket because Riley always wears new and expensive clothes. He looks at Ethan with wide eyes and gestures to the material.

"This is clean, right?"

Ethan chokes out a laugh. "Ungrateful bastard."

Riley smiles and then does something else that shocks Ethan. He pulls the collar up to his face, covering his nose as he smells it.

"Smells like cigarettes and cheap booze."

He grins and Ethan lets out a short laugh, making a note in his head to wash his jacket. He can't remember the last he washed it. Probably never.

Riley approaches his side and sits next to him with his legs dangling off the edge of the pier like a child. Neither of them says anything but it's okay. It's a comforting kind of silence as they look out at the landscape.

"We better get back to the flat," Ethan suggests. He can feel Riley's eyes on him, but he doesn't look at him. They're now behind on the investigation and Ethan doesn't want to waste any more time.

"Yeah, we probably should."

"This has been a complete waste of fucking time."

"No, not really."

He feels Riley's head rest on his shoulder as he shifts closer. Ethan darts his eyes to the side to look at him, too scared to move his head in case it disturbs him. Riley's hair grazes his neck as he faces the lake. It smells nice. A strange sweet but masculine smell. He still has that look of content on his face. The rising sun reflects a light-yellow tint off Riley's skin. It highlights the blue in his irises, making them seem almost inhuman. A small smile tugs at Ethan's lips and he looks back out to where Riley's looking.

"You smell like smoke," Riley says with a slight smirk in his voice.

"Sorry."

Are they watching the sunrise together? With Riley wearing his jacket? Seems like something they would do if they were a couple.

Chapter Thirteen

Anna makes her way down the rows upon rows of shelving, each stacked with sealed containers holding evidence of cold cases that they hope to resurface and miraculously solve. Each one feels like a reminder of their failings.

She looks between the plastic boxes and the scrap piece of paper in her hand which reads:

Natalie Brown,

February 25th, 2008

She halts, wiping her head up and down to confirm that it's the right box. Carla was murdered on the 25th of February 2024. That's not a coincidence. She screws up the piece of paper and shoves it in her pocket. Anna reaches out and grabs the container with both hands, yanking it out from between two other boxes. She shakes off the dust and then makes her way out to check it out of storage. It feels like it's been minutes but really, it's hours later when she finds herself sat in the conference room eating a soggy sandwich as she begins to sort through the contents.

"What are you doing?" Lucas asks, appearing in the doorway.

"And where the hell have you been?"

"Out for lunch. Now you?"

"Just looking into this cold case."

"Why? We've already got a case on the go," he says gesturing to the whiteboard which has notes scribbled on it along with images of Carla's corpse. She shoots him a testing look. "Ma'am," he adds.

"I think this case is linked to Carla's murder."

"How?" he asks intrigued.

"Here's how."

She places a finger on the crime scene photo and slides it across the table towards him.

"Who is this?"

"Natalie Brown. Ethan's mother."

His head whips up. "And her heart was?"

"Missing. Never found. And neither was her killer. Not to mention she was murdered on the 25th of February as well."

Lucas rubs the bottom of his chin back and forward.

"And Ethan never told you about this?"

"Nope. I found out through Riley."

"Huh. Sounds like he's been trying to hide this."

"Why do you think that is?"

"Because he's guilty."

"He was ten when his mother was murdered."

"And? Doesn't mean he couldn't have done it."

She shrugs, turning to look at the rest of the paperwork.

"Do you know what else I found?" she asks, and he perks up, his interest growing. "Ethan found his mother's body but guess who found him." She pauses for the sake of being dramatic as she leans into Lucas a little closer. "Carla Milhouse." His mouth opens but nothing comes out. "I know. It says in the first responder's report by that Carla arrived at the house and found Ethan with his mother's dead body. Police were already called to the house because of a domestic disturbance. Apparently, Carla was a family friend."

He scratches his chin. "It's a bit odd that Carla was friends with his mother and then years later they end up working together as detectives."

"Well, it actually makes a lot of sense," she says, and he frowns prompting her to explain. "About two years ago, Carla was in charge of a drug raid, and it was just a fluke that Ethan was one of the uniformed officers on that raid too. After they met, Carla started to pay extra interest in him. Training him, helping him pass his Sergeant's exam, and then demanding that he gets stationed with her. I always thought it was because she fancied him but now."

She gestures to the files.

"Do you think he knows?"

She thinks for a moment. "Probably not. He was quite young when Carla was in his life and who honestly remembers their mother's friends."

She can see his brain working overtime as a deep frown crinkles his forehead and around his eyes.

"It can't be a coincidence that Ethan's mum was murdered…"

"...with her heart ripped out."

"With her heart ripped out, and then exactly sixteen years later Carla is murdered the same way."

"Precisely," Anna confirms.

"Do you think he did it?"

"God no! But the killer *is* linked to Ethan somehow and I'm going to find out how."

A knock at the door interrupts them.

"Come in," Anna calls and Oliver peers around the door with a file in hand. "Is that the post-mortem?" she says gesturing to it, and he nods.

"Milly's explained it to me," Oliver says. "Just what we suspected. The killer started cutting into her chest whilst she was alive. She passed out at some point and then the killer used an electric saw to cut the ribcage open to get the heart out."

"Sounds like our killer has a lot of aggression," Anna airs her thoughts out loud.

Oliver hesitates in handing over the file.

"What's wrong?" Lucas asks.

"They found something else," he says with a sigh as he hands over the file to Anna.

Keeping her eyes fixed on Oliver's expression, she grabs the file and opens it. She begins to skim-read trying to find the most shocking thing about Carla's post-mortem. Her finger finds it, and she stops breathing. She feels Lucas close beside her, peering over her shoulder.

"This has to be a mistake," she says to no one in particular.

Oliver shakes her head. "Are you sure?" Anna asks looking up at him.

"Milly is certain."

"Shit!"

Anna knocks into Oliver as she races out the conference room and tears down the hallway towards Ash's office. She bursts through his door, causing him to shoot her a look of shock and disappointment from behind his desk. She notices the phone in his hand that's pressed to his ear.

"We need to talk. Now," she whispers. By now, Lucas has caught up and is standing beside her.

"Something's come up, I'll speak to you later," he says before hanging up the phone. "What the hell do you think you're doing?"

"It's urgent," she says out of breath. He gestures for her to continue. "First of all, there's more than one victim by this killer."

She explains everything to him concerning Natalie's murder and then hands him Carla's post-mortem file. They all stand in silence as the wrinkles on Ash's face crinkle into a frown. She calculates how long it'd take for him to get to the point where his expression will lift into a state of surprise, which it does. He glances between them and the file.

"Right."

"What would you like us to do?"

He thinks for a moment, leaving Anna waiting in silence. "Keep this under wraps. No one needs to know, not even Ethan. Don't show your hand too soon, understood?"

"Yes sir," they both say in uniform.

"No one needs to know about Natalie's murder either. I don't want the press finding out about this. In fact, we should just be focusing our attention on Carla's murder. Not some cold case," he says discarding the file on his desk.

"But Sir –"

"You shouldn't even have dug up this cold case," he says, not quite shouting but enough to shock her into silence. She bites her bottom lip to prevent saying something that'll get her fired and loops her finger inside the ring around her neck. "Leave it alone and focus all your attention on Carla's homicide."

"Can I ask why, Sir?" Lucas asks.

"Because if the press finds out that there's been a killer walking around on the loose for sixteen years, our department will be ripped apart and under investigation for its failings. You'll cause mass panic and for what? Some small chance that this is the same killer?"

"It is the same killer," she growls through gritted teeth.

"The profiles are different and there's too much of a gap between them."

"Both their hearts were ripped out."

"Coincidence."

"On the same day."

"You've only got two things linking these cases together. You need a lot more than that if you're going to make this stick and cause a national scandal and panic."

"I could if –"

"I said to drop it! Understood?"

"Yes Sir," she snarls before coming forward and snatching the files without giving him any eye contact. She storms out with Lucas at her heels.

"We're not going to leave it are we?" he asks.

"Of course not."

Chapter Fourteen

Ethan's back there again. The sound of running water pouring over the sides of the tub. His footsteps on the creaking old wooden floorboards. The sound of his feet in thick red liquid. He looks down at his mother's body lying in a pool of her own blood.

"Ethan," he hears Carla's voice.

The body on the floor switches to Carla's. The same position. The same place. The same sound of running water. The same ripped-open chest, hollow look in her eyes, and mouth pried open in a silent scream. He closes his eyes.

"Ethan," she says again a mixture of both his mother's voice and Carla's.

He opens his eyes, now feeling shorter as he looks up at the large door in front of him.

"He is my son!" Natalie shouts at someone who Ethan can't see.

Ethan can only see his mother through the gap between the door and the wall. He steps forward, looking up at her but she doesn't see him. Her eyes full of hatred are aimed at someone out of sight.

He hears mumbling but he can't work out what the other person says. That's when his mother sees him. She looks at him with wide eyes and an open mouth. "Ethan."

His eyes fling open as his body jumps. It's that dream again that feels so real. He gasps, looking around at Riley's living room. He's back at the flat. Ethan struggled to ride the bike back with his injuries and Riley sat on the back. He drove slowly and took regular breaks meaning it took them almost the whole morning to get home. As soon as they'd gotten back, Riley had insisted on wrapping Ethan's bruises with icepacks and bandages. He looks down to see that Riley has placed a thin blanket over his torso. He pulls it back to look at the bandages. It still feels sore as he repositions himself on the sofa.

He then hears Riley's mumbled voice coming from the kitchen. He stirs, trying to sit up and that's when the pain he'd been so blissfully unaware of hits him. Struggling to sit up, he looks over the back of the sofa. Riley darts around the kitchen placing mugs and dishes in the sink.

"I trust him," he says in a hushed voice. "That was an accident." He pauses. "He's not going to hurt me," he hisses louder this time.

Oh no, Ethan thinks to himself, *he's hallucinating*.

"Riley," Ethan hears his own shaky voice call. Riley looks around at him with wide eyes. "Who are you talking to?"

"Hey," Vincent's voice bellows as his head pops around from behind the kitchen wall. "Sleeping Beauty's awake."

Instinct kicks in and Ethan tries to jump to his feet. He stumbles and falls head-first onto the floor.

"Are you okay?" Riley's voice calls.

He recovers, using the coffee table to help him climb to his feet. Riley rushes over, face full of concern with outstretched arms ready to catch him. He's now conscious that he's shirtless.

"What the fuck are you doing here?" he hisses, looking past Riley at Vincent.

"I could ask you the same thing," Vincent appeases, leaning against the wall.

"I'm sure Riley's already filled you in on that."

"Hm."

"Where's my shirt?" Ethan asks, now looking at Riley.

"I'll just go and grab it," he says, turning and darting away.

An awkward silence crawls in as he looks everywhere but at Vincent.

"I don't think it's a good idea, you know," he says, his voice startling Ethan. Vincent slurps his drink.

"What isn't?"

"You, staying here with Riley."

"Why?"

"Well, it just seems like everyone around you drops dead." There's a coldness to his voice. "First your mother and now your partner. A bit odd, don't you think?"

"I'm surprised you remember about my mum's death."

"We all lived in a small town, it's not something you easily forget."

Ethan looks into the kitchen, relieved to see that Riley has removed all their notes and files. He sharpens his eyes and straightens his back to gain height.

"I don't think what Riley does is any of your business."

Vincent adjusts himself, mimicking his stance.

"Have you thought about how all of this," Vincent says gesturing his hands into the empty space, "is affecting Riley's illness? How the stress isn't good for his condition?"

"How the fuck am I bad for his condition?"

Vincent draws out the silence for dramatic effect. "Do you have the faintest idea about schizophrenia? How it works?"

"No, but…"

"You're not capable of looking after him."

"And you are?"

"Well, I am a doctor."

"And why do you care?"

"Excuse me?"

"Why the fuck do you care what Riley does?"

A flicker of something flashes across his face before the sound of Riley's footsteps down the hallway interrupts them. They both turn to look at him.

"Found it," Riley says, coming into the room holding Ethan's white shirt and offering it to him. "I washed it and dried it for you."

Ethan pulls it on over his head, grunting at every slight movement. He looks at Riley who is glancing between them as he brings his hand to his mouth and bites the ends of his nails. Ethan notices that Riley is still wearing his leather jacket even though the flat is warm.

"What's going on?" Riley asks.

"We…"

"I was just saying that I better go," Vincent interjects.

"Oh, okay, Vinny," Riley mutters sounding disappointed.

"Vinny?" Ethan mimics.

Vincent takes one last swig out of his mug before placing it down on the table and then approaching Riley with a charming smile.

"Thanks for having me," he says, wrapping one hand on Riley's waist and pulling him in to place his lips to the side of Riley's face.

Ethan gets it now, and his body tenses in repulsion. He notices Vincent's disapproving eyes as he looks the jacket up and down.

"I'll see you out," Riley says as he goes to follow him.

"I'm sure he can find his own way out, unless he's a dumb shit," Ethan snarls. Riley turns to shoot him a glare, but he ignores it. "Or do you need me to draw you a map?"

"That's okay, I know my way around," he says with a wink before turning to Riley with that smile again. "Call me later, okay?"

Riley nods. They're both silent as they listen to Vincent's footsteps fade down the stairs, followed by the front door opening and closing.

"Why do you have to be like that?" Riley snaps, spinning around to look at him.

"I don't trust him."

"Why?"

"I don't trust anyone with a name like Vincent."

"You don't trust anyone at all."

Ethan crosses his arms and sharpens his glare.

"What was that about anyway?" Ethan demands.

"What?"
"That!" he says gesturing towards the air that Vincent has vacated. "The whole, '*Thanks for having me*' and then that kiss."
He tries to hide his jealousy but it's difficult.
"It's a kiss on the cheek, what's weird about that? He's just being nice."
"Yeah, sure, he's just being nice."
"Why does everyone have to have an alternative motive with you?"
"So, you're telling me that there's absolutely nothing going on between you two?"
"What's it got to do with you anyway?"
They stare at each other, and Ethan can't decode Riley's emotions from under his scowl. He's right though, it has nothing to do with him because they're not a couple anymore. Not through Ethan's choice, but because Riley left him. He holds his glare thinking about the way Vincent had placed his hand on Riley's back and kissed the side of his face. There was no hesitance. Like someone who's been that close before. Maybe even closer.
"You're fucking him, aren't you?"
Riley's mouth drops open in shock. "That is none of your business!"
"Is he the reason?"
"The reason for what?"
"The reason you fucking left me!"
"I left you?" he repeats in disbelief.
"Yes, you! You fucked off to university and cut me off!"
"I was in a mental institute," he says narrowing his eyes. "Not that you cared about that."
"What the fuck does that mean?"
"You never came to see me. Hell, you never even showed up after I was discharged."
Ethan's body tenses and he clenches his fists to relieve some

of his anger.

"And how the fuck was I to know that you were in a mental institute? I didn't even know about your schizophrenia until now!"

"That's a lie! My father told you what happened to me, and you told him that you didn't want to see me anymore."

"Bullshit! Your dad never told me jackshit!" Ethan shouts and Riley shakes his head. "You were the one who said that you didn't want to see me anymore!"

"When the hell did I say that?"

"Don't act dumb, your...," Ethan stops feeling as though a veil has been lifted in his mind. *Your dad told me that you didn't want to see me anymore.* The same way Riley's dad told him that Ethan didn't want to see him because of his schizophrenia, and they both believed him. He always knew how much Riley's dad hated him, but he didn't think he'd go this far.

"You didn't say that," Ethan says, trailing off.

"Well, duh!" he snaps.

He thinks about how much this would hurt Riley. To be betrayed by his own father. Ethan knows what that's like. Is it better for Riley to be hurt by him or by his dad?

"I'm sorry," he chokes. He can see by the look on Riley's face that he wasn't expecting that. *I'm sorry I ever listened to your fucking dad*, is what he really wants to say. "I was young and stupid back then."

Riley's shoulders slump and his body deflates. Ethan watches his expression. Exhaustion. Hurt. He'd always pushed Riley back before because he thought that he left him and that he didn't want him. The truth is they both never ended things and now every emotion that Ethan's suppressed is racing to the surface. The need to comfort him overcomes Ethan. He steps forward, closing the gap between them but as he does, Riley steps backwards.

"Let's just leave the past in the past. Okay?"

"Okay," Ethan agrees, but his mind revisits the very reason

why this argument started. "Are you though?"

"Am I what?"

"Seeing Vincent?" he asks and Riley glares at him. "I need to know for the investigation. I need to know who is coming in and out of this flat and why."

"Because you don't trust anyone," he says with a hint of sarcasm, and Ethan nods in agreement. Riley crosses his arms and he doesn't answer straight away, his glare still fixed on his face. "There's nothing going on between me and Vinny."

"You can tell me if there is."

"There isn't."

"Riley –"

"Look, Vinny is just my father's friend, okay? My father gets him to check in on me from time to time because he lives closer. Happy?"

"Thank you," he says with a sigh of relief. An uncomfortable silence creeps in as they stand in front of one another.

"What's next then?" Riley asks.

Ethan's eyes flicker to the kitchen clock. "Fuck, how is it 10 pm! Why didn't you wake me earlier?"

"You needed to rest."

"Not for 24 hours!"

"Well actually, you've been out for three days."

"Three days!"

"You took quite the hit, Ethan, your body needed to rest."

He's right, but Ethan can sleep after Carla's killer is caught. "Well, we better catch up," he says pulling out the kitchen chair and falling into it. Riley doesn't respond, so Ethan looks up at him as he shifts from one leg to the other. "What's wrong?"

"Nothing, it's just." He pauses as he tries to formulate a sentence. "I have a sleeping pattern."

"A sleeping pattern," Ethan laughs.

"Yeah, because of my schizophrenia," he explains, and Ethan drops his smirk. "I need a regular pattern with a good amount of sleep."

Ethan thinks about what Vincent said and how he's determined to prove him wrong.

"Go to bed now then."

"Are you going to be okay?"

"I'll be fine, just go."

Riley doesn't move and looks around the living room. "What if I sleep on the sofa instead?"

"Why?"

"In case you need me for anything."

"No, just go to your bed. I'm sure that's way more comfortable."

"But –"

"Go," Ethan insists, but he still doesn't move.

"I don't want to be alone right now."

He gets it now. Ethan gestures to the sofa and watches as he lies fully clothed on it, rearranging the cushions, and shifting from one side to the other, questions race through his mind. Riley never left him. For all those years Ethan believed that he didn't want him anymore and he carried around that hurt. Does Riley feel the same hurt and anger as he did? And does this mean that he still has feelings for Ethan?

***

The hands on the clock seem to jump between digits faster than Ethan reads. The reports only throw up more questions than answers.

"Aw, he's sleeping," he hears Carla's voice say. He looks over at her as she leans over Riley. "He looks kind of cute actually. Less psychopathic murderer vibes."

"Get away from him."

"Someone's defensive," she says, and he ignores her. "Don't you think it's at all possible that Riley is doing all this," she says stepping forward and gesturing to the board, "to get your attention?"

"Why not just use the phone?"

"Because a serial killer doesn't think logically."

"He's not a serial killer!"

"By killing me, the killer thinks they're getting your attention. Now you know that Riley didn't leave you, just how upset do you think he was when he thought you left him? And what better way to get back in contact with you than to kill your partner?"

If she had asked him a few days ago, he would have said yes, but not now. "Riley didn't do any of this."

"How can you be so sure?"

"Because I am! So, shut up. I'm not talking to you anyway."

"Oh, you're not still mad at me, are you?"

"Yes."

"Don't be like that, Ethan. Not with me."

He looks at her chestnut-coloured eyes which are glazed over. "You lied to me."

"I never wanted to hurt you," she says sitting down on the chair next to him.

"That makes no sense."

"It will."

A flash of a memory triggers in his head. She said that the night she went missing. He can still hear her voice as if she was here saying it to him now.

"I never wanted to hurt you," she cried as mascara ran from her eyes.

"What happened that night?" he asks the hallucination.

"Now, you know why I can't answer that."

"Right, of course."

"But I'm sure it'll come back to you at some point." He turns his attention back to the case file. "Don't you think you've been staring at your mother's dead body long enough?" she says.

"What else am I supposed to do?"

She smiles at him. "Remember what I taught you?"

"Always bring cake to work on a Friday?"

"No."

"Right, I know, clear my mind and go back to the beginning."

He closes his eyes and takes in deep breaths, cleansing his brain of all his thoughts and then visualises that moment.

"I can't pinpoint when you were taken, but Natalie was murdered in her home." He gets up and walks out into the hallway. "If I'm the killer and I'm about to kill her, why would I do it in the house with a potential witness?" He pauses. "Crime of passion. I don't walk in with the intention to murder her, but something provokes me to do so."

"And what does that mean?"

"Forensics found no signs of a break-in."

"Meaning," she prompts twirling her wrists around in a circular motion.

"She knew and trusted the killer to let them in."

"Uh huh, and what else does it say in the report?"

"Natalie's bags were packed. And she was in the middle of packing mine."

"She was leaving."

"But why?" he asks with a frown.

"Seems pretty obvious why they suspected your dad though." She pauses. "Are you sure he didn't do it? I mean, he did hit you as a child."

"No, I know he didn't do this."

"Then who else would be pissed off that Natalie was leaving?"

He walks over to the bathroom and turns on the light. "Who would Natalie trust to let in the house?" he mumbles to himself.

"What friends did she have at the time?"

"The only ones I remember are Riley's parents. But why would they care if Natalie was leaving or not?"

"I never did trust that family. Their son was a right weirdo."

"Watch it!"

"Not Riley, the other one. His older brother. God, what was his name?"

"Josh."

"Right!"

"I can't argue with you there." He stares at the bathroom floor imagining his mother's dead body lying there. "You know who else would have probably been mad that Natalie was leaving?" he says. "You."

Carla's drunken voice echoes in his head. "I'm sorry, Ethan. I never wanted to hurt you!" she cried.

Why was she apologising to him? What if she had killed his mother? What if that made him do something stupid. Like kill her.

Chapter Fifteen

Riley looks around. There's nothing but darkness; a black void he finds himself falling backwards into it. He tries to reach out to grab him. Ethan. He's standing in front of Riley with outstretched arms. But it's pointless. He's falling and there's nothing either of them can do about it. The force of gravity pulling him away from Ethan. Away from everything.

He wakes up, gasping and clinging to a sofa cushion in tight fists. Cold sweat soaks his clothes. He tries to figure out the dream and why he keeps having it; what it means; but most importantly, was Ethan reaching out to save him, or were his arms outstretched because he's the one who pushed Riley?

***

Ethan leans against the kitchen worktop staring down at his mobile which has the website Mind up on it, when he hears Riley drop off the sofa and wander into the kitchen. Ethan locks his phone, getting rid of it. After he'd exhausted his brain on the investigation, he decided to look up schizophrenia to try and prove Vincent wrong about him not being able to look after Riley.

"Hey," Ethan says.

"Hey. Have you slept?"

"I can sleep when this is over," he says and then looks at Riley. "Everything okay?"

"I'm fine," Riley mumbles, opening the fridge and pulling out a bottle of water. "Anything new?" he asks gesturing to the board.

"No closer than before." Ethan analyses his face. "Seriously, what's wrong?"

"Nothing!"

Ethan gives him a look. "I feel like you're hiding things from me."

"Like what?"

"You tell me," Ethan challenges, placing his hands down on the kitchen table and maintaining eye contact with him.

Riley fidgets on the spot. "I keep having this dream," he reveals finally. "It's the same dream over and over again."

"What's the dream about?" Ethan asks, leaning on the table and looking him dead in the eyes.

Riley looks up from the ground and his eyes search Ethan's. "You."

He can't suppress the smirk spreading across his lips. "Oh really?" Ethan says, raising an eyebrow.

Riley chokes out a laugh. "It's not that kind of dream."

"Oh," Ethan says, and he would be lying if he said he wasn't disappointed. "What is it then?"

He shrugs. "I don't know, it's stupid."

"Tell me."

There's a pause as they look at each other and he can see Riley is debating going ahead with saying it. "I'm falling," Riley mumbles but doesn't continue.

"From what?"

"That's just it, nothing. There's nothing around me. Just me, you, and darkness, and I'm falling back into darkness."

"And where do I fit in?"

"Well, that's the other thing. I can't decide if in the dream, you're trying to save me or if you pushed me."

He doesn't know how to respond to that. He's never believed that dreams are symbolic or having meaning as such, but they do resemble your emotional state and as much as Ethan hates it, Riley doesn't trust him.

"It's only a dream, Riley."

"I know, but I thought I should mention it." There's another pause and Ethan can see that there's more to this story.

"What else is on your mind?" Ethan asks.

"I think I could – I could be having a relapse."

"What makes you think that?"

"I've been getting some symptoms lately."

"Like what?" he asks but Riley doesn't answer as he hangs his head low. "Are you getting more hallucinations?"

"More than usual."

Ethan digests the information. "Well, if you are, we'll get through it. Together." Riley flashes a weak smile and it soon vanishes. "Tea?"

Before Riley answers, Ethan fills up the kettle whilst keeping an eye on him. Ethan can see he's scared. His feet shift on the spot. Ethan can't imagine how he must be feeling. How isolating it must be to see or hear things that aren't there. He doesn't know how to make it go away or how to help. Then he remembers something his mum used to do when he was younger. He was scared of dogs for a while when he was young, and his mum told him to name them. Psychologically, it works. It normalises it and builds a comfortable connection. The word hallucination or relapse can be intimidating.

"Why don't we call it something else?" Ethan suggests.

"What do you mean?"

"Well, instead of using the medical terms, why don't we call your hallucinations something less clinical."

"Like what?"

He sighs. "Um, I don't know. What if we call them… blips?"

"Blips?"

"Yeah."

He pauses, staring at Ethan with wide eyes. He doesn't know what Riley's thinking or whether he should have even suggested it. Eventually, Riley flashes a faint smile and says, "It's just a blip."

As the kettle boils, Ethan looks in the sink. Nothing. No washing. No bubbles. Not even wet. "Did you eat last night?" he asks looking around at Riley.

"Um," he mumbles, with that faint line creasing in the middle of his forehead. "I don't know. I don't think so. I must have forgotten."

Ethan remembers reading that because of his condition, he can skip meals.

"You know what, let's go out and get something to eat."

Riley hesitates. "No, I'm okay."

"Yeah, well, it'll be good for me to eat something."

Ethan knows too well that people in pain are reluctant to help themselves but will go out of their way for others.

Riley's eyes look up at the ceiling for a few seconds. "There's a nice café down the road."

***

Ethan suggests walking to get some fresh air and he's right, the walk does make Riley feel better somehow. Although a walk doesn't just cure mental health conditions, no matter how many you've been on. When they get into the café, he sits Riley down in a booth and throws a menu at him.

"Order whatever you like, I'll pay."

"I thought you didn't have a job."

Ethan shoots him a look. "Cheeky bastard."

Riley grins. "I'm right though. I'll pay."

"What do you want?"

"Just a tea."

He fires Riley another look. "What about food?"

"I'm okay."

"If you're not going to pick something, then I'll have to choose for you."

He doesn't say anything as Ethan gets up with the menu and heads towards the counter. A million worst-case scenarios enter his mind. What if Ethan forgets that he's vegan? What if he doesn't like what he orders? What if it offends him? Riley jumps to his feet and follows after him. A young overly tanned waitress approaches them from the other side of the bar.

"How can I help you?" she says in a monotone voice.

"Tea and what are you eating?" Ethan asks him.

"I said I'm fine."

"No, you're eating something."

"Wait, do I know you two?" the waitress asks.

They both look at her.

"I don't think…," Riley begins.

"Oh my God, you're them!" she shrieks.

"Who?" Ethan asks frowning.

"You're the two guys from that video. Yeah, you're that detective and you're that suspect he tackled!"

Riley deflates and he feels Ethan's body tense beside him.

"Oh, that's great," Ethan mumbles.

"Lucy!" the waitress calls and another waitress appears beside her. "It's them from that video!"

"Oh my God!" her friend screeches.

"Wait, are we famous now?" Riley asks Ethan who looks like he could die.

It doesn't take the first waitress long before she pulls out her mobile and aims her camera lens at them.

"Have you found The Heart Snatcher yet, Detective?" she announces like she's some kind of a reporter.

Ethan stares at them blankly. "The who?"

"The Heart Snatcher, that's what the press are calling the killer."

"Don't call him that!" Ethan snaps. "Giving sickos like him a name only fuels his killings."

"So, the killer is a him?"

"Stop fucking recording. It's an offence to record someone without consent."

"And why are you two out together? I thought you were a suspect?"

"I don't…," Riley begins.

"Not anymore, no," Ethan cuts in.

"Oh, so are you assisting on the case?"

"No comment."

"Are you two friends?"

"Enemy to friends?" her friend chips.

"Oh, are you enemies to lovers!" the first waitress shrieks.

"That's even better!" her friend exclaims.

"Please stop recording," Riley says, and he knows that it sounds pathetic.

"Put the fucking phone down!" Ethan snaps.

"Can we go home and eat the leftover oranges?" Riley says to him. Ethan looks to him and Riley wonders if he's already forgotten about their code word.

"Let's just go," Ethan says, turning to walk away.

"One more thing, Detective!" the waitress shouts and Ethan stops, but Riley's already walking towards the door. "Do you believe that the police abuse their powers with brutality?"

"No comment," he hears Ethan say.

Riley turns his head to look back at Ethan before he crashes into a pillar. But it's not a pillar. He halts, staring at the man in shock. "Oh, I'm so sorry."

"It's fine."

Then he realises that he's spilt the man's coffee down himself. "No, it's not, um, here, let me help you." He tries to help clean the man's shirt but realises he's only sponging the liquid around. The man chokes out a laugh. "Yeah, I'm not really helping, am I?" Riley laughs unnaturally.

"Not really," the man laughs and Riley's thankful at how understanding he is about the situation. He looks around at Ethan who's still standing by the counter staring at him with wide eyes, before looking around the room and scratching the back of his neck. The two girls behind the counter are still holding up a mobile, beaming with excitement.

Riley turns back to the man. "Um, let us buy you another one."

"No, it's okay."

"It's the least I can do." Riley smiles at the man.

Ethan appears by his side. "Come on, Riley, let's go."

Ethan grabs his arm and tries to pull him away, but Riley resists against him.

"But I spilt his drink. We should buy him another one."

He gestures to the man, but Ethan doesn't look at him, he just looks at Riley.

"No, we don't, it's fine," he says dragging Riley away.

Riley looks back to the man. "I'm sorry," he says to him before turning to Ethan. "That was kind of rude, Ethan."

Ethan pulls him closer, wrapping his arm around the back of his neck and hustles him towards the door. Riley looks around at the others in the café staring at them but when Riley looks at someone in particular, their eyes dart away. His heart sinks. He knows this look. He's seen it too many times before. He notices one girl use her finger to spin loops around her head before giggling. He looks back at the two girls behind the counter still filming and grinning. Then he feels the air hit him as Ethan ushers him out the door.

Standing on the pavement, Ethan pulls away and places both his hands on either side of Riley's arms, looking him in the eyes. "Wait here," he says before heading back towards the door. He opens it and shouts inside. "Go fuck yourselves!"

He slams the door and turns to Riley. The vision of Ethan begins to blur through the liquid swelling in his eyes.

"That man wasn't there, was he?" Riley whimpers. He knows the answer.

"It's just a blip. Remember?"

"Just a blip," Riley murmurs as he hangs his head low, but already the word 'blip' is losing its novelty.

He feels Ethan's hand on his shoulder. "Come on, let's go home. They serve crap coffee here anyway."

Riley chokes out a laugh and nods. It's strange how good Ethan is at somehow making him feel better.

Chapter Sixteen

Ethan slams the door of the flat and races up the stairs to turn on the television.

"What are you doing?" Riley asks.

"Shh!"

The sound of the news reporter's voice fills the room. A yellow banner at the bottom of the screen running from one side to the other has the words 'BREAKING NEWS' across it.

"- police are no closer to finding out who murdered Carla Milhouse, but if you're just tuning in, we now have some disturbing intel that some viewers may find upsetting," the news reporter says with a flare of the dramatic in her voice. "Carla Milhouse's heart was removed from her body but still has not been located."

Both their head whip around to look at each other. "Shit," Ethan says.

"How did they?"

"Warning, viewers may find the following images disturbing," the reporter says before the screen shows the gruesome images of Carla's body next to the lake.

"How did they get those images?" Riley asks concerned.

"Must have been a leak," Ethan says through gritted teeth.

"Is that common?"

"With high-profile cases like this, yes," he answers without taking his eyes off the screen.

"The police and media are now calling this killer 'The Heart Snatcher'," the reporter continues.

"Fucking great!"

"I guess what those girls said is true then."

"It's so fucked up to give this sick bastard a nickname! No one ever remembers the victims's names."

The last part comes out weak. No one remembers Natalie's

name or even her son who found her mutilated body, but this son-of-a-bitch will most likely go down in history. Then life just carries on.

"Maybe we shouldn't watch this," Riley suggests.

"Yeah, because turning off the TV will make it go away," he hears Carla say and Ethan turns to see her leaning against the fridge in the kitchen. "You seriously trust this guy after all this?" she asks.

"Shut up," he warns and then he remembers that Riley's still here and turns back to him. He stares at Ethan with a concerned look.

"The police have also connected Carla Milhouse's case to a homicide sixteen years ago," the news reporter goes on and that grabs his attention again. "Natalie Brown was murdered in her home on 25th February 2008. Her heart was also removed. The killer was never found."

"How the fuck did they know that?" he shouts and then notices the look on Riley's face. There's guilt in his expression. "Riley, what did you do?"

"I thought they knew."

"Who?"

"Anna," he says. Ethan pinches the bridge of his nose in frustration. "I didn't know! I thought she knew!"

"So, you told her?" He nods. "Great! So, now the police are looking into both murders!"

"How is that a bad thing?"

"Because that means the press knows what's happening too which means the killer knows what's happening!"

"Oh."

Ethan flicks off the TV and begins pacing backwards and forwards with Riley at his heels.

"What the fuck are you doing?" Ethan snaps, spinning around to face him. Riley doesn't say anything but his eyes glaze over and Ethan wants to curl up and die for snapping at him like that after what's just happened at the café. "It's okay, I'm sorry," he says and without thinking, he pulls Riley into him and embraces him, placing his hand on the back of Riley's head.

"It's all a bit of a mess, isn't it?" Riley says, his voice muffled as his face is buried into Ethan's T-shirt.

"We're going to be okay." He pulls back and releases Riley, realising that he still hasn't eaten. Ethan goes to the kitchen that has now become their personal little detective office. "I'll cook you something here."

The best Ethan can manage is beans on toast, although Riley doesn't complain as he finishes his last few bites at the kitchen table whilst Ethan finishes pinning the last of his mother's case file notes that were of any relevance.

"Right, what's left for us to do now?" Riley asks, pushing away his plate.

"Just this," he replies, revealing the scribbled notes from Carla. "I'm still not sure what this means."

Ethan examines the sequence of numbers that don't seem to have a formula or purpose as Riley joins his side, peering over his shoulder.

"Could be coordinates for somewhere?" Riley suggests.

"No, I already tried that."

"Could be a cypher, then?"

"Maybe."

"Or phone numbers?"

"Why the fuck would it be phone numbers?"

Riley shrugs.

He blocks off sections of the numbers in his mind and imagines them separated. Then it clicks. He spins around to face Riley.

"Dates!" they both say in sync with each other.

Riley's eyes light up with the same excitement that Ethan feels. A small smile tugs at the ends of Ethan's lips, admiring how much Riley sounds like a detective. Although, he's not sure whether it's a good thing or not. Ethan places the paper on the table and grabs a pen. He circles the numbers in the formation of dates with DD/MM/YYYY.

"Definitely dates!" he confirms.

The sound of slow clapping draws Ethan's eyes past Riley to Carla who's leaning up against the wall behind him with a smirk on her face.

"Why would she write it like that, though?" Riley asks, bringing his attention back.

"That's just how we write things out when we first record notes. None formulated and then later we rewrite it clearer."

"What do they mean?" Riley asks.

Ethan looks at the first date. 25/02/2008.

"The day Natalie died...," he mutters to no one in particular. The next date he writes out is 25/02/2009. Then 25/02/2010 and then 25/02/2011. He doesn't need to read any more to know what the rest of the dates will say. His stomach drops. "Get your laptop!" he demands.

Riley darts off and retrieves his laptop from his bedroom, sitting back at the table with it in front of him. Ethan stands behind him, leaning over his shoulder close to his face as he boots up the device.

"What are we looking for?" he asks.

"I need you to search the newspaper archives for these dates, apart from the first one."

He already knows the significance of the first date. Riley opens the browser and searches for the most popular newspaper. The homepage opens.

"Type 26/02/2009 along with missing persons in the search bar," he says pointing to the notes.

"But Carla wrote 25/02/2009?"

"The papers will need a day to print so whatever happened on the 25th will be printed on the 26th." Riley does as he says without a word. A list of missing persons appears. "Scroll through."

It still surprises Ethan how many people go missing in the UK every day. Someone is reported missing approximately every 90 seconds. Although most are found, dead or alive, others are never found. Riley scrolls the page and Ethan's eyes examine every small thumbnail image of the person who went missing. The killer has a type.

"Stop!" Ethan exclaims, leaning over Riley and placing his hand over his to stop him. "There," he mutters, using Riley's hand to move the mouse and click on the thumbnail of a woman with blonde hair and similar facial features to both Carla and Natalie.

"Sarah Wilson," Riley says. "Went missing in London and was last seen leaving work at 3 am. Single mother to a son," he says, his voice trailing off at the end.

"Next," Ethan snaps, grabbing the notes and calling out the next date for Riley to type in. He scrolls through but can't find a woman of similar age or with blonde hair. "Pull these ones up," Ethan says pointing to three potential females that all have darker hair. He examines the first one. No child. "No." He reads the next one. "No." Then the next one. A woman named Chloe Blakemore. Went missing in Devon. Mother to a young son.

"That's the one." He looks down at the next date. "Next!" he orders again, but he knows what they're going to find, and he can see in Riley's eyes that he knows too.

Stephanie Bennett. Went missing in Manchester. Mother to a son.

"Next!"

Mandy Lovell. Went missing in Nottingham. Single mother to a son.

"Next."

"Ethan…," Riley says.

"Next!"

He does what Ethan says and the next woman appears in the

search fitting the profile perfectly.

"Ne..."

Riley gets up and begins to pace as he runs his hand through his hair. Ethan sits in his chair and begins searching for the rest of the dates.

"You don't think," Riley says but doesn't finish.

"I don't *think*, I *know* this is our killer."

"There's one each year, that's sixteen victims, Ethan. Sixteen women," he says in disbelief. "I mean, how the hell did this not flag up with the police?"

"Because they're across different counties, they're missing not found dead, and there's no real evidence linking them. Plus...," he says but is too ashamed to continue his sentence.

"Plus, what?"

Ethan pinches the bridge of his nose. "If the families don't have the money to pay for a search party, and the police don't have the funds to continue searching for them, then..."

"Then what? They just get forgotten about?"

He doesn't say anything. He doesn't like it any more than Riley does but it's the way it goes.

"How can you be okay with that?" Riley whines.

"I'm not!" he yells. "Do you have any idea how many people go missing a year? How many unsolved murders there are? How many rape cases we have to deal with day in and day out? And we don't have the funds to keep investigating cases from years earlier. It's all fine for people to scream about defunding the police and then bitch about the fact that we're not solving enough cases!"

They stare at each other as a toxic silence fills the atmosphere.

"Doesn't make it right that innocent people get forgotten about."

He knows that Riley is right. He's stuck between his morals and his job because both are pulling him in different directions.

"I know."

"This is way over my head, Ethan."

"I get it. Even for me this is –"

"No, you don't get it. I can't do this," he says in a drawn-out way and Ethan doesn't respond as he holds his breath. "I just can't."

Riley walks out and a few seconds later, the front door opens and slams shut.

***

Riley sits on the waiting room chair after his hour-long drive back to his hometown, Guildford, Surrey. The screen light on his mobile illuminates his face as he watches the endless video loop of him and Ethan in the café.

"It's the least I can do," his voice says through the mobile speakers as he tries to aid an invisible man. Riley closes his eyes and rubs his forehead.

"Come on, Riley, let's go," Ethan's voice says through the mobile.

"But I spilt his drink. We should buy him another one."

He opens his eyes to see the comments at the bottom of the screen spring up.

'It's obvious that he's The Heart Snatcher!'

'He's psycho! Lock him up!'

He switches off his mobile and looks down the hallway before climbing to his feet. Feeling lightheaded and fuzzy, he wonders if he'll make it to her before passing out. He goes to the counter and explains why he's here. The receptionist gestures for him to pass through. He follows the coloured signs before approaching the ward he's looking for.

"Debbie, did you eat my sandwich?" he hears a familiar female voice say to a colleague and he smiles.

He catches a glimpse of her black hair as she shuffles a medical trolley through a ward full of beds and sings a jolly song that makes the patients lying in their beds smile and laugh.

"You should go on Britain's Got Talent," one patient says.

"Watch this space," she responds with a wink.

He watches from a distance as she attends to a patient, taking their blood pressure and smiling whilst doing it.

"Can I help you?" a nurse asks approaching him.

"I – I'm here to see Elizabeth," he explains and the nurse's eyes light up.

"Oh, it's you. I recognise you from her photographs," the nurse says, and he wonders how many photos his mother has shown her colleagues. "Lizzie, your son is here!"

Elizabeth turns and beams at him before a concerned look clouds her face. She rushes over to him.

"What's wrong?" she asks, her voice full of worry.

"Nothing, I'm fine, why?"

"Do you feel okay? No negative symptoms? Are you eating and drinking enough? Getting enough sleep?"

"I said I'm fine."

"Then, why are you here?" she asks, and he's filled with guilt that he doesn't visit his mother nearly as much as he should. "Not that I'm not thrilled to see you, of course!"

"I just wanted to see you."

Her smile widens. "Aw! Nice jacket by the way," she says, tugging at the open collar, reminding him that he's still wearing Ethan's coat. "Is it new?"

"Sort of."

"Huh, I've never seen you in anything like it before."

"How's dad?" he asks clearing his throat.

"Oh, he's fine, he's been doing some operations in East Sussex."

"That's quite far to go."

"Ah it's fine, we're both doing some work there over the next week. Plus, we can always just stay in our holiday cabin if we need to." She pauses reading his dampened expression. "What's wrong, honey?" He shrugs. "You don't seem like your usual self. Are you stressed or worried about anything?"

Like you wouldn't believe, he thinks to himself.

"No," he says, and she raises an eyebrow. "Well, I guess a little."

"This isn't because of everything that's going on with," she says and then leans in closer to whisper, "the murder." Riley shrugs. "It's going to be okay. You didn't do anything, so you have nothing to worry about."

"It's not that."

"Then what is it?"

"I just – what if doing the right thing means not doing what's right for you?"

She frowns. "Are you still taking your meds?"

"Yes," he grumbles.

"Sorry, it's just that made no sense!"

His body deflates. "I don't know what to do anymore."

She gives him a pitiful look and places her hand on the side of his face.

"Look, whatever it is that you're struggling with, you already know what to do, and I trust you that you always make the right decision."

He looks at her and hates himself for not appreciating her sooner.

"If anything ever happened to you, I would want someone to do everything in their power to get justice," he says and that's what he's going to do for the victims of those women.

Her face crinkles in confusion and he realises that she has no idea what he's talking about.

"You've been a massive help," he says, giving her a quick kiss on the cheek. "Thank you."

"Always happy to help!"

"I don't have long," he says checking his watch knowing that he needs to get back to his flat now feeling more determined to help Ethan find out what happened to all those missing women. "But did you want to get lunch?" he asks, and her smile grows.

He remembers his and Ethan's argument and he wouldn't be surprised if Ethan had run off and left him. After all, Ethan was the one who left him before.

Chapter Seventeen

Ethan bought some beer as soon as Riley left and discarded his leftover takeaway when it started to stink out the flat. He looks over Carla's notes whilst taking a swig from the bottle. Why did these missing women not get enough media publicity? Why wasn't there more of a search party for them? The malty, caramelised smell of his drink burning both his nostrils and throat. A scent that reminds him of every time he was beaten by his father because he 'deserved it'. In a way, he's punishing himself all over again.

He hears the sound of the front door open and close, followed by footsteps up the stairs. Riley peers around the corner and they both look at each other.

"You're still here," Riley says surprised.

"Do you not want me to be?"

"No!" he blurts before clearing his throat. "I just thought you might have, I don't know, left or something, after our argument."

"Wouldn't call *that* an argument."

"Disagreement then. I'm sorry."

"For what?"

"About our *disagreement*. I just – I was –"

"Forget it," Ethan says as he discards the apology by waving his hand. Riley smiles but neither of them moves. He eyes Riley who's still wearing his jacket. It's odd that he's still choosing to wear it over his own fancy coat. "Have you now claimed that for yourself?"

"Oh," he says looking down at himself. "I was going to wash it for you before giving it back to you."

"Keep it," he says waving his hand in the air. "Looks good on you."

Riley beams at the compliment. "I'm still going to wash it though. I put my hand in something sticky in the right pocket," he explains, and Ethan chokes out a laugh.

All Ethan wants to do is tell him how handsome he thinks Riley looks in his jacket, but instead he asks, "Where did you go?"

"Just out."

"Out?"

"Yeah," Riley says with a shrug.

"Huh. You're not hiding things from me, right?"

"No, of course not. I went to see my mum."

"Oh okay. So, what's wrong then?"

"Nothing."

He gives Riley a look and watches as he starts to chew off the remainder of his nails.

"I wish you wouldn't do that," Ethan scorns.

"Do what?"

"Bite your nails!" he says, leaning over and forcing his hand away from his mouth. "Now, tell me what's going on."

"They - they think I'm The Heart Snatcher."

"Who?"

"Everyone."

Ethan frowns so Riley gets out his mobile and holds the screen out to show him. He pinches the bridge of his nose and squeezes his eyes shut when he sees the video of them at the café.

"All the comments are full of people who think I did it."

"Fuck them!" he exclaims, and Riley looks at him surprised. "Fuck all of them!"

"So, you don't think I did it?"

Their eyes lock together and he's telling the truth when he says, "I know you didn't do it."

There's a brief smile that flashes across Riley's face. "I can't just walk away from this now."

"Does that mean you're back on the case?" Ethan asks.

"If you'll still have me."

Ethan picks up the case file and hands it out to him as he leans in close to Riley. "Oh, I'll still take you."

Riley gives him a suggestive look as his lips stretch into a smirk. It vanishes when he takes the file and the thought that a serial killer is still brutally murdering women kills the moment.

Ethan prints out and pins the new victims to the board followed by all the details about their disappearance from online research which is in short supply. Riley taps away on his mobile and Ethan's not sure if he should ask him what he's doing.

"Do you mind if I find out what happened to you?" he mutters to the sixteen faces staring back at him on the board. It seems like a respectful thing to do. "I just wish we could somehow get access to their case files," he says louder to Riley.

"The other victims?" he asks and Ethan nods. "Is there a chance that any of these women are still alive?"

"No."

It sounds emotionless, but it's a fact. He knows that each of these women is dead, it's just about finding their bodies and their killer now.

"There is one thing I don't understand," Ethan says. "Each woman was a mother to a son. Except Carla."

"What does that mean?"

"I don't know," he examines each of the woman's profiles. "I mean Carla doesn't fit the killer's profile. Why kill women who have a child and then kill someone who doesn't?"

"Because of you, we already know that. The killer murdered Carla to get to you."

"Yeah, but it's still strange. The child is important to him. It's a strong part of his MO. He wouldn't just stop caring about that."

"Or she. The killer could be a she."

"Right, of course."

"Are you sure Carla didn't have a child? Maybe one she gave up for adoption?"

Ethan shakes his head. "No, even the initial evaluation would have picked up that she had carried and given birth to a child. It would have been the first thing Anna said to me when I was in the morgue."

"Do you think the killer took all these women's hearts too?"

"Yes. The three things that seem to be important to him…"

"Or her."

"…is that *their* victims have a son, they have to be killed on the same day each year and the killer has to remove their heart."

"But why?"

"I think it's some kind of ritual or something. I just need to figure out how the killer targets and finds his victims."

"We could go and talk to their families."

"We can't do that," Ethan scoffs.

"Why not?"

"Because I'm suspended and you're not a detective."

"We could say that we're amateur journalists?"

Ethan sighs. "Even so, how would we even find any of these women's families?"

"Well, our victim from last year, Charlotte Spring has a sister called Jennifer Spring in London who is looking after her son."

"How the fuck do you know that?"

"Social media," he says, turning his mobile around to show him.

"How did you find her?" he asks eagerly, rushing over to get a better look at the screen by peering over his shoulder.

"All I did was type in our victim's name and I found this 'Find Charlotte' account on socials set up by Jennifer."

'Our victim'. Now he really is talking like a detective.

"You're a genius!" Ethan announces. He looks at Riley and their eyes are fixed on one another. Ethan's gaze wanders down to Riley's lips. He clears his throat and quickly adverts his eyes. "Do you know where she lives?"

"No, but the location tag on her last post says that she's at a park not too far from us."

"You're not suggesting…"

"It's worth a shot."

It would be strange for them to turn up out of the blue and start asking questions without a police or journalist ID badge, but Riley's right, it's worth a shot.

"Fine, but I'll probably need my jacket back now," Ethan requests.

***

It's overcast but no rain, although Riley insisted on bringing an umbrella just in case. There's also a chill in the air as Ethan makes his way through the park which is filled with the noises of screaming kids and chatting parents. It almost makes him feel sick as he takes a drag of his cigarette. It's not a life he ever planned on pursuing; children that is. Riley tags behind him holding his phone with the woman's profile picture up. He feels like he's some kind of stalker, but he has to get answers.

"There!" Riley says just as Ethan spots her sat alone on a bench in front of the children's playground. "So, how do we approach this without looking like a couple of strange men in a park?"

Ethan ignores him and decides to go ahead despite hearing Riley call his name repeatedly. If he thinks too much about it, he'll turn around and go home. He discards his cigarette butt on top of a bin and approaches the bench. He stands in front of it, facing Jennifer, Charlotte's sister. She flicks her light brown hair off her face as she looks up at him wearing a frown.

"May I?" Ethan asks gesturing to the space next to her.

She nods and shuffles along the bench despite there being more than enough room. He drops into the space next to her, resting his elbows on his knees. Both his and her eyes are fixed forward, facing the play area. Children clamber on the obstacles and on the swing sets without fear of falling, without fear of pain.

"Which one's yours?" he asks, glancing in her direction. When she doesn't respond straight away, he looks at her, rigid in her seat.

"What do you want?" she finally snaps. It's then that he notices the heavy bags under her green eyes.

"Just making friendly conversation," he says with a shrug.

"If you want my number, then the answer is no."

"Ew." It's an automatic response. He realises how she's taken it as her glare hardens. "What I mean is, I'm not here to ask for your number."

"Well, I didn't see you come with a kid, so what do you want?"

"I want to ask you about Charlotte."

Her frown lifts and her mouth makes an O shape. The sound of kids playing and screaming fills the silence as he watches her collect her thoughts.

"Wh - what about her?" she says, stumbling over her words.

"She went missing last year, right?"

"Who are you?"

"We're just a couple of amateur journalists who want to help find her."

"We?"

He looks over at Riley who's stood where he left him. He gives a nod for him to come over and Riley makes his way to them.

"Sorry, I should have introduced myself," he says, turning back to Jennifer. "My name's Ethan and this," he says gesturing to Riley as he approaches them, "is Riley."

Riley gives a short nod to Jennifer before taking a seat on the other side of Ethan.

"And why are you two so interested in what happened to Charlotte?"

"We want to help," Riley says.

"Why?"

"We came across her missing person account on social media and we want to help by shedding some light on her disappearance," Ethan explains. She doesn't say anything but looks back towards the play area. "We want to know why the police and media stopped looking for her."

She scoffs a laugh. "Isn't it obvious? They think she ran away or committed suicide or something."

"Why would they think that?"

"Because," she begins but stops as her voice breaks. He can see the tears swelling in her eyes and he hears the lump in her throat. "My sister suffered with depression. She would have episodes of extreme downs. Suicidal thoughts, and all that."

Out of the corner of his eye, he can see Riley's hand clasp over his wrist.

"But you don't believe she ran away or killed herself?" Ethan asks.

"Of course not! I mean, she was getting better, you know," Jennifer says as she looks at him properly for the first time. Tears shimmer down her cheeks. "It's just easier for the police to blame her condition than to actually get off their asses and do something!"

"I know how that feels," Riley mutters.

"Did she get help for her mental illness?"

"She was seeing a psychiatrist and was doing well. Look, Charlotte wasn't perfect, but she was a damn good mother. It isn't easy bringing up a child on your own."

"What happened to the father?" Riley asks but then adds, "if you don't mind me asking."

"He died before the birth and his family don't want anything to do with either of them."

"And now you're looking after him?" Ethan asks but it comes out like a statement.

She nods and more tears spill out from her eyes. "He's not been the same since she went missing."

"I know how that feels," Ethan mutters.

"Auntie Jennifer!" a child's voice calls.

He turns his head to see a young boy running towards them. Light brown hair and blue eyes that mimic the ones he saw in Charlotte's photo. Jennifer collects herself, wiping away her tears as he approaches her. Ethan watches as the boy beams up at his auntie but he can see through the mask. He can see the difference between this boy compared to the rest of the kids. People – even children – have a certain posture and movement once they experience trauma whether that's physical or mental.

"Can we go and get ice cream now?" the boy asks.

"Um, I'm just talking with these nice men at the moment, sweetie."

"It's okay, I think we're done now," Ethan says standing up. He feels Riley follow after and watches as Jennifer stands as well.

"So, what happens now?" she asks, wrapping her arm around the boy.

Ethan's mouth opens but no words follow. He doesn't know what to tell her.

"We'll be in touch if we find anything," Riley says and it's usually a response that Ethan would have said.

Ethan looks down at the boy, who stares up at him with rounded eyes. There's a hole in him; a certain void that Ethan can see in his eyes. It's one that he sees every time he looks in the mirror. He crouches down to the boy's level.

"What ice cream are you going to get?" Ethan asks in a soft tone.

"Chocolate," the boy says, swaying slightly from side to side.

"That sounds nice."

"Me and mummy would always get chocolate ice cream together."

That pain in his chest returns and for the first time in Ethan's life, he sees his ten-year-old self right in front of him. Ethan forces a smile as best he can as his eyes begin to sting. He stands back up, pulling out his wallet and hands Jennifer a note.

"For your trouble," he says.

"I can't..."

"Just take it and get the boy two scoops."

She flashes a smile before accepting the money. "Please find out what happened to my sister."

He's torn between wanting to promise her that he will and giving his usual response to those kinds of questions. "I promise I'll try."

But the thing is, he already knows what's happened to her.

Chapter Eighteen

On the way back from the park, Ethan and Riley retreat into a small, quiet café. They both pull up the collar of their coats and keep their heads down as they make their way to a booth in the back corner and order table service to avoid bumping into people after what happened at the last café. They spend the rest of the afternoon searching for each of the victims's families on Riley's mobile. Some of them still have a missing person account for their loved ones but most of them have died off over time. They send messages to each of the accounts saying the same thing that they said to Jennifer. Some message back straight away with their desperate tones radiating through the screen and some call them with desperation in their voices. Ethan feels bad for taking advantage of their situation, but he keeps telling himself that he is only trying to help.

"Okay, thank you. Bye," Ethan says into his mobile, before looking up at Riley who's staring at him from the opposite side of the table.

"Another one?"

He looks into Riley's eager eyes; eager to know if this girl is the same as the other victims. He nods and looks away.

"What was it this time?" he hears Riley ask.

"Post-partum psychosis. Apparently, her family reported her missing a few times, but she'd always come back."

"Not this time."

He shakes his head and looks around the café at the people who are too busy and self-absorbed in their own lives to notice them or what they're talking about. The sound of murmured voices from multiple conversations drowns out his and Riley's words. The rain now hammering on the roof also helps disguise their conversation.

"So, the killer is targeting people with mental health issues too," Riley whispers.

"It seems that way," Ethan says examining the way Riley's mouth opens and closes as if trying to get out words.

"Why, do you think…"

He leans forward and hushes his voice.

"Probably because it makes it easier for the killer to go unnoticed. By targeting victims who are classed as high risk to themselves, the killer knows that the police will presume that they've run away or killed themselves. They won't look into it being a kidnapping or murder. He can keep killing without a risk of being caught."

He stares at Riley as he says the words.

"Is there anything else I can get you?" a waitress asks as she approaches the table.

"Just the bill," Ethan says as she collects their empty, stained mugs. He looks out the window, noticing how dark it is as day turns to evening.

He notices how she eyes them both as if trying to recall how she knows them. He turns his head in the opposite direction. After the waitress returns with the bill, he pays and then shuffles out of the booth chair, followed by Riley.

Ethan holds the door open for him as Riley pulls up his umbrella over his head and Ethan lights up a cigarette to relieve his stress. They make their way back to the flat, with him under the umbrella and Ethan on the outside as water soaks his hair and runs down his face. Riley gestures the umbrella towards him but he waves his hand away and flicks his cigarette butt. He'd have to crouch down to get under it anyway. They make their way past all the night owls and drunken club-goers who shout unformulated words and sentences. It's not until they get to the bus stop down the road that it's quieter and no one's around. There's no shelter at this one, only a post with a bus sign on it.

"Next bus is in ten minutes," Ethan says, reading the sign. He looks at Riley. "Are you okay?"

"Just thinking," he says with a shrug.

"About?"

"How all those women - mentally ill women - went missing and the police haven't done anything about it."

"Our killer has been smart."

"Or the police are dumb." Ethan gives him a look. "I mean, we figured it out."

"The killer chose victims that are a flight risk and has somehow disposed of their bodies where they won't be found. Our killer is *smart*."

"You're right. I guess I just feel like it's – it's," he says but stutters as he tries to find the right words.

"It's personal to you," Ethan finishes for him and Riley nods to clarify. "You never talk about your, you know."

"Schizophrenia? You can say the word, you know."

"I know," he says feeling stupid for treating the word as if it was taboo. "You can talk to me about your schizophrenia if you want."

"I don't know. It's kind of personal."

"Too personal to tell me?"

"Yes."

"I don't think there's much we don't know about each other. I mean, I have seen you naked."

"That was eight years ago."

Ethan bends under the umbrella bringing them closer together. "I still remember. Everything."

His eyes look Riley up and down before returning to his face. Riley's cheeks flash red before choking out an awkward laugh.

"I remember everything too," Riley says shifting a little closer. Ethan can feel Riley's breath on his neck.

"Oh, really?"

"Yeah. Like how you left me when I needed you the most."

The last sentence trails off and there's pain to his voice as he pulls back.

"Riley, about what happened when we were teenagers. I want you to know that –"

"Shh," Riley interrupts, snapping his head to the side.

"Okay, fine then," Ethan mutters as he ducks out of the umbrella.

"No, Ethan."

"It's fine."

"No, you don't understand."

"I get it."

"I wasn't talking to you!"

Ethan frowns at the stupid excuse but then it clicks. "Oh." Riley doesn't move and it doesn't even look like he's breathing. "Are you… hearing things?"

His shoulders slump. "It's hard to explain."

"Try."

"Sometimes I can make them go away by shh-ing them. It makes them stop."

"By shh-ing them?"

"You think I'm mad, don't you?"

Ethan analyses him for a moment. If this had happened last week or even a few days ago, he would have run in the opposite direction. But he's wiser now. He knows Riley and, in a way, he finds it quite endearing. He ducks back under the umbrella, hearing the raindrops drip on the fabric over his head. His face inches away from Riley's as rainwater drips from the ends of his hair.

"I hope so. Normal people scare me." Riley stares at him surprised before breathing out a laugh. "Tell me about it."

"About my hallucinations?" he asks and Ethan nods. "Now that is personal."

"You don't have to tell me if you don't want to."

Riley's eyes flicker between the ground and his face. "It's just stupid things."

"Like what?"

“I kind of get this running commentary, like someone’s reading out what’s happening to me as it’s happening.”

“Oh, that’s not so bad.”

“It’s mostly harmless now. Not like when I had psychosis. The hallucinations were more aggressive.”

“Does it happen a lot?”

“Sometimes. Not all the time. The meds help stop negative symptoms and control most of the positive symptoms,” Riley explains. Ethan frowns. What the fuck are negative and positive symptoms? Riley looks at his face and sighs, as if reading his mind. “Negative symptoms are depression and loss of motivation. Positive symptoms are hallucinations, audio-hallucinations, delusions, that sort of thing.”

“That doesn’t sound very positive,” he says not understanding why they would call it that.

Riley laughs. “No, it doesn’t mean positive as in good, it means symptoms of schizophrenia that add to my life. Negative symptoms take away from my life.”

“Oh!” Ethan exclaims. Riley smirks still amused. “I am trying to get my head around all of this,” Ethan adds.

“I can see that,” Riley says and there it is, the first hint of love in Riley’s eyes. For a moment he looks at Ethan in the same way he did when they were teenagers. As soon as it’s there, it’s gone again. His gaze shifts to look past Ethan and his expression drops.

“Maybe, we should just walk home,” he says turning with the umbrella and knocking the back of Ethan’s head with it.

Riley storms on ahead and he has to jog to keep up with him.

“Are you okay?” Ethan calls after him.

“I’m fine.”

He doesn’t stop moving as he answers.

“Did I ask too many questions?” Ethan asks.

“No.”

“Is it because of what happened when we were teenagers?”

"No!"

Riley turns to cross the road. He clearly doesn't see how close or how fast the car is going until he's already in its path. But Ethan does.

"Riley!" he shouts as he lunges forward, grabbing at his coat and yanking him back onto the pavement.

Riley stumbles backwards, dropping the umbrella as he falls to the ground. Ethan holds him by the shoulders, keeping him in safety. The car's engine revs, and the driver blasts his horn as he races past them.

"Dickhead!" Ethan shouts at the driver and flips him off. He then feels the throbbing in his muscles from where he'd pulled Riley back with his injured arm. His whole body still aches from the motorbike accident. He turns back to Riley who looks dazed. Ethan stoops down in front of him.

"Are you okay?" Ethan asks, holding his face in both his hands. Riley nods. "What the hell were you thinking?"

Riley shrugs and Ethan gives him a look.

"I just thought I saw something, that's all," Riley says sitting up.

"Saw what?"

"It doesn't matter."

"Yes, it does!"

"Leave it!"

"Tell me!"

Riley doesn't say anything for a few seconds before opening his mouth. "I saw," he begins and pauses. "It was just a hallucination."

"And you were trying to get away from it?" Ethan says with pity in his voice. He now understands why they say people with schizophrenia are more likely to hurt themselves than others. He climbs to his feet and then helps Riley up. "What was it?"

"If I tell you what it is and where it is, then you'll look in its direction which will fuel my hallucination."

"I promise I won't look." He gives him a glare and Ethan uses one finger to draw a cross over his chest. Riley sighs.

"I used to see this cloaked figured when I had psychosis. Like a demon. And it used to follow me around."

"And that's what you saw?" He nods. "And is it here now?"

"Yes."

"Where?"

He hesitates, shifting on the spot. "Over in the alley just to the left behind me." Ethan presumes that he means his left and he can't help but look over. He feels a whack on his arm. £You promised!"

"Riley, that's not a hallucination."

He doesn't take his eyes off the cloaked dark figure lurking on the outskirts of the alley, just like Riley said. He sees Riley in the corner of his eye looking between them both.

"You can see it too?" he asks.

"Unfortunately."

"So, it's real?"

"Either that or we're both going mad."

Ethan charges past him, heading straight for the figure. As he does, it moves back and becomes engulfed by shadows and camouflages.

"Hey!" he calls but it's useless. "Stay here!" he shouts back to Riley before sprinting after it down the alley.

Specks of rain spray into his eyes as he runs down the alley, blurring his vision. He doesn't lose sight of the cloaked figure. Ethan would have been able to catch up to the figure, but his body succumbs to his injuries. His run evolves into a fast limp because of the pain in the side of his abdomen. The figure knocks over bins, leaving a wake of destruction in his path which Ethan manages to dodge and jump over. A container hits Ethan making him waver and stumble as he staggers onwards.

The figure charges out from the alley and onto the pavement where the streets are lined with nightclubs. Ethan follows them into a crowd of drunk and disorderly teenagers. He loses sight of the figure as they become engulfed in the horde. He can only see a sliver of the cloak through the gaps between people. He pushes them out of the way and squeezes through the mass of shouting drunks, spilling their drinks all over him and themselves. Ethan's foot gets caught in something and he looks down at the black material wrapped around his shin. He picks it up and spins around on the spot, trying to search the faces of the crowd for anyone he recognises or anyone who looks suspicious. He emerges out from the herd and into a clearing to see better. There's nothing. The killer is gone.

"Riley," he whispers and tears back through the alley from where he'd come from. Ethan tries to retrace his steps back to where he left him, struggling to remember the route. He eventually finds his way to the familiar road and sees the umbrella lying on the ground. There's no Riley.

"Riley!" he shouts.

"Ethan," Riley's voice calls back in the distance.

He turns and hobbles in the direction of his voice as he calls his name over and over again. Each time Riley calls back, his voice becomes louder and clearer. He turns on his mobile torch and a beam of light pierces the darkness. As he rounds a corner, he runs into something which he realises a few seconds later is a someone.

"Jesus, can you not shine that thing at me!" Riley exclaims trying to shield his eyes from the torch.

"Fucking hell! Don't do that!"

"Do what?"

"Run off!"

"You were the one who ran off."

"I told you to stay where you were."

"I couldn't just leave you," he says and there's a hint of emotion in his voice that resembles worry. He looks down at Ethan's hand. "What's that?"

"The cloak," he clarifies, walking out of the alley and onto the street back with all the drunks.

"Do you think that's the, you know?"

"The killer's cloak? Most likely."

"Why would the killer be following us?"

"I don't know," Ethan mutters examining the material in his hand.

It's nothing special. Just an ordinary black piece of fabric with a hood. Ethan decides to approach a nearby group.

"Hey!" he calls, grabbing their attention one by one as they all have delayed responses depending on how much they've had to drink. "Did you see anyone in a black cloak pass through here?"

"A - a what?" a man slurs as he turns to face Ethan. He can smell the stench of alcohol on the man's breath as he leans in a little too close to Ethan. He steps back to try and distance himself from the scent that reminds him of his abusive dad.

"A cloak."

"A cloak?" the man laughs.

"Yes, a fucking cloak! This," he shouts waving the material in the air. "Did you or did you not see who it was?"

The man sways side to side as he looks between him and then at Riley, who Ethan's just realised is standing close behind him.

"I saw you," he says looking at Riley.

"That's not helpful," Ethan says.

"I remember - I saw - cloak - then you - him."

What Ethan gathers from that fragmented speech is that he saw someone in a cloak, then Ethan and then Riley.

"Let's just leave," Riley says to Ethan, placing his hand on his upper arm to lead him away. "I don't think he knows anything."

"Hey! That's not polite!" the drunk man slurs.

Riley glances between the man and Ethan. "It wasn't an insult."

"You think I'm stupid, don't you?" he shouts, and Riley doesn't answer. "Don't you!"

Everything escalates and the drunken man pushes Riley so hard that he falls backwards onto the ground, letting out a slight whine. Ethan grabs the man's arm and twists it backwards. His mouth drops open in pain and his friends around him fall silent.

"Touch him again and I'll break both your arms," Ethan growls.

"Leave it," Riley pleads from behind but his voice is calm. "Let's not add assault to our growing list of accusations."

Ethan releases his arm but keeps his glare aimed at him.

"Now, piss off or I'll arrest you all for being drunk and disorderly as well as assault."

"Whoa, you're the police?" another drunk person slurs.

"I'm a detective. Now fuck off!"

The group disperses mumbling to one another.

"You're a suspended detective," Riley informs him.

"Well, they don't know that."

Ethan helps him to his feet and Riley attempts to wipe the dirt and rainwater from his clothes.

"Great! This is a new coat, now look at it!" he exclaims.

"We've got bigger problems," Ethan mutters as he begins to pace back and forth in front of Riley. He clutches the cloak in his fist. "How long have you been seeing this cloaked person?"

"I told you, when I had psychosis about eight years ago."

"No, when did you start seeing it again recently?"

"About, maybe, a few days ago. No more than a week ago."

"So, since Carla was murdered."

"Could be a coincidence."

"I don't believe in coincidences."

"But it could be."

"Right, because it just so happens that a serial killer murdered my partner and now, we're being stalked by someone dressing up as one of your hallucinations."

Riley looks up to the sky as he thinks it through. "Good point."

"Who else have you talked to about your hallucinations?"

"No one, why?"

"Because the killer is someone who knows about your hallucination of the cloaked demon. That's why they're dressed like this so that you'd think it wasn't real," Ethan says, stopping to look at him. There's a moment of dread as realisation sets in. "Now think, who else knows?"

"Um, just my parents. Probably my brother too."

"Is that all?"

"Vinny."

"Right."

"And my psychiatrist."

"Anyone else?" he shakes his head. "Right, well that narrows it down."

"It can't be any of them!" Riley interjects.

"And why not?"

"Because – because it just can't!"

"No one else knows about that hallucination."

"Your detective friends do. It states on my medical file what hallucinations I suffer from, and I bet they've all read it."

"Fine, so Lucas, Anna and Ash also know."

There's a whole team of detectives working on Carla's case who know too but he leaves that out to save Riley embarrassment. There's a drawn-out silence as Ethan's brain tries to think why the killer would do this. To see where they go? To monitor them? But why dress up as Riley's hallucination?

"I'm not crazy," Riley snivels and looks at him. "I thought I was relapsing."

Riley's eyes glaze over. His leg twitches as he bites his quivering bottom lip. That's when Ethan realises. "How many times have you seen that person?"

He doesn't answer straight away as he begins to chew along his nails. "Everyday."

Ethan saw the link between Riley's illness and the victims

but because the victims are all female, he didn't think that Riley could be a potential target. Now he knows that was a mistake. The killer is targeting Ethan by destroying anyone close to him and Riley is the last person alive who he loves. This proves that not only is he a potential target; he's the next victim.

"All the victims had mental health illnesses," Ethan utters.

"Because they were easy targets." He pauses. "I'm a –"

"Don't!" he shouts.

"Ethan."

He comes forwards and takes hold of Riley's face. "Nothing is going to happen to you! I won't let it."

Chapter Nineteen

As he pours the plant-based milk into the mug of decaf tea, Ethan stares at all the faces of the victims with a feeling of dread in his stomach at the thought that Riley's face could join them on the board. He tears himself away and sits cross-legged next to him on the sofa. He hands him the mug.

"Here you go."

"Thanks," Riley says cradling it with both hands.

"How are you feeling now?"

"As good as someone can who's going to be dead soon," he says sipping his tea.

"Don't say that!" They stare at each other. "I told you; I'm not going to let anything happen to you."

"And how do you plan on doing that?"

"By finding this son-of-a-bitch. In the meantime, it's best if you don't go anywhere alone. I'd prefer you not to go out at all, but I can't exactly keep you caged here."

"I have an app on my phone."

"What?"

"An app that tracks my location. If you download it, you can add me and see where I am."

"I can't do that."

"I want you to."

Ethan sighs, hating that they have to do this, but they really do have to do this.

"Fine." Ethan looks at his face as Riley's head hangs low. If something was to happen to him, he'd die believing the lie that his dad told him and thinking Ethan didn't love him. "Riley, about when –"

"Do you mind if I make a phone call?" Riley asks.

He shrugs. "Fine by me. Why?"

"I just need to call my parents," he says putting down his mug and getting up from the sofa to grab the phone.

"Your parents," Ethan repeats.

It was Riley's dad who separated them when they were teenagers. And why would Riley's dad be getting his friend, Vincent, to keep checking in on Riley? His dad also knows about Riley's hallucinations. Ethan jumps to his feet.

"Actually," he says placing his hand over the phone to stop Riley dialling. "Why don't we go and see them?"

"Seriously?" he scoffs.

"Why not?"

"You hate my parents."

"No, I don't."

"Well, you hate my father."

"He hates me too if I remember rightly." Riley gives him a look. "I was thinking that we could have a chat with them and see if they remember anything about Natalie and Carla."

"Why would my parents know anything?" Riley questions, crossing his arms.

"They knew Natalie, right? And we already know that Carla hid a lot from me about Natalie. I mean, what else don't I know?" It's half a lie and half the truth. Riley doesn't say anything as he holds the phone in the air. "It's just a casual chat. Only a few questions." He doesn't respond. "Riley, please."

Riley places down the phone. "Okay. We can talk to them if you want but I'm not sure how much help they'll be."

"It's worth a shot."

"Fine, we'll go tomorrow morning."

"Thank you."

Riley looks him up and down. "You don't have anything else to wear?"

"Well, no, my belongings are still in my flat, remember?"

"Those are the only clothes you have?" Ethan nods and Riley rolls his lips, scowling at his clothing. "You don't want to buy some more clothes? You can't keep wearing the same ones all the time."

He supposes that's right, but he knows the real reason why Riley is asking. His parents are upper-class snobs and even though Riley thankfully never inherited their snobbish ways, he's still conscious of what they think for some reason.

***

The next day Riley drives them to the Darlington house in his black expensive car and Ethan's gaze is fixated out the window for the whole journey, watching how the hills, fields and forestry engulfs the cities created by man. After a quick trip to the shop and a change of clothes into a nicer version of what Ethan was already wearing, they were on the hour-long drive to their hometown. The crappy music on the radio fills the void between them. He recognises some of the landscape as they close in on Shere in Guildford. The town in which he once lived now feels unbearably nostalgic. Most of his memories here were negative.

Riley's parents live further from the town, out in the vast countryside. The house emerges into view as Riley drives up to the large black gates that are open, much to Ethan's surprise. The car crunches across the gravel, skidding around the grass island in the middle. The house – or mansion as Ethan used to call it – looks down on him, causing him to sink a little lower in his seat. Riley stops the car and looks at him. His expression changes to concern.

"We don't have to do this," Riley says. "We can just turn around and go home."

Ethan's taken aback by the word 'home'. Does he think that his flat is now Ethan's home too? He looks past Riley at the house. As a shadow moves across the large windows, Ethan wonders if it's too late for that now. He looks back to Riley. "I'm fine."

Riley flashes Ethan a sympathetic smile before Ethan's attention is drawn back to the house as the front door swings open and Vincent strides down the grey concrete steps towards the car. He opens Riley's door and leans down to look inside.

"Well, this is a pleasant surprise," he beams at Riley.

"What are you, a fucking chauffeur?" Ethan says, leaning across and scowling at Vincent, who returns the look.

"Mum and Dad aren't expecting us. I've not told them about Ethan's, you know, situation," Riley explains.

"Oh, right, you mean how he's freeloading off you?"

Ethan's jaw clenches.

"Have you told them? That, you know, Ethan's back?"

Vincent laughs. "No, I thought I'd let you have the honour of that."

He stands up straight allowing Riley to get out the car. Ethan jumps out his side and follows them, but before he's even shut the car door, Vincent is leading Riley up the steps with his hand on his lower back. Ethan's hands form into tight fists.

The steps seem smaller than Ethan remembers, but the two pillars on either side, supporting the porch are still as intruding. Vincent opens the door and ushers Riley inside. He would have walked in front of Vincent to stop him going in after Riley, but a memory resurfaces, pinning him to the spot.

He remembers the last time he was here. How Riley's dad had shouted in Ethan's face and told him that Riley didn't want to see him anymore before slamming the door on him.

"You coming or what?" Vincent spits.

He snaps out of it and with one deep breath, he walks inside the house that he hasn't been in since he was eighteen.

All he can hear is the echo of his shoes on the solid wooden floor. When he was younger, he hated how much the sound drew attention to him. Some things don't change.

Vincent budges past him, walking alongside Riley down the hallway towards the kitchen. Ethan follows after, his body hunched forward with hands stuffed in the pockets of his jacket. The half panelled, half wallpapered walls seem to close in on him.

"Lizzie?" Vincent calls. "Riley's here to see you."

As he rounds the corner into the kitchen, he catches a glimpse of Riley's mum, Elizabeth, as she rushes over to Riley with open arms wearing a floral dress and an apron. Glossy black hair in perfect curls with matching black makeup framing her green eyes. *A picture-perfect mother*, he thinks.

"Riley!" she screeches, wrapping her arms around Riley's neck in a suffocating way and squeezing her eyes shut.

"Okay, that's enough," Riley mumbles trying to separate himself from her.

Ethan crosses his arms across his chest. Riley doesn't know how lucky he is. Elizabeth opens her eyes as she's about to let go, but then she catches sight of Ethan. She double takes and her eyes widen.

"Ethan?" she says in disbelief, before pushing her own son to one side. "Ethan!" she screeches in the same way she did with Riley. She runs up to him and engulfs him in a hug, pinning his arms in an uncomfortable position. She releases him but keeps both hands on either side of his arms. "Oh my God, it really is you! Look how much you've grown!" She looks him up and down with beaming eyes. "Wow, how long has it been?"

Ethan's mouth opens to answer but he's cut off immediately.

"I have to get Martin! I must tell him that you're here!" Elizabeth exclaims before rushing away and shouting, "Martin!" down the hallway.

He looks at Riley whose cheeks blush red.

"Your mum hasn't changed then," Ethan says.

Riley shakes his head. Muffled voices down the hallway grow closer. He turns, just as Elizabeth drags Martin into the kitchen.

"Look! Look who it is!" she says waving her arms towards Ethan.

Martin's face drops before hardening. "Oh, you're here."

It's the same words he used when Ethan turned up on the night of Riley's leaving party. Some things don't change.

"Yes, isn't it great!" she goes on, not sensing her husband's disapproving tone.

Martin and Riley both exchange a look that Ethan can't quite decipher. Vincent is still leaning against the wall with his arms crossed. A small smirk of amusement on his lips.

"Where did he come from?" Martin asks, looking at his son but nodding towards Ethan as if he were a stray puppy that Riley had found.

"It's – it's a long story," Riley stutters.

"You clearly haven't been on social media lately," Vincent says with amusement.

Riley's eyes widen as him and Ethan exchange a look, remembering the viral video of Ethan tackling him to the ground.

"Right, well, this calls for a celebration! I'm making biscuits!" Elizabeth announces.

"No, you don't have to…" both Riley and Ethan say in unison.

"Is that necessary, Lizzie?" Martin barks.

"Of course! Now, you boys go and sit in the living room, and I'll join you in just a sec," she says gesturing for them to leave. When no one moves, she waves her hands and adds, "Hurry now, we've got a lot of catching up to do."

Riley is the first to move, then Ethan, followed by Martin and Vincent, as they exit the kitchen and into the living room. It's decorated the same as Ethan remembers, with the same red wallpaper, fancy beige sofas and a red rug in the middle of the three sofas all looking in on one another. Riley sits on one sofa opposite Martin. Vincent takes a seat on the other one. Ethan lingers in the middle, looking between each one. Riley shifts along, signalling for him to sit. Ethan perches himself down on the edge of the sofa next to him, both elbows resting on his knees as he avoids eye contact. None of them talk for what feels like forever before Elizabeth enters.

"Right," she says approaching them with a tray full of drinks.

"Here we are."

She places a glass of whiskey on the glass coffee table in front of Martin and then the same with Vincent. She then places a glass of water in front of Riley and a glass of what Ethan presumes is orange juice in front of him. He looks between the glass and her.

"You always used to like orange juice when you were younger," she explains.

"He's twenty-six, Mum," Riley utters.

"And? Adults can still like juice!"

"It's fine," Ethan says before adding, "Thank you," with a smile.

Elizabeth plumps herself down on the sofa next to her husband.

"So, how did this amazing reunion happen?" she asks beaming at them both.

Ethan and Riley exchange a look.

"Um, well, actually, Ethan's staying with me for a while," Riley clarifies but he's cut short by Elizabeth's screech.

"Oh wonderful!" she exclaims.

Martin's face hardens. "How did that happen, then?"

"Well, uh," Riley stutters. Ethan would help him out but even he can't think of a lie quick enough. Thankfully Elizabeth interrupts.

"So, what do you do now, Ethan?" she asks, perching on the edge of her seat.

The silence swallows him, and he feels all their eyes on him.

"I'm," he says but his voice is cracked. He tries again. "I'm a Detective Sergeant."

Was, he thinks to himself.

Elizabeth's eyes light up.

"Wow, that's amazing! Isn't that amazing, Martin?" she says nudging him.

He scowls, looking between them both. "Weren't you arrested recently, Riley?"

Ethan feels Vincent's eyes shifting between them all, as the silence returns but before either Ethan or Riley can answer, Martin continues, "Something tells me that your arrest has something to do with this *coincidental* reunion."

"Oh, don't be silly. Ethan would never arrest Riley. He knows Riley never hurt that girl. Right, Ethan?"

"I, um," he stammers.

"Ethan wasn't the arresting officer," Riley jumps in. "He also did try to defend me against the other detectives," he explains, laying the lie on too thick.

Ethan looks at him, wondering how Riley could lie so effortlessly. He catches Vincent's face, looking at Riley with a confusing and hurtful scowl. He turns away shaking his head. After all, it was Vincent who vouched for Riley's character, not Ethan.

"See!" Elizabeth exclaims. "I think it's awful what happened to that girl, don't you think?"

There's a lump in Ethan's throat that stops any words from exiting his mouth.

"That's actually why we're here," Riley says leaning forward.

"What do you mean?" Martin says.

Now it's time for Ethan to take hold of the conversation. "We think that Carla's murder might be linked to Natalie's."

Martin's frown deepens and Elizabeth's eyes look like they might pop out of her skull as her mouth parts.

"You mean your mother?" Martin croaks out. Ethan nods.

"How so?" Vincent says, leaning forward and sharing the same expression as Martin.

"Yeah, I mean, she's been dead for," Elizabeth begins in a high-pitched voice, pausing to try and work out the maths. "Like, sixteen years!" She looks at Ethan and realisation crosses her face. "No offense, I know she was your mother."

He waves his hand and discards the apology.

"What makes you think that it's the same killer?" Martin says in a sharp tone.

Ethan cocks his head to the side. "I didn't say that."

The air grows cold as they look at each other. Ethan's mouth opens but then he feels Riley's hand on his knee. He looks down at it before looking back to Martin, who mimics his eye trail.

"That woman, Carla, was friends with Natalie, right?" Riley asks.

"I vaguely remember her," he says.

"Oh yes, I remember them both very well!" Lizzie jumps in.

"Well, Carla was also Ethan's partner."

"Work partner," Ethan adds.

"Oh!" Elizabeth says as if not knowing what to do with the information.

"Obviously, we were kids when Natalie passed away so, we were wondering if there was anything you could tell us about them both," Ethan says and then holds his breath.

Riley still hasn't taken his hand off his knee and Ethan's not sure if he's picking up on his dad's disapproving eyes or whether he's choosing to ignore it.

"Why?" Martin bites.

Ethan looks between all three of them.

"You don't think it's a little strange that Carla and Natalie were friends all those years ago and then they both end up murdered on the exact same day?"

He watches as their minds process the information.

"Yeah, well, that's just a coincidence. Right?" Lizzie says with an unsteady tone.

"I don't believe in coincidences."

"Do you remember anything about either of them?" Riley asks.

"Sure," Elizabeth says before taking a deep breath. "Well, Carla was always a little strange. A bit of a free spirit who befriended your mother. And Natalie she was extremely pretty. I mean all the guys fancied her," she chuckles. "Didn't they?" she adds, turning to Martin.

He grunts in response as he picks up the newspaper on the coffee table and opens it. Ethan's not sure how useful this information is but she's the only one offering up something, so he listens.

"Natalie was very kind too. A little shy and maybe a little odd, but a really nice lady," Elizabeth says. She pauses looking up at the ceiling and then her eyes light up as they return to him. "Oh, and she *adored* you!" Ethan feels a tug on his heart, and it must show on his face because Elizabeth's mouth spreads into a smile. "She absolutely loved you! Well, both of them did! Everything was Ethan this and Ethan that," she laughs.

Ethan notices Martin knocking his knee against hers. Her expression drops.

"It's such a shame what happened to her," she continues with the type of emotion that can't be faked. Her eyes widen. "Oh, the biscuits!" She jumps up and rushes out to the kitchen. Leaving them with the two people who aren't talking. Riley clears his throat.

"Dad, do you remember anything?" he asks.

"Not much," Martin mumbles, flicking the page in his newspaper.

"I'm sorry, is my dead mother inconveniencing you?" Ethan snaps and he feels Riley's hand find his knee again. Martin's face looks up over the newspaper.

"Excuse me?"

"What Ethan means is that it'll only take ten minutes of your time," Riley explains in a low voice. Martin's eyes flick down to Riley's hand on his knee again.

"I think it's the least we can do," Vincent says and his voice startles Ethan. He'd almost forgotten that he was there.

Martin looks between them before sighing and folding up his newspaper. "What do you want to know?"

"Did she have any friends, enemies, anyone at all who was

close to her?" Ethan asks.

Martin gets the same line down the middle of his forehead when he's thinking as Riley, except it's cute on Riley. He hopes that's the only thing Riley's inherited from his dad.

"I think it's pretty obvious what happened to your mother," he remarks.

"What's that supposed to mean?" Ethan barks.

"Well, after she died there were rumours…"

"I know about the rumours," Ethan interjects.

"There you go, you have your answer then!"

"My dad didn't kill my mum!"

Martin scoffs a laugh. "And how do you know that?"

"He wasn't there the night she died."

"Oh, so you remember that?"

"What's that supposed to mean?"

"I think it's very coincidental that you don't remember what happened but you're so adamant that your dad didn't do it."

"I just know," Ethan says with certainty.

"Well, I wouldn't be surprised if it was him. I mean if you can beat your own wife and child…"

"What?" Ethan shouts, ignoring Riley's hand that's now gripping his knee even harder.

"You heard."

"My dad never laid a hand on my mum."

"Oh please, she was always in and out of my A&E!"

"What?" Ethan whispers.

"Broken arm, cracked rib, bruising all over her; you name it, she had it!" Martin snarls. "Oh, and don't give me the bullshit she gave me about falling down the stairs or any of that crap."

Ethan can feel his face cripple into a frown. No, he doesn't remember his dad ever hurting his mum. That's something he would remember. His dad beat him after his mum died.

"There were other rumours too," Vincent chips in.

"What rumours?" Riley asks. Ethan is too caught up in what

Martin's said to even digest what Vincent's words.

"I'm not sure if I should say this, and I don't want you to think badly of your mum, Ethan."

"Spit it out," Ethan snaps.

Vincent takes a deep breath. "Well, she used to work at the pub in town. One day I was in there when your dad came in and asked for her because she'd told him that she was working, but she wasn't there."

"What are you trying to say?" Ethan says with a tone that warns him not to say it. Ethan knows what he's implying. He knows about those rumours too; that his mum was a cheating whore.

"I'm just saying that it's a possibility that maybe she was seeing someone else, and your dad got mad…"

"He didn't do it!" Ethan shouts. "And Natalie wouldn't have done that!"

"Well, there's only one other person it could be," Martin says, drawing Ethan's attention back to him. He waits for Martin to continue. "The only other person they found in that house that night."

It's a punch in gut. He remembers those rumours too. He opens his mouth to speak but before he has time, Riley's on his feet, standing in front of Ethan.

"That's enough!" Riley shouts.

Martin rises, mimicking his son's movement. They glare at each other, and Vincent is the first to try and defuse the situation.

"Okay, okay," he says, standing up. "I think we all need to calm down and cool off."

"That's fine, we're leaving now anyway," Riley says without breaking his glare that's fixated on his father.

Ethan hears the door behind him open. "What's going on?" Elizabeth asks.

After a moment, Riley breaks eye contact to turn to his mum. "We have to leave now," he says in a flat tone.

"Already!" she exclaims.

"Sorry, Mum, I really am."

Riley grabs Ethan's wrist and pulls him to his feet.

"Well, at least take these for the road," she says and as Ethan turns to face her, he sees that she's holding a plate full of biscuits.

"I don't..."

"Please."

Riley looks between the plate and her face with a sigh. "Fine."

She beams before disappearing into the kitchen.

"Riley, a word," Martin says appearing by his side and grabbing the top of his arm to drag him into the kitchen.

Riley doesn't say anything but allows his dad to lead him away from Ethan's side. Vincent budges past Ethan and follows after them. He turns to him just before he disappears through the door.

"Family stuff, I'm sure you understand," he says, closing the door behind him. In other words, it's none of his business.

Just before the door meets the frame, Ethan jams his foot in between so that there's a slight gap.

"What the hell do you think you're doing?" he hears Martin say.

"What?" Riley snaps.

"Letting him stay with you."

"It's only temporarily."

"It's still not a good idea!"

"He's right, Riley," Vincent chimes in. "I mean, what if he finds out that we all lied?"

Ethan frowns.

"He won't, it's fine!" Riley says.

"If he finds out about our false statement, you have no alibi for the night that woman was murdered. You'll go to prison, Riley!" Martin says in a repressed shout.

Ethan swings open the door. All four of them look at him with wide eyes. Elizabeth is scooping the biscuits into a tub whilst

Martin and Riley stand at ends with each other with Vincent in the middle like a referee.

"We're still talking!" Martin snaps.

"Oh, I heard," Ethan says with a bite to his voice. "Continue."

Chapter Twenty

"It's not what you think!" Riley exclaims, rushing forward towards him.

"You lied to me!" Ethan says and he's surprised at the pain in his own voice. Riley's face drops as he goes within himself.

"You don't understand, Ethan," Elizabeth says. "If we hadn't said that Riley was with us the night Carla was murdered, he'd still be in that awful place!"

"So, you lied? You all gave a false statement!" he says in disbelief looking at each and every one of them.

"We did what we had to do," Martin mutters.

"Don't blame them, I was the one who lied at the police station and then asked them to go along with it," Vincent explains.

"How heroic of you," he says. "You do realise that you can all go to prison for this?"

"How?" she asks.

"Obstructing the course of justice," he bursts out. "Being an accessory to murder…"

He doesn't realise what he's indicated until he looks at the hurt on Riley's face.

"Look, we all know that Riley didn't do anything," Martin exclaims.

"Oh, and let me guess, that's why you've been getting him," Ethan says jabbing his finger at Vincent. "To keep an eye on Riley. To make sure I don't find out about all this!"

"What?" Martin says frowning.

"You know what I mean! You, getting Vincent to keep checking in on Riley all the time."

Martin's face cripples into a frown as he turns to look at Vincent. "What the hell is he talking about?"

Ethan looks at Vincent who scowls at him. Then he looks at

Riley who stares up at him with guilt all over his face, his body rigid. The pieces come together in his head.

"Oh, you've got to be joking," Ethan utters, the fury written in his face.

"With you and Elizabeth working a lot and with everything going on with Riley with these accusations, I thought I'd check in on him for you and make sure he's okay," Vincent explains in an innocent tone that makes Ethan feel sick.

"Oh, that's so nice of you, Vinny," Elizabeth beams.

Ethan and Riley still haven't broken eye contact. Riley shakes his head a little, silently begging him not to say anything.

"Yes, how nice of you to lend a helping hand," Ethan spits. He can't bring himself to even look in Vincent's direction.

"We've got to go," Riley announces, spinning around to face his family.

Ethan doesn't say anything as he turns and storms out, leaving them in the kitchen. He charges out of the house and past the car, walking aimlessly.

"Hey!" Riley calls from behind. "Where the hell are you going?"

"Away from here!"

He hears footsteps pound on the grass behind him and feels a hand grab his wrist. Ethan turns, pulling his arm away from Riley's touch as if it was now poison. There's silence between them and Ethan waits for him to speak first.

"Let's just get in the car and go home," Riley says with a shaky voice.

"With you? No fucking way!"

A flicker of pain crosses Riley's face. "I can explain everything."

"You lied to me! Twice!"

"I didn't lie to you."

Ethan scoffs a laugh. "You lied to the other detectives – and to me – about where you were the night Carla died."

"I lied to the other detectives, but I never told you that I was with them the night she died. Vincent told you that."

"But you let me believe it."

"I know and I'm so –"

"So, where were you?"

Riley sighs. "I was at home in my flat all night."

"Alone?"

He doesn't answer.

"Riley!" a voice calls.

They both turn their heads towards the house as Vincent walks down the steps. Riley turns back to face Ethan. Another piece clicks into place for him.

"Oh God, you were with him that night, weren't you?" Ethan says now feeling sicker. "That's why you lied at the station because you didn't want your parents to know."

"If my dad ever finds out, he'll kill him… and then me."

"But why the fuck did you lie to me?"

"Again, I never lied to you about him."

"You told me that your dad gets Vincent to check in on you and that's why he's always in your fucking flat. You told me there was nothing going on between you both!"

"Okay, maybe I lied a little."

"A little?"

Riley turns his head away and Ethan can see that he's clenching his jaw. "Why does it matter?"

"It matters because we we're supposed to be honest with each other. We're supposed to trust each other!"

"You can trust me."

"Can I?"

Silence fills the space between them as they stare at each other.

"I don't have to tell you anything about me and Vinny," Riley mumbles. "It has nothing to do with Carla's murder and it has nothing to do with you."

"Clearly," Ethan snaps.

Riley narrows his eyes. "Let's not forget, you were the one who left me," he says with a painfilled voice before turning and walking towards the car.

Ethan watches him walk away, remembering that Riley thinks that he rejected him all those years ago. Riley approaches Vincent and he watches how Vincent brings himself closer towards him. Ethan can't hear anything they're saying but he tries to lipread. He knows Vincent is asking how Riley is but that's as far as he gets. Ethan marches back towards the car and interrupts whatever it was that they were saying.

"Riley, are we going or what?" he barks, opening the passenger side of the car.

Riley gives a quick glance at Ethan and then back to Vincent muttering a simple, "Yeah."

"Call me when you get home," Vincent says, opening the car door for him. "You know how much I worry about you."

Ethan mimics his words under his breath, feeling childish for doing so afterwards. Riley gets in the car and Vincent shuts the door for him. Ethan's about to get in when he hears Lizzie's voice.

"Wait, wait, wait!" she shouts bursting out the front door and down the steps holding the tub of biscuits. Ethan's surprised as she rushes around the car to him, holding out the tub. "For the journey."

Ethan flashes a weak smile and takes the tub.

"You're not going to say anything, are you? About, you know," she asks.

He thinks for a moment. He should tell Anna what he's discovered today but convinces himself that she wouldn't even believe him if he did say anything. After all, it's not like they trust him anymore either. He shakes his head and Lizzie smiles with relief.

"I worry about him," she confesses, her voice hushed.

"Who?"

"Riley. He's, not exactly social." She sighs. "Well, not since his," she points to her head. "He did tell you about his illness, right?"

He gets the feeling she's dancing around the word.

"His schizophrenia?" he says, and she nods. "Yes, he did."

"Is he drinking enough water? Eating enough? Sleeping enough But not too much, though, because that's also not good."

"He's okay, don't worry."

A wide smile spreads across her face. Ethan glances to where Vincent was standing but there's an empty space now.

"I used to worry about him, all alone in that flat. He never dates and he doesn't have any friends." *That's what you think*, Ethan thinks to himself, resisting the urge to say it out loud. "That's why I'm so happy that he has you again!" she continues, beaming up at him.

Ethan glances towards the house. "I'm sure your husband disagrees."

"Oh, just ignore, Martin. He can be funny like that. He also worries about Riley but in a different way. He doesn't want Riley having any kind of stress."

"Right, and he thinks I'm causing him stress?"

She shrugs. "Maybe, but I don't think that. I think you're good for Riley."

"What makes you think that?" he chokes out a laugh as he says it. He's not good for Riley and he wouldn't blame her for saying it.

"Because the happiest I ever saw him was when you were in his life."

That tug on his heart pulls again and a knot ties itself in the pit of his stomach. Riley's car roars to life and he knows it's a signal to wrap it up. She smiles at Ethan before reaching out with one hand to stroke back a piece of stray hair that's fallen onto his face. "Your mum would be so proud of you."

Before Ethan can react, she wraps her arms around him one

last time. "Look after him," she whispers.

"I'll try."

He's gotten used to not promising things to people. It's the number one rule as a detective. She releases him and flashes one last smile before walking away. She waves to Riley through the car window and blows a kiss. He watches her walk back up the steps and into the house. Then he sees Martin scowl at him from the window and it prompts Ethan to get into the car and get the hell out of this place.

Chapter Twenty-One

They haven't said a word since leaving the house. Riley keeps his eyes fixed to the road and both hands tight around the steering wheel. In a way, the silence is comforting, it's better than arguing or shouting at each other. But Ethan can't help but feel Riley's anger, hurt and worry radiate from him. Ethan takes out his packet of cigarettes.

"Not in my car!" Riley snaps.

He grumbles, shoving them back into his pocket. Maybe he was wrong for what he said and maybe he did overreact, especially considering Riley thinks that he left him.

"I'm sorry about before," Ethan mutters and he watches from the corner of his eye as Riley glances at him with wide eyes. "I didn't mean to get."

Ethan tries to find the next words but the only word that comes into his head is 'jealous'. He can't even bear the thought of Riley in that way with anyone else. The car grinds to a halt. Ethan's head whips forward and then back against the seat.

"What the fuck?" he exclaims, looking across at Riley. He stares out the window and Ethan wonders if he's having another episode, or blip as they call it now.

"Do you know where we are?" Riley asks looking at him with rounded eyes.

He frowns. "Why? Are you lost or something?"

"Do you not recognise it?" Ethan looks around. Of course, he knows where they are, but he's surprised that Riley does. He looks back to him. A smile spreads across Riley's face. He then pulls the car onto the grass side. "Come on," he says unbuckling his seatbelt and jumping out of the car.

His eyes follow Riley and he contemplates telling him that they should go home but he sees this as an opportunity to have a cigarette, so he gets out after him. He follows Riley as he makes his way into the woodland, pushing aside the branches that now hang low. Ethan lingers on the outskirts lighting up his cig. It's now all overgrown and the path is impossible to find. Not like when they were teenagers. Seems like the council has let this place go since they've grown up.

"Riley, where are you going?" Ethan asks, puffing smoke into the air. He knows that he wants to go into the woodland because it was where they used to go when they were teenagers, but he's not sure why.

"To our spot."

"Do we have time for this right now?"

He's shocked that Riley still calls it that. He's also tempted to revisit old memories, but there's too much going on right now.

"I just want to see if it's still here," he says powering on ahead.

Ethan gets it now and he'd be lying if he said he wasn't curious too. "It probably isn't," Ethan calls after him.

"It might be."

"It won't."

"Only one way to find out."

He's got a point, so, Ethan follows, discarding the rest of his cigarette. They make their way through the thick undergrowth of the woodland. Shards of sunlight penetrates through the leaves of the overhanging trees, creating lines of yellow light across the forest. Small insects fly high overhead as if dancing above them. Bright colours of yellow and green fill his eyes.

He keeps his eyes on Riley the whole time. They reach the wooden bridge that Ethan remembers but it seems smaller now. The bridge allows them to cross a stream that runs through the middle of the forest. Although, he's sure that they could just jump across it now. Riley takes his time walking across the wooden slates. They dispute which way to go from there. Riley's convinced that they used to turn left after the bridge. Ethan knows that it was right. He persuades Riley to take his direction, which they later realise is wrong and they backtrack to Riley's route.

They reach the clearing and see it. It is still here even after all this time. An old wooden plank with a tired rope tied at either end and then hung from a tree branch. A construction he and Riley made when they were teenagers in an attempt to make a swing.

Riley looks up at him with a grin. "Told you."

"I wouldn't say it is safe though."

"Only one way to find out."

Riley makes his way over to it and lowers himself onto the plank of wood. Both hands grip the rope and his body tenses. He sways and the branch creaks.

"Seems okay to me," he comments looking up at Ethan as he approaches.

Something about the way Riley looks sparks an image in his head of when he was sixteen. He remembers when they first made the swing and Riley sat on it to test it. How Ethan had tormented him that it would break. How nothing is ever built to last and how overtime everything becomes broken. But it didn't break, and here it is still. He remembers them joking around together on the grass and how they had their first kiss under the branches of this oak tree.

He thinks back to how innocent Riley was back then. Before he got schizophrenia, before Ethan became a detective, and before all this mess happened. He wonders where those two teenagers disappeared to over the last few years and if they could ever come back. So, he decides to take a page out of Riley's book.

"Only one way to find out," Ethan utters. He takes hold of the rope on either side and tugs it backwards, ignoring the twinge of his once dislocated arm.

"What the hell are you doing?" Riley panics.

"Seeing if it breaks."

There's a high-pitched screech as the swing is pulled back as far as Ethan dares to take it before letting go. It creaks but doesn't break as it swings forward and then back again.

"Told you," Riley says. Ethan pushes the swing as it comes back to him again. This time harder but it still doesn't break. He half expected it to. "See." Riley tilts his head backwards, looking at him upside down with a smug smirk as he swings back and forth.

Ethan grins. "Fine, what about this then?"

He grabs the swing to pull it to a halt. He removes Riley from the seat and sits in his place. Ethan slides one hand around his waist and guides him onto his lap. Riley looks at him surprised, his body rigid and awkward as he positions himself sideways across his lap. Ethan feels the twitch of pain in his side and the aching in his legs as he digs his heels into the dirt, pushing the swing as far back as gravity will allow. He leans in close to Riley's ear.

"Hold on," he whispers before lifting his legs up.

Riley's arms wrap around him and Ethan grunts from the pain of his bruises as their bodies press against each other. His hand grasping at the fabric of Ethan's jacket and the other onto the rope of the swing. He buries his face in between Ethan's neck and shoulder. It swings back and forth in a fluid motion. He watches as Riley's face peers out, as if surprised to not be lying on the ground. He lets out a sigh of relief and Ethan smiles down at him. He kicks his tired legs to swing higher and faster and they both laugh as they try to hold onto the swing and to each other as best they can. It's a smile Ethan's not seen for a while and it's a laugh he's not heard for years.

Ethan's mind is playing in a way that he thought was lost, like a child again. His eyes are fixed on Riley's, watching how they seem to transform into an even deeper shade of blue. The branch and swing continue to creak. Not in a way that it might break, but in a way of being brought back to life again. Like the rekindling of lost innocence, childhood laughter, and the feeling of being young and in love again.

Chapter Twenty-Two

Anna squints against the burning sunshine and places her hand above her eyes to shield them. She misses the tall buildings and the shade they offered back in London as she stares across a clear field of patchy brown short grass. In the distance, some hills cast shadows against the clear blue sky and the outline of bare trees surrounding the bottom.

"Any luck?" Lucas calls from behind her.

"No, just a load of green shit," she says turning to look down on him from the large rock she's standing on. He hangs on the car door, his arm resting on the top of it.

"Face it, we're lost!"

"We're not lost," she says, her voice trailing off into hopelessness. She looks at the vast landscape again and hooks her finger inside the ring hanging from her necklace. An insect lands on her neck. She slaps it in an attempt to squash the fly, but it gets away. "God, I hate the countryside!"

She jumps down from the rock and marches back to the car.

"If we're not lost, then which way are we going?"

She looks around doing a full 360 on the spot. "That way!" she says randomly pointing her finger in any direction.

His gaze lingers on the rock in the middle of the field as she goes around to the passenger side of the car.

"Why is there a rock in the middle of nowhere?"

"It's Guildford, does anything make sense here!"

They drive around for almost an hour before reaching a small town that's surrounded by hills.

"Find somewhere to park, I need coffee," she says.

He pulls the car into a narrow parking space, and she doesn't wait for him as she makes her way into the closest café.

"Black coffee," she orders to the young man behind the counter and then she turns to take in her surroundings. Presuming that the boy who served her would be too young to know a Colin Brown, she turns and leans across the counter to the older woman next to the machines. "Hi, sorry, do you happen to know where I could find a Colin Brown?"

"Colin Brown?"

"Yes. I have his address here, but I can't seem to find it," she says pulling out the scrap piece of paper from her jacket pocket. She holds it out to her, but the woman shrugs.

"Sorry, don't know him."

"You must know him! His wife was murdered here sixteen years ago! His son Ethan found the body."

The woman stares at him with a wide-eyed expression. "I've just moved here, lovie."

Anna lets out a frustrated growl.

"I know where he lives," a voice says from behind her. She turns to look at the man in his later forties wearing a cap and a worn-out jacket.

"You know Colin Brown?"

"Every local knows him and what happened."

"Where can I find him?"

"Go to the end of this road, turn left, second right, house at the end."

"Right!" she says spinning around and repeating the set of instructions under her breath as she swipes her coffee from the young man and takes a swig of it. Lucas swings open the door as she approaches it. "Back in the car," she demands, brushing past him.

"Did you get me a coffee?"

She shoves the coffee into his abdomen.

"You've already had some of this!"

"Stop your moaning!"

They both get in the car and after taking several wrong turns, they find themselves parked in front of a small, terraced house. She climbs out of the car and pushes open the small black gate which is hanging on its last hinge. The grass is overgrown and floods the narrow concrete pathway leading to the front door, an old children's bike lying amongst the sea of green. She knocks on the splintered wooden door and feels the need to watch her hands. No answer. She knocks harder.

"Maybe he's not in," Lucas suggests.

Then there's the rumble of heavy footsteps that seems to shake the front door. It swings open.

"What do you want?" a large man with dark hair groans and she steps back to avoid the wave of alcohol that radiates off him.

"Colin Brown?" she asks the man who doesn't resemble Ethan in the slightest.

"Yeah, what do you want?"

"DI Anna Jones," she says producing her ID badge. "But you can call me Anna." He gives her a blank look. "And this is DS Lucas Turner, but you can call him Luc."

"Why are you here?"

"We just want to talk to you about your wife Natalie Brown."

His head perks up in surprise. "You mean dead wife," he grunts.

"Yes."

"Why?"

"May we come in?"

He glares between them before moving aside. Anna squeezes past him through the doorway into the dark house, followed by Lucas. The old wooden floorboards creak beneath her feet and her high heels echo around the derelict space. She takes in the mess of beer cans, crisp packets and dirty clothing on the floor that's layered with thick dust and tangled hair. The air feels suffocating and humid, laced with the tang of stale beer. She looks around the living room, noting the empty mantlepiece.

"Now what's this about Natalie?" Colin asks throwing himself onto the sofa.

Lucas looks down at the sofa, wiping away crumbs before

perching himself on the edge.

"We think her murder might be –," Lucas begins but Anna cuts him off.

"We're just giving her case a look over. You know, just procedure," she says with a shrug.

"I didn't kill her."

"I didn't say you did."

"We just want to ask you a few questions," Lucas explains in a professional tone.

"Well, I don't know anything different to what I told the police sixteen years ago."

"The police never asked the right questions back then," Anna says.

"And what questions would that be?" he asks, raising an eyebrow.

"Do you remember anyone who was close to Natalie or paid a particular interest in her?"

His eyes form slits as a frown bridges the gap between his eyebrows. "Not really."

"Anyone at all?"

"Well, there was just Carla really."

"And I'm presuming you've heard on the news that she was murdered recently."

"I don't watch the news but there's been talk around the town."

"Bit coincidental, don't you think?"

He shrugs. "I guess."

"Especially given their certain connection."

He frowns, so she produces a piece of paper from her jacket, unfolds it and holds it out in front of him. His eyes igniting with realisation and fury.

"How dare you!" he exclaims. She retracts the piece of paper and conceals it in her jacket. "How dare you come here and start bringing up the past!"

“We did some digging and found that you got a restraining order against Carla after Natalie died? You practically forced her to leave town.”

“She was nothing but a bitch! Natalie should have stayed the fuck away from her!”

“Do you speak to your son?” she asks spinning on her heels to watch his reaction as it turns stone cold.

“I have nothing to do with that boy!”

“Yes, I noticed there were no pictures of him or your wife anywhere.”

“And?”

“You don’t get along with Ethan then?” Lucas asks.

“Haven’t seen him for over ten years.”

“Over ten years? That would have made him like sixteen.”

“So?”

“Why are you estranged from him?”

“That boy was nothing but trouble! Couldn’t do anything right, useless piece of shit!”

“Ah, I get it,” Anna agrees overemphasising her enthusiasm to understand him. “I’ve only worked with him for a while and already he’s a pain in my ass.”

Colin barks out a bitter laugh. “So, you get what I mean then.”

“Oh yeah! Never listens, always causing trouble.”

“Yeah well, it didn’t matter what I did, I couldn’t knock any sense into that boy!” he exclaims picking up his can of beer from the floor and draining it.

“Huh, I see,” she utters as the word ‘knock’ mulls over in her brain. “What about his friend?”

“What friend?”

“Riley.”

“Ah, the Darlington kid.”

“Do you remember much about him?”

“Odd boy from an odd family. Not much to talk about.”

“Why were they odd?” Lucas asks.

"The so-called perfect little family!" he spits. "At least that's the image they like to give, but they're no different from the rest of us."

"I know the type. Bet they've got a lot of secrets," she coaxes, taking a stab in the dark.

"The family is crawling with them."

"Oh really?"

"Their eldest son is on drugs; the father's been having affairs; and we all know their youngest was taken to a psychiatric hospital."

"How much of that is just small-town gossip though?"

"Oh, it's all legit!"

"So why did you let your son hang around with a boy from a family like that?"

"Wasn't my choice! It was Natalie who always took Ethan there. I never liked it."

"Huh. When did Ethan meet Riley?"

"I don't know," he says with a sigh as if bored with this conversation. "I guess when they were like eight. Maybe nine."

"And Carla would go with them too?"

His eyes sharpen. "Yes, but only because Natalie let her."

"I see. Do you mind if I use the bathroom?"

Colin waves his hand towards the door. Her heels clunk along the floorboards as she climbs the stairs. Wandering down the hallway, she opens the door to the bathroom and moves onto the next one. The door at the end of the hallway is already ajar and using one finger, she pushes it open, causing the wood to creak in protest. The room is painted a pale blue and has a single bed inside. She looks at the door which has a broken lock and handle. Running one finger along the edge of the door she feels the splintered wood and gash in the side of it. Like someone had barricaded it shut and someone else broke it open.

Stepping inside the small room, she tries to put herself in Ethan's shoes; a child's shoes. She goes over to the dusty and discoloured bed. She gets on her knees and lifts up the covers to look under the bed. She begins to pull out rubbish and pieces of clutter. Everything is covered in cobwebs. A spider runs out making her jump back, but she continues. Anna's fingertips touch some paper, and she pulls it out to view it fully. She stares down at the drawings, feeling a sting swell behind her eyes. They're all drawn by a child, each one showing a stick woman lying beside a bathtub, red pencil scribbled all around her. Placing them down, she keeps digging under the bed, pulling out items of clothing which she discards. She stops when she pulls out a piece of material with dark burgundy stains on it. She unfolds the fabric, revealing a teenager's size T-shirt with bloodstains on the back of it. She pokes her finger through one of the slits in the back. Small holes on the material created from years of beatings by a metal belt.

Some people don't deserve the chance to have children, she thinks. Her hand goes to her stomach. She can see the blood running down her legs and feel her body letting go of the one thing she's always wanted. That maternal instinct of protection and care has never left her even though she doesn't have a child anymore.

"What are you doing?" a voice asks from behind, making her jump.

She turns, relieved to see Lucas standing in the doorway.

"You scared the shit out of me!" she shouts, climbing to her feet.

"Why are you in here?"

"Just looking around," she replies discarding the shirt and wiping her eyes before Lucas notices. "I think we've got everything we need for now."

"This has been a complete waste of time," he grumbles.

"Not entirely."

"He hasn't told us anything useful."

"I think you'll find he's told us a lot without knowing it."

Lucas frowns so she continues. “I’ve done the maths. Ethan and Riley met a year or two before Natalie was murdered. Now Carla.”

“You think it’s linked to the Darlington family?”

“I think it’s too much of a coincidence.”

“So, Riley murdered Natalie as well as Carla?”

“Riley would have been ten when Natalie died. Do you honestly believe that a ten-year-old could cut out a grown woman’s heart?”

“Children have been known to kill.”

“I guess so. Either way this all links back to that family and I’m going to find out how.”

Chapter Twenty-Three

The next day Riley goes to work as he's taken too many sick days and holidays. But he texts every so often to let Ethan know that he's still alive and that he hasn't seen the cloaked figure. Meanwhile, Ethan tries to figure out how the killer finds his victims. He decides to call Jennifer for some more information.

"Hello?" she says through the phone.

"Hi Jennifer, it's Ethan."

"Have you found anything?"

His heart sinks. "No, not yet sorry."

"Oh," she says sounding more deflated. This part of his job never gets any easier.

"I just have a few more questions about your sister."

"Okay?"

"Did she talk about anyone in particular before she die –" he stops himself and covers it with a cough. "- she went missing?"

"Not really, why?"

He glances up at the board of women who went missing from different places across different counties. One was last seen shopping in a supermarket, and another was last seen walking her dog in the morning.

"Was there anyone new in her life? A new area she'd go to for a walk or anything."

There's silence on the other end of the phone and he wonders if she's lost signal or is just thinking.

"She had a new support group."

"Support group?"

"Yeah, for her mental health. You know, they'd meet, chat, do some workshops, that sort of thing."

"Was it an NHS one?"

"No, it was a private one."

"And what was it called?"

"God, what was it called, mind... meet... and something." She pauses but Ethan doesn't say anything, eager to give her time to remember it. "Mind Meet and Greet!" she blurts out.

He scribbles it down. "You've been a massive help, thank you."

"Are you any closer to finding out what happened?"

"Yes," he says, and this time he means it. He hears her sigh of relief from the other end of the phone. "I'll speak to you soon, okay?"

"Okay. Bye."

He hangs up and begins researching the support group on Riley's laptop. A text flags up on his phone from Riley. *On my way home now x*

Ethan's surprised to see a kiss at the end but it still makes him smile. He writes out a quick response but keeps deleting and rewriting the tiny X at the end of his message. His finger lingers on the send button before firing it off. *See you soon x*

He stuffs one of Elizabeth's biscuits in his mouth as he opens up the Life 360 app, or as he likes to call it, The Stalker app and finds Riley's location. He's down the road and heading in this direction. He looks at the laptop screen and frowns at it, trying to gather as much information about this support group as he can. They meet once a week, and the group is run by someone who Ethan doesn't recognise so they can't be their killer. This is definitely where the killer finds their victims. He checks his app, seeing Riley only a few feet away from the front door. Moments later, he hears it open and shut, followed by footsteps up the stairs.

"Hey, what have I missed?" Riley asks hurrying into the kitchen.

"Do you recall a mental health support group called Mind Meet and Greet?"

Riley frowns. "Not really, why?"

"Would you tell me if you had?"

They stare at each other. "I'm not lying to you, Ethan."

"But you have done. You lied to me about your sugar daddy."

"Sugar daddy?" he questions with a frown. His expression lifts with realisation. "Vincent is not my sugar daddy."

"Why else would you be with him?"

"Maybe because he cares about me and doesn't just leave me," he says with a bite to his voice. Ethan sighs, lowering his head. "I'm not lying to you anymore. I promise."

There's something sincere in the way he says it that makes Ethan believe it.

"Whilst we're on that subject, there is one thing I need to know," Ethan says, and Riley waits for him to continue. "Were you with *him* the whole night Carla died?"

Ethan doesn't want to know but he has to ask. Riley shifts from one leg to the other.

"Yes."

"Like between 1 am and 3 am?"

His eyes narrow. "Yes."

Ethan's body cringes and tries to clear the disgusting image from his mind. At least he can rule Vincent out as a suspect, because, despite the lies Riley has told him, he believes and trusts Riley.

"Biscuit?" Ethan offers out the tub of biscuits Riley's mother had made as he bites into one. He shakes his head, but Ethan doesn't retract his offer. Riley grabs one and bites into it.

"So, you don't recognise the support group then?"

"No, why?"

"Because Charlotte started going to that group before she disappeared."

"But there are hundreds of mental health support groups. The killer probably went to them all!"

"Most likely. Our killer crossed counties which means he most likely targeted different mental health groups within each area." He looks at Riley who has large dark bags under his eyes and a withdrawn face. "Have you taken your meds today?"

"I think so, I can't really remember."

"I think you should take some," Ethan says, grabbing a blister pack and handing it out to Riley.

"What are you a doctor now?" he hears Carla say from behind him. His body tenses at the sound of her voice.

Riley hesitates before giving an unconvincing nod and taking them. "Fine," he mutters, piercing the foil and taking a tablet out.

"Oh yeah, just swallow some more pills, that'll help!" Carla scoffs.

He ignores her, getting a bottle of water out of the fridge and handing it to Riley. After Riley swallows them, he hands the blister pack and water back to Ethan. He turns around and looks at the hallucination of Carla. What if he is like Riley? What if his medication could help? Ethan takes out a couple of pills and throws them into his mouth. He swings his head back allowing the tablets to hit the back of his throat and then downs the water.

"Well, that wasn't a good idea," she says half serious and half amused. He glares at her as he places down the bottle and blister pack.

Riley seems better and more alert as he makes note of the support group and adds it to the board. Ethan doesn't take his eyes off him as he gets out a bottle of beer from the fridge and opens it. Riley's got a lot of energy as his leg twitches, but Ethan guesses that's a side effect of the medication.

"Is he okay?" Carla asks, appearing next to Ethan and leaning against the counter.

"He's fine."

"Are you sure he's not, you know, losing it?"

He flips her off before taking a mouthful of his drink.

"Should you really be drinking after you've just taken someone else's medication?" she asks with a smirk.

"Are you a doctor now too?" he hisses in a low voice. He looks at Riley whose shoulders seem to stiffen, and Ethan worries that he heard him.

"I think you need your head examined."

Her smile widens and his glare sharpens. "I'm starting to see why you were murdered."

"Steady, you're already a suspect."

"Yeah, and I'm the one trying to find out who did this to you," he says, becoming aware that he's having a full conversation with her now in front of Riley. Either Riley is too caught up in the investigation or he's choosing to ignore Ethan's delusions.

"Oh, I won't be holding my breath then. You two don't stand a chance of solving this. I mean, you," she says pointing at him. "An alcoholic with mummy and daddy issues. And him." She jabs a finger in Riley's direction. "A sad, lonely schizophrenic."

"Shut the fuck up," Ethan growls, his voice louder this time. He knows Riley heard that, but he doesn't say anything. He doesn't even flinch.

"Aw, getting defensive, are we?" Carla torments.

"No."

"Trying to stick up for your little boyfriend."

Ethan's mouth opens to protest.

"Shut up," Riley exclaims, spinning around to look in his direction. But he's not looking at Ethan. He's looking at Carla. "I'm trying to concentrate."

Ethan and Carla both stare at Riley in shock. She looks at Ethan with large round eyes as a grin replaces the look of surprise on her face.

"Things just got interesting," she chimes with amusement in her voice.

He frowns between Riley and Carla. "You can see her?" Ethan asks.

"Yes, and she's very annoying. How you both never killed each other, I'll never know," Riley says.

"Well, we still don't know if one of us did," she says gesturing at Ethan as she approaches him.

All Ethan can do is gawp with his mouth open as Carla stands in front of Riley and shifts from side to side, watching as his eyes follow her exact movements. Ethan still hasn't blinked, watching them both. A sick feeling churns in his stomach and his head feels light on his shoulders. He puts down his drink.

"This isn't right. This can't be happening," Ethan says in disbelief.

"Oh, but it is," she says with a smile.

How can they both see her? She's dead. They can't both be interacting with the same hallucination. Can they?

"See, I told you that you shouldn't have taken his meds," she says to Ethan.

"You took my medication?" Riley asks, looking at him.

"Only a couple," he says with a shrug.

"You idiot!"

Carla chokes out a laugh. "I like this guy," she says looking at Ethan and then she eyes Riley from head to toe before stepping closer. "Finally, someone I can have some fun with."

He watches as Riley's face flashes red. Is he blushing? Ethan goes to move forward but stumbles, just managing to grab the table in front of him to steady himself. His chest feels tight, and his breathing is laborious, coming out in shallow gasps.

"And what do you like to do for fun?" he hears Carla ask.

"I paint, play piano, go dancing."

"Oh," she says.

Ethan's head feels like a balloon that could explode at any moment. Everything around him seems out of sync, as if his body and mind aren't connected. The sound of music fills his ears, but he can't remember what the song is called, and he doesn't know if it was Riley or Carla who decided to put it on. He looks up at them now dancing together.

"What the fuck is going on?" he mutters to no one in particular. He stares at them, not understanding what's happening. What he does know is that Carla doesn't exist. "Stop," Ethan tries to shout but it comes out weak. "Riley, stop!"

Riley spins Carla around so that her back is against his front and they're both looking in his direction. His arms wrapped around her.

"You have to stop. She's not really here," Ethan says, but they both just laugh.

"I think someone's jealous," Carla sings.

She spins back around towards Riley and continues dancing. Ethan tries to grab Carla's clothing to pull her back, but he misses. For some reason his hand and eyes are not synced.

"Stop!" Ethan shouts. Riley's back is to him as Carla looks over his shoulder at Ethan. Her arms wrapped around his neck. "Fucking stop!"

"Fine," Carla says raising an eyebrow. "You want him? Take him."

She pushes Riley away and he falls back into Ethan. He scrambles to catch Riley, who laughs uncontrollably, struggling to steady himself as he uses Ethan's arms for balance. Carla giggles watching them.

"You think this is fucking funny?" he shouts at her.

"Oh, this is the most fun I've had since you started hallucinating me."

Riley twists around in Ethan's arms to face him. "Dance with me," he requests, taking Ethan by surprise.

Before he has time to refuse or accept the invitation, he feels Riley's hands slide onto his waist, one hand going in the dip on Ethan's back and pulling him in so both their bodies press against each other. Ethan now finds it harder to breathe. He's not sure why but he slides his hands onto Riley's hips, fastening their bodies together. He still feels dizzy and sick, and the dancing isn't helping. Looking over Riley's shoulder, he sees Carla standing there with a grin on her face and he still has no idea what's going on.

Their dancing is clunky and out of tune from the music and

from each other. Riley moves his head in front of Ethan's, so their foreheads are pressed together. His gaze lifts as a smirk tugs at his lips.

"In those eight years, did you ever miss me?" Riley asks.

Ethan's caught out by the question and his heartbeat quickens. "Maybe. Did you?"

"Maybe," Riley says still smirking. Ethan's skin begins to burn up under his clothes. "Did you ever think about me?"

Their eyes lock and their lips are inches away from each other.

"All the time," Ethan hears himself say.

Ethan can feel himself lean forward but something's not right. Riley's pupils are unusually wide. He stops and pulls his head back to allow light to shine on them, but they still seem dilated. It's a look that Ethan has seen many times in his line of work. Substance abuse.

"What's wrong?" Riley asks but he doesn't seem alarmed.

Ethan takes his face in his hands to inspect his eyes closer. Riley chokes out a laugh with a smile spreading across his face.

"Your pupils are dilated," Ethan says.

"Aw, thank you!"

"No, it means something's not right." Ethan pauses trying to work it out. It's as though Riley's drunk, but he doesn't drink alcohol. "What have you drunk? What have you taken?" he asks but Riley isn't listening. He looks spaced out and distant. "Riley, this is serious. I need you to tell me what you've taken."

Riley beams as if now awake. "Just my meds. Like you told me to, Doctor," he teases, winking at him.

"That's not right, it's like you're – you're – drugged."

"Drugged?"

"Yes, like you're high"

"Don't be stupid, Ethan," Carla says from behind Riley who now also looks drugged. "You've been with him the whole time; have you seen him take any drugs?"

"No, but –"

"But?"

The penny drops. "You've been spiked!"

Riley looks both surprised and spaced out, before it's replaced by a smirk that begins to spread across his lips, growing wider into a laugh. Then Carla begins to laugh as well.

"Riley, this is fucking serious!" Ethan shouts but that makes Riley laugh more. His eyes become enlarged, and he howls with laughter.

"So, what? It's no big deal. It's just drugs," she says. That doesn't sound like Carla, but then again, she is a hallucination.

"Stop laughing!" Ethan shouts at him, grabbing hold of his arms to get Riley to look directly at him. He doesn't know what else to do to get him to see how dangerous this is.

"Oh, stop being so serious and dance with me," Riley insists, grabbing Ethan by the waist and pulling him in.

"No, Riley," Ethan commands, hardening his grip on him and forcing Riley to stay in place.

"Oh, come on. It's funny!"

"You won't think it's funny later."

"I think it's bloody hilarious."

"Come on, don't be a kill joy," Carla says peering over Riley's shoulder.

"Yeah, Detective, let's have some fun."

Riley throws himself forward but Ethan's quick to move back before he can kiss him. He holds Riley back by his forearms. He attempts to wiggle free, but Ethan tightens his grip, holding him in place.

"No, Riley, this isn't what you want."

"But it is what I want."

"No, it's not," he says but he's not sure if he's reminding Riley of that fact or himself.

Everything around him tilts fighting to stay in control of his intoxicated brain. He pushes Riley back to put distance between them. Everything seems to stretch further away from him, like an elastic band being pulled. He looks at Riley who seems to sway from side to side but Ethan's not sure if that's him or Riley.

"Why do you always have to *kill* the mood, Ethan?" Carla asks and there's something in the way she says 'kill' that makes his body tense. She smirks. "Like you *kill* everything good in your life."

He senses a change in the mood as Carla's tone lowers. It feels more sinister now.

"Don't…"

"Aw, poor little Ethan," she mocks. "Mummy's dead, daddy used to beat on you, and now even your own colleagues are sick of your shit!"

"Carla," Riley starts but doesn't finish as he almost falls backwards.

She steps towards Ethan, and he glares at her, half warning her to not say another word but also daring her to do so.

"I mean, even your own parents couldn't love you, what hope did you have that anyone else would?"

"Shut up, Carla," Ethan growls. Her smile grows.

"Why? Because you don't want to hear the truth? You don't want him to know the truth?" She turns to Riley. "Have you ever thought that it's possible for a ten-year-old boy to kill their own mother? Children have killed their parents before," she says, shifting her gaze to Ethan. His hand forms into a fist as her tone begins to rise. "Maybe, just maybe, that's why your dad hated you so much. Maybe that's why he hit you because he knew you killed your own mother. Just like you killed me!" she shouts, and something erupts inside Ethan.

"Shut up!" he screams, stepping forward and thrashing his arm through the air.

He freezes and time feels like it freezes with him. Ethan and Carla's eyes lock, both wide with shock. Her hands pressed tight to her chest. Ethan and Riley's heads tilt sideways in sync. Red liquid gushes out from her chest, trickling down her torso and spilling onto the floor.

Ethan looks down at the organ palpitating in his hands, veins throbbing as blood drips from his stained red hands. Their eyes lock together as her body falls towards the ground and Riley rushes to her side. Blood pours onto the floor and pools around her. Ethan looks back at the heart in his hands. Horrified, he drops it and the organ splats on the floor.

"It's not real. None of this is real," he mutters to himself.

He staggers towards Riley, looking over as Carla's body falls limp. Her face freezes in a state of pain. The same way she looked when they found her body by the river.

"What have you done?" Riley asks with a shaky voice.

He grabs both of Riley's upper arms and forces him to his feet. He resists, trying to pull back but Ethan holds him in place.

"Riley, listen to me. This isn't real!"

"What do we do?"

"Nothing. There's nothing to do."

"There's a dead girl in our flat! We have to do something!"

"It's not fucking real!"

Riley's expression is filled with horror. He does believe this is real and Ethan's not going to change that.

***

Everything escalates into a nightmare. One minute he's dancing with Carla and the next thing Riley knows he's staring down at her heartless corpse.

"Run, Riley," a voice shouts.

Riley pushes Ethan but can't shake him off as he backs into the living room. He squirms and struggles in Ethan's arms. Their footing gets caught on each other and they stumble backwards knocking into the living room table. They both crash to the ground along with the table as it cracks and glass shatters around them. Riley clambers to his feet and races out of the living room. He stops watching as the hallway rotates round and round and round. The doors on each side turn up overhead and then down under his feet in a repetitive motion.

"Riley!" he hears Ethan's voice call. As the door circles back round to the left side of the hallway, Riley throws himself inside and locks the door just in time as Ethan begins to bang on it from the other side. "Riley, open the door!"

"No!"

"I'm trying to help you, now open the fucking door!"

Riley places his hands over his ears. "Stop it! Just stop!"

"Congratulations!" a voice says. He pulls his hands away and looks around confused before staring up at his own reflection in the cabinet mirror. *"You are exactly what they think you are; crazy!"* his reflection says, speaking words that do not exit his mouth.

"I'm not…"

"What if they're right?" Riley doesn't answer, just stares at his reflection who grins a him as dark shadows form under his eyes. *"What if you did kill them? All of them."*

"I didn't -"

"All sixteen."

"No."

"Carla."

"Stop it!"

"Natalie."

"Please stop," he begs, placing his hands over his ears to try and block it out.

"You know, I don't know what Ethan sees in you. You're pathetic!"

"Please…"

"You should leave. You'll be doing Ethan a favour if you did. He's better off without you."

"I can't…"

"Better yet, you should kill yourself." Riley looks up, staring his reflection in the eyes.

"I can't just leave Ethan like that."

His reflection scoffs a laugh. *"What the hell makes you think he'd care? He'd be thrilled that you're dead. You won't be a problem to him anymore. He'd be free of you."*

"He needs me…"

"He doesn't need you! What makes you think he needs you?"

"Stop it!"

"No one would miss you."

"I said stop it!" Riley shouts, slamming his hands against the mirror. Once, then twice, then three times. The glass shatters more and more each time, defragmenting his reflection until he can't even see it anymore. Broken glass falls into the sink.

He steps back, gasping for air. He looks at the glass in the sink that's stained red. A cool liquid runs down his hands and drips from his fingertips. He brings his hands up to look at them.

"See? There is blood on your hands."

Chapter Twenty-Four

Ethan breaks down the door after hearing shouting and the sound of shattering glass. He's horrified to find Riley standing in the middle of the bathroom with red liquid pouring out of his palms.

"Riley," he calls but he doesn't react as he stares down at his bloody hands.

He tries to take Riley's hands in his, but he starts to push against Ethan. He has no choice but to restrain him by wrapping both his arms around him. Riley kicks and tries to wiggle free from his grasp.

"Let me go!"

"Calm down!"

"Get off me!"

He grabs the tie from the robe that's hanging from one of the pegs and just manages to wrap it around Riley's wrists as he continues to fight him. He then shoves him over to the sink and turns on the cold tap to rinse off Riley's wounds. Everything around him is spinning and nothing feels real. He grabs the hand towel and wraps it around Riley's hands. Eventually, Riley loses energy and becomes limp, allowing Ethan to carry him into the living room, stepping on broken glass from the shattered coffee table as he lays Riley on the sofa. Hours pass into the night as he monitors Riley. There are beads of sweat running down Riley's skin, so Ethan decides to give him water as well as drinking glasses of the stuff himself. Fluid can help drugs pass through the system quicker but not by much. He unbuttons the top of Riley's shirt to try and help with the heat.

Ethan comes down from his high quicker than Riley, even though he still feels sick and disorientated. Over the next few hours, Ethan's had to try and keep him restrained. It's for his own safety, so he didn't hurt himself. Red seeps through the towels around his hands. His breathing is heavy as he pants shallow breaths. He can see Riley's pulse beating through the skin on his neck and he's hot to touch. He tries wrapping ice in a tea towel to put on Riley's skin to cool him but the ice melts and has no effect. Ethan also tries cold wet rags to keep his heat down, but the fabric warms within minutes.

Ethan removes the rag off his forehead and lays the back of his hand to Riley's skin. Even before his hand makes contact, Ethan can feel the heat radiating off him. Riley squirms, uncomfortable in his own skin as he tries to claw at his clothing from under the bloody towel.

"It's okay," he tries to reassure Riley. There's nothing more Ethan can do, and he hates the feeling of being so helpless. The ice and rags aren't working.

Ethan slides his hands under Riley's body and lifts him up. He curls in his arms as his head folds inwards on Ethan's shoulder. He missteps as he carries Riley to the bathroom feeling as though his arms might give out as his injured arm pulses from straining. He's careful to mind Riley's head as he goes through the door. He climbs into the tub and manages to turn the showerhead on, making sure it's as cold as it can be without giving them both hypothermia. The water hits both of them. Riley's body jumps from the shock at first but then he lets out a breath of relief. His body relaxes in Ethan's arms, and he seems calmer.

He holds Riley there for a while, under the pouring water. Both their clothes soak up the water and cling to their skin. Ethan's clothing drags, weighing heavy on him. His body grows weak as his bruises throb, so he lets Riley down, making sure he's okay on his feet before letting go. At first, Riley squirms as if to free himself but Ethan wraps his arms around him to hold him still. Riley's body deflates and he just stands there, letting the water hit his head and trail down his body.

It seems like the drugs are coming out of his system and the effects are wearing off. It's been about nine hours since the symptoms first started, although it seems a lot longer, but Riley seems better. After a while, Ethan lets him go and shuts off the shower. Riley looks up at him with round eyes and he rests his back against the tiled wall as if exhausted. Ethan helps him out of the tub and into his bedroom, sitting him on the bed. Riley doesn't move and his body is rigid. He just sits on the bed staring out into space. His eyes are open but he's not there. There's nothing Ethan can do to bring him out of it, he just has to be patient.

He unties the bonds around his wrists and then gets out Riley's PJs. Ethan helps him change into them as discreetly as he can. Afterwards, he lays Riley on the bed. He stares up at the ceiling, still spaced out. Ethan watches him for a while, sitting on the chair opposite the bed. His clothes are still heavy, and water drips off him onto the carpet. The cardboard box under Riley's bed is poking out from under the overhanging sheet. Ethan's tempted to look but he knows that would destroy any trust they've only just managed to salvage. He stays there until Riley falls asleep before he walks out the bedroom, leaving the door open in case Riley needs him. Ethan goes into the living room, looking at the broken glass and the mess around him, but he still feels sick and dizzy, so he collapses onto the sofa.

He must have fallen asleep because, before he knows it, his eyes fling open to see Carla standing hunched over him. Her face close to his.

"Oh good, you're awake," she says with a lack of emotion. "I thought you might have died."

He frowns at her. "Why do you care?"

"Because we've got a case to solve."

He sits up, forcing her to back away as if being pushed by an invisible wall.

"What chance do I stand with my mummy and daddy issues," he says, shooting her a glare.

"Oh please, I was drugged!"

"How were you drugged?"

“Hello?” she says reaching forward and tapping his forehead. “Remember, I only exist in here, stupid. You were drugged, so I was drugged.”

He supposes that makes sense but at the same time nothing about this makes sense. He crawls up from the sofa and looks around at the mess as Carla collapses into the armchair. He feels burnt out and like he could fall asleep again.

“How long have I been out?” he asks staring at the clock in the kitchen. The clock says it’s early evening but he’s sure he fell asleep at about ten o’clock.

“About eighteen hours,” she says with a shrug.

“Great, another day I’ve slept through.”

“Burn out and fatigue after a high is normal.”

Crouching down, he begins to collect the bigger shards of glass in his hand. He tries to think who could have done this to Riley.

“Whoever drugged you both is clearly the killer,” she says.

“No shit.”

“What drug do you think the killer used?” Carla asks.

He thinks about the symptoms both him and Riley had experienced: Hallucinations, high temperature, nausea, paranoia, mood swings, arousal. The high lasted about nine hours and he’s suffering from extreme fatigue.

“LSD,” he guesses. “It was probably something like acid.”

“And why would the killer do that?”

He tries to think what the motive behind it could be. It makes sense for the killer to use LSD. The effects of it are similar to symptoms of schizophrenia. He wonders how long Riley’s been experiencing these effects, thinking it’s his condition.

“Whoever did this, knows their stuff. They knew to give him a drug that mimicked his condition so we wouldn’t know. Just like the killer knew to dress up like one of his hallucinations,” he says, airing his thoughts out loud.

“But why would they do it?”

"Throw us off the investigation? Get us to turn on each other?"

As the thoughts roll over in his mind, he tries to clean the place up, picking up the broken glass in the bathroom and putting the furniture back where it belongs. He doesn't want Riley to come out to a mess. He doesn't need that.

"And how do you think the killer spiked you?"

"Could have been put in our food or drink."

"That would mean the killer has been in this flat."

Ethan goes to the kitchen and looks around. The half empty tin of homemade biscuits from Riley's mother sitting on the counter. One has a bite taken out of it. He goes over and bins the whole tin before moving onto the cupboards. He tears through them and the fridge, pulling out tins and cartons of food. Anything that isn't sealed goes into a black bag.

As Ethan ties up the bag, he thinks back to when the trip first started. How Riley seemed happy and wanted to dance. How he had come onto Ethan and how something could have happened between them. Something almost did happen between them. Ethan can't shake that thought. The thought of what they would have done if he hadn't noticed that Riley was drugged. Even though they've had sex before, it wouldn't have been consensual this time, and that would mean…

"Oh, come on, Ethan, let's not forget that you were drugged too. Neither of you was able to give consent. It wouldn't have been your fault," Carla says.

He supposes that's true, but he still can't bear the thought. He hates himself for not realising sooner. He then remembers Riley's cut hands, so he grabs his jacket and heads for the door.

"Where are you going?" Carla calls after him.

"To get some fucking bandages!"

Chapter Twenty-Five

Anna takes a sip of the coffee that she'd forgotten about, screwing her face up at the revolting cold taste. She then decides to ditch the rest of the contents into the soil of her desk plant.

"Ma'am," Lucas calls as he approaches her desk holding a file. "We need to talk."

"About?"

"In private."

"Why not here?"

"Because," he says but doesn't give a reason, so she gives him a look and crosses her arms. "I just thought you might be interested in what exactly Ethan's been up to since his suspension."

He takes out the contents of the file and slaps a wad of A4 photographs onto the wooden surface in front of her. Anna's eyes widen as she looks from the photos to Lucas's smug expression.

"In the conference room," she barks, grabbing the photos and concealing them away from prying eyes. She guides him into the room and slams the door shut behind him. "How did you get these?" she demands holding up the photos. Lucas doesn't answer. "Have you been spying on him."

"I just so happened to be in their street at the time."

Anna flicks through the photos. There are photos of Ethan and Riley talking in the park with some woman; a photo of them almost being hit by a car; and she stops on the photo of both of them in a mid-dance pose with their arms wrapped around each other and foreheads together.

"Huh, I never took you for a peeping Tom," she says with a smirk as she holds up the photo of Ethan and Riley. He rolls his eyes.

"I wasn't spying on them for that reason."

"Then why were you?"

"I don't trust either of them and I know they have something to do with Carla's murder."

"Right, and what the hell is going on in this one?" she asks holding up a mid-action shot of them running around the flat and seemingly arguing with someone else who isn't in the room.

Lucas shrugs. "If you ask me, I think they're both off their rockers!"

"What is all this supposed to prove?"

"It proves that Ethan is still investigating this case and is having an affair with our number one suspect."

"Really?" She pauses to examine the photos. "Because all I see is two people out for a walk in a park; all I see is someone almost getting hit by a car; and all I see is two people dancing together. Hardly an affair, Lucas. I mean, it's not like you've got any photos of them at it! You have nothing."

He looks deflated and drained.

"But," she adds, piquing his interest. "You're right, Ethan is most certainly investigating Carla's case and he probably is doing our suspect, but you can't spy on them. This will never warrant an arrest."

"What do we do?"

"Be patient. Give them enough rope and they'll hang themselves. Gather your evidence and when you've got them - and I mean really got them - with something concrete, then we make an arrest. But if I see one detective or journalist with any of these photos, I'm coming for you. I know there's already a rat in here somewhere."

"Why are you protecting him?"

"I'm not!" she bursts out. "I'm protecting our case. Do not show your hand too soon."

The door swings open and Ash bursts through.

"What do you want?" Anna snaps.

"I need to speak to you. Now."

He just looks at her unblinking with a certain look on his face that she recognises all too well.

"No," she utters, shaking her head. He nods. "Shit!"

"I think it's time we paid these two a visit," Lucas says, holding up the photograph of Ethan and Riley.

Chapter Twenty-Six

Ethan checks on Riley in the bedroom who's still sleeping and thankfully still alive. He's been in bed for the last twenty-four hours but Ethan guesses that it's better to just let Riley rest. He leaves him to sleep throughout the remainder of the night whilst Ethan pins their notes back on the board, putting their investigation back together through to the early morning. He hears the floorboards creak and looks around to see Riley lingering between the hallway and the living room. He stops and shifts from one foot to the other.

"Hey," Ethan utters.

"Hi," he replies in an uneven tone.

"How do you feel?"

"Better" he rasps, and Ethan knows it's a lie. "Thank you." That awkward silence creeps back in. "What happened?"

"We were spiked."

"How?"

"Could have been in anything."

"Did you find it?"

"No, but I got rid of any unsealed food or drink," he says filling up a glass of water and putting it on the table in front of him. "Who's been in this flat in the last couple of weeks?"

"Just my dad, Vinny, and my landlord. My psychiatrist checked in on me too. Why?"

"Just curious."

"It couldn't have been any of them. Maybe the killer broke in whilst we were out."

"Maybe," Ethan agrees although he thinks it's unlikely.

"What do you think it was?"

"LSD." Ethan holds out a blister pack of Riley's neuroleptic meds. "You should take these."

Riley holds up his towel-wrapped hands.

"Oh, right. I better take a look at that," Ethan says pulling out a chair for Riley. He goes to the bathroom and fetches the tweezers, joining Riley at the table.

He's careful as he unwraps the towel, taking note of every pain-filled flinch on Riley's face as he does so. He pulls away the last layer to reveal a mass of blood and cuts that are laced with tiny pieces of broken glass.

"I've got to take you to A&E."

Panic radiates off Riley. "No, please don't."

"Why not?"

"Because – because I can't," he stutters. Ethan glares, wanting a better reason than that. "If they know what happened - what I did - they'll keep me in! They'll lock me up!"

He's not sure what that means but Riley's terrified response is enough for him to drop it.

"Fine," he sighs.

Riley's hands rest in Ethan's as he plucks the glass out piece by piece from the cuts, using a damp rag to wipe away rising blood. Riley winces when Ethan has to dig deeper into the wound to fish out some of the shards that have embedded themselves in Riley's flesh.

"What the hell happened?" Riley asks. "I mean we both saw *her*."

"I know."

"How is that –" he says but stops to wince as Ethan digs the tweezers in, "- possible?"

"Have you ever heard of Folie a deux?"

"I've heard a little about it."

"What have you heard?"

"It's where two or more people can share psychosis when isolated together."

He grimaces as Ethan extracts a piece of glass.

"Especially when stressed," Ethan says.

"That was intense."

Ethan nods in agreement. "It's best if we don't have any visitors and we don't meet with anyone. Not even your parents, okay?" he insists, glancing in his direction. "And all this stays between you and me."

"I won't tell anyone, I promise."

"I mean it. Not even your dad," he demands and when Riley frowns, Ethan adds, "or your mum." He pulls out one last shard and then wipes Riley's hands with the cloth. "You need to run your hands under the cold tap."

Riley does as he says whilst Ethan collects the bandages he bought earlier. He wraps them around Riley's hands, not looking at his face as he does so.

"You can't even look at me now, can you?" he hears Riley ask. Ethan looks up and opens his mouth, but no words follow, so he adverts his eyes back to Riley's hands. "I'm sorry."

Ethan looks up at him for longer this time, frowning. "What are you sorry for?"

"Everything."

"It's not your fault you were drugged."

"I know, but –"

"If anything, it's my fault," Ethan cuts in, pulling the knot on the bandage to hold it in place. Riley looks at him surprised. "I should have noticed sooner that you were drugged. I mean, what would have happened if I hadn't?"

Riley touches his hand and Ethan's head whips up.

"But you did," Riley reassures and offers a sympathetic smile.

Ethan's expression hardens and he pulls his hand away. "Not soon enough."

Riley's mouth opens but a knock at the door interrupts them. Riley startles in his chair and they both don't move.

"I've got it," Ethan says as he goes to the front door.

He peers through the peephole but sees no one. He frowns, turning the key to unlock it but leaves the door chain on. The links pull tight as he opens the door and peers through the gap.

No one's there. His eyes go down to the cardboard box that's sat on the top step. Ethan retracts and unhooks the chain to open the door fully. He inspects the plain box with caution. Using his foot, he nudges it and jumps back as if expecting it to explode. A man across the road stares at him bemused.

"Morning!" Ethan calls and waves his hand with too much enthusiasm.

The man moves along, looking over his shoulder to give him a sceptical look. Ethan crouches down, seeing scribbled handwriting on the side which reads, *'For Skipper XX'*

"Anna," Ethan mutters, grabbing the box and closing the door behind him as he heads back up to the kitchen.

"What the hell is that?" Riley asks jumping backwards.

"Relax, it's just a parcel from Anna," he says, going to the knife block and collecting one.

Riley's phone buzzes and he struggles to pick it up off the counter with his bandaged hands.

"Hello?" he says, pressing the mobile to the side of his face using both hands as support. He turns away from Ethan, so he can listen to whoever is on the other end. "Vinny, I'm okay."

Ethan rolls his eyes and stabs the box down the middle, splitting it open.

"Why what's wrong? No, I haven't seen the news, why?" he hears Riley say with panic in his voice. "What!"

He throws down the mobile and lunges for the remote control.

"Riley, what's wro…"

The 'breaking news' banner and a reporter appear on the screen.

"A woman's body has been found this morning," the female news reporter announces standing in front of a housing estate. "Her heart missing from her chest," she continues, with a flare of drama in her voice.

"What is…" Ethan begins but trails off as the image changes to a photo taken in selfie style of a woman with a little boy whose face has been blurred out. “Jennifer,” he breathes.

“The body of Jennifer Spring was found in her home in her bathroom earlier today. The police believe this to be the work of The Heart Snatcher.”

In her bathroom. The image of his own mother’s body lying in their bathroom flashes across his mind. He looks down at the box that’s still in his hands. Everything around him blurs. He peels back the now loose flap of cardboard.

“Ethan?” he hears Riley say but it feels far away and muffled as if through glass.

He loses control of his arms, causing the box to slip from his hands. As it hits the ground, red liquid spills across the floor before a red lump splats on the wooden surface. The heart drips blood as veins and arteries bulge from the organ. He stares at Riley who looks down at the heart and stumbles backwards.

“Riley,” Ethan calls as he rushes across the living room towards him, grabbing him by his upper arms and forcing Riley to look at him, his face seemingly drained of all blood, and his eyes wide in fear and shock. His body trembles beneath Ethan’s grasp.

“No, no, not again,” he stutters.

“Riley, it’s okay.” Riley’s breathing increases, coming out in short gasps of air. “You need to calm down,” he pacifies but it doesn’t work. “Calm the fuck down!” Ethan shouts. It’s the best way to deal with someone in this circumstance. Riley’s body stiffens and his breathing is shocked into normal again, but his bottom lip still quivers.

“Everything is going to be okay, but you have to listen to me, okay?” Ethan says, and Riley gives a shaky, hesitant nod. “Okay, good.”

Riley’s body trembles when Ethan let’s go as if he was the only thing holding Riley together. Ethan turns to face the mess behind him.

“Oh, what are you going to do now, Ethan?” he hears Carla

say from the kitchen. "You can't call Anna because it looks too suspicious. Let's face it, how are you two going to explain this," she says gesturing to all the chaos.

"We've got to get rid of it," he mutters to himself.

He rushes into the kitchen and finds some gloves, pulling them on. Grabbing the box, he places it alongside the heart and nudges it inside. He seals it before dumping it into the bag and removing his gloves.

"I've got to get rid of this. You just sit tight."

Ethan turns to leave but then feels Riley's hand on his arm.

"You can't leave me here alone," Riley begs.

"You'll be fine."

"What if the killer comes here? What if I'm next? What if –"

"Riley stop!" Ethan shouts, staring him in the eyes. "I'll lock the door and if you need me, phone me."

Ethan walks away leaving Riley rigid in the middle of the room.

***

Ethan enters through the front door still in autopilot. It feels like his brain is shutting down and blocking out realism. He almost doesn't recognise the sound of scrubbing as he climbs the stairs and enters the living room. The TV entertaining itself on the other side of the room. He stops and looks at the floor.

"Riley, leave it. I'll clean it up," Ethan says, going to the kitchen.

"It's fine," Riley grunts, as he continues to scrub backwards and forwards in repeated motions.

"Well, you're not going to get it out like that."

Ethan collects baking soda, vinegar, and a couple of dry cloths from the kitchen before turning back to Riley who's standing upright on his knees, staring at him.

"Take this and soak a toothbrush in it," Ethan demands, holding out the vinegar.

Riley doesn't move for a moment before he grabs the vinegar and makes his way to the bathroom. Ethan gets down on his knees and wipes away the warm soapy water that Riley was using and then pours a thin layer of baking soda over the dried blood. He massages the area with another dry cloth. Ethan doesn't hear Riley return but can feel him behind him, watching every move he makes.

"How do you know that?" Riley asks.

"Know what?"

"How to get blood out of the floor?"

"I'm a detective," he says as if Riley was stupid for thinking that was strange. "You got the toothbrush?"

A toothbrush appears in the air beside him. He grabs it and scrubs the bristles against the blood stains. Riley moves around him and gets down on his knees opposite Ethan holding another toothbrush that he also soaked in vinegar. They both scrub at the floor, neither of them saying a word. The sound of the TV fills the silence.

"The young woman, Jennifer Spring, was murdered late last night and the police are still yet to locate her heart."

"What did you do with it?" Riley mumbles. Ethan doesn't respond, so Riley repeats himself.

"I dumped it near to her home. Close enough that they'll find it. Far away enough so I didn't get caught. Then I set fire to the box somewhere else."

"Why?"

"That box has the word 'Skipper' on it. It could trace back to me."

"Oh."

They fall back into silence as the scrubbing sounds fill the space between them.

"Detectives believe that this is linked to DI Carla Milhouse and Natalie Brown's murder, all of which are believed to be the work of The Heart Snatcher."

Ethan grunts and rolls his eyes at the nickname as he continues scrubbing until the bubbles stop. He then wipes away the surface to reveal nothing, but the image of her heart and the blood is still burned in his head. Ethan looks Riley up and down, and then looks down at himself. Their clothes are stained red. He then looks at his bloody hands.

"It's all my fault," Ethan utters, his voice crackled. "She's dead because I – I –"

"Did your job," Riley interjects.

Ethan looks up, surprised to see a blurred vision of him.

"If we hadn't gone and spoken to her, she could still be alive."

Riley doesn't say anything, but his eyes also begin to fill with water.

"Come on, Ethan!" Carla's voice exclaims. "There's only one person to blame for all this and it isn't you."

"I can't –"

"Now, pick yourself back up again and get this motherfucker!" He doesn't move. "Ethan get up!"

"I don't –"

"For Jennifer, Natalie. For me."

Her voice fills with an emotion that motivates him to climb to his feet, but his legs shake beneath his weight.

"Now what?" Riley asks and he doesn't seem to acknowledge Carla's presence, so Ethan presumes that their folie a deux was substance induced. He looks at Riley's clothes and then down at his own.

"Take off your clothes," Ethan demands.

"What?"

"We need to get rid of them. Now."

Riley stares at him with wide blue eyes. "What? Right here? Right now?"

"Yes. Then go and wash yourself in the bathroom."

Ethan turns around to face the wall so he's not looking. He kicks off his shoes and unbuckles his belt. As Ethan pulls down his jeans, he groans from the pain in his side and is conscious that Riley heard him, so he glances over his shoulder. He catches a glimpse of Riley's face before Riley whips his head away. He pulls his shirt up over his head revealing his bare back as Riley's shirt glides over his skin. Ethan turns back around as he tears his jeans off each foot. Neither of them says a word, as the sound of clothing being removed fills the space between them. Ethan hears the bag rustle and then Riley's footsteps as he walks down the hallway to the bathroom. The door slams shut. Ethan lets out a breath of air as he gathers his removed clothing and shoves it in the black bag. He ties it up before going to his bedroom to put on fresh clothes and then leaving to get rid of the evidence.

Chapter Twenty-Seven

"Riley?" Ethan calls his name as he runs up the stairs. He doesn't get a response.

He goes in the living room. Ethan looks around. Riley isn't there. He marches back into the hallway. He looks at the front door. Riley's shoes are placed side-by-side next to the door and his coat is hanging from a hanger. He frowns. Riley's here but he doesn't know where. Concern starts to swell inside him.

"Riley?" Ethan calls again. No response. He goes to Riley's door and knocks. "Riley?"

Still nothing. Ethan's pulse quickens. He pulls the handle on Riley's door. It's unlocked. "I'm coming in."

Ethan opens the door and rushes in. Nothing. Riley isn't there. He looks around the room. Riley's bed is neatly made up, even the corners at the end of his duvet are tucked under. Everything in the room looks like it's in place. His frown deepens. "Riley?" Ethan calls again, this time even louder.

A short knocking sound alerts him to the wardrobe. The most horrible images of Riley being tied up and beaten race through his head.

Ethan hurries over and swings open the wardrobe doors. A gush of air escapes his mouth as he sees Riley curled up in a ball, sitting on the floor of the wardrobe. He looks up at Ethan with glazed-over ocean eyes. Ethan crouches to the ground to get to Riley's level.

"Are you okay?" It's a stupid question and Ethan knows it.

Riley shakes his head. Ethan's eyes scan over him. He looks so vulnerable. Like a child scared of the dark. He slides himself into the wardrobe beside Riley who stares at him wide-eyed. He pulls the wardrobe doors shut, closing them both in.

He doesn't say anything and neither does Riley. They don't need to. He just wants to show Riley that whatever he's going through, they'll go through it together. Riley shifts over closer to him so they're side by side and he rests his head on Ethan's shoulder. He finds himself wrapping his arm around Riley and he buries his face deeper between Ethan's neck and shoulder. That sweet masculine scent smothering his nostrils as warmth and comfort replace the cold space.

He's not sure how long they've been in the wardrobe before a loud knock on the door echoes up through the building. He feels Riley's body startle. Ethan pushes open the doors and staggers out.

"Stay here," Ethan says as he goes to the front door. An unsettling feeling swells in the pit of his stomach. He looks through the peep hole.

"Shit," Ethan mutters under his breath, squeezing the bridge of his nose with his fingers.

"Who is it?" Riley asks and Ethan turns to see him on the stairs.

"My colleagues." Riley's face fills with worry. "Don't worry, I'll handle it," he says, taking in a deep breath before swinging the door open.

"And what can I do for you, Detective Inspector?" he says with a hint of bitterness.

"We need to speak with you," Lucas replies.

"I wasn't asking you," Ethan says shooting him a glare, which he returns.

"Just need to ask you some more questions," Anna says. "Shouldn't be too long."

Ethan hesitates. He doesn't have to comply; he could just shut the door and there would be very little they could do about it. But he wants to know what they've got to say.

"Where's your friend?" Lucas asks.

Ethan turns around to find an empty space on the stairs where Riley once was. He frowns before turning back to them.

"Fine, you better come in," he says opening the door wider

and stepping to the side.

Once they've entered, he closes the door and shoots ahead of them up the stairs. He walks into the kitchen to find Riley holding a black bag and Carla's notes are gone. He's clever for thinking about that, but the panic shows in his eyes when Anna and Lucas walk in. He ties the bag causing the plastic to crinkle.

"Nice flat," Anna says looking around. She sticks her nose out and sniffs the air like a hound dog. "Been cooking, Skipper?"

"No."

"Huh. Smells like vinegar."

"I spilt some earlier."

"What's that?" Lucas asks gesturing to the bag in Riley's hands.

Riley's eyes widen further, and Ethan can see that he's stopped breathing. A primal reflex humans do when they feel under threat.

"Rubbish," Ethan answers for him. "What else do you think it is?"

They both glare at each other.

"What happened to your hands, Riley?" Anna asks.

"Just - just an accident," Riley stutters.

"What kind of accident?"

"I need to buy more oranges from the shop," he whispers. His eyes flicker to Ethan and back to Anna and Lucas who frown at each other.

"Okay?"

"He cut his hands when clearing up a broken glass that I dropped," Ethan interrupts. "Right, Riley?"

He nods and his shoulders loosen.

"You seem nervous," she says turning her attention back to Riley.

"Why are you so nervous?" Lucas asks.

"Why do you think?" Riley replies with a shaky voice.

"You tell us."

"Well, I was attacked, arrested, and interrogated by you all so, I'm sorry if I seem a little jittery," he explains with a hint of sarcasm and annoyance in his voice. His and Ethan's eyes meet, but Ethan adverts his gaze as the feeling of guilt twists in the pit of his stomach.

Anna lowers her head whilst Lucas keeps the same stern expression.

"Can we see what's in the bag?" he asks. Ethan scowls at him.

"Why?" Riley asks.

"If you've got nothing to hide then you won't mind us seeing what's in the bag."

"I'm sorry, I didn't see a warrant when you came in," Ethan snaps.

"It's fine," Riley says and Ethan's head whips round to look at him.

Every muscle in Ethan's body tenses and he holds his breath as he watches Riley untie the bag and open it. But he's right; all that's in there is rubbish. Ethan frowns and Lucas mimics his expression as he steps forward to get a closer look. He shifts aside some rubbish on the top layer.

"Are you done?" Riley asks. Lucas's gaze lifts to glare at him. "Or did you want to go through the rest of my rubbish?"

Ethan smirks and he hears Anna snuffle a laugh. Lucas steps back, his face red from either embarrassment or anger.

"Can we ask you some questions, Ethan?" Lucas cuts straight to the chase, turning to him. "You know, alone."

Ethan looks at Riley who instinctively does the same.

"I guess that's my cue," he sighs, shifting his body past Lucas and Anna.

"Don't go too far, we need to question you too," Lucas bursts out before Riley can disappear.

Riley turns back with a worried expression.

"Don't worry, we won't handcuff you again. Unless you want me to," Anna chips in with a wink.

Ethan notices that Riley's face flashes red before he retreats.

Ethan's glare follows him out the door. He turns as Lucas opens their dishwasher and peers inside.

"What the fuck are you doing?"

"Nothing," he replies with a shrug, as he closes it and analyses the rest of the kitchen.

"What's this about?" Ethan asks, turning to Anna.

"Can we sit down?" she says with a calming tone.

Ethan gestures to the chairs at the dining table. He lets them sit first before sitting opposite them both. He waits for the questions; for the photo; for the endless twisted words designed to trick him into incriminating himself. He should know, after all, he uses the exact same tactics.

"Just to go over a few things, you were friends with Carla Milhouse, correct?" Lucas queries.

"Cut the crap," Ethan bites.

"Excuse me?"

"I know what you're doing so let's just cut to the chase."

"Fine. Do you know a Jennifer Spring?" Anna asks taking over the conversation.

"Never heard of her."

Lucas slides a photo of the woman across the table. "Do you recognise her?"

Ethan snatches the photo and squints at it. Long enough to convince them that he's actually looked at it, but not too long to display any emotions.

"Never seen her before," he comments with a shrug, throwing the photo on the table.

He leans back, hooking one arm around the back of the chair. Their eyes search him, and he knows that they're looking for any sign of emotion.

"Are you sure you don't want to take another look?" Lucas says, sliding the photo back across the table.

Ethan holds his gaze. "What's this about anyway?"

"Just answer the question."

"I just did," Ethan bites. "Now, are you going to tell me what this is about?"

"You're telling me you haven't been watching the news lately?"

"Not really."

"She was murdered," Anna says, looking at him with unblinking eyes and he knows she's analysing his response.

Ethan frowns, faking his expression of confusion. "Right, and what's this got to do with Carla's homicide?"

"Jennifer's heart was also removed."

"Ah, like Carla's," Ethan points out, pretending that this is all new information to him. "I get the link now."

"Where were you last night?"

"Here."

"The whole night?"

"Yes."

"Can anyone vouch for that?"

"Riley."

"But you do sleep, right? It's not like you were gazing into each other's eyes all night," Lucas mocks.

"Oh, you sound jealous," Ethan replies and judging by the look on his face, he's not amused.

"Alright, smart-ass, how do you explain this then?" Lucas asks, pulling out another photo. One that does spark an emotion too strong to suppress. As he stares down at the photo, the real-life memory of his mother's body lying on the bathroom floor in her blood resurfaces in his mind. "See the resemblance?" Ethan hears him ask.

He looks up at Lucas whose eyes burn into him. He then looks across to Anna who has that look on her face, guilt.

"You never told us your mother was murdered in the same way as Carla," Lucas accuses.

"Should I have done?"

"Yes," Anna interjects, switching her facial expression to a scowl. "Why didn't you tell us?"

"I didn't think it was relevant."

"Not relevant!" Lucas blurts. "Your mother and partner murdered in exactly the same way, on the same day and you don't think it's relevant."

"It was sixteen years ago."

"And?"

"It could have helped with our investigation," she says. "Is there anything you can tell us about the night your mum was murdered?"

"I don't remember anything about that night."

"You honestly expect us to believe that?" Lucas snaps.

"I was ten," he reminds them, and they glance at each other. "The brain tends to block out traumatising memories such as finding your mother's dead body. So, unless you have some questions I can actually answer," he says, pushing away the photo. "I think we're done."

"We need to speak to Riley."

"Why?"

"He might know something."

"He doesn't."

"Right, because he tells you everything?"

"Yes."

"It's just protocol," Anna insists.

"Fine," he says as he goes to get up, but she's quicker than him.

"I'll get him," Anna says, jumping to her feet and disappearing before Ethan's even off the seat.

They sit in silence for a few seconds before Lucas opens his mouth.

"So, you don't have an alibi for both Carla's and Jennifer's homicide then?" Lucas asks.

Ethan half-closes his eyes, knowing how bad it all looks.

"I didn't kill them," he mutters.

"I don't believe you."

Ethan looks at him with wide eyes. Lucas's glare is fixed in place. He doesn't even notice Anna has returned with Riley until she sits back in the chair in front of him and he feels Riley sit in the chair next to him. He looks at Riley who seems so small with hunched forward shoulders and hands pressed together stuffed in the gap between his upper legs.

"We're done questioning you now, Ethan," Anna says.

"I'm not leaving." Lucas and Anna look at him with shock at Ethan's urgency to protect Riley. "You can get fucked if you think I'm leaving him with you two."

"We need to question him without you, so fuck off!" Lucas says and his tone tells Ethan that he's running out of patience.

Anna raises a hand to him, indicating for him to calm down.

"He's right, you have to leave," she says as a matter of fact.

"I'm not going anywhere," he growls. He and Anna glare at each other. "I can stay while you question him."

"How do you figure that?" Lucas spits.

"Because I'm his appropriate adult," he says and watches as both their faces drop into realisation. "If he wants a friend or family member here with him whilst he's being questioned, then you have to oblige because of his mental health condition. It's protocol."

Anna and Lucas exchange a look before she turns to Riley. "Do you want Mr Ethan Brown here as your appropriate adult?"

Ethan watches in the corner of his eye as Riley squirms in his seat, glancing between them all. His final gaze lands on Ethan.

"Yes, please," Riley requests.

Lucas shakes his head, rubbing his forehead.

"Fine," Anna bites crossing her legs and shifting more in his direction. "Where were you last night?"

He doesn't answer straight away. Ethan can see his brain working like clockwork trying to think of the right thing to say. That small line creases in the middle of his forehead. Ethan presses his leg against his. Riley peers up at him and he gives a nod to encourage Riley to answer.

"Here," he confirms.

"Can anyone vouch for that?"

"I can," Ethan interjects.

"A bit of a coincidence that the only alibi you both have is each other," Lucas says frowning.

"Well, we do live together," he says.

"Did you know a Jennifer Spring, Riley?" Anna asks, redirecting the conversation back to him.

"N – no," he stutters.

Anna slides the same image of Jennifer across the table. "Do you recognise this woman?"

"No," he answers shaking his head.

Riley doesn't look at the image, his eyes fixed on Anna. Ethan tenses at how suspicious he's acting. If it were Ethan interrogating him, he would be convinced it was him too. He looks across at Lucas whose frown deepens, analysing Riley.

"Are you sure?" Lucas says holding the image of Jennifer's dead body up in front of him.

And there it is: the flicker of emotion that they've been trying to trigger. Riley's body retreats within himself, as if trying to disappear. Guilt spreads across his face.

"N- no."

"And what about this one?" he says holding up the image of Carla with Jennifer's image. "Or this one?" he adds holding up Natalie's image.

Ethan looks at him in the corner of his eye. Riley's body sways forward and backwards with his hand clasped over his wrist. Then he notices Riley's fingertips digging into his scars as if trying to reopen them.

"He said no!" Ethan shouts knocking Lucas's hands down. They glare at each other.

"Why are you nervous, Riley?" Anna coaxes as she stretches

out her arms across the table towards him to close the gap. "Do you know something? Because if you do, Riley, you need to tell us. We can help you."

"Are you experiencing a mental breakdown?" Lucas asks but it doesn't sound like a question. As Riley's mouth opens, Lucas cuts back in taking his mobile out of his pocket. "You two have a habit of staying in the limelight."

He turns the screen of his mobile around to show a video.

"It's the least I can do," Riley's voice on the video comes through. A pause. "Come on, Riley, let's go," he hears himself say.

He closes his eyes not wanting to look at the scene that unfolded in the café that has now gone viral on social media thanks to those two girls.

"You see, I think you know exactly what happened to them!" Lucas barks and then holds up Jennifer's image again, shoving it towards him.

"And we know you're lying to us," Anna adds in a calm tone as she produces a photograph of him and Riley in the park talking to Jennifer. Ethan scowls at her, knowing exactly why they waited to show Riley that photo and not when it was just him.

"Get the fuck out!" Ethan shouts, standing up so fast that the chair falls onto the floor behind him.

"We're not done yet," Lucas snaps, standing up to challenge him.

"Yes, we fucking are!"

"We still need to ask him questions."

"What the fuck is wrong with you! He's sick, can't you see that? Just because it's an illness you don't understand, doesn't mean it's not real!"

He hears Anna get up from her chair.

"We're done… for now," she says. He shifts his eyes to look at her. "Make sure you both don't go anywhere, Skipper, because this isn't over."

“Well, I suggest next time you want to talk to us, you go through lawyers.”

Lucas’s eyes search past Ethan.

“Nice knife block, but I think you’re missing one,” he says. Ethan doesn’t look behind him, but now it makes sense to him as to why Lucas was looking in their dishwasher.

They exchange a glare before he follows after Anna. Ethan follows them out, not out of politeness, but to make sure they leave without stopping.

Ethan watches as she gets in the driver’s side of the car with Lucas scowling from the passenger’s side. He watches as the car stays stationary. Two shadowed figures sit still in the car with the occasional movement. Ethan waits until the car moves away from the pavement before he slams the door and locks it. He rushes upstairs back to Riley. He’s standing over by the window with the curtain pulled back.

“What do we do now?” Riley asks.

“Where did you put all our notes?”

“In here,” Riley says going over to the kitchen and pulling out the bin. “I knew they’d want to see whatever I was holding so I put our investigation in a bag and switched them.”

“Huh, clever,” Ethan says as he takes out the cork board and notes. The red seeping through his bandages catches Ethan’s eye. “I should probably change those,” he says gesturing to them and then going to the kitchen to retrieve the left-over bandages.

He looks at the knife block. He knew that the knife had been missing for days but thought nothing of it before. He looks over at Riley as he takes a seat at the table. Ethan sits opposite him and unravels the layers to reveal his cut hands. It’s worse than he thought. The cuts somehow seem bigger and won’t stop bleeding.

“Shit,” he mutters, rubbing his face. “You have to go to A&E.”

“No, I can’t!” he shouts, almost jumping out of his seat.

“Riley, you need stitches!”

“I’m fine.”

“No, you’re not, I’m taking you to A&E!” Riley deflates back into his chair. Ethan holds both his hands. “Look, I’m not going to let anything happen to you. I promise.”

Chapter Twenty-Eight

After an agonising five-hour wait in A&E and about four cigarettes later, Riley gets seen by a doctor. He leads them into an individual bay structured with turquoise curtains. Ethan stays by Riley's side the whole time as the doctor stitches his flesh back together and then bandages his hands. Riley sits on the edge of the bed with his legs dangling off the side.

"All done," the doctor announces at last.

"Great, so we can leave now," Ethan says, grabbing Riley's jacket from the bed.

"Not quite."

Riley looks up at him with dread.

"Why not?" Ethan asks.

"We just need a consultant to perform a psychological assessment," the doctor explains.

"It was just an accident," Ethan contends. "It was nothing to do with his condition. He just cut his hands whilst clearing up a broken glass."

"I don't think you get those kind of cuts from just that," the doctor states with a knowing look.

"He's fine!"

"It's just a mental health assessment, to be sure."

Riley looks up at Ethan with unblinking eyes. Ethan reaches across and places his hand over Riley's. "You'll be okay," he whispers before turning back to the doctor. "Can I stay with him?"

"If that's what Riley wants," he says as a half question looking at Riley now.

Riley's head bobs up and down. "Yes, please."

"Great, I'll be back in a bit."

They wait in silence until the doctor returns with a consultant psychiatrist to ask Riley a series of questions. She asks him about his feelings, symptoms, physical health, relationships etc. all of which he answers clearly and without hesitation. Riley seems more confident as the conversation goes on, so Ethan takes a step backwards.

"Strange, isn't it?" Carla asks him from behind. Ethan turns around to face her.

"What is?" he mutters under his breath.

"Well, Riley seems fine now, but based on everything that's happened, anyone on the outside would say that he's relapsing."

His body turns rigid as realisation floods over him. The LSD imitates Riley's hallucinations; the missing knife; and Jennifer's heart turning up on their doorstep.

"The killer's trying to frame him," he breathes looking over at Riley who's just finished talking to the consultant.

Riley is given his outpatient forms and Ethan is silent as he fills them out. Riley's voice takes him out of his thoughts, but Ethan doesn't catch what he says as he stares at him waiting for an answer.

"I'm sorry, what?" Ethan asks.

"I said, I'm done." Riley slides off the bed and grabs his coat. Ethan follows by his side as they head towards the reception desk with Riley's forms. "Are you okay?" he asks. Ethan looks at him as Riley eyes him with a sceptical look.

"I'm fine," he blurts, not able to hide his true emotions. He looks away and a tall, dark-haired man in the waiting room catches his eye. "What the fuck is your sugar daddy doing here?"

"I – he messaged earlier and was wondering because I wasn't at my flat and I didn't want him to worry so I told him what happened," Riley stutters.

"When the fuck did you do that?"

"In the waiting room whilst you were having a cigarette."

"Great," Ethan bites.

"I'm just going to hand these in," he says but he's already walking away.

Vincent clocks them and heads towards Riley, but Ethan intercepts his path.

"What the fuck is going on?" Vincent exclaims.

"Riley hurt himself and now I'm taking him back home," Ethan explains.

"You?" Vincent snaps. "You're not taking him anywhere. You're the reason he got hurt in the first place!"

"That's bullshit!"

"Is it?" he says, and a short silence falls between them. "If you hadn't involved Riley in this, he wouldn't be here. He wouldn't be relapsing. If you had just bloody left him alone…"

"You love him."

The words fall out his mouth realising that the only thing Vincent is guilty of is being in love with Martin's son. Vincent stares at him with unblinking eyes.

"You – you don't know anything."

"I know it must be hard to be in love with your best friend's son."

His expression of shock turns to anger. They both turn as Riley approaches them from the other side of the lobby.

"I would have done a better job of looking after him than you," Vincent mutters and it's a way of having the last word. A final jab at Ethan and it works because he knows it's true.

Vincent steps in front of Ethan to greet Riley but he walks past him, his eyes fixed on Ethan.

"Riley!" Lizzie calls and Ethan turns to see her along with Martin approaching them.

"You told his parents," Ethan mutters shooting Vincent a glare.

"Of course," he replies, returning the look.

Lizzie engulfs Riley in a hug and then pulls back and places her hands on either side of his face. "Are you okay? What happened?"

"I'm fine," he says, retracting out of her touch.

"Come on, Riley, we're taking you back with us," Martin

demands, stepping forward and grabbing Riley's arm.

Riley's mouth drops open for a few seconds before talking. "But I want to go home."

"We are taking you home."

"But I want to go with Ethan."

"Martin," Lizzie begins.

"I think it's for the best," Ethan hears himself say. They all look at him stunned.

"What?" Riley asks.

Ethan looks between the other three faces still staring at them and he could have sworn he saw Martin smile. Ethan ushers Riley away out of hearing range. They stop by the exit and Riley looks at him waiting for him to explain.

"I think it's better if you go with them," Ethan says.

"Why?" he asks and his voice cracks with pain that makes Ethan's chest ache.

He knows what the killer's plan is now and he knows that what Vincent has said is right. He needs to get Riley away from him. Jennifer's heart was in a box labelled 'Skipper' meaning the killer is most likely someone connected to Ethan. He straightens his expression to disguise any hurt.

"I'm done with all of this. I'm done with you."

"What the hell does that mean?"

"I don't need any of this right now," Ethan barks.

"Of what?"

"Your schizophrenia!"

Riley withdraws into himself and his face crumbles. "You don't mean that," he whimpers, shaking his head.

"I don't want you anymore. I told you it was over years ago and nothing's changed. My feelings haven't changed."

"I thought we were a team?"

"Well, you thought wrong." He pauses. "I'll pack my bags tonight and be gone by the morning."

Riley's mouth opens but no words follow.

"Riley," he hears Martin's voice say from behind him. "We're leaving. Now."

He looks at Ethan, his eyes pleading for Ethan to do something. Ethan steps aside as Martin marches past him and grabs Riley's arm.

"You stay the hell away from him," he demands, pointing his finger at Ethan. "This is all your fault!"

"Don't worry, I'll be gone by the morning."

"Good! Don't come back."

As Martin pulls him away, Riley resists. "But I'm fine! I don't need to go with you."

"Of course, you're going to say that, you're sick and you won't admit it!"

"I'm not relapsing! I've just had my mental health assessment and they've discharged me."

"You mean the mental health assessment that you know how to answer and lie on?" Vincent chips in approaching them from the side.

"Ethan, tell them," Riley begs. Ethan doesn't say anything as he watches Riley's face dissolve into betrayal. "Ethan!"

They're not going to believe the word of someone who's mentally ill and Ethan needs them to take Riley as far away from him as possible. Martin has no problem dragging Riley away who is too focused on Ethan. Vincent follows after, going on the other side of Riley as he and Martin guide him out the sliding doors. Elizabeth steps towards Ethan with a smile.

"Thank you," she says.

"For what?"

"For doing the right thing."

She reaches out and tucks a piece of Ethan's stray hair behind his ear, brushing the side of his face before turning around and following after her husband. Ethan watches as Elizabeth catches up to them outside. Riley looks over his shoulder at him as one final plead. Ethan feels a tear run down his cheek. He thinks about running after them. Stopping them and then taking Riley home. It's all he wants. But then the doors slide close, and he's gone.

Chapter Twenty-Nine

Riley sits on the stool in front of his parent's piano. He usually paints when he feels like this but as he doesn't have his art supplies, he settles for music. The feeling of betrayal swells inside him and he releases the frustration with each key he pushes in formation to the classical song he'd memorised so well he didn't need the notes anymore. The music drowns out the raised voices of his parents arguing in the kitchen, and he feels the throbbing pain pulsing through his fingers and hands which feels strangely satisfying.

How could Ethan just let him go? He doesn't care about Riley. Ethan doesn't want him. He left him before, and Riley feels stupid for believing he might stick around this time. He feels someone sit on the stool next to him, and he stops to look beside him.

"I taught you that song," Vincent says, smiling like some proud parent. "How are you feeling now?"

Riley ignores him and continues.

"That bad," he hears Vincent say before he then pushes the keys on his side of the piano. Vincent's hand wanders to the middle and grazes his. Riley stops and moves his hands off the piano and into his lap.

Vincent's hand finds his knee. "Talk to me. You know you can tell me anything."

Riley feels the sting in his eyes.

"You're relapsing, aren't you?" Vincent coaxes.

"I'm fine."

"Riley, you're ill and that's okay."

Riley gets up from the stool to put distance between them. "I'm not relapsing!"

"Riley, it's okay," he says following him and placing his hands on either side of Riley's face.

He moves back out of Vincent's touch. "You don't believe me."

"How else do you explain everything that's happened?"

"Because I was drugged!"

"Drugged?"

"Yes. The killer has been drugging me and posing as one of my hallucinations to make me think I'm relapsing but I'm not," Riley explains. Vincent's face softens into sympathy and worry, and Riley knows what he's thinking. "Look, I know how this sounds…"

"Sound like you're relapsing."

"I'm not paranoid, Vinny!"

He wraps both his arms around Riley and pulls him in. He doesn't hug back but just stands in his embrace.

"Everything's going to be fine. I'm going to look after you now, okay?" Vinny reassures, stroking the back of his head. "I think you should stay with me tonight, okay?"

Riley wriggles free from his arms. "No, I'm going home."

"What? Back to *him*?"

"Yes."

"He doesn't want you anymore, Riley! And you need someone who'll actually look after you. You need someone like – like –"

"Like who?" Riley snaps. Vincent looks down and Riley realises what he is implying. "We're not a thing anymore. I told you it was over. For good this time."

"The only reason you ended things was because *he* decided to come back. You can't just use me like that."

"I never used you!"

They stare at each other as the sound of Riley's parents arguing fills the space between them.

"Please, Riley, just stay here with me tonight."

Riley knows that he should, but he needs to confront Ethan. Some things need to be said and there are questions that need to be answered.

"I can't," Riley mutters and then marches towards the kitchen.

His parents turn to look at him stunned as he swings the door open.

"Riley, go sit back down," Martin demands.

"No, I'm going home."

"No, you're not!"

"You can't stop me."

Martin turns to Elizabeth. "And you're just going to let this happen?"

"If it's what Riley wants."

"You can't be serious!"

"We're both on the night shift tonight anyway so we can't watch him. It's better that he goes back to his flat with Ethan."

"I can watch him for you," Vincent's voice says from behind. Riley jumps.

"See? Vincent can watch him!" Martin exclaims.

"I don't need watching," Riley argues.

"And why can't Ethan watch him?" Elizabeth protests.

"Yeah, because he did such a great job before!" Vinny mutters.

"What happened wasn't his fault!" Riley shouts.

"Look, I don't want that guy anywhere near you!" Martin demands.

"Why? What's your problem with him anyway?"

"Riley," Vincent beckons, and Riley feels his hand on his shoulder. He shrugs it off, stepping forward to confront his father.

"He's not good for your condition!" Martin shouts back.

"Oh, come on, it's not about that and you know it! You've always hated Ethan, even when we were teenagers."

"He's just not good for you."

"And you know what's good for me?"

"Yes. Everything I do, I do to protect you!"

"Martin…" Elizabeth tries to interject.

"Is that why you think you had the right to take me away from him today?" Riley shouts and he's aware of how his voice is crippled with pain.

"Yes! And that's exactly why I told him to leave you alone when you were teenagers. And I'd do it all again to protect you!"

His mouth opens but he can't find the words. Silence fills the space between them as they stare at each other.

"You told him to leave me?" Riley mutters.

Martin's face drops, realising what he's just let out. Riley thinks about the day his dad came to see him in the psychiatric hospital and told him that Ethan didn't want to see him anymore. He thinks back to when Ethan accused him of breaking up with him. Hurt erupts into rage.

"You were the one who told Ethan that I didn't want to see him anymore!"

Martin doesn't say anything.

"Oh, that's not true, is it Martin?" Elizabeth says in disbelief.

"I did what I had to do," he says in a low voice.

"But why?" Lizzie asks.

"I knew that kid was trouble from the moment he stepped into my house! I was just protecting our son."

"Protecting me from what? From being happy!" Riley shouts.

"He's Riley's friend," she says.

"Oh, wake up, Lizzie!" Martin says turning to her. "How do you not realise what the hell was going on under your own roof?"

She looks at Riley and then back to Martin. "But Ethan used to just sleep on our sofa."

"Well, he didn't spend much time there!"

She looks at Riley with disapproving eyes. "Oh, Riley!"

"Look, the point is you lied!" Riley exclaims to his father.

"And I had good reason to!"

"No, you didn't," Lizzie says, and they both turn to her shocked. She looks at Riley. "I'm mad as hell that you lied to me, but you," she says turning to her husband, "you didn't tell me either and you had no right to interfere in our son's life."

"I was protecting him!"

"I'm with Martin on this one," Vincent says.

"No one asked you!" Riley shouts spinning on his heels to face him.

He feels a hand grab his arm, forcing him back around.

"Do not speak to him like that!" his father shouts down in his face.

"Let him go, Martin!" she shouts but his grip tightens. "Martin!"

He loosens his clutch just enough for Riley to free himself and he heads straight for the door. He isn't being controlled anymore. Vincent tries to catch his arm but misses by inches.

"Riley!" he hears Elizabeth call after him. He doesn't stop, not even for her.

"I've got him," he hears Vincent say as footsteps chase after him.

Riley rushes towards the front door, grabbing his parent's car keys. He manages to open it before Vincent's hands grab hold of him and spin him around to face him.

"Let go!" he demands as Vincent's hands tighten around his upper arms, holding him in place.

"No, Riley."

"I'm not staying here!"

"It's okay. Your dad was only looking out for you."

"Looking out for me?" he questions in disbelief.

"He just cares about you," Vincent says, and all Riley wants to do is to get away from him and this place. "Calm down!"

"How the hell do you expect me to calm down!" He tries to wiggle himself free but then freezes on the spot as realisation sets in. "You knew…"

"Knew what?"

"That my dad lied to separate me and Ethan." Vincent doesn't respond but looks down at the ground. "You knew and you didn't tell me!"

"It was for the best."

“For whom? You? Just so you could get me into bed!”

“It’s not like that, Riley!” Vincent’s hands move from his upper arms to either side of his face, forcing him to look him in the eyes.

As soon as Riley notices his dad standing behind Vincent, Martin pulls him off Riley and throws him into the wall.

“What the fuck has been going on?” he shouts looking between them both.

“Martin, it’s not what you think,” Vincent tries to explain.

“How much did you hear?” Riley rasps.

“All of it!” Martin snaps, shooting him a look that Riley never wants to see again.

His eyes wander past his dad as his mother stands in the hallway with her mouth dropped open and her face crinkled with both disgust and horror.

“Martin,” he begins, stopping to duck Martin’s fist, which slams into the wall instead.

“My son – you’ve been – with my son,” Lizzie rambles to no one in particular.

“Get out of my fucking house!” he shouts at Vincent.

Something in his mother’s eyes snaps. She arms herself with one of the umbrellas sticking out of the basket near where the coats hang. She then uses it as a baton to whack Vincent repeatedly.

“He. Is. Half. Your. Age!” she screams, emphasising each word in time with her blows.

Vincent raises his arms in defence and lets out a string of curses whilst Martin seems surprised by the outburst. Riley rushes forward and grabs the umbrella as she swings it back. He forces it and her arms down.

“I said get out of my fucking house!” Martin repeats, raising his fist to take another swing at Vincent.

Vincent jumps to the side and Martin stumbles forward. Riley’s head twists to one side, and a burning sensation spreads around his cheek bone. He looks back to his dad, tears already filling his eye sockets as he touches the skin on his face that's already starting to swell. Martin gawps at him with his mouth dropped open and then looks down at his trembling fist. His mother's eyes stare at him unblinking with both hands clasped over her mouth.

"I – I didn't mean," Martin stutters.

Riley squeezes the car keys in the palm of his hand, and they sink into his skin. He turns and bolts out of the door, as he hears his mother cry his name.

Chapter Thirty

Ethan sifts through the investigation notes which he fished out from the black bin Riley hid from Lucas. He lays them across the kitchen table, ignoring the landline with a cigarette hanging out of his mouth. Upon the fifth ring, Ethan decides to answer the phone, ditching his cig in the sink.

"What?" he shouts into it.

"Ethan?" a female voice says through it. "Is Riley there?"

"Who the fuck is this?"

"It's Lizzie."

"Oh."

"Is Riley there?"

"No, why would he be here, he's with you?" he asks with confusion in his voice. She doesn't answer and all he can hear is sirens in the background. "Why can I hear police sirens?"

"Oh, that, well, we had a slight incident here."

"What kind of an incident?"

"Oh, nothing really. Just a domestic disturbance but if you ask me, I think the neighbours are overreacting."

"Right. So, where's Riley?" She doesn't answer and panic erupts in him. "Where the fuck is Riley?" He hears the front door open and then slam close, followed by footsteps and Riley appearing in the doorway. Ethan sighs with relief. "Never mind, he's here."

"Oh good! Can I talk to him?"

Ethan holds out the phone to him. "It's your mum," he says. Riley walks over, takes the phone and slams it down before then pulling out the cable. Ethan eyes him. "What the fuck is going on?"

"Nothing."

"I thought you were staying at your mum and dad's?"

"Yeah well," he mutters, adjusting his skewed clothing.

Something's changed. Ethan can see it in his body and can hear it in his tone. Riley's eyes seem softer, looking at him in a way that's familiar. Ethan notices the dark bruise and raised skin around his cheekbone.

"Jesus, what happened?" Ethan asks taking his face in his hands and inspecting the injury.

Riley inhales before meeting his eyes. At first there's an expression of love which changes to anger. His eyebrows lower over his eyes and he pushes Ethan's hands off his face.

"Why didn't you tell me?" Riley demands.

"Tell you what?"

"About what my dad said to you when we were teenagers."

Shit. "You're going to have to be more specific."

"Bloody hell, Ethan, I'm not doing this with you!" he shouts. "You know what I mean."

Ethan sighs. "Fine. I didn't tell you because I didn't want you to get hurt."

"You didn't want to hurt me?" he repeats. "You don't think that lie hurt me? You don't think that believing for years that you left me, hurt me every single day!"

"We don't have time for this, Riley!" Ethan shouts walking away. He can't do this with him. Not now. "In case you haven't noticed, there's a serial killer still out there!"

He feels Riley's hand on his arm pulling Ethan back to look at him. "No, this has waited long enough!"

Ethan shrugs off his hand. "Just go back to your parents. You're safer there, okay?"

"I'm safer with you."

Ethan scoffs a laugh. "Don't you get it? I'm the reason you're in danger!"

"That's not true and you know it!"

Riley's watery blue eyes search his.

"Please, Riley, just go," he says, losing the strength to withhold this battle.

"Do you want me to go?"

"Well, that's what I said."

"No. I mean, do you *really* want me to go, or is it just because you think I'm better off without you?" Ethan doesn't respond. Riley steps forward, closing the gap. "If you tell me that you want me out of your life then fine, I'll leave. But I'm not leaving you if you're just trying to play the hero."

Ethan doesn't speak and he refuses to look at him. Riley turns and marches towards his bedroom.

"I thought you wanted to talk about this?" Ethan calls after him.

After a few seconds, Ethan goes after him just as Riley reappears in the hallway holding the box from under his bed. He takes the lid off, keeping eye contact with him.

"I kept everything. This," he says picking up a cinema ticket out of the box, "is from the first time we went to the cinema together. This." He picks out a photo which has multiple images of them on it. "Is when we got our ID photos done and we messed around in the photo booth. And this." He holds up a crinkled sticky note. "Is the first note you left for me on my bedside. I held onto all these things because I never stopped thinking about you."

Ethan stares down at the rest of the contents in the box between them that's filled with bits and pieces that make up their relationship and teenage years.

"And what about Vincent?" Ethan asks.

"What about him?"

"Well, you're with him, aren't you?"

"It's over."

"And what was *it*, anyway?"

"A mistake." The silence engulfs them and their eyes lock.

"It's definitely over?"

"Yes."

"Good."

Ethan rushes forward, taking hold of either side of Riley's face in his hands and pressing his lips to his mouth in an impatient kiss. He hears the sound of the box dropping on the ground as Riley's hands cover his. Their bodies are tense as the love they'd carry for so long ignites. *You're putting him in danger,* the thought appears in his mind. *Let him go.*

He goes to draw back but Riley's hands clutch the collar on his jacket to pull Ethan back to him, silencing any logical thought in Ethan's head. Wrapping one arm around Riley's waist, Ethan spoons him in, pressing their bodies together and moulding into one. Riley wraps both his arms around his neck, and Ethan tightens his grip around his body. Running both hands up his back, Ethan catches his shirt as it lifts. He slides his hands up under his clothing, tracing Riley's skin with his fingertips. Riley's mouth opens, breaking the kiss as he gasps.

Ethan moves his lips down, kissing along Riley's jawline and down his neck. He feels Riley's body tense in his arms and feels Riley's hands run through his leather jacket, pulling it off his shoulders. Ethan releases his grip on him to slide it off his arms, groaning from the bruises that still haven't completely healed. As the jacket falls onto the floor behind him, they collide together again. He can feel Riley's hands fumble at his belt, hearing it rattle as he struggles to release the catch with his injured hands, and loosening Ethan's jeans around his waist.

Stop, that voice inside Ethan's head demands. He pulls back as he grabs Riley's hands, stopping them going any further.

"Wait," he rasps, out of breath. Riley's body freezes. Their faces still close together. "Are you sure this is what you really want?" Ethan asks. He needs to make sure before taking this any further.

Riley pauses for a moment, staring at him. "Yeah. Do you?"

Ethan lets out a short breath of air and nods. Riley smiles before falling straight back into it as they kiss and begin tearing at each other's clothing that gets in the way. The only thing slowing them down is both their injuries. Riley's bandaged hands make their way under Ethan's clothes, touching his bare skin with his fingertips. Ethan grunts and twitches as Riley's hand presses against one of his bruises. Riley removes his hand and lifts Ethan's shirt, grazing his soft lips along the dark blue pigment on Ethan's chest and stomach. Ethan closes his eyes and allows the pleasure to overpower the pain.

Riley struggles to pull Ethan's shirt over his arms and head with his injured hands and Ethan groans from the ache in his side. Then there's relief as his body relaxes and the shirt drops onto the floor. Tearing through the buttons on Riley's shirt, Ethan kicks off his shoes and backs Riley into the bedroom, slamming the door close behind them.

Chapter Thirty-One

Ethan stirs in amongst the sheets, moving on his side and stretching his arm across the bed, grasping nothing but sheets. Riley's scent is wrapped around him as if he was still on his body. It comes back to him in snippets, remembering both his and Riley's bodies intertwined together, the feel of his body, his touch, and the way he moved.

He forces his eyes open, and they adjust to the darkness. He looks at the clock realising that it's just gone midnight. But there's nothing around him, only an empty space. With half-closed eyes, Ethan lifts his head from the pillow and looks around the room. Nothing.

"Riley?" he calls. No response.

It's then he becomes aware that he's naked lying across Riley's skewed sheets. He slides off the bed, dragging the covers with him, his bare feet finding the floor. The carpet feels cold as he searches for his discarded clothes in the dark, pulling them on one by one. His belt rattles as he pulls up his jeans. He fumbles around for his shirt and shoes but can't find them. Then he remembers that they were taken off in the hallway.

He staggers out the bedroom, his bare feet hitting the hard wooden floor and it shocks his body in an icy way that's familiar. He heaves his T-shirt on over his head feeling the tension in his injured arm and torso. He collects his shoes and jacket off the floor, staring down at the broken glass just a short distance away from him. His eyes stray to the bathroom. The sound of running water echoes around the gloomy flat.

"Riley?" he calls, watching as the water spills out from under the bathroom door and into the hallway.

The door creaks as he pushes it open with eyes unblinking from fear of what he might find on the other side. He stares down at the bathtub as it overflows with water. He imagines his mother's body lying there on the cold tiles, but there's nothing. Just water.

Something deep within his brain feels like it's being triggered. A buried memory resurfacing as his eyes shift towards the living room. The argument he overheard. That night returns to him in small snippets, growing stronger. His bare feet move across the cold wooden floor, the hem of his jeans dragging at his heel.

"He is my son!" Natalie shouts.

"Well, he's my son too!" a voice shouts back. Carla's voice.

Natalie turns to see Ethan through the crack in the door. Her eyes widen and her jaw drops.

"Ethan…" she says, her voice trailing off.

Carla steps into view staring at him in the exact same way. A coldness spreads over his body like it did the night Carla went missing. The argument replaying in his head with more fragments falling into place. They were outside the club as her body swayed from side to side.

"I never wanted to hurt you, Ethan," her drunken voice slurred.

"You lied to me!" he shouted back. "You all lied to me!"

"It wasn't like that!"

"What? Do you just expect to tell me all this now so we can play mother and son!"

Her eyes fill with water and then Ethan is snapped back into the present as the hallucination of Carla stands in front of him. She flashes him a crooked smile.

"And now you know the truth," she whispers, reaching up and tucking a loose strand of hair behind his ear.

A loud thump on the door takes him out of his mind and takes her away from him. He looks down the hallway towards the stairs and when he looks back, she's gone. Another loud thump on the front door echoes upstairs. He looks at the stairs again and forces himself to move towards them. He swings open the door.

"Anna?" he says, frowning.

"I'm so sorry, Skipper," she says staring up at him with round glistening eyes.

He looks past her, and his mouth opens with no noise to follow. The street is lit up with blue lights as police cars surround the flat. Lucas is leaning up against the car with an emotionless expression. His eyes focus back to Anna.

"What's happened?" he asks.

"We need to come in."

"What the fuck's happened?" he shouts, and she doesn't answer. "Where's Riley?"

A flicker of shock flashes across her face. "That's what I was about to ask you."

Ethan frowns. "Why?"

"Do you have any idea where he is?"

"No," he snaps. "Now tell me what the fuck this is about!"

She doesn't answer. His eyes shift back to the police cars and officers surrounding the area. They only bring this much reinforcement when they make an arrest on a dangerous suspect.

***

It's not long before the flat is invaded with forensics dressed in white suits from head to toe, with Anna and Lucas joining them. Officers are posted outside the flat and Ethan finds himself caught up in the middle of it all.

"Don't fucking touch that!" Ethan shouts from the living room to the kitchen as Lucas examines a piece of paper from his and Riley's investigation with gloved hands.

Lucas shoots him a glare. "You don't think this was something we should have been aware of?"

"Didn't think it'd be relevant to you."

He scoffs a laugh. "Right, so instead you had some schizophrenic help you."

"Don't fucking call him that!" Ethan shouts launching himself forward, only to be caught by Anna who steps in front of him.

"I've turned off the bath tap but forensics have taken photos of it running for the record," Milly says as she enters the room wearing a forensic suit.

"I want this place secure. Everyone has to leave!" she demands. "That means you, Skipper."

"I'm not fucking going anywhere!" Ethan exclaims.

"You can't be here, Ethan."

"She's right," Milly chimes in. "I need the scene uncontaminated."

"I've been living here for the last two weeks; I think I've already contaminated it!"

"Oh, I bet you have," Lucas mutters.

"What the fuck did you say?"

"Ethan, we need to sit down and talk," Anna says with that soft tone in her voice.

"Then talk!"

"In private. Let us take you back to the office," she says placing her hand on his arm to lead him away. He pulls back.

"No! Tell me what's going on right now!"

"Where's Riley?" Lucas asks.

"I told you; I don't know."

"Covering for him makes you an accessory to murder, so if you know where he is, you need to tell us now," Anna says.

"I don't know where he is and even if I did, I wouldn't tell you!"

Anna's face hardens.

"Call missing persons. Put an alert out for him," she says to another officer, who's already pulled out her mobile and is dialling the number.

"Something bad has happened to him," Ethan says, drawing Anna's attention back to him. "Don't you get it, he's in danger!"

"What makes you think that?" Lucas snarls.

"Because of the bath."

"The bath?"

"The killer was in here; they took Riley and ran the bath just to fuck with my head."

"And where were you?"

"In bed," he says, feeling stupid for allowing him to fall asleep.

"And how did you not wake up?"

"Because the killer waited in the flat and when Riley got up to get some water, they probably grabbed him from behind and covered his mouth. Hence, why there's a broken glass in the hallway."

"Right, and do you have any proof of this?" Anna asks.

"You have read my mother's case file, haven't you? She was found with the bath running."

"That's another thing we need to tell you," she says, taking in a deep breath and pulling out a piece of paper from her jacket pocket which she unfolds. "When we conducted Carla's post-mortem, we ran her DNA through the system and found that she shares a genetic link to you meaning –"

"She was my biological mother," he finishes for her, and her eyes widen.

"You knew?"

He nods, only coming to terms with it all himself. It feels like a pit has opened up in his stomach and his head feels light yet heavy at the same time. He snaps out of it remembering that he needs to stay focused for Riley.

"We don't have time for this! The killer's got Riley, we have to do something."

"Or he's gone on the run."

"He isn't the fucking killer!"

"Well, they do say love is blind," she says with slight bitterness. Some emotion of shock or disbelief must have flickered across his face because she continues. "We know everything, Ethan."

"You don't know shit!"

"We know that whoever killed your mum must be the same person who murdered Carla and Jennifer. We know that you and Riley are more than just friends. And we know that his obsession with you led to him murdering all three of them."

"Speculation," he says, sounding like one of the stupid lawyers he hates so much.

"Lucas, do you have the folder?" she asks, outstretching a hand as he places a file in her open palm. She then pulls out a series of photographs. The first one is of him and Carla. "We found these on Riley's camera. He was stalking you both before making his move." She flicks through them, each photo a different day leading up to Carla's murder.

"We've also had you both under surveillance for the last couple of weeks," he hears Lucas say as the images change to a series of photos featuring him and Riley.

Ethan shakes his head, trying to get rid of the dizziness. His knees buckle and he struggles to maintain his balance.

"Riley couldn't have…"

"The knife at the crime scene used to kill Jennifer and take out her heart has Riley's fingerprints all over it. Forensics also found traces of Carla's blood in the gap between the handle and blade."

Ethan looks over to the knife block and clutches the fabric of his shirt around his stomach, now thinking that the knife Riley used to prepare his food was the same one used to end Carla's life. He shakes his head again.

"It doesn't make any sense," Ethan groans.

"Here we go again," Lucas mumbles, rolling his eyes.

"How doesn't it?" Anna asks.

"Why would he murder Carla, bring the knife back to his flat to then murder Jennifer with it and leave it at the crime scene?" He pauses. "One minute he's a criminal mastermind and the next he's some amateur. It doesn't make sense."

She crosses her arms and stares at him with an alarmingly calm yet stern look. "Have you noticed any signs of psychosis in

Riley?"

"Oh, not fucking this again!"

"Well, the videos on social media prove that he is."

"Doesn't mean he's dangerous. He just gets slight episodes from time to time."

"We also got his reports from his psychiatrist and a lot of Riley's symptoms are consistent with psychosis which explains why his actions are contradicting each other."

His jaw drops. "You got his confidential reports from -"

"Don't," she interrupts. "We had good reasons for getting those files. I did what I had to do."

"You bitch," he hears himself say.

"Out of line, Ethan!" Lucas exclaims coming to her side.

"He's a fucking murderer, Ethan! At least I'm trying to solve Carla's homicide whilst you've been shagging him!" Anna shouts.

The space and silence between them now feel toxic and he's fully aware of Lucas, Milly and all the others in the room listening to every single word. The forensics going through every part of the flat, tearing apart his and Riley's life the same way Anna's been doing behind his back this whole time.

"Congratulations, Ma'am," he bites. "Congratulations on tearing my whole fucking life apart."

She doesn't answer although her mouth opens as if to say something. There's betrayal in their friendship now and he watches as the realisation of that sets in her eyes.

"Ethan," he hears Lucas say. Ethan doesn't look at him. "If you know where he is, you need to tell us. Now."

"What? So, you can arrest him for something he didn't do?"

"No, so I can put a psycho where he belongs; behind bars!"

Ethan's hand forms a tight fist.

"I'm still suspended, right?" he says to Anna.

"Yeah, why?"

"Good."

Ethan doesn't dwell on his next actions as he throws his clenched fist at Lucas's face. His head cracks to one side as he stumbles backwards. Ethan can feel the weight of the room looking at him, but he doesn't care.

"Ethan!" Anna shouts at him, pushing him back.

Lucas regains his balance and launches forward but before he can get close to him, Anna steps in front and pushes him back.

"Stop!" she shouts at Lucas like he's a trained dog. He does as she says but his scowl is fixed on Ethan. She turns back to him. "What the hell is wrong with you?"

"Me? What about that bastard?"

"You can't just go around punching everyone in the face!"

"Why the fuck do you care, anyway?"

"Suspension or no suspension, I'm still responsible for you!" There's a moment of silence as they stare at each other.

Milly creeps between them all and hands Lucas a tissue to cover his bloody nose.

"Can't have you bleeding all over my scene," she explains. He looks down at it for a few seconds before accepting it and holding it to his nose.

"The killer is trying to set Riley up. To make him look like the murderer," Ethan says calmer but through gritted teeth.

"How do you know that?"

"I just know!" Ethan exclaims, running his hands through his hair. "That's why the killer chose to set him up, because it's all so easy for us to believe that someone with schizophrenia did all this! That's why the killer drugged Riley with LSD to make it look like his illness…"

"LSD?" she repeats.

"I found out that someone's been spiking him with LSD."

"Got any evidence of that?"

He shakes his head, and she rolls her eyes.

"It's the truth! The killer must have taken Riley's camera and used it to stalk me to make it look like it was Riley."

"Are you actually listening to yourself right now?" she asks with a bitter laugh.

"It has to be someone close to Riley," Ethan rambles turning around to think. "Someone who has access to this flat, someone who Riley would have lent his camera to. Someone like…"

He places both his hands on the cabinet, staring at the framed photo of Riley with Martin and Elizabeth in front of their wooden cabin by the lake. The slow realisation dawns in his mind. His shoulders stiffen.

"Please stop with all this, you're only making it harder on yourself," she says.

"You're right," he sighs. He turns to look at Anna who wears an expression of surprise. "You're right, it is Riley."

"Do you know where he is?" she asks, her tone and face softening.

He shakes his head and this time tears swell in his eyes because he really doesn't know. He feels his mobile buzz in his pocket for too long to be a text message. He pulls it out and he freezes when the caller ID flashes with Riley's name. It's too late for him to hide it now, Anna's already seen it.

"Answer it," she commands. He looks up at her. "Be calm. Don't let onto him that you know anything. Find out where he is."

He'll do as she says not because he's tricking Riley, but because he needs to trick the real killer. He answers.

"Riley?" he says into the phone.

The other side is silent for a few seconds.

"Ethan?" Riley's cracked voice echoes out the phone. He sounds scared and Ethan's heart breaks. He pauses, debating his next words carefully.

"Are you okay?"

"I guess."

"Um, before I forget, the oranges in the kitchen have gone bad so don't eat them," Ethan says. He pauses waiting for an answer but all he can hear is Riley's breathing. He watches as Anna and Lucas exchange a frown of confusion across the kitchen. "Riley, do you understand what I'm trying to tell you?"

"Y-yes," he stutters.

Lucas reaches for one of the oranges on the kitchen counter and examines it before turning to Anna with a shrug.

"Look, I need to see you. Where are you?" Ethan pleads.

"Do you remember our conversation? The one when I asked you if you had ever killed or saved anyone before?"

"I understand. Just stay where you are, I'll be there soon."

There's a pause.

"Ethan don't, it's a tra…"

The line cuts dead but Ethan still holds the phone to the side of his face as the long beep screeches in his ear and tears leak from his eyes.

"Where is he?" Anna asks.

He thinks for a moment. If he tells them, they'll rush to the scene, causing the killer to act quickly which would either mean them arresting Riley or finding his dead body. He needs to buy himself time first before involving them. A plan forms in his head.

"There's a café we used to go to, he's there."

"You sure?"

Ethan nods.

"If you're tricking us, Ethan, I swear to God, I'll kill you!" Lucas barks.

"I'm not tricking you. He's there."

"Right, let's go," Anna says. "You stay here, Skipper."

He nods.

"Not like you to not argue back?" Lucas says.

"I don't want to see the man who murdered my partner. Just do what you got to do," Ethan says and the tear that drops from his eye convinces them that he's genuine.

They both leave and Ethan waits until the sirens fade away

into the distance before he moves. Only forensics are still in the flat.

"Where are you going?" Milly asks.

He looks at her with wide eyes. "Out for some fresh air."

He doesn't wait around. He walks out of the flat and jumps on his motorbike feeling every bruise on his body strain as if warning him not to go. He knows it's a trap set out by the killer, and he knows the end game, but he has to get to Riley, even if it kills him.

Chapter Thirty-Two

Ethan parks his motorbike down the road and stumbles the rest of the way to the cabin, not wanting to alert the killer. The gravel beneath his feet crunches with every footstep and the silhouette of the cabin emerges into view. A single light shines from one of the windows, penetrating the darkness of the early morning. The morning moon still hangs low in the dark blue sky. Trees overhang above him as if trying to stop him. No sign of Riley.

His mobile vibrates in his pocket, and he pulls it out.

"Anna."

"You fucking liar!"

"Let me explain."

"No, you fucking lied to me! That makes you an accessory to murder you son-of-a-bitch!"

"The Darlington's cabin."

"What?"

"Riley is at his mum and dad's cabin."

"Eth – breaking – can't –"

The line cuts and the no signal icon at the top of his phone is the reason. He can only hope that she heard what he said. He hasn't got time to try and get a signal or wait for help. He walks up the creaking wooden steps onto the porch. The door is ajar. He pushes it open and peers inside. Darkness. Ethan steps in. The moonlight highlighting the outline of the sofa and other shadows that look like dark figures waiting for him.

He steps through, feeling every wooden floorboard under his feet cry out. The killer would use a secure room, out of sight so they didn't get caught. He walks around the cabin, checking each room and even moving furniture out from the walls in search for any hidden compartments. He returns to the living room and looks at the rug on the floor. Stepping off it, he crouches down to pull back the material. Dust scatters in the air and stings his eyes.

He squints, turning his head away until it clears. He looks down at the now exposed floor. The wooden boards in the middle are raised and Ethan carefully opens the lid on the hatch. The hinges screech as he lifts it, begging him not to go in there. But he must.

He uses the small wooden ladder to the side to climb down into the darkness. He can't even make out shapes down here. He pulls out his mobile and switches on the torch. A single beam of light strikes the darkness and Ethan pursues onwards. The first object he encounters is a shelving unit. The metal instruments lined up in size order along the shelf glisten from the reflection of the torch. A scalpel and an electric surgical saw are the ones that stand out the most.

He shines his torch further along and freezes to the spot. The light penetrates through a glass jar, outlining the shape of a heart inside. He moves the torch along to the next jar. Then the next jar. Then the next jar. Each one is filled with organ preservation liquid and has a name tag hanging from the lid. He walks over to a jar, staring at the organ encased inside. The name Natalie Brown is written on the brown paper tag. He shines his light on the one next to it. Carla Milhouse. His eyes sting as water fills up inside his sockets. He chokes out a grunt, placing both hands on the shelf to steady himself.

His head flings up as the sound of creaking wood from the ladder vibrates through him. Ethan grabs his mobile and switches off the torch, plunging himself into darkness. He holds his breath, staring aimlessly into the nothingness, waiting like prey.

"Oh, Detective," a voice mocks and he's not surprised by who the voice belongs to.

He hears a light switch flick on, and an orange glow flashes on and off, throwing him momentarily into light and then darkness over and over again. Footsteps clunk along the floor towards him.

Ethan lunges for the scalpel on the shelf and retreats backwards. There's nowhere to run. There's only fight or die. He slides the blade under his sleeve to conceal it and waits for the light to stable itself.

The orange glow illuminates the room. He looks around at all the faces that he'd come to know through missing person photos pinned on a cork board. They all stand around the room circling the operating table next to him, a line of surgical instruments on a metal trolley. Dried, brown blood stains the walls, flooring, and ceiling around him. He looks forward to come face to face with his mother who has a hole in her chest. Then they all disappear, and his eyes meet the killer standing before him, a few feet away.

"There you are," Vincent croons as his mouth spreads into a sinister grin, his hands behind his back and his posture raised.

"Where's Riley?" Ethan asks, trying to steady his breathing.

Vincent's eyes look past him, and he follows them, turning on the spot to see Riley on the ground behind him. Grey parcel tape circles his head, covering his mouth. His hands are bound together with rope, keeping him tied to an old rusty pipeline that runs down the wall. His eyes are wide and full of water with dark rings around them. A bruise around one eye.

Ethan looks back to Vincent who hasn't moved except for one hand that comes out from behind his back to reveal a handgun. Ethan's facial expressions must have betrayed him as Vincent says, "Oh, don't worry about this. It's just to ensure that you behave."

He wedges the gun into the back of his trouser waist band.

"It's so nice of you to join us," Vincent beams. "The final part of my ritual will now be complete."

Vincent steps forward, running his finger along the shelves as he admires his collection of hearts. Ethan takes a subtle step back. He tightens his grip on the scalpel, ready to strike. He glances back to Riley, noticing that both Riley's hands are shifting back and forward in formation. He looks at the rope that's now frayed in one place and the old screw that's half sticking out from the pipe. He needs to buy time. Give Riley a chance to escape.

"Your mum died, didn't she?" Ethan croaks as he looks back

to Vincent. "That's why you murder mothers who have a son." There is unease in Vincent's expression. "Oh, come on. You know you *want* to tell me all about it and I *want* to know. Tell me just how clever you are."

Something in Vincent's eyes lights up. Serial killers like Vincent love the attention and they certainly love to talk about themselves.

"Well, I suppose I should start at the beginning, if you want to know so desperately," he teases grinning and enjoying a long pause for dramatic effect. "My mother was sick."

"Let me guess, something to do with her heart?" Vincent shoots Ethan an angry look and Ethan realises Vincent wants to tell the story himself.

"She died waiting for a heart transplant," Vincent explains, "I watched her die right in front of me." He takes another step forward. There's no emotion to his voice, it's almost as if he's reading a shopping list. "My father didn't stick around when I was born so I had to live with my grandparents and all I was to them was a painful reminder of what had happened to their daughter."

"They abused you," Ethan says, coming out as a half question. Vincent clenches his jaw. Ethan knows because it was the same with his father.

"The day I saw their dead, rotting bodies was the only day in that house when I smiled." A smirk spreads across his mouth again as if reliving the memory. "You see, it isn't impossible for a child to commit murder," he adds and watches Ethan's expression. "I told myself that I wanted to be a doctor to save people like my mother, but that was never true. I even tried dissecting the neighbour's cat in the name of science as a teenager, but nothing quite filled that urge. That was until your mother moved into town."

"Let me guess, she reminded you of your mum."

"There was something about the way she looked, the way she

moved, the way she smelled that was just too, irresistible."

Ethan glances behind at Riley.

"And the way she was with you," Vincent adds, drawing his attention back to him. "But the night I came round to see her, she was packing yours and her bags, and I couldn't let her leave."

"So, you killed her."

"You know, at the time I wasn't sure why I cut out her heart after I killed her. Now, it seems so obvious," he says, running his fingertip along Natalie's glass jar. "It's so she can never leave me. None of them can." He pauses. "And then there's you." Vincent's eyes snap back to Ethan. "When I saw you at Natalie's funeral, it was the first time in my life when I didn't feel alone." Vincent closes the gap. "Because I saw myself in you."

Ethan stumbles back, grabbing the operating table to steady himself.

"You see, we're the same, you and me," Vincent continues.

"I'm nothing like you."

"Yes, you are!" he says with excitement, grabbing both the sides of Ethan face. "We both carry that same hollow void."

Ethan thinks about the boy in the park and how he saw himself in him, the same way Vincent sees himself in Ethan.

"That's why you became a detective. And don't give me the crap that it's because you wanted to save people like your mother, because that's the same lie I told myself. No, no, it's so you can take back control. To play God," he says, and Ethan doesn't say anything because it's true. "Face it, Detective, wherever you go, I go; whatever you do, I do; whoever you fuck, well," he says glancing over at Riley and back to Ethan. "You get the point."

He doesn't look at Riley. He can't. Ethan doesn't need to hallucinate Carla to remember what she taught him. Detach yourself emotionally.

"So, what? You kept tabs on me. Followed me around like a sick puppy."

"I watched you grow up and I waited for you to display some

sort of sign – any sign – that you had the same urges as me. Even after you left our small town and went to London, I followed you." He pauses. "And that's when I saw you with her."

"Carla."

"Natalie's so-called friend. But it wasn't until I saw the way she looked at you that I knew. Some would mistake it for romance. No, no, no," he says waving his hands around. "It was undoubtedly the look of a mother to a son."

Vincent grins and Ethan knows how much he's enjoying every second of this. It's not just about the kill anymore, it's about the foreplay.

"You knew," Ethan says, and he doesn't need to elaborate for them both to know what he means.

"I remembered the rumours that went around. How long it had taken Natalie to fall pregnant with you and how Carla was always around you like a moth to a flame. So, I used my position as a doctor to look up Natalie's and Carla's medical records and guess what I found."

"That Carla donated her eggs to Natalie."

"It didn't seem fair, Detective. You got another chance of a mother, and I didn't!" he shouts, closing the gap between them again. He can feel Vincent's breath on his face and the spit that comes out with his words. Ethan turns his head away. Vincent snaps back into calm just as quickly as he exploded into rage. "But then, I realised how perfect she was for my ritual. You both were." He places both his hands on Ethan's face again.

"But you couldn't kill her and get away with it, could you?" Ethan says, his voice shaky. "She was a detective, and you knew that it wasn't going to be as easy to get away with it like the others. And you needed to make sure you got away with it."

Vincent smiles, clearly impressed.

"That's where he comes in," he says pointing his finger towards Riley. "It was easy really. All I had to do was tell Riley the night before that a walk would do his mental health good.

Give him a trail to follow and make sure Carla's body was there waiting for him. You and your detectives did the rest for me."

"But you were with Riley the night Carla was murdered," Ethan questions, the only thing not making sense.

"Oh, that was easy too. All I had to do was slip him a sleeping pill and be there while he fell asleep and then back before he woke up."

"Huh. The girls in the café filming Riley's episode?"

"I guess I just got lucky."

"And the drugs?"

"I put them in Riley's bottled water," he gushes as his body jumps with excitement. The same water Ethan used to take Riley's tablets. "Like I said, it was easy really." Vincent looks over at Riley who's now stopped trying to free himself with Vincent's attention on him. "Don't take it personally, it wasn't all fake between us. But you did choose him, you see, so in a way you deserve this."

"You've staged all of this so that Riley goes down for killing Natalie, Carla, Jennifer, all of them, and now you're going to set him up for killing me." Ethan's voice shakes as he watches a single tear trail down Riley's cheek.

"It's that simple. Almost too easy." Vincent walks over to Riley and leans his head in close, his lips inches away from his ear, "because who will ever believe a schizophrenic like you?"

Ethan's grip on the scalpel tightens. It's his only chance to strike. He raises his arm and lunges forward, but Vincent is already on his feet facing Ethan. A gun clicks in his hand.

"I really wouldn't do that," Vincent warns, directing the barrel of the gun at Riley's head. "Enough chatting, now get on the table." Ethan doesn't move. "Do it now!" Vincent shouts shoving the gun closer towards Riley.

"You won't shoot him; you need him to take the fall for all this."

"Don't underestimate me." Ethan steps back, knocking into

the operating table. He glances behind at it. "You see, the gun is just to keep you under control, and if I have to shoot you first to get your heart," he says, pointing the gun at Ethan. "I will."

Even Ethan didn't see Riley move until both his hands were already around Vincent's arm, pushing up towards the ceiling. The blast of a bullet being fired deafens him. Ethan drops to the ground, but the whole world blurs as though moving in slow motion. His hands collapse over his ears as the sound of gunfire explodes into the air. Then, the world falls into silence.

Chapter Thirty-Three

For a moment, Ethan thinks he's dead. That he must be dead. But he releases a mouthful of air, and he knows he's still breathing. His hands are still over his ears as he crouches on the ground. Dust falls from the ceiling, misting the air around him.

Looking up, he sees Riley and Vincent fighting over the gun that's still in both their hands. Both their arms raised in the air letting out one, then two, then three gunshots. The sound of the gun firing pierces the air. It's difficult for Ethan to see what's happening, but the fight continues. Vincent knocks Riley unsteady by punching him in the gut and he releases his grasp on the gun. Riley falls to the ground, the back of his head hitting the hard floor. His face winces in pain. Ethan feels the scalpel in his hand and lunges towards Vincent, striking him in the back. Vincent turns to look at Ethan with crazed eyes and elbows him in the side of his abdomen reawakening the pain from his bruises. He stumbles but keeps his composure. Vincent strikes him again, kicking his leg up and winding Ethan. He swings his fist, but this time, Ethan ducks and charges forward, grabbing Vincent by the waist and pushing him against the wall. He throws a punch which hits Ethan in the face. He grabs Vincent by the throat whose eyes fill with rage and his face cripples into the monster he truly is.

Vincent's knee rises and kicks him in his groin. Ethan releases his grip, grunting as he stumbles back. He grabs Ethan by the collar and throws him through the shelving unit, but Ethan keeps hold of him and pulls Vincent down with him. They crash to the ground, tearing through the jars of hearts. The glasses smash and liquid explodes out along with tiny shards. The hearts splat onto the hard ground all around him.

Ethan's disorientated and his body aches as pain surges through him. His mouth opens to cry out, but he can't even utter a sound. He feels a force turn him over onto his back and a heavy pressure weighs down on him from above. Ethan hears the sound of an electric saw, and he squints at the shine of a blade coming towards him. His eyes ping open, and he grabs Vincent's hands, pushing against him. Vincent presses down on top of Ethan's abdomen with the electric saw spinning its way towards his chest. Vincent forces his weight down harder. He has the advantage of gravity, and Ethan knows that it's a losing battle, but that doesn't stop him fighting for every second of his life.

The thought of death has crossed his mind many times before. But now he's staring it in the face. People often say your life flashes before your eyes. That's not true. Only a few thoughts race through his mind. He doesn't believe in heaven, but the thought that he might see his mum again is comforting. He wonders if he'll see Carla again, too. But then he thinks of Riley and leaving him behind. What will happen to him?

The blades tear through the fabric of his shirt. Ethan cries out as the saw rips into his skin and blood splatters up on Vincent's face. Ethan's eyes widen as Vincent's head cracks to the side and he falls to the ground beside Ethan with the bloody surgical saw spinning circles on the ground near them. Riley stands where Vincent once was, holding a plank of wood. He stumbles back, dropping the wood. Ethan pants, examining the gash across his chest. It's not deep enough to kill him. The gun. Ethan looks around, finding it lying under the table. He scrambles towards it before Vincent can gather himself.

The cold metal hits Ethan's hand as he grasps it, jumping to his feet. Ethan points the gun at Vincent, but there's only an empty space. He spins around.

"Where is he?" he shouts to Riley who still has tape wrapped around his head.

The hatch door slams shut. Ethan bolts towards the ladder, shoving the gun into the back of his jeans. He pushes the door up and it half opens before slamming against something heavy. He's pushed back, and the door drops. Ethan drives his upper body strength against the hatch. The burden of something above weighs on him. Every muscle in his arms pulses and his body aches as he pushes up. A gap emerges and he manages to crawl his way through the small break. It's enough to fling the hatch open, sending both the cabinet and Vincent across the living room.

He staggers to his feet just as Vincent runs out the front door. Serial killers need control and the moment they lose it, they flee. Ethan races after him, using every muscle in his legs as he chases him across the grass. Vincent heads straight for the pier that's looking out onto the lake. He knows that Ethan can't swim and it's his only chance to get away.

He pulls the gun from his back pocket as his feet pound on the wood of the pier.

"Stop!" he shouts. Vincent doesn't. He fires a warning shot into the air. The sound echoes throughout the early morning air and Vincent's silhouette halts, both arms raised in shock. "I said stop!" Ethan shouts, holding the gun out in front of him, at Vincent.

Vincent turns to face him, both arms still raised. His calmness is alarming.

"Come on, Detective, I know you can't follow me," he says taking a step back towards the edge of the pier.

"Don't fucking move!" Ethan jabs the gun in his direction. "You've lost. It's over."

Vincent stops, with that smile still tugging at his lips.

"Ethan," he hears Riley's voice whisper from behind him. Ethan glances round at him as he stumbles forward onto the pier, but he doesn't look at him for long as his eyes go back to Vincent. "Put the gun down."

"I can't," he says to Riley still looking at Vincent.

"You have her eyes," Vincent taunts. Ethan frowns, so he continues, "Carla. You've got her eyes." Why is he antagonising him? He's not in a position to do so and Ethan's already tempted to shoot this bastard. "Do you want to know exactly what I did to her, Detective?"

"Shut the fuck up," Ethan growls, warning him. But that smile spreads across his face.

"It wasn't quick. It was slow and painful."

Ethan's hands tighten around the gun, his finger closer on the trigger.

"Ethan, put the gun down," Riley's voice begs, but he doesn't look at him.

"She put up a fight, just like Natalie."

"Shut up!" Riley shouts and Ethan's surprised that those words didn't come out of his mouth instead. He's too busy contemplating whether to shoot him. Vincent wants this. He wants Ethan to shoot him. To him, death by the police is a better way to go than going to prison.

"Ethan don't shoot him, Carla wouldn't want this," Riley says.

"Wouldn't she?" Vincent taunts cocking his head to the side.

He struggles to fight the urge to pull the trigger. His finger pushing against the metal, feeling the pressure against his fingertip.

"He killed them, Riley. My mum, Carla, and Jennifer. All of them," Ethan says to Riley, still not looking at him as he tries to justify his actions before doing it.

"I know, but you don't want blood on your hands."

"I don't fucking care!"

"If you do it, you'll go to prison. There's no turning back."

"I don't care," Ethan shouts again but there is pain in his voice now.

"I do," he says. Ethan looks at Riley's pleading eyes as he approaches him, still stumbling forward with his hands across his stomach. "I still need you."

Ethan has two choices. His past or future. He can shoot Vincent and get justice for both his mum and Carla, or he can have a future with Riley. He remembers the conversation him and

Riley had the last time they were here. When Riley asked him if he had ever killed anyone before and if he had ever saved a person's life. And now he's faced with that choice.

"Riley, look away. I don't want you to see this," Ethan says, looking back to Vincent because he can't bring himself to look at Riley anymore.

"No, Ethan, please."

"Look away!"

"Don't!"

Ethan wants to shoot. He really does. But something inside him stops his finger from pulling the trigger. Maybe it's the fact that Riley is here or some last shred of morality he has. He feels Riley next to him. He feels Riley's bloody hands slide onto Ethan's. He looks at Riley's face, and into those blue eyes. His hands guide Ethan's down, lowering the gun so it's pointing at the ground, away from Vincent. His vision of Riley begins to blur through the tears in his eyes. The gun slips from Ethan's grasp and into Riley's hands. He hears Riley breathe a sigh of relief.

The sound of sirens echoes in the distance, drawing his attention to the road. Anna must have heard what he said on the phone. Vincent's smile drops. The sky is now turning a light blue as dawn approaches.

"You've lost," he says to Vincent.

He sees the decision in Vincent's eyes and before he's even moved, Ethan's already running towards him.

"Don't!" Ethan shouts as Vincent turns and jumps from the end of the pier. He follows after.

"Ethan!" he hears Riley call just before he plunges into the icy, dark water.

The sirens muffle as his ears fill with water. Everything blurs into little balls of H2O and darkness. His legs kick, and his throbbing arms punch the transparent force that submerges him. Panic takes over. The vision of his mother by the running bath; the image of Carla's body by the river.

His fingertip brushes a piece of fabric. He clings to it. It's Vincent's shirt. He tries to push Ethan away, but he grabs hold of Vincent's shoulders half trying to stop him getting away and half in a blind panic to not drown. They struggle with each other in a frantic push and pull fight for survival. The water thrashing around them. Ethan knows how this will end. It's live or die together. He wraps his arm around Vincent's neck, to keep them both locked together. He tries to pry Ethan's arm away with his nails digging into his flesh. They sink lower into the depths of the water. The void swallowing them both. His lungs pulse quicker as his heart pounds against his ribcage. He breathes out his final breath.

A splash and wave within the water ricochets into them. Two hands grab his shoulders and pull him back. He doesn't let go of Vincent who is giving up the fight. He feels the water evacuating from around him as he's pulled up towards the sky. He gasps for air and chokes on it as if his body is now rejecting survival. He feels the ground beneath him as he's pulled onto land. He drags Vincent with him. As he scurries across the ground, he flips Vincent over to see if he's still breathing. He's alive. Unfortunately. Riley drags himself up and out of the water. He holds his side as he stumbles forward. Water dripping from his clothes.

"Now you've lost," Ethan says to Vincent as he gets to his feet, leaving Vincent lying on the ground.

He looks dazed, staring up at the sky. Then he smiles.

"Have I, Detective?" Vincent says and there's an eerie tone to his voice that tells Ethan that he knows something he doesn't.

He looks at Riley who stumbles backwards away from Ethan's side. The sirens are now louder, closing in on them. Vincent erupts into laughter.

"What's funny?" Ethan shouts but that makes him laugh harder. Ethan bends down and grabs him by his collar. "What's so fucking funny!"

Ethan squints against the blue lights radiating from the police cars skidding across the grass in front of the cabin.

"I'm surprised that you were able to do that in your condition," Vincent torments but not to Ethan. He's looking at Riley. "I guess adrenaline really does do incredible things for the human body."

"What the fuck are you talking about!"

"Whilst you were so fixated on the gun down in the hatch," Vincent drawls to Ethan. "You didn't even notice the knife."

Vincent's smile expands and Ethan's eyes widen, remembering how Riley and Vincent had struggled with the gun and the way Riley fell back onto the ground. How Riley stumbled onto the pier. The blood on his hands. The way he was holding his stomach.

He spins towards Riley who's got his hand over his lower abdomen. Red liquid seeps through the gaps in between Riley's fingers. Blood and water gather on the ground in front of him. Ethan's eyes go to Riley's pale face and wide blue eyes. Blue flashing lights from the police car light up his face in an all too familiar way, the lake behind him as water spills onto the earth.

"I didn't want to alarm you," Riley mutters, stumbling backwards.

"Riley!" Ethan shouts.

He rushes towards him as Riley begins to fall backwards. Ethan wraps his arms around him, catching him and lowering him to the ground. He rests the back of Riley's head on the soil. His eyes don't look at Ethan as they stare up into nothingness.

Ethan lifts up his shirt to see the damage. It's worse than he imagined. There is a slice across Riley's skin with two pieces of flesh wide open. Dark red liquid seeps out of the gash. His hands shake above the wound, trying to think how to stop the bleeding. He looks up towards the police cars with an open mouth. He wants to call for help, but he can't get his voice working. He hears Vincent choke on his own laughter.

"Ethan?" he hears Anna call as she emerges into view. She

stares at Vincent, then him, and Riley. “Over here!” she shouts to the others. “We need an ambulance!”

Anna rushes over to them, pulling Vincent to his feet as he continues to laugh at them. Oliver gets out of one of the police cars and runs towards Ethan, collapsing on the ground opposite him and beside Riley.

“Stab wound or gun shot?” Oliver asks. Ethan’s mouth opens again but nothing comes out. He stares at the wound. “Knife wound or bullet wound, Ethan!” he shouts again. That kicks Ethan’s mind into working.

“Knife wound,” he blurts out.

Oliver uses both his hands to force Riley’s mouth open and he puts his finger inside. Taking it out he inspects it.

“No blood,” he says, and Ethan knows that’s a good sign. It means there’s no internal bleeding or damaged organs.

“There’s so much blood.”

Oliver doesn’t waste much time in taking off his coat and scrunching it up. He pushes it onto the wound. Then he grabs Ethan’s trembling hands and puts them on the jacket. “Hold this on the wound and push down as hard as you can.”

Ethan presses the jacket to the wound. Riley bawls with agony and his hand grabs at Ethan’s arm. He eases off the pressure.

“Ethan, you have to press harder.”

“I can’t, I’m hurting him.”

“Better than him dying!”

Ethan presses down harder, trying to ignore Riley’s cries as he throws his head back.

“Don’t let him close his eyes. I’ll help the ambulance through,” Oliver orders as he gets up, running back over to the police cars.

He watches as Oliver runs. Lucas is here also, looking over at Ethan with wide eyes. Ethan turns his attention back to his hands pressing Oliver’s jacket on the wound. There’s so much blood, but Ethan keeps reminding himself that it looks like a lot because of how sticky it is. He realises that Riley's silent now. His eyes go to Riley's face. He looks in shock with little expression on his face. But his eyelids droop.

"No," Ethan yells using one of his hands to tap the side of his face. It alerts him and Riley's eyes widen. "Just keep looking at me," he says leaning over closer to Riley's face. "Focus on me."

Riley's mouth opens as if to say something but only a short gurgling noise comes out.

"It's okay, I'll do the talking," Ethan says but now he doesn't know what to say. He weighs down harder on the wound, peering around to see an ambulance making its way through the police cars. Oliver and Lucas guide it through and run towards them. Oliver joins his side whilst Lucas stands over them. His mouth opens and closes.

"Riley Darlington, you're under arrest on suspicion of murdering Carla Milhouse," Lucas orders.

"You've got to be fucking joking!" Ethan shouts up at him.

"Anything you say can and will be used against you…"

Ethan glares at him shaking his head before focusing his attention on Riley as Lucas finishes off telling him his rights. Ethan doesn't want the last thing he hears to be his arrest.

"I love you," Ethan whispers, looking him straight in the eyes. He knows that Lucas and Oliver are there, but he doesn't care. "I've always loved you, Riley."

Riley struggles to stay awake, and his mouth opens as if to say something, but no words follow. His head falls to the side as his eyelids drop.

"No, don't!" Ethan shouts taking hold of his face in his bloody hands to prop his head up. But his eyes are closed, and his head is heavy in his hands. "Riley, please don't leave me," he begs, however useless his pleas are.

Ethan feels someone tug on his shirt, pulling him backwards. He tries to hold onto Riley as he's dragged away from him, but he can't. He tries to stand but his knees buckle. He crumbles, only being supported by Oliver who stands behind him with his arms looped under his armpits. Ethan watches helplessly as paramedics rush to his side. His body lying lifeless and limp, the same way Carla's body lay by the river. The same way he found his mother's body. Just like Carla and Natalie, Riley is gone.

Chapter Thirty-Four

The paramedics take Riley away in the ambulance and Ethan's not waiting around either. He leaves the crime scene, much to Lucas's despair. He even tries to stop Ethan's motorbike as he speeds away after the ambulance. There's only one hospital close to this area where they'd take Riley. So, he heads there, dumping the bike on the side of the road. He rushes into the reception, making the nurse behind the counter jump back from the desk.

"Mr Riley Darlington, I'm looking for a Riley Darlington." The words rush out of his mouth.

She eyes him up and down as if debating whether he's on drugs or not. "Sir, you need to calm down."

"Is he here?"

They have to tell him that. They can tell him if there's a patient under that name in the hospital.

"He came in about ten minutes ago."

"Is he okay? Is he going to be okay?" Ethan begs but he knows she won't tell him that.

"What's your relationship to the patient?"

Ethan stutters because even he doesn't know the answer to that question. Her eyes narrow. "I'm his roommate. Friend. Partner!" He blurts out.

"I'm sorry, I can only give out patient details to the next of kin."

"Please, I just need to know if he's okay."

"Sorry, there's nothing I can do," she says, vacating the counter.

"Ethan," Oliver's voice calls from behind him. Ethan turns to look at him. "You shouldn't have left the scene!"

"They won't tell me anything," he whimpers, then Oliver's face softens, looking past him at the nurse as she walks down the hallway.

He rushes past Ethan and chases after her. He watches from a distance as Oliver pulls her aside and flashes his DC identification. They talk but he can't hear what they're saying. She walks away and Oliver makes his way back to him.

"He passed out from blood loss but he's breathing," he explains. Ethan breathes out a sigh of relief. "They've taken him into surgery, and he'll need a blood transfusion but, his blood type is B negative which -"

"Is one of the rarest blood groups," Ethan finishes.

Everything begins to blur and all the noises around him amplify. The exhaustion hits him as the adrenaline wears off.

"Ethan?" Oliver says concerned, but his words sound distorted.

His breathing increases and snowballs out of control. His knees cave, and his body tumbles to the ground. The wall behind him weakens the fall as his back hits it. Oliver lowers himself to his level, crouching down in front of him.

"It's going to be okay, Ethan."

But it doesn't help. It feels like suffocating. Like it doesn't matter how hard he tries to gasp for air, there is none. "Look at me, focus on me," he says, and Ethan tries but he can't. "Ethan, breathe!" he shouts, and the volume of his voice shocks his breathing into restarting.

A nurse rushes down the hallway to the counter.

"We need another surgeon to the operating theatre. Now!" she shouts.

Lines crease on Oliver's forehead and Ethan mimics his expression. Why would they need another surgeon? Then he remembers what hospital he's at. He remembers that Riley's parents get transferred around from different hospitals in this area. Surgeons can't perform operations on people they know.

"I've got to go," he panics, struggling to his feet. Oliver looks shocked at his sudden urgency to leave.

"Why?"

"I can't be here when they're here."

"Who?"

Ethan tries to back away down the hall, but then he sees him. A man wearing surgical overalls charges down the hallway.

"What the hell happened to my son?" Martin shouts.

Oliver spins around towards him. "What?"

"Tell me why the hell *my son* is lying on *my* operating table."

Oliver's eyes are round. "You're Riley's dad," he says coming out more as a question.

Ethan wonders why Riley's dad went straight for them but then he looks down at himself. Of course, he went towards them, he's covered in blood. Riley's blood. The colour of his shirt has now changed to a dark reddish brown and the blood on his hands clings to his skin, forming web-like threads across each of his fingers. Martin looks at Ethan and their eyes meet.

"What the hell have you done to my son?"

Ethan shakes his head and stumbles back but as he does, Martin steps forward. Oliver steps between them, facing towards Martin.

"DS Brown…"

"I know who that is! He's the runt who attached himself to my son."

Ethan figures he deserved that.

"Mr Darlington, you need to calm down," Oliver says trying to pacify the situation. He gestures as if to lead him away. "Why don't we go…"

"What did you do?" Martin shouts, his eyes fixated on Ethan.

"Mr Darlington, please…"

"This is your fault! You did this."

He knows it's his fault, but he isn't going to be told it by some over-privileged bastard with a silver spoon up his arse.

"Go fuck yourself!" Ethan shouts.

Oliver looks around at him shocked but doesn't have enough time to say something before he has to stop Martin as he lunges himself towards Ethan. His hands in tight fists. He struggles to hold him back.

"What the hell did you do?"

"Martin?" another voice calls from down the hallway. They all turn to look.

"Who the hell is this?" Oliver asks.

"Riley's mum," Ethan replies, his voice monotone.

"Great!"

"What's happened?" she whines. Then her eyes go from Martin to Ethan. "Ethan?" He doesn't respond but her eyes go to his blood-soaked clothes. Her hand goes to her mouth. "Oh my God, are you hurt?"

She rushes towards him, but his automatic response is to step back. Oliver steps in front of him again. She tries to push him aside, stepping closer to Ethan. "You look hurt. I can help you."

"Fuck him!" Martin shouts and that draws her attention back to him. "He's the reason our son is on an operating table!"

Her eyes seem to widen with more horror than surprise now and her skin turns paler. "Why? What the hell has happened to Riley?" she shouts, looking between them all, but her final look is on Ethan.

"Come on Lizzie, we all knew something like this would happen. Right Ethan?" Martin spits, looking at him.

"What's happened?" she shouts again, staring at him.

"Can we please go somewhere quiet? And I'll explain everything," Oliver says, trying to mitigate the situation.

"No, I'm asking him," she says pointing at Ethan. Her voice is torn between hurt and anger. He can't speak, so she steps towards him. "What happened to Riley?"

Ethan lets out a string of noises and stutters that resemble no words. But at least he tries.

"I told you, Lizzie. I told you he was bad for Riley," Martin exclaims.

She reaches forward and takes each side of Ethan's face. "No,

I know you wouldn't have hurt Riley so tell me what happened, and we can sort this. It'll be okay."

He's not sure if she's in shock or if she believes that he had no part in Riley's injury. Her fingers rub his skin, and he realises that she's trying to rub the blood off his face.

"Don't fucking help him!"

Oliver pushes her back and steps in-between again. "Mrs Darlington -"

"Don't touch me!"

She now goes for Oliver, and he jumps back shocked. "Jesus Christ!"

"I don't want to talk to you, I'm talking to him!"

That's when Ethan notices Martin coming towards him. "You should have stayed away from him!"

He's right and Ethan knows it. Oliver jumps in front of him again, attempting to keep them both back.

"Oliver?" Anna's voice sounds through the reception doors. He breathes a sigh of relief.

"Anna, a little help here," he begs.

She rushes over. "Who's this?"

"Riley's parents," Ethan mutters.

She turns to face them. "Mr and Mrs Darlington, your son was involved in an incident."

"What kind of incident?" Elizabeth interrupts.

"I think it's best if you let my colleague take you both somewhere in private?"

There's something in her voice that is calming but stern which is the only thing keeping them both under control.

"What about him?" Martin says pointing to Ethan.

"We have no reason to believe that DS Brown caused the incident."

"We should get someone to check over him," he hears Lizzie say as Anna ushers Ethan away, leaving Oliver with Riley's parents.

"Are you okay?" she asks as Ethan watches Oliver guide Riley's parents down the hallway. He shakes his head. How can he be okay right now? "Why don't we get you cleaned up?" she suggests.

Ethan looks down at himself. He can now feel the blood seeping through his top and the wet on his skin. He nods, now feeling sick and wanting to scrub himself clean. But he feels guilty. As if he doesn't deserve to rid himself of what he's done. He can wash off the blood physically, but Riley's blood will always be on his hands, and on Vincent's.

As the thought enters his head, he sees him. Vincent lies on a gurney with two paramedics either side wheeling him through the front doors. All Ethan sees is red, and Anna isn't quick enough to hold him back as he lunges towards him.

"I'll fucking kill you!" he shouts as he jumps on top of the gurney, wrapping his hands around Vincent's neck.

His eyes widen, grabbing Ethan's hands to try and pry them off. Then a smile creeps along his mouth. Images of his mother's body flash across his mind. Then Carla's. And then Riley's. Screams and shouts echo around the hospital. He knows Anna is shouting at him, begging him to let go. She tries to pull him off, but he holds his grasp around Vincent's neck. It takes three men from hospital security to pull him off Vincent. His legs give in and its only security holding him up as he watches the paramedics rush onwards still looking stunned at what just happened. Vincent's laughter erupting out from him and echoing down the hall.

"What the fuck is wrong with you?" Anna shouts in his face.

It feels as though everything around him caves in as his vision distorts, still staring after Vincent's gurney. His whole world crashes to the ground.

Chapter Thirty-Five

After the incident at the hospital reception, Anna forced him to be checked over by a doctor, telling him that he might be experiencing some breakdown or might have hit his head. Ethan knows that she's just looking for reasons to justify his attack on Vincent other than pure hatred. Ethan sits on the edge of a bed as a doctor checks the flesh wound on his chest and cleans it up in a curtained-off area within A&E. When the doctor finishes, Ethan struggles to get himself into a spare shirt provided by the hospital. He stares blankly at the light blue fabric with the image of Riley's stab wound printed on his brain. The look on his face as he collapsed. Ethan can't help but feel like he let him down. The curtains part, and a familiar face enters.

"Is he okay?" Anna asks.

"Nothing serious and no mental damage," the doctor explains.

"Oh, there's definitely some kind of mental damage," she utters. He still hasn't met her eye. "Can I have a moment with him, please?"

The doctor nods and leaves without hesitation. He feels Anna's eyes heavy on him, but he still refuses to look at her.

"What the hell were you thinking?" she asks in a parent-like voice. For some reason, it reminds him of both his mother and Carla. "Answer me, Skipper."

He looks at her, and she's even got that disappointed look on her face that reminds him of them.

"How's Riley?" he utters.

"In surgery."

"And *him*?"

"He's fine."

"Shame."

"I need to question you about what happened."

Ethan places his head in his hands before telling her

everything. There's no point in denying anything now. He tells her about his and Riley's investigation, what happened when he got to the cabin, and how they ended up by the lake when she arrived. She nods and he can see her trying to digest all the information he's regurgitated at her.

"So, you and Riley *were* in a relationship?"

"I don't know what we were," he mutters, his voice trailing off. He frowns at the question he just answered. That's what she picked up on? He looks at her as the penny starts to drop. "Wait, you don't think I'm lying for him, do you?"

Anna exhales, avoiding his eyes. "I think that we see what we want to see sometimes. You know, our brains can lie to us to shield us from getting hurt."

The curtain draws back again, and this time Ash appears. "Have you questioned him yet?"

"Just finished."

"Have you told him?"

"No."

"Told me what?" he asks half not wanting to know. It could be about Riley. He could be dead.

"It's Vincent," she says. "His account of what happened is different to yours."

"Of course, it is because he's a fucking liar!" Ethan shouts. She raises her hand to beckon him to calm down. "What's he fucking said?"

"That him and Riley met, they argued about you and him, then you turned up and…"

"And then what?"

"Riley pulled the gun on you both."

"Bullshit!"

"Then he tried to cut out your heart, so Vincent struggled with him and during the fight, Vincent said he feared for his life so he…"

"Stabbed him."

"In self-defence."

Ethan shakes his head, placing his head in his hands. He knows what he saw, and he knows that what Vincent said is a lie, but the reconstructed version of events plays out in his mind.

"It's not true."

"Well, his injuries seem consistent with being attacked, like the massive gash on the back of his head," Ash says.

"Riley only did that to protect me when that sicko tried to cut out my heart! See," Ethan shouts, pulling his shirt down to show them the injury. "Riley's the one who was stabbed. He's the victim here!"

"I think if a schizophrenic attacked me, I would have stabbed him in self-defence too."

Ethan shakes his head. "If you don't believe Riley then fine, but what about me? Do you not believe me?"

Ash and Anna exchange a look before turning back to him.

"You're too emotionally involved, and all our evidence proves that Riley killed Carla."

"Your so-called evidence, doesn't prove jack shit!"

"See what I mean?"

"But Vincent was laughing at the crime scene, that doesn't exactly scream victim, does it!"

"Isn't enough to make him our Heart Snatcher either."

He doesn't answer her as he stares at the ground through the gap between his two hands. His, Riley's and Vincent's DNA are all over that cabin so there's no evidence against Vincent. He fool-proofed his plan airtight and there's nothing Ethan can do about it.

"I should have killed him," Ethan utters. "When I had the gun, I should have killed him."

"I'm going to pretend I didn't hear that," she says.

"Covering for Riley makes you an accessory to murder," he hears Ash say. Ethan exhales knowing that they've failed. Vincent still gets away with murder and managed to somehow pin all this on them. "We have to take you in."

"Fine," he breathes and gets to his feet.

He grabs his jacket that's slung over the bed and as he does so, he hears a clang hit the floor beneath him. He gawps down at his mobile lying at his feet.

"Are you okay?" Anna asks.

His head whips back to her. "I have proof," he whispers.

"Proof of what?" Ash asks.

"Proof that Riley was at his flat at the time of Jennifer's murder; proof that Vincent set him up; proof of everything."

"Show us then," she says.

"Only if you let me talk to Vincent."

"No way!" Ash jumps in.

"I can get a confession out of him. I know how his sick mind works now."

"You're still suspended, Ethan."

"No, you suspended me on personal reasons for grief. That grief period ended at midnight. Technically you can reinstate me as a working DS."

"Still doesn't change the fact that you're too emotionally involved to work on this case."

"Anna, please trust me," he says looking at her with pleading eyes and she stares back at him with a torn expression.

"Nothing's changed, you're still not allowed on this case!" Ash demands.

"Didn't stop him before," Anna says with a shrug. "And if he's got proof then I say we hear him out." Ash and Anna exchange a look before looking back to him.

***

Anna is the first to enter the interrogation room, making both Vincent's and his lawyer's head whip around at the same time. As Ethan walks through after her, his face lights up.

"Detective," Vincent says, sounding half pleased and half

surprised. "Strange for you to sit in on my interview."

Ethan closes the door and puts his back to it, keeping a safe distance from him, not because Ethan's scared of him but of what he might do to Vincent. Already, he imagines using his face as a punching bag.

"DS Brown is now officially reinstated," Anna says sitting in the chair opposite them on the other side of the table and unwrapping the recorder to set it up. "As you are aware, this is a formal interview concerning the homicide of Natalie Brown, Carla Milhouse and Jennifer Spring, so, this interview will be recorded and anything you say can and will be used against you."

"I understand," Vincent consents, placing his clasped hands in front of him on the table. She then reads the date, time, and place of the interview.

"Please introduce yourself for the record."

"Dr Vincent Hale."

"Should he still be here? Due to his personal involvement," Vincent's lawyer says.

"We have no reason to believe that DS Brown's view is corrupt."

His lawyer opens his mouth but Vincent cuts in. "He can be here," he says, smiling at Ethan with an amused look on his smug face. "I have nothing to hide."

Ethan sharpens his eyes. "Tell her," he demands and notices Anna's body tense. "Tell her everything you told me at the cabin."

"Why did you come here, Detective?" he asks.

"That's not –"

"Why don't you sit down?"

Vincent kicks the chair opposite him out from under the table.

"After you tell her."

Vincent's head tilts back and his eyelids subside.

"How's Riley?" he asks and every muscle in Ethan's body tenses.

"Don't you fucking say his name!" Ethan snarls launching forward but he's stopped by the chair and table blocking his path. It only seems to amuse Vincent as a smile perks at the end of his lips.

"Should your Sergeant be talking to my client like that?" the lawyer says with a warning in his tone.

"Ethan," Anna warns. Turning around to mouth the words 'shut up'.

"I just want to know how he is," Vincent says with fake innocence in his voice.

"Don't do that!" Ethan snaps.

"Do what?"

"Pretend that you care about him when you're the reason he's in fucking hospital."

"I would never hurt Riley."

"You're the one who fucking stabbed him!"

"Which was an act of self-defence," his lawyer interjects.

"Of course," Anna agrees.

"My client was attacked and hit on the back of the head which he needed stitches for. I'm sure he just wants to go home, not be verbally abused by an officer."

"My Sergeant isn't being abusive or insulting towards your client. Interviews can get heated sometimes, but we all know where the line is. Right, Ethan?"

Ethan leans forward on the table. "I know you spiked Riley with LSD to make it look like his schizophrenia; I know you set Riley up to find Carla's body; and I know you murdered Natalie and Carla along with countless other victims."

"You're nuts," Vincent snaps.

"Fascinating story. Where's the evidence?" the lawyer mocks.

Ethan can feel his hands shaking, so he grips the back of the chair tighter to calm them. He reminds himself of his and Anna's plan but it's difficult to play along when all he wants to do is kill this man. He closes his eyes and tries to steady his breathing.

"Don't worry," Anna says. "We've got a forensics team in that cabin now gathering evidence. Fingerprints, DNA, you name it. So, if you really are innocent, you'll have nothing to worry about."

"Don't forget I was down there when I was attacked," Vincent says.

He opens his eyes again to see Carla standing at the back of the room, leaning against the wall.

"Right, but why would your fingerprints be on all the jars of hearts?" Anna asks. Vincent's silent, staring into blank space as he contemplates his next words.

"You don't have to answer that," his lawyer says.

"Of course not," she agrees.

Carla gives a nod and it's all he needs. He knows what she'd be telling him, and he knows what he has to do. He starts to laugh.

"Is he okay?" the lawyer asks Anna with concern. Ethan laughs harder.

"What's so funny?" Vincent shouts.

"This!" Ethan says gesturing to the air. "Your whole so-called master plan. I mean, it's laughable really."

Vincent's head tilts. "What's so amusing about it?"

"You think you were being so clever, covering your tracks and setting Riley up for it all, but you're just… *pathetic*."

"Insulting my client!" the lawyer exclaims.

"Hypothetically," Vincent says ignoring his lawyer. "If what you're saying is true, I've been pretty clever. Hypothetically, that is."

Anna gives a theatrical shrug that makes Ethan laugh for real.

"Really?" he says, crossing his arms and cocking his head. "Because I figured it out. It wasn't difficult. So, what makes you think that with our forensics team, resources, and all the other detectives looking into this case that they won't figure it out too?"

"Because they're not as smart as we are," Vincent says leaning forward in his chair with a sinister grin.

"I think we should take a break," his lawyer suggests, glancing between him and Anna.

"Hypothetically though, right Vincent?" Anna mocks.

"Of course."

"You see that's where you're wrong. There's no we; *I* am smarter than you," Ethan says leaning forward over the table.

"No, we're equals. We're the same."

"I'm better."

"No, you're not!" he shouts.

He watches the anger build inside Vincent, that's displayed on his face.

"Don't say anything else," the lawyer warns Vincent.

"It's kind of sad really; that you're supposed to be some genius serial killer and yet you're letting some stupid little schizophrenic take the credit for your work." Serial killers like Vincent don't like being belittled.

"I -"

"Really, Riley's the mastermind in all this," Anna chips in.

"No, he's fucking not!"

"Oh yes, he is," Anna teases. "I mean, he managed to kill a grown woman when he was ten, got away with it and was killing for sixteen years. He even convinced Ethan that he was innocent. I'd say Riley's a genius."

Vincent's body trembles with rage. Serial killers like him also don't like others taking credit for their work. Anna rises out of her chair and waves her arms around dramatically.

"Riley will go down as Britain's most notorious serial killer. Psychologists will be jumping at the chance to interview him; to analyse his brain; people will be talking about him for years even after he dies," she says emphasising every word. "He'll be famous," she adds to dig the knife in.

Ethan can see by the look on his face that they've got to him. All he needs to do is give one final push. He leans in close over

Vincent.

"And I'll be the famous detective who caught him, whilst you'll be forgotten about. Because I'm smarter than you, better than you."

Vincent does as he planned; he explodes into anger. Jumping up from his seat, Vincent grabs hold of Ethan's jacket collar.

"No! I'm the one who bested all of you! I'm the one who killed all those women and got away with it! I'm the one who killed both your mothers and ruined you! I did!"

Ethan's lips curl into a smile. *Finally*.

He watches as it dawns in Vincent's eyes what he just admitted to. His confession. Ethan notices how still he looks, not even his shoulders or chest move as if he's not breathing. It's a primal instinct to limit your movement as much as possible when in self-defence, which even means holding your breath.

"No, I bested you," Ethan whispers.

"Don't say another word!" his lawyer shouts jumping to his feet.

"Vincent Hale, you're under arrest for the murder of Carla, Natalie and Jennifer," Anna announces. Satisfied, Ethan turns to leave, flashing Vincent one last victory smirk.

"I'll fucking kill you!" he hears Vincent shout.

Ethan turns to see him lunging towards him. An expression of pure evil and hate is displayed on his face. He grabs Vincent's arm and twists it back. He lets out a cry of pain and Ethan can feel a smile tug at the corner of his mouth. He hears a clanging noise and looks at Anna as she pulls out her handcuffs.

"Can I?" Ethan asks.

She smiles smugly and holds out the cuffs. Ethan takes them and fastens the metal around Vincent's wrists, tightening them as much as possible behind his back. He passes him over to Anna. "He's all yours."

As Ethan walks out, he hears Anna read him the rest of his rights. He stumbles down the hallway. It all hits him at once.

Everything. It's all over now but there's a hole still left inside him. He still doesn't know if Riley is going to make it through surgery. He leaves the police station, determined to get back to the hospital. He has to know if he made it.

Chapter Thirty-Six

Ethan must have fallen asleep whilst lying across those plastic waiting room chairs in the hospital, because the next time he opens his eyes, there's a new receptionist on the desk. He frowns as he hears the faint sound of magazine pages turning. He strains his eyes to look above his head, managing to make out a pair of legs in the seat next to him. He shifts trying to see who it is, but his whole body aches.

"Hey, you're awake," Lucas chimes, putting down the magazine and straightening in his chair. The vision of him is upside down as Ethan looks up him, head still resting on the seat.

"What the fuck are you doing here?"

Lucas shrugs and Ethan notices a bandage across the dip in his left arm. His frown deepens as he sits up to get a better look.

"You gave blood," Ethan says, half a question, half a statement.

"I'm O negative," he confirms. "A perfect match for someone who's B negative and needs blood after being stabbed. Funny coincidence, right?"

He doesn't know what to say, except for the obvious question.

"Is he," Ethan begins but doesn't finish.

"He's out of surgery and in the recovery room."

The back of Ethan's head hits the wall behind him as he lets out a sigh of relief. It feels like a weight has lifted off his body, and he can breathe again.

"Recovery room," he utters. "So, he's going to be, okay?"

"Yes, but they want to keep him in for a day or so to monitor him. You can go and see him if you like?"

There's nothing Ethan wants more than to see him, but there's two people he doesn't want to see.

"Are Riley's parents still here?" Ethan asks and Lucas nods. "I'll wait then."

"You can't hide from them forever. Plus, I think Riley needs to see you."

"How do you know that?"

"A couple of hours after he was taken into the recovery room, I had to go in and get his statement. All he did was ask for you before I was pushed out by his parents telling me that he needed to rest."

"Is that why you've been waiting around here? To get his statement?"

"Partly," Lucas says with a shrug. "I also figured you might need a friend right now."

"I thought you hated me?"

"I think you're an arrogant bastard," he chuckles, half-joking. Ethan chokes out a laugh. "But you're not all bad."

"Yeah, neither are you. I guess."

"Oh, did I just get a compliment from Ethan Brown?" Lucas asks with a smirk.

"Don't make it weird."

"Right," he laughs.

They sit side by side on the chairs both looking straight ahead.

"Sorry I punched you," Ethan apologises but not very well.

"I'm sorry I deserved it."

"Yeah, you did."

"I just wanted to help; to earn my place as a Sergeant."

"I get that."

"There's one thing I don't understand," he says, and Ethan waits for him to continue. "Why you're still sat here talking to me?"

Lucas gives him a look and he knows he needs to stop delaying.

"What room number?" Ethan asks.

"32."

He staggers to his feet and navigates his way down the hallway, trying to find the right room. He finds it and lingers outside, staring at the closed wooden door. He raises his shaky fist and knocks.

"Come in," Lizzie's voice calls from behind the door.

He takes a deep breath and opens the door into the dark room that's lit by a dim lamp emitting an orange glow. Riley's parents look round as he enters. He stays back and keeps the door open in case they decide to kick him out.

Riley's mum is stood closest to him with her husband behind her next to the top of Riley's hospital bed. They look withdrawn and tired. Heavy bags under their bloodshot eyes. Ethan looks from Elizabeth to Martin who scowls at him. Ethan can't see Riley's face. His body is just a lump under a sheet with a mass of black hair at the top and his arm hung over the covers. He's lying on his side, curled in the foetal position. Tubes and wires going in and out of him. A fluid bag to the side of his bed and a long clear tube going into his hand.

"How is he?" Ethan manages to ask but he can't bring his voice above a whisper.

The silence is painful and drawn out. They both exchange a look.

"You can ask him yourself," Lizzie says stepping to the side to let him through.

"He's fine, no thanks to you," Martin mutters as he turns his attention back to Riley.

Lizzie's head whips around to scowl at him. Martin strokes the top of Riley's head and forehead, as if he could somehow cure his son's mental illness with his touch. Ethan can't imagine what that's like. To have all that money, all that medical knowledge, and still not be able to fix your son's illness. Ethan doesn't like the guy, but seeing him with Riley in this moment, he can understand why he acted the way he did.

"Is that Ethan?" Riley asks as the covers stir.

"Yes, he's come to see if you're okay, Sweetie," Lizzie jumps in before Martin can speak.

"I want to see him."

"You need your rest," Martin demands.

"I need to see him!" Riley protests, trying to sit up.

Ethan rushes towards the bed, not caring as he pushes Martin aside. "Riley, I'm here," he reassures Riley, taking and caressing his hand, worried that he might knock the tube going into his vein.

Riley's blue irises seem duller and his skin paler than usual. A sick pale, not his usual glowing skin. He looks so vulnerable and fragile, like he could somehow break in half.

"Ethan," he breathes.

"He needs to rest," Martin repeats through his teeth.

"He asked to see me," Ethan snaps. "And as long as he wants me here, I'm staying."

"But –"

"Oh, shut up, Martin," Lizzie blurts out, causing him to look at her in shock. She looks at Ethan. "If you need us, we'll be in the canteen."

She beams at him as she grabs Martin's arm and leads him away. Ethan makes an effort to return the smile back to her as they leave, closing the door behind them. He tries to swallow down the lump in his throat, turning back to Riley.

"How are you feeling?" Ethan asks.

He's quiet for a moment, as he stares up at Ethan with watery eyes. "Like I've been stabbed."

"Well, that's ironic," he says, and they both choke out a hesitant laugh. It's nothing to joke about, but it's their way of dealing with it. "What happened with Vincent?" he asks, his expression now changing to panic.

"Don't worry, he's been arrested. We got him. He can't hurt you anymore."

Riley is silent for a moment, staring into space. "What about the other detectives? What about my –"

"Your name's been cleared. You remember that Stalker app

you made me link to your phone so I could see your location?" he asks and Riley nods. "It showed that you were nowhere near Jennifer when she was murdered. That was how I got Anna to believe that you were innocent and then we got Vincent to confess."

It's like someone has lifted a load off him physically and mentally. His body relaxing into the bed and his face lightening. Ethan tries to think of what to say. How does he sum it all up with words after all they've been through? He notices Riley looking up at him with a smirk.

"What?" Ethan asks.

"You told me you loved me."

Shit. He forgot about that. "Oh yeah. Well, people say stupid shit in a crisis."

"You're not getting out of it that easy."

He laughs. That knot retying itself in the pit of his stomach. He thinks for a moment as silence fills the air.

"I know you were stabbed and all, but, um," he stutters, trying to string together a sentence. "I don't want you to say it if you don't, you know, want to. But if you feel it - if you feel the same, then you could say it back."

Now he sounds like an idiot, but he waits for Riley's response. A grin spreads across his face. "Do I have to say it for you to know?"

Ethan lets out a sigh of relief that's merged with a short laugh. "It would still be nice to hear it."

Their eyes lock and he finds himself leaning over and gently kissing Riley's forehead. As he retreats, Riley's lips find his and he leans into the kiss, embracing every second. Their lips part just enough for Riley to say, "I've always loved you, Ethan."

High heels click on the floor as the door swings open. Ethan stands upright, and spin around.

"Anna," Ethan coughs, as if she hadn't just walked in on him kissing Riley. A smile begins to surface on her face.

"Sorry, I just came to see how Riley's doing," she says still smiling.

Riley clears his throat. "Yeah, I'm doing better now, thank you."

"Oh, I bet you are," Anna smirks, raising an eyebrow. She turns to Ethan. "Have you told him the good news?"

Ethan nods. "Y- yes," he croaks trying to get his voice working.

Anna walks over to him, placing her hand on Ethan's back as she looks round at Riley. "I think I speak for everyone when I say that we owe you a massive apology."

Riley's eyes dart between Ethan and Anna. "It's okay."

"No, it's not," Ethan interjects.

"Well, you can expect a formal apology letter from the station," she says.

"Really, it's fine. There's only one person to blame," he says. "He's the one who had you all fooled."

"Everyone except Ethan."

"Yeah well, that's just because he's a better detective than the rest of you."

"Is that so?" she smiles. Ethan grins at her. "Good job we kept your desk then."

"Doesn't Lucas have it?"

"I guess I'll have to kick him off when you come back," she says with a wink. "How does first thing Monday sound?"

He smiles before realising. "Oh, I think it'll have to wait a couple of weeks first." She frowns. "Someone's got to look after Riley whilst he recovers."

"Of course," Anna says with a wide smile. "Oh, I've also got this for you too."

She pulls out an envelope in a clear evidence bag.

"What is it?"

"We found it with Carla's belongings in her room. It's for you."

He sees his name scribbled across the envelope. "Don't you need it for evidence?"

"Yeah, we did, hence why I'm only giving it to you now. It's yours."

He takes the bag and looks at the already torn envelope. "You opened it."

"Of course," she confesses with a catty smile.

He turns back to Riley. "I'm just going to get some air; will you be okay on your own for a bit?"

Riley gives a reluctant nod.

"Don't worry, I'll look after him," Anna says smiling between them.

"That's what I'm worried about."

"I could actually use some rest," Riley requests.

With that hint, Anna takes a step back. "I'll be around if you need me," she says before turning to Ethan. "And I mean, both of you," she adds. "It's good to have you back, Skipper."

She disappears and Ethan takes Riley's hand to kiss the only patch of skin that's exposed. Ethan waits until Riley closes his eyes before moving towards the door, looking back at him before closing it.

Chapter Thirty-Seven

Ethan walks along the bank of the lake near the Darlington's cabin as the afternoon sun penetrates through the trees creating sunbeams. He watches as the underwater search team dive under, looking for the victims. Already, several body bags are lined up on shore with a forensics team securing them. Milly is among them. She looks across at him and signals with two fingers that she's got her eyes on him. He offers her a crooked smile.

"We've got another one," a diver shouts; another one of Vincent's victims; another innocent mother.

He sits on the grass and stares at the folded letter in his hands. He takes a deep breath, turning the paper and unfolding it. Carla's handwriting is scribbled all over it and he begins to read it.

'*Dear Ethan,*

There's so much I want to tell you, but I'm scared you'll only hate me for the truth, so I'm writing this letter in hopes that maybe one day I'll build up the courage to give it to you. Kind of cowardly, really, isn't it?

"I want to tell you, how proud I am of you," the hallucination of Carla says, tears swelling in her eyes. "And just how much I love you. But most importantly, how proud I know Natalie would be of you. She loved you more than anything and giving her the opportunity to have you was the greatest gift I could have given anyone, and I'm so glad I did. Although you are biologically mine, you will always be Natalie's son. I see a mix of both of us in you. I guess that's the beauty of motherhood."

Water falling from his eyes smudges the letter in his trembling hands. He looks at Carla, tears trailing down her face. He folds the letter, trying to steady his shaky breathing.

"Don't worry, I'll tell her all about you when I get there." Carla reaches out and tucks a stray piece of hair behind his ear.

She gets up and all he can do is watch her as she walks

towards the lake to join the others. Her feet step into the water, followed by her legs and waist as the liquid engulfs her. Her hair falling on top of the water's surface before she disappears, and he knows that she's gone. Forever. He sits in silence, watching the gentle ripples ricochet across the lake, feeling somehow at peace that both his mother's live on through him.

THE END

ACKNOWLEDGEMENTS

Thank you to my wonderful parents for always encouraging me to chase my dreams and for believing in me. I am who I am today because of your love and guidance.

Thank you to my darling husband, Chris, for all your love and support, and for consoling me when I doubted myself. Thank you for listening to me ramble on about this book for the last ten years.

To the rest of my lovely family, thank you from the bottom of my heart. Thank you to my brother, Craig, and sister, Amy, for all your encouragement and faith. Thank you to my sisters-in-law who are more like sisters to me, Zoe and Danielle. Thank you to my wonderful gran, Noma, for all your love.

A special thanks to my writing girls, Belinda, Laila and Sarah, for helping me become a better writer and for believing in this book.

To my incredible editor, Belinda Stuebinger at The Raven's Script, for your excitement towards this book and for developing it further with me. Your advice and patience have been remarkable.

Thank you to my amazing sensitivity reader, Kathryn Wheeler, for all your guidance and support as well as your enthusiasm for this book.

Lastly, thank you to all my work friends, Anya, Catherine, Ian, Carlie, Sophie, Wendy, Chloe, Sam, Lisa, Jane, and Elaine (and our office dog Alfie, of course) for all your excitement for this book.

It's been a long journey and I couldn't have done it without you all.

ABOUT THE AUTHOR

T. H. Carrington is a new crime fiction author, and *The Heart Snatcher* is her debut novel. After graduating from her Master's in Creative Writing and Publishing at Bournemouth University, she now has a full-time job as a social media executive. She has a love for crime fiction as well as true crime documentaries. When she isn't writing or reading, you can find her sightseeing with her husband, gardening, or painting.

Follow her on social media:
Instagram: @thcarrington
TikTok: @thcarrington

Printed in Great Britain
by Amazon

42577773R00195